George A. Aitken

**The Spectator**

Vol V

George A. Aitken

**The Spectator**
*Vol V*

ISBN/EAN: 9783741103599

Manufactured in Europe, USA, Canada, Australia, Japa

Cover: Foto ©Andreas Hilbeck / pixelio.de

Manufactured and distributed by brebook publishing software
(www.brebook.com)

George A. Aitken

**The Spectator**

# THE SPECTATOR

WITH INTRODUCTION AND NOTES
BY
## GEORGE A. AITKEN
AUTHOR OF 'THE LIFE OF RICHARD STEELE' ETC.

*IN SIX VOLUMES*

*VOLUME THE FIFTH*

LONDON
GEORGE ROUTLEDGE & SONS, Limited
NEW YORK: E. P DUTTON & CO

RICHARD CLAY & SONS, LIMITED,
BREAD STREET HILL, E.C., AND
BUNGAY, SUFFOLK.

# NOTE

The present edition is reproduced unabridged from the edition in eight volumes published by Mr. JOHN C. NIMMO in 1898.

G. R. & S., Ld.

# THE SPECTATOR

No. 401.    *Tuesday, June 10, 1712*    [BUDGELL

*In amore hæc omnia insunt vitia: Injuriæ,*
*Suspiciones, inimicitiæ, induciæ,*
*Bellum, pax rursum.*    TER., *Eun.*, Act i, sc. 1

I SHALL publish, for the entertainment of this day, an odd sort of a packet, which I have just received from one of my female correspondents.

MR SPECTATOR,—Since you have often confessed that you are not displeased your paper should sometimes convey the complaints of distressed lovers to each other, I am in hopes you will favour one who gives you an undoubted instance of her reformation, and at the same time a convincing proof of the happy influence your labours have had over the most incorrigible part of the most incorrigible sex. You must know, sir, I am one of that species of women, whom you have often characterised under the name of Jilts, and that I send you these lines, as well to do public penance for having so long continued in a known error, as to beg pardon of the party offended. I the rather choose this way, because it in some measure answers the terms on which he intimated the breach between us might possibly be made up, as you will see by the letter he sent me the next day after I had discarded him; which I thought fit to send you a copy of, that you might the better know the whole case.

I must further acquaint you, that before I jilted him there had been the greatest intimacy between us for an year and half together, during all which time I cherished his hopes and indulged his flame. I leave you to guess after this what must be his surprise when, upon his pressing for my full consent one day, I told him I wondered what could make him fancy he had ever any place in my affections. His own sex allow him sense, and all ours good-breeding. His person is such as might, without vanity, make him believe himself not incapable to be beloved. Our fortunes indeed, weighed in the nice scale of interest, are not exactly equal, which by the way was the true cause of my jilting him, and I had the assurance to acquaint him with the following maxim, that I should always believe that man's passion to be the most violent who could offer me the largest settlement. I have since changed my opinion, and have endeavoured to let him know so much by several letters, but the barbarous man has refused them all; so that I have no way left of writing to him, but by your assistance. If we can bring him about once more, I promise to send you all gloves and favours, and shall desire the favour of Sir Roger and yourself to stand as god-fathers to my first boy. I am, Sir,

Your most obedient most humble Servant,

AMORET

### 'PHILANDER to AMORET

'MADAM,—I am so surprised at the question you were pleased to ask me yesterday, that I am still at a loss what to say to it. At least my answer would be too long to trouble you with, as it would come from a person who, it seems, is so very indifferent to you. Instead of it, I shall only recommend to your consideration the opinion of one whose senti-ments on these matters I have often heard you say are extremely just. "A generous and constant pas-sion", says your favourite author[1], "in an agreeable lover, where there is not too great a disparity in their circumstances, is the greatest blessing that can befall a person beloved; and if overlooked in one, may per-haps never be found in another."

'I do not, however, at all despair of being very shortly much better beloved by you than Antenor is at present; since whenever my fortune shall exceed his, you were pleased to intimate your passion would increase accordingly.

'The world has seen me shamefully lose that time to please a fickle woman, which might have been employed much more to my credit and advantage in other pursuits. I shall therefore take the liberty to acquaint you, however harsh it may sound in a lady's

[1] Cicero.

ears, that though your love fit should happen to return, unless you could contrive a way to make your recantation as well known to the public, as they are already apprised of the manner with which you have treated me, you shall never more see

PHILANDER '

'AMORET *to* PHILANDER

'SIR,—Upon reflection I find the injury I have done both to you and myself to be so great, that though the part I now act may appear contrary to that decorum usually observed by our sex, yet I purposely break through all rules, that my repentance may in some measure equal my crime. I assure you, that in my present hopes of recovering you, I look upon Antenor's estate with contempt. The fop was here yesterday in a gilt chariot and new liveries, but I refused to see him. Though I dread to meet your eyes after what has passed, I flatter myself that amidst all their confusion you will discover such a tenderness in mine, as none can imitate but those who love. I shall be all this month at Lady D——'s in the country; but the woods, the fields, and gardens without Philander, afford no pleasures to the unhappy

AMORET '

I must desire you, dear Mr Spectator, to publish this my letter to Philander as soon as possible, and to assure him that I know nothing at all of the death of his rich uncle in Gloucestershire.　　　　X.

No. 402.　　*Wednesday, June 11, 1712*　　[STEELE

*quæ*
. . . *sibi spectator tradit.*

HOR., *Ars Poet.* 181 [1]

WERE I to publish all the advertisements I receive from different hands and persons of different circumstances and quality, the very mention of them, without reflections on the several subjects, would raise all the passions which can be felt by human mind.

---

[1] The folio issue has no motto.

As instances of this, I shall give you two or three letters, the writers of which can have no recourse to any legal power for redress, and seem to have written rather to vent their sorrow than to receive consolation.

MR SPECTATOR,—I am a young woman of beauty and quality, and suitably married to a gentleman who dotes on me; but this person of mine is the object of an unjust passion in a nobleman who is very intimate with my husband. This friendship gives him very easy access and frequent opportunities of entertaining me apart. My heart is in the utmost anguish, and my face is covered over with confusion when I impart to you another circumstance, which is, that my mother, the most mercenary of all women, is gained by this false friend of my husband to solicit me for him. I am frequently chid by the poor believing man, my husband, for showing an impatience of his friend's company; and I am never alone with my mother but she tells me stories of the discretionary part of the world, and such a one, and such a one, who are guilty of as much as she advises me to. She laughs at my astonishment, and seems to hint to me, that as virtuous as she has always appeared, I am not the daughter of her husband. It is possible that printing this letter may relieve me from the unnatural importunity of my mother, and the perfidious courtship of my husband's friend. I have an unfeigned love of virtue, and am resolved to preserve my innocence. The only way I can think of to avoid the fatal consequences of the discovery of this matter is to fly away for ever, which I must do to avoid my husband's fatal resentment against the man who attempts to abuse him, and the shame of exposing a parent to infamy. The persons concerned will know these circumstances relate to 'em; and though the regard to virtue is dead in them, I have some hopes from their fear of shame upon reading this in your paper; which I conjure you to do if you have any compassion for injured virtue.

SYLVIA

MR SPECTATOR,—I am the husband of a woman of merit, but am fallen in love, as they call it, with a lady of her acquaintance, who is going to be married to a gentleman who deserves her. I am in a trust relating to this lady's fortune, which makes my concurrence in this matter necessary; but I have so irresistible a rage and envy rise in me when I consider his future happiness, that against all reason, equity, and common justice, I am ever playing mean tricks to suspend the nuptials. I have no manner of hopes for myself; Emilia, for so I'll call her, is a woman of the most strict virtue; her lover is a gentleman who of all others I could wish my friend; but envy and jealousy, though placed so unjustly, waste my very being, and with the torment and sense of a demon, I am ever cursing what I cannot but approve. I wish it were the beginning of repentance, that I sit down and describe my present disposition with so hellish an aspect; but at present the destruction of these two excellent persons would be more welcome to me than their happiness. Mr Spectator, pray let me have a paper on these terrible groundless sufferings, and do all you can to exorcise crowds who are in some degree possessed as I am.

CANNIBAL

MR. SPECTATOR,—I have no other means but this to express my thanks to one man, and my resentment against another. My circumstances are as follows : I have been for five years last past courted by a gentleman of greater fortune than I ought to expect, as the market for women goes. You must, to be sure, have observed people who live in that sort of way, as all their friends reckon it will be a match, and are marked out by all the world for each other. In this view we have been regarded for some time, and I have above these three years loved him tenderly. As he is very careful of his fortune, I always thought he lived in a near manner to lay up what he thought was wanting in my fortune to make up what he might expect in another. Within few months I have observed his carriage very much altered, and he has affected a certain art of getting me alone, and talking with a mighty profusion of passionate words : how I am not to be resisted longer, how irresistible his wishes are, and the like. As long as I have been acquainted with

him, I could not on such occasions say downright t
him : 'You know you may make me yours when yo
please.' But the other night he, with great franknes
and impudence, explained to me that he thought of m
only as a mistress. I answered this declaration as i
deserved; upon which he only doubled the terms o
which he proposed my yielding. When my ange
heightened upon him, he told me he was sorry he ha
made so little use of the unguarded hours we had bee
together so remote from company, 'as indeed', con
tinued he, 'so we are at present'. I flew from hir
to a neighbouring gentlewoman's house, and thoug
her husband was in the room, threw myself on
couch, and burst into a passion of tears. My frien
desired her husband to leave the room, but, said he
'There is something so extraordinary in this, that
will partake in the affliction, and be it what it will
she is so much your friend, that she knows she ma
command what services I can do her.' The man sat
down by me and spoke so like a brother, that I tol
him my whole affliction. He spoke of the injury don
me with so much indignation, and animated me agains
the love he said he saw I had for the wretch, wh
would have betrayed me with so much reason an
humanity to my weakness, that I doubt not of m
perseverance. His wife and he are my comforters, an
I am under no more restraint in their company than i
I were alone; and I doubt not but in a small tim
contempt and hatred will take place of the remain
of affection to a rascal.

I am, Sir,
Your affectionate Reader,
DORINDA

MR SPECTATOR,—I had the misfortune to be an uncl
before I knew my nephews from my nieces, and no'
we are grown up to better acquaintance they den
me the respect they owe. One upbraids me wit
being their familiar, another will hardly be persuade
that I am an uncle, a third calls me Little Uncle, an
a fourth tells me there is no duty at all due to a
uncle. I have a brother-in-law whose son will wi
all my affection, unless you shall think this worthy c

your cognisance, and will be pleased to prescribe some
rules for our future reciprocal behaviour.   It will be
worthy the particularity of your genius to lay down
rules for his conduct, who was, as it were, born an
old man; in which you will much oblige,
                        Sir,
            Your most obedient Servant,
   T.                           CORNELIUS NEPOS


No. 403.      *Thursday, June 12, 1712*      [ADDISON

*Qui mores hominum multorum vidit.*
                        HOR., *Ars Poet.* 142

WHEN I consider this great city in its several
quarters and divisions, I look upon it as an aggregate
of various nations distinguished from each other by
their respective customs, manners, and interests.
The courts of two countries do not so much differ
from one another as the court and city in their peculiar ways of life and conversation.   In short, the
inhabitants of St James's, notwithstanding they live
under the same laws and speak the same language,
are a distinct people from those of Cheapside, who are
likewise removed from those of the Temple, on the one
side and those of Smithfield on the other, by several
climates and degrees in their ways of thinking and
conversing together.

For this reason, when any public affair is upon the
anvil, I love to hear the reflections that arise upon it
in the several districts and parishes of London and
Westminster, and to ramble up and down a whole
day together in order to make myself acquainted with
the opinions of my ingenious countrymen.   By this
means I know the faces of all the principal politicians
within the bills of mortality; and as every coffee-
house has some particular statesman belonging to it
who is the mouth of the street where he lives, I
always take care to place myself near him in order
to know his judgment on the present posture of
affairs.   The last progress that I made with this

intention was about three months ago, when we had
a current report of the King of France's death. As
I foresaw this would produce a new face of things
in Europe, and many curious speculations in our
British coffee-houses, I was very desirous to learn
the thoughts of our most eminent politicians on that
occasion.

That I might begin as near the fountain-head as
possible, I first of all called in at St James's [1], where
I found the whole outward room in a buzz of politics.
The speculations were but very indifferent towards
the door, but grew finer as you advanced to the upper
end of the room, and were so very much improved by
a knot of theorists, who sat in the inner room within
the steams of the coffee-pot, that I there heard the
whole Spanish monarchy disposed of, and all the line
of Bourbon provided for in less than a quarter of an
hour.

I afterwards called in at Giles's, where I saw a
board of French gentlemen sitting upon the life and
death of their *Grand Monarque.* Those among them
who had espoused the Whig interest, very positively
affirmed that he departed this life about a week since,
and therefore proceeded without any further delay to
the release of their friends on the galleys and to their
own re-establishment, but finding they could not
agree among themselves, I proceeded on my intended
progress.

Upon my arrival at Jenny Man's [2], I saw an alert
young fellow that cocked his hat upon a friend of his
who entered just at the same time with myself, and
accosted him after the following manner : ' Well,
Jack, the old prig is dead at last. Sharp's the word.
Now or never, boy. Up to the walls of Paris
directly.' With several other deep reflections of the
same nature.

I met with very little variation in the politics between Charing Cross and Covent Garden. And upon
my going into Will's I found their discourse was

[1] See No. 1.          [2] See No. 109.

gone off from the death of the French king to that
of Monsieur Boileau [1], Racine, Corneille, and several
other poets, whom they regretted on this occasion,
as persons who would have obliged the world with
very noble elegies on the death of so great a prince
and so eminent a patron of learning.

At a coffee-house near the Temple I found a couple
of young gentlemen engaged very smartly in a dispute on the succession to the Spanish monarchy. One
of them seemed to have been retained as advocate
for the Duke of Anjou, the other for his Imperial
Majesty [2]. They were both for regulating the title
to that kingdom by the statute laws of England, but
finding them going out of my depth, I passed forward
to 'Paul's Churchyard, where I listened with great
attention to a learned man, who gave the company
an account of the deplorable state of France during
the minority of the deceased king.

I then turned on my right hand into Fish Street,
where the chief politician of that quarter, upon hearing the news (after having taken a pipe of tobacco,
and ruminated for some time) : ' If ', says he, ' the
King of France is certainly dead, we shall have plenty
of mackerel this season; our fishery will not be disturbed by privateers, as it has been for these ten
years past.' He afterwards considered how the death
of this great man would affect our pilchards, and by
several other remarks infused a general joy into his
whole audience.

I afterwards entered a by-coffee-house that stood
at the upper end of a narrow lane, where I met with
a nonjuror, engaged very warmly with a laceman
who was the great support of a neighbouring con-
venticle. The matter in debate was, whether the
late French king was most like Augustus Cæsar or
Nero. The controversy was carried on with great
heat on both sides, and as each of them looked upon
me very frequently during the course of their debate,

[1] Boileau died in 1711, a few months before this paper was written.
[2] Philip V of Spain and the Archduke Charles.

I was under some apprehension that they would appeal to me, and therefore laid down my penny at the bar, and made the best of my way to Cheapside.

I here gazed upon the signs for some time before I found one to my purpose. The first object I met in the coffee-room was a person who expressed a great grief for the death of the French king; but upon his explaining himself, I found his sorrow did not arise from the loss of the monarch, but for his having sold out of the bank about three days before he heard the news of it : upon which a haberdasher [1], who was the oracle of the coffee-house, and had his circle of admirers about him, called several to witness that he had declared his opinion about a week before that the French king was certainly dead; to which he added, that considering the late advices we had received from France, it was impossible that it could be otherwise. As he was laying these together, and dictating to his hearers with great authority, there came in a gentleman from Garraway's, who told us that there were several letters from France just come in, with advice that the king was in good health, and was gone out a hunting the very morning the post came away : upon which the haberdasher stole off his hat that hung upon a wooden peg by him, and retired to his shop with great confusion. This intelligence put a stop to my travels, which I had prosecuted with much [2] satisfaction; not being a little pleased to hear so many different opinions upon so great an event, and to observe how naturally upon such a piece of news every one is apt to consider it with a regard to his own particular interest and advantage.                                        L.

---

[1] This haberdasher is the counterpart of Addison's 'Political Upholsterer' in the *Tatler* (Nos. 155, 160).
[2] 'Great' (folio).

No. 404.    *Friday, June 13, 1712*    [BUDGELL [1]

*Non omnia possumus omnes.* VIRG., *Eclog.* viii, 63[2]

NATURE does nothing in vain; the Creator of the universe has appointed everything to a certain use and purpose, and determined it to a settled course and sphere of action, from which, if it in the least deviates, it becomes unfit to answer those ends for which it was designed. In like manner it is in the dispositions of society, the civil economy is formed in a chain as well as the natural; and in either case the breach but of one link puts the whole in some disorder. It is, I think, pretty plain, that most of the absurdity and ridicule we meet with in the world is generally owing to the impertinent affection of excelling in characters men are not fit for, and for which Nature never designed them.

Every man has one or more qualities which may make him useful both to himself and others. Nature never fails of pointing them out, and while the infant continues under her guardianship, she brings him on in his way, and then offers herself for a guide in what remains of the journey; if he proceeds in that course, he can hardly miscarry. Nature makes good her engagements; for as she never promises what she is not able to perform, so she never fails of performing what she promises. But the misfortune is, men despise what they may be masters of, and affect what they are not fit for; they reckon themselves already possessed of what their genius inclined them to, and so bend all their ambition to excel in what is out of their reach : thus they destroy the use of their natural talents, in the same manner as covetous men do their quiet and repose; they can enjoy no satisfaction

[1] Or perhaps Pope. There is much uncertainty about the authorship of papers signed 'Z'. See Nos. 408, 425, 467.
[2] The motto in the folio number was Virgil's

Continuo has leges æternaque fœdera certis

in what they have, because of the absurd inclination
they are possessed with for what they have not.

Cleanthes had good sense, a great memory, and a
constitution capable of the closest application : in a
word there was no profession in which Cleanthes
might not have made a very good figure; but this
won't satisfy him, he takes up an unaccountable fondness for the character of a fine gentleman; all his
thoughts are bent upon this, instead of attending
a dissection, frequenting the courts of justice, or
studying the Fathers. Cleanthes reads plays, dances,
dresses, and spends his time in drawing-rooms, instead
of being a good lawyer, divine, or physician; Cleanthes is a downright coxcomb, and will remain to
all that knew him a contemptible example of talents
misapplied. It is to this affectation the world owes
its whole race of coxcombs. Nature in her whole
drama never drew such a part; she has sometimes
made a fool, but a coxcomb is always of a man's
own making, by applying his talents otherwise than
Nature designed, who ever bears an high resentment
for being put out of her course, and never fails of
taking her revenge on those that do so. Opposing
her tendency in the application of a man's parts, has
the same success as declining from her course in the
production of vegetables, by the assistance of art and
an hotbed : we may possibly extort an unwilling
plant, or an untimely salad; but how weak, how
tasteless and insipid! Just as insipid as the poetry
of Valerio : Valerio had an universal character, was
genteel, had learning, thought justly, spoke correctly;
'twas believed there was nothing in which Valerio did
not excel; and 'twas so far true, that there was but
one; Valerio had no genius for poetry, yet he's resolved to be a poet; he writes verses, and takes great
pains to convince the town that Valerio is not that
extraordinary person he was taken for.

If men would be content to graft upon Nature, and
assist her operations, what mighty effects might we
expect! Tully would not stand so much alone in

oratory, Virgil in poetry, or Cæsar in war. To build upon Nature, is laying the foundation upon a rock; everything disposes itself into order as it were of course, and the whole work is half done as soon as undertaken. Cicero's genius inclined him to oratory, Virgil's to follow the train of the muses; they piously obeyed the admonition, and were rewarded. Had Virgil attended the Bar, his modest and ingenuous virtue would surely have made but a very indifferent figure; and Tully's declamatory inclination would have been as useless in poetry. Nature, if left to herself, leads us on in the best course, but will do nothing by compulsion and constraint; and if we are not satisfied to go her way, we are always the greatest sufferers by it.

Wherever Nature designs a production, she always disposes seeds proper for it, which are as absolutely necessary to the formation of any moral or intellectual excellence, as they are to the being and growth of plants; and I know not by what fate and folly it is, that men are taught not to reckon him equally absurd that will write verses in spite of Nature, with that gardener that should undertake to raise a jonquil or tulip without the help of their respective seeds.

As there is no good or bad quality that does not affect both sexes, so it is not to be imagined but the fair sex must have suffered by an affectation of this nature, at least as much as the other. The ill effect of it is in none so conspicuous as in the two opposite characters of Cælia and Iras; Cælia has all the charms of person, together with an abundant sweetness of nature, but wants wit, and has a very ill voice : Iras is ugly and ungenteel, but has wit and good sense. If Cælia would be silent, her beholders would adore her; if Iras would talk, her hearers would admire her; but Cælia's tongue runs incessantly, while Iras gives herself silent airs and soft languors; so that it is difficult to persuade one's self that Cælia has beauty and Iras wit : each neglects her own excellence, and is ambitious of the other's character; Iras would be

thought to have as much beauty as Cælia, and Cælia
as much wit as Iras.

The great misfortune of this affectation is, that
men not only lose a good quality, but also contract
a bad one.   They not only are unfit for what they
were designed, but they assign themselves to what
they are not fit for; and instead of making a very
good figure one way, make a very ridiculous one
another.   If Semanthe would have been satisfied with
her natural complexion, she might still have been
celebrated by the name of the Olive Beauty;[1] but
Semanthe has taken up an affectation to white and
red, and is now distinguished by the character of the
lady that paints so well.   In a word, could the world
be reformed to the obedience of that famed dictate,
' follow Nature ', which the oracle of Delphos pronounced to Cicero when he consulted what course of
studies he should pursue, we should see almost every
man as eminent in his proper sphere as Tully was in
his, and should in a very short time find impertinence
and affectation banished from among the women, and
coxcombs and false characters from among the men.
For my part, I could never consider this preposterous
repugnancy to Nature any otherwise than not only as
the greatest folly, but also one of the most heinous
crimes, since it is a direct opposition to the disposition of Providence, and (as Tully expresses it),
like the sin of the giants, an actual rebellion against
Heaven.                                                      Z.

No. 405.      Saturday, June 14, 1712      [ADDISON

Οἱ δὲ πανημέριοι μολπῇ θεὸν ἱλάσκοντο,
Καλὸν ἀείδοντες παιήονα κοῦροι ᾿Αχαιῶν,
Μέλποντες ᾿Εκάεργον. ὁ δὲ φρένα τέρπετ᾿ ἀκουων.
HOM., Iliad i, 472

I AM very sorry to find by the opera bills for this
day, that we are likely to lose the greatest performer
in dramatic music that is now living, or that perhaps
ever appeared upon a stage.   I need not acquaint my

[1] See No. 396.

reader that I am speaking of Signior Nicolini[1]. The town is highly obliged to that excellent artist, for having shown us the Italian music in its perfection, as well as for that generous approbation he lately gave to an opera of our own country, in which the composer endeavoured to do justice to the beauty of the words, by following that noble example which has been set him by the greatest foreign masters in that art.

I could heartily wish there was the same application and endeavours to cultivate and improve our church music, as have been lately bestowed on that of the stage. Our composers have one very great incitement to it. They are sure to meet with excellent words, and, at the same time, a wonderful variety of them. There is no passion that is not finely expressed in those parts of the inspired writings which are proper for divine songs and anthems.

There is a certain coldness and indifference in the phrases of our European languages, when they are compared with the Oriental forms of speech; and it happens very luckily, that the Hebrew idioms run into the English tongue with a particular grace and beauty. Our language has received innumerable elegances and improvements, from that infusion of Hebraism, which are derived to it out of the poetical passages in Holy Writ. They give a force and energy

[1] See No. 5. The folio issue had the following advertisement: 'At the Queen's Theatre in the Haymarket, this present Saturday, being the 14th day of June, Signor Cavaliero Nicolino Grimaldi will take his leave of England, in the opera of "Antiochus." And by reason of the hot weather, the waterfall will play all the time.—Boxes, 8s.; Pit. 5s.; First Gallery, 2s. 6d.; Upper Gallery, 1s. 6d.; Boxes upon the Stage, half a guinea. To begin exactly at seven.' In No. 115 of the *Tatler*, Steele spoke in high praise of Nicolini: 'An actor who, by the grace and propriety of his action and gesture, does honour to an human figure, as much as the other (a tumbler) vilifies and degrades it.' Cibber says that Nicolini, 'by pleasing the eye as well as the ear, filled us with a more various and rational delight'. He was again in England in 1715. Hughes, in a letter to Nicolini dated February 4, 1710, says he had told Steele of the obliging manner in which the singer had spoken of Mr Bickerstaff, saying that he much wished to learn English, if only that he might have the pleasure of reading the *Tatler*. Steele much appreciated the compliment (*Correspondence of John Hughes*, 1773, i, 33).

to our expressions, warm and animate our language,
and convey our thoughts in more ardent and intense
phrases, than any that are to be met with in our own
tongue.　There is something so pathetic in this kind
of diction, that it often sets the mind in a flame, and
makes our hearts burn within us.　How cold and
dead does a prayer appear, that is composed in the
most elegant and polite forms of speech which are
natural to our tongue, when it is not heightened by
that solemnity of phrase which may be drawn from
the Sacred Writings.　It has been said by some of
the ancients, that if the gods were to talk with men,
they would certainly speak in Plato's style; but I
think we may say, with justice, that when mortals
converse with their Creator, they cannot do it in so
proper a style as in that of the Holy Scriptures.

If any one would judge of the beauties of poetry
that are to be met with in the Divine Writings, and
examine how kindly the Hebrew manners of speech
mix and incorporate with the English language; after
having perused the book of Psalms, let him read a
literal translation of Horace or Pindar.　He will find
in these two last such an absurdity and confusion of
style with such a comparative poverty of imagination,
as will make him very sensible of what I have been
here advancing.

Since we have therefore such a treasury of words,
so beautiful in themselves and so proper for the airs
of music, I cannot but wonder that persons of distinction should give so little attention and encouragement
to that kind of music, which would have its foundation in reason, and which would improve our virtue
in proportion as it raised our delight.　The passions
that are excited by ordinary compositions, generally
flow from such silly and absurd occasions, that a man
is ashamed to reflect upon them seriously; but the
fear, the love, the sorrow, the indignation that are
awakened in the mind by hymns and anthems, make
the heart better, and proceed from such causes as are
altogether reasonable and praiseworthy.　Pleasure

and duty go hand in hand, and the greater our satisfaction is, the greater is our religion.

Music among those who were styled the chosen people was a religious art. The songs of Sion, which we have reason to believe were in high repute among the courts of the Eastern monarchs, were nothing else but psalms and pieces of poetry that adored or celebrated the Supreme Being. The greatest conqueror in this holy nation, after the manner of the old Grecian lyrics, did not only compose the words of his divine odes, but generally set them to music himself. After which, his works, though they were consecrated to the tabernacle, became the national entertainment, as well as the devotion of his people.

The first original of the drama was a religious worship consisting only of a chorus, which was nothing else but an hymn to a deity. As luxury and voluptuousness prevailed over innocence and religion, this form of worship degenerated into tragedies; in which, however, the chorus so far remembered its first office, as to brand everything that was vicious, and recommend everything that was laudable, to intercede with Heaven for the innocent, and to implore its vengeance on the criminal.

Homer and Hesiod intimate to us how this art should be applied, when they represent the muses as surrounding Jupiter, and warbling their hymns about his throne. I might show, from innumerable passages in ancient writers, not only that vocal and instrumental music were made use of in their religious worship, but that their most favourite diversions were filled with songs and hymns to their respective deities. Had we frequent entertainments of this nature among us, they would not a little purify and exalt our passions, give our thoughts a proper turn, and cherish those divine impulses in the soul, which every one feels that has not stifled them by sensual and immoderate pleasures.

Music, when thus applied, raises noble hints in the mind of the hearer, and fills it with great conceptions.

It strengthens devotion, and advances praise into
rapture. It lengthens out every act of worship, and
produces more lasting and permanent impressions in
the mind, than those which accompany any transient
form of words that are uttered in the ordinary method
of religious worship.                                   O.


No. 406.    *Monday, June* 16, 1712    [STEELE

*Hæc studia adolescentiam alunt, senectutem oblectant, secundas res
ornant, adversis solatium et perfugium præbent; delectant domi, non
impediunt foris: pernoctant nobiscum, peregrinantur, rusticantur.*
                                                        TULL.

THE following letters bear a pleasing image of the
joys and satisfactions of private life. The first is
from a gentleman to a friend, for whom he has a very
great respect, and to whom he communicates the satisfaction he takes in retirement; the other is a letter to
me, occasioned by an ode written by my Lapland
lover [1]; this correspondent is so kind as to translate
another of Scheffer's songs in a very agreeable manner. I publish them together that the young and old
may find something in the same paper which may
be suitable to their respective taste in solitude; for
I know no fault in the description of ardent desires
provided they are honourable.


DEAR SIR,—You have obliged me with a very kind
letter; by which I find you shift the scene of your
life from the town to the country, and enjoy that
mixed state which wise men both delight in, and are
qualified for. Methinks most of the philosophers and
moralists have run too much into extremes in praising entirely either solitude or public life; in the
former, men generally grow useless by too much rest,
and in the latter are destroyed by too much precipita-
tion : as waters lying still putrefy and are good for
nothing; and running violently on, do but the more
mischief in their passage to others, and are swallowed
up and lost the sooner themselves. Those who, like

[1] See No. 366.

you, can make themselves useful to all states, should
be like gentle streams, that not only glide through
lonely vales and forests amidst the flocks and shepherds, but visit populous towns in their course, and
are at once of ornament and service to them. But
there is another sort of people who seem designed for
solitude, those I mean who have more to hide than
to show : as for my own part, I am one of those of
whom Seneca says, 'Tum umbratiles sunt, ut putent
in turbido esse quicquid in luce est' (Some men, like
pictures, are fitter for a corner than a full light); and
I believe such as have a natural bent to solitude are
like waters which may be forced into fountains, and
exalted to a great height, may make a much nobler
figure, and a much louder noise, but after all run more
smoothly, equally, and plentifully, in their own natural
course upon the ground. The consideration of this
would make me very well contented with the possession
only of that quiet which Cowley calls the companion
of obscurity[1]; but whoever has the muses too for
his companions can never be idle enough to be uneasy.
Thus, sir, you see I would flatter myself into a good
opinion of my own way of living : Plutarch just now
told me that 'tis in human life as in a game at tables,
one may wish he had the highest cast, but if his
chance be otherwise, he is even to play it as well as
he can, and make the best of it.

I am, Sir,<br>Your most obliged and most humble Servant

MR. SPECTATOR,—The town being so well pleased with
the fine picture of artless love which nature inspired
the Laplander to paint in the ode you lately printed,
we were in hopes that the ingenious translator would
have obliged it with the other also which Scheffer has
given us; but since he has not, a much inferior hand
has ventured to send you this.

It is a custom with the Northern lovers to divert
themselves with a song whilst they journey through
the fenny moors to pay a visit to their mistresses.

---

[1] Here wrapped in the arms of quiet let me lie,
Quiet, companion of obscurity.
　　　　　Cowley's *Essays :* 'Of Obscurity'.

This is addressed by the lover to his reindeer, which is the creature that in that country supplies the want of horses. The circumstances which successively present themselves to him in his way are, I believe you will think, naturally interwoven. The anxiety of absence, the gloominess of the roads, and his resolution of frequenting only those, since those only can carry him to the object of his desires; the dissatisfaction he expresses even at the greatest swiftness with which he is carried, and his joyful surprise at an unexpected sight of his mistress as she is bathing, seem beautifully described in the original.

If all those pretty images of rural nature are lost in the imitation, yet possibly you may think fit to let this supply the place of a long letter, when want of leisure or indisposition for writing will not permit our being entertained by your own hand. I propose such a time, because though it is natural to have a fondness for what one does one's self, yet I assure you I would not have anything of mine displace a single line of yours.

I

Haste, my reindeer, and let us nimbly go
Our amorous journey through this dreary waste:
Haste, my reindeer, still, still thou art too slow,
Impetuous love demands the lightning's haste.

II

Around us far the rushy moors are spread:
Soon will the sun withdraw his cheerful ray;
Darkling and tired we shall the marshes tread,
No lay unsung to cheat the tedious way.

III

The watery length of these unjoyous moors
Does all the flowery meadows' pride excel;
Through these I fly to her my soul adores;
Ye flowery meadows, empty pride, farewell.

IV

Each moment from the charmer I'm confined,
My breast is tortured with impatient fires;
Fly, my reindeer; fly swifter than the wind,
Thy tardy feet wing with my fierce desires.

V

Our pleasing toil will then be soon o erpaid,
And thou, in wonder lost, shalt view my fair,
Admire each feature of the lovely maid,
Her artless charms, her bloom, her sprightly air

VI

But lo! with graceful motion there she swims,
Gently removing each ambitious wave;
The crowding waves transported clasp her limbs:
When, when, oh when, shall I such freedoms have!

VII

In vain, you envious streams, so fast you flow,
To hide her from a lover's ardent gaze:
From every touch you more transparent grow,
And all revealed the beauteous wanton plays.

T.

No. 407.      *Tuesday, June* 17, 1712      [ADDISON
*Abest facundis gratia dictis.*   OVID, *Met.* xiii, 127

MOST foreign writers who have given any character
of the English nation, whatever vices they ascribe to
it, allow in general that the people are naturally
modest.  It proceeds perhaps from this our national
virtue, that our orators are observed to make use of
less gesture or action than those of other countries.
Our preachers stand stock-still in the pulpit, and will
not so much as move a finger to set off the best sermons in the world.  We meet with the same speaking statues at our bars, and in all public places of
debate.  Our words flow from us in a smooth continued stream, without those strainings of the voice,
motions of the body, and majesty of the hand, which
are so much celebrated in the orators of Greece and
Rome.  We can talk of life and death in cold blood,
and keep our temper in a discourse which turns upon
everything that is dear to us.  Though our zeal breaks
out in the finest tropes and figures, it is not able to
stir a limb about us.  I have heard it observed more
than once by those who have seen Italy, that an un-
travelled Englishman cannot relish all the beauties
of Italian pictures, because the postures which are

expressed in them are often such as are peculiar to that country. One who has not seen an Italian in the pulpit, will not know what to make of that noble gesture in Raphael's picture of St Paul preaching at Athens, where the Apostle is represented as lifting up both his arms, and pouring out the thunder of his rhetoric amidst an audience of Pagan philosophers [1].

It is certain that proper gestures and vehement exertions of the voice cannot be too much studied by a public orator. They are a kind of comment to what he utters, and enforce everything he says, with weak hearers, better than the strongest argument he can make use of. They keep the audience awake, and fix their attention to what is delivered to them, at the same time that they show the speaker is in earnest, and affected himself with what he so passionately recommends to others. Violent gesture and vociferation naturally shake the hearts of the ignorant, and fill them with a kind of religious horror. Nothing is more frequent than to see women weep and tremble at the sight of a moving preacher, though he is placed quite out of their hearing; as in England we very frequently see people lulled asleep with solid and elaborate discourses of piety, who would be warmed and transported out of themselves by the bellowings and distortions of enthusiasm.

If nonsense, when accompanied with such an emotion of voice and body, has such an influence on men's minds, what might we not expect from many of those admirable discourses which are printed in our tongue, were they delivered with a becoming fervour, and with the most agreeable graces of voice and gesture?

We are told that the great Latin orator very much impaired his health by this *laterum contentio*, this vehemence of action, with which he used to deliver himself. The Greek orator [2] was likewise so very

---

[1] *Acts*, chap. xvii.
[2] Demosthenes, whose banishment was caused by his speech *De Corona*.

famous for this particular in rhetoric, that one of his antagonists [1], whom he had banished from Athens, reading over the oration which had procured his banishment, and seeing his friends admire it, could not forbear asking them, if they were so much affected by the bare reading of it, how much more they would have been alarmed had they heard him actually throwing out such a storm of eloquence?

How cold and dead a figure, in comparison of these two great men, does an orator often make at the British Bar, holding up his head with the most insipid serenity, and stroking the sides of a long wig that reaches down to his middle? The truth of it is, there is often nothing more ridiculous than the gestures of an English speaker; you see some of them running their hands into their pockets as far as ever they can thrust them, and others looking with great attention on a piece of paper that has nothing written on it; you may see many a smart rhetorician turning his hat in his hands, moulding it into several different cocks, examining sometimes the lining of it, and sometimes the button, during the whole course of his harangue. A deaf man would think he was cheapening a beaver when perhaps he is talking of the fate of the British nation. I remember, when I was a young man, and used to frequent Westminster Hall, there was a counsellor who never pleaded without a piece of pack-thread in his hand, which he used to twist about a thumb, or a finger, all the while he was speaking: the wags of those days used to call it the thread of his discourse, for he was not able to utter a word without it. One of his clients, who was more merry than wise, stole it from him one day in the midst of his pleading, but he had better have let it alone, for he lost his cause by his jest.

I have all along acknowledged myself to be a dumb man, and therefore may be thought a very improper person to give rules for oratory; but I believe every one will agree with me in this, that we ought either

[1] Æschines.

to lay aside all kinds of gesture (which seems to be very suitable to the genius of our nation), or at least to make use of such only as are graceful and expressive. O.

No. 408. *Wednesday, June 18, 1712* [POPE [1]

*Decet affectus animi neque se nimium erigere, nec subjacere serviliter.*
TULL., *de Finibus*

MR. SPECTATOR,—I have always been a very great lover of your speculations, as well in regard to the subject, as to your manner of treating it. Human nature I always thought the most useful object of human reason, and to make the consideration of it pleasant and entertaining I always thought the best employment of human wit. Other parts of philosophy may perhaps make us wiser, but this not only answers that end, but makes us better too. Hence it was that the Oracle pronounced Socrates the wisest of all men living, because he judiciously made choice of human nature for the object of his thoughts; an inquiry into which as much exceeds all other learning, as it is of more consequence to adjust the true nature and measures of right and wrong, than to settle the distance of the planets, and compute the times of their circumvolutions.

One good effect that will immediately arise from a near observation of human nature is, that we shall cease to wonder at those actions which men are used to reckon wholly unaccountable; for as nothing is produced without a cause, so by observing the nature and course of the passions, we shall be able to trace every action from its first conception to its death. We shall no more admire at the proceedings of Cataline or Tiberius, when we know the one was actuated by a cruel jealousy, the other by a furious ambition; for the actions of men follow their passions as naturally as light does heat, or as any other effect flows from its cause; reason must be employed in adjusting the passions, but they must ever remain the principles of action.

[1] Or possibly Budgell. See No. 404.

The strange and absurd variety that is so apparent in men's actions, shows plainly they can never proceed immediately from reason; so pure a fountain emits no such troubled waters. They must necessarily arise from the passions, which are to the mind as the winds to a ship, they only can move it, and they too often destroy it; if fair and gentle they guide it into the harbour, if contrary and furious they overset it in the waves. In the same manner is the mind assisted or endangered by the passions: reason must then take the place of pilot, and can never fail of securing her charge if she be not wanting to herself. The strength of the passions will never be accepted as an excuse for complying with them; they were designed for subjection, and if a man suffers them to get the upper hand, he then betrays the liberty of his own soul.

As Nature has framed the several species of beings as it were in a chain, so man seems to be placed as the middle link between angels and brutes. Hence he participates both of flesh and spirit by an admirable tie, which in him occasions perpetual war of passions; and as a man inclines to the angelic or brute part of his constitution, he is then denominated good or bad, virtuous or wicked; if love, mercy, and good-nature prevail, they speak him of the angel; if hatred, cruelty, and envy predominate, they declare his kindred to the brute. Hence it was that some of the ancients imagined, that as men in this life inclined more to the angel or the brute, so after their death they should transmigrate into the one or the other; and it would be no unpleasant notion to consider the several species of brutes, into which we may imagine that tyrants, misers, the proud, malicious, and ill-natured might be changed.

As a consequence of this original, all passions are in all men, but all appear not in all; constitution, education, custom of the country, reason, and the like causes, may improve or abate the strength of them, but still the seeds remain, which are ever ready to sprout forth upon the least encouragement. I have heard a story of a good religious man, who, having been bred with the milk of a goat, was very modest in public by a careful reflection he made on his actions, but he frequently had an hour in secret, wherein he had his frisks and capers; and if we had an opportunity of examining the retirement of the strictest philosophers, no doubt but we should find perpetual returns of those passions they so artfully conceal from the public. I remember Machiavel observes [1], that every state should entertain a perpetual jealousy of its neighbours, that so it should never be unprovided when an emergency happens; in like manner should the reason be perpetually on its guard against the passions, and never suffer them to carry on any design that may be destructive of its security; yet at the same time it must be careful, that it don't so far break their strength as to render them contemptible, and consequently itself unguarded.

The understanding being of itself too slow and lazy to exert itself into action, it's necessary it should be put in motion by the gentle gales of the passions, which may preserve it from stagnating and corruption; for they are as necessary to the health of the mind, as the circulation of the animal spirits is to the health of the body; they keep it in life, and strength, and vigour; nor is it possible for the mind to perform its offices without their assistance. These motions are given us with our being, they are little spirits that are born and die with us; to some they are mild, easy, and gentle, to others wayward and unruly, yet never too strong for the reins of reason and the guidance of judgment.

We may generally observe a pretty nice proportion between the strength of reason and passion; the greatest geniuses have commonly the strongest affections, as, on the other hand, the weaker understandings have generally the weaker passions; and 'tis fit the fury of the coursers should not be too great for the strength of the charioteer. Young men whose passions are not a little unruly, give small hopes of their ever being considerable; the fire of youth will of course abate, and is a fault, if it be a fault, that mends every day; but surely unless a man has fire in youth, he can hardly have warmth in old age. We must therefore be very cautious, lest while we think to regulate the passions, we should quite extinguish them, which

[1] *The Prince*, chap. xiv.

is putting out the light of the soul; for to be without passion, or to be hurried away with it, makes a man equally blind. The extraordinary severity used in most of our schools has this fatal effect, it breaks the spring of the mind, and most certainly destroys more good geniuses than it can possibly improve. And surely 'tis a mighty mistake that the passions should be so entirely subdued; for little irregularities are sometimes not only to be borne with, but to be cultivated too, since they are frequently attended with the greatest perfections. All great geniuses have faults mixed with their virtues, and resemble the flaming bush which has thorns amongst lights.

Since therefore the passions are the principles of human actions, we must endeavour to manage them so as to retain their vigour, yet keep them under strict command; we must govern them rather like free subjects than slaves, lest while we intend to make them obedient, they become abject, and unfit for those great purposes to which they were designed. For my part I must confess, I could never have any regard to that sect of philosophers, who so much insisted upon an absolute indifference and vacancy from all passion; for it seems to me a thing very inconsistent for a man to divest himself of humanity, in order to acquire tranquillity of mind, and to eradicate the very principles of action, because it's possible they may produce ill effects.

I am, Sir,<br>
Your affectionate Admirer,

Z.                                                      T. B.

No. 409.      *Thursday, June 19, 1712*      [ADDISON

*Musæo contingere cuncta lepore.*  LUCR. i, 933

GRACIAN [1] very often recommends ' the fine taste ', as the utmost perfection of an accomplished man. As this word arises very often in conversation, I shall endeavour to give some account of it, and to lay down

[1] See No. 293. Gracian introduced into Spanish prose that false taste for conceits with which Gongora had infected Spanish poetry. Among his works were a prose tract, *The Hero*, an *Art of Poetry*, and the *Criticon*.

rules how we may know whether we are possessed of it, and how we may acquire that fine taste of writing, which is so much talked of among the polite world.

Most languages make use of this metaphor, to express that faculty of the mind, which distinguishes all the most concealed faults and nicest perfections in writing. We may be sure this metaphor would not have been so general in all tongues, had there not been a very great conformity between that mental taste, which is the subject of this paper, and that sensitive taste which gives us a relish of every different flavour that affects the palate. Accordingly we find, there are as many degrees of refinement in the intellectual faculty, as in the sense, which is marked out by this common denomination.

I knew a person who possessed the one in so great a perfection, that after having tasted ten different kinds of tea, he would distinguish, without seeing the colour of it, the particular sort which was offered him; and not only so, but any two sorts of them that were mixed together in an equal proportion; nay, he has carried the experiment so far, as upon tasting the composition of three different sorts, to name the parcels from whence the three several ingredients were taken. A man of a fine taste in writing will discern, after the same manner, not only the general beauties and imperfections of an author, but discover the several ways of thinking and expressing himself, which diversify him from all other authors, with the several foreign infusions of thought and language, and the particular authors from whom they were borrowed.

After having thus far explained what is generally meant by a fine taste in writing, and shown the propriety of the metaphor which is used on this occasion, I think I may define it to be ' that faculty of the soul which discerns the beauties of an author with pleasure, and the imperfections with dislike.' If a man would know whether he is possessed of this faculty, I would have him read over the celebrated works of antiquity, which have stood the test of so many different ages and countries, or those works among the moderns which have the sanction of the politer part of our contemporaries. If upon the perusal of such writings he does not find himself delighted in an extraordinary manner; or if, upon reading the admired passages in such authors, he finds a coldness and indifference in his thoughts, he ought to conclude, not (as is too usual among tasteless readers) that the author wants those perfections which have been admired in him, but that he himself wants the faculty of discovering them.

He should, in the second place, be very careful to observe whether he tastes the distinguishing perfections, or, if I may be allowed to call them so, the specific qualities of the author whom he peruses; whether he is particularly pleased with Livy for his manner of telling a story, with Sallust for his entering into those internal principles of action which arise from the characters and manners of the persons he describes, or with Tacitus for his displaying those outward motives of safety and interest which give birth to the whole series of transactions which he relates.

He may likewise consider how differently he is affected by the same thought, which presents itself in a great writer, from what he is when he finds it delivered by a person of an ordinary genius. For there is as much difference in apprehending a thought clothed in Cicero's language, and that of a common author, as in seeing an object by the light of a taper or by the light of the sun.

It is very difficult to lay down rules for the acquirement of such a taste as that I am here speaking of. The faculty must in some degree be born with us, and it very often happens that those who have other qualities in perfection are wholly void of this. One of the most eminent mathematicians of the age has assured me, that the greatest pleasure he took in reading Virgil was in examining Æneas' voyage by the map; as I question not but many a modern com-

piler of history would be delighted with little more in
that divine author than in the bare matters of fact.

But notwithstanding this faculty must in some
measure be born with us, there are several methods
for cultivating and improving it, and without which
it will be very uncertain and of little use to the person that possesses it.  The most natural method for
this purpose is to be conversant among the writings
of the most polite authors.  A man who has any
relish for fine writing either discovers new beauties
or receives stronger impressions from the masterly
strokes of a great author every time he peruses him :
besides that he naturally wears himself into the same
manner of speaking and thinking.

Conversation with men of a polite genius is another
method for improving our natural taste.  It is impossible for a man of the greatest parts to consider anything in its whole extent and in all its variety of
lights.  Every man, besides those general observations which are to be made upon an author, forms
several reflections that are peculiar to his own manner of thinking; so that conversation will naturally
furnish us with hints which we did not attend to, and
make us enjoy other men's parts and reflections as
well as our own.  This is the best reason I can give
for the observation which several have made, that
men of great genius in the same way of writing seldom rise up singly, but at certain periods of time
appear together, and in a body; as they did at Rome
in the reign of Augustus, and in Greece about the age
of Socrates.  I cannot think that Corneille, Racine,
Molière, Boileau, La Fontaine, Bruyère, Bossu, or
the Daciers, would have written so well as they have
done had they not been friends and contemporaries.

It is likewise necessary, for a man who would form
to himself a finished taste of good writing, to be well
versed in the works of the best critics, both ancient
and modern.  I must confess that I could wish there
were authors of this kind who, beside the mechanical
rules which a man of very little taste may discourse

upon, would enter into the very spirit and soul of fine writing, and show us the several sources of that pleasure which rises in the mind upon the perusal of a noble work. Thus although in poetry it be absolutely necessary that the unities of time, place, and action, with other points of the same nature, should be thoroughly explained and understood, there is still something more essential to the art, something that elevates and astonishes the fancy, and gives a greatness of mind to the reader, which few of the critics besides Longinus have considered.

Our general taste in England is for epigram, turns of wit, and forced conceits, which have no manner of influence, either for the bettering or enlarging the mind of him who reads them, and have been carefully avoided by the greatest writers, both among the ancients and moderns. I have endeavoured in several of my speculations to banish this Gothic taste, which has taken possession among us. I entertained the town for a week together with an essay upon wit[1], in which I endeavoured to detect several of those false kinds which have been admired in the different ages of the world; and at the same time to show wherein the nature of true wit consists. I afterwards gave an instance of the great force which lies in a natural simplicity of thought to affect the mind of the reader, from such vulgar pieces as have little else besides this single qualification to recommend them. I have likewise examined the works of the greatest poet which our nation, or, perhaps, any other, has produced, and particularised most of those rational and manly beauties which give a value to that divine work[2]. I shall next Saturday enter upon an essay ' On the Pleasures of the Imagination[3] ', which, though it shall consider that subject at large, will perhaps suggest to the reader what it is that gives a beauty to many passages of the finest writers,

1 Nos. 58, 61, 62, &c.
2 The papers on *Paradise Lost*, which appeared between Nos. 267 and 369.                              3 Nos. 411–421.

both in prose and verse. As an undertaking of this
nature is entirely new, I question not but it will be
received with candour.          O.

No. 410.    *Friday, June 20, 1712*    [TICKELL [1]

*Dum foris sunt, nihil videtur mundius,*
*Nec magis compositum quidquam, nec magis elegans:*
*Quæ, cum amatore suo cum cœnant, liguriunt,*
*Harum videre ingluviem, sordes, inopiam:*
*Quam inhonestæ solæ sint domi, atque avidæ cibi,*
*Quo pacto ex jure hesterno panem atrum vorent.*
*Nosse omnia hæc, salus est adolescentulis.*
                      TER., *Eun.*, Act v, sc. 4

WILL HONEYCOMB, who disguises his present decay
by visiting the wenches of the town only by way of
humour, told us that the last rainy night he, with
Sir Roger de Coverley, was driven into the Temple
cloister, whither had escaped also a lady most exactly
dressed from head to foot. Will made no scruple to
acquaint us that she saluted him very familiarly by
his name, and turning immediately to the knight, she
said she supposed that was his good friend Sir
Roger de Coverley; upon which nothing less could
follow than Sir Roger's approach to salutation, with
' Madam, the same at your service '. She was
dressed in a black tabby mantua and petticoat, without ribbons; her linen striped muslin, and in the
whole in an agreeable second mourning; decent

---

[1] This paper, sometimes attributed to Steele, is generally believed
to have been written by Tickell. Johnson and others have supposed
that Addison was so annoyed at the suggestion that Sir Roger de
Coverley could have any equivocal relations with a woman of bad
character, that he decided to kill off the knight to prevent such a
thing occurring again. But the fact is, that four months elapsed
after the publication of this paper, before Addison wrote his account
of Sir Roger's death (No. 517); and by that time the discontinuance
of the *Spectator* had been resolved upon, and the knight's death was
only the first of a series of papers designed to dispose of the various
members of the club. In No. 544 Steele said that the story in this
paper had been misunderstood; the circumstance of the young woman
at the tavern was intended as an instance of the simplicity and
innocence of Sir Roger's mind, which made him think it an easy
matter to reclaim the girl, and not as inclination in him to be guilty
with her. There is really nothing in the paper to warrant us in saying
that this explanation is forced.

dresses being often affected by the creatures of the
town, at once consulting cheapness and the pretension to modesty.  She went on with a familiar, easy
air, ' Your friend, Mr Honeycomb, is a little surprised to see a woman here alone and unattended;
but I dismissed my coach at the gate and tripped it
down to my counsel's chambers, for lawyers' fees
take up too much of a small disputed jointure to
admit any other expenses but mere necessaries.'  Mr
Honeycomb begged they might have the honour of
setting her down, for Sir Roger's servant was gone
to call a coach.  In the interim the footman returned with no coach to be had; and there appeared
nothing to be done but trusting herself with Mr
Honeycomb and his friend, to wait at the tavern at
the gate for a coach, or be subjected to all the impertinence she must meet with in that public place.
Mr Honeycomb being a man of honour determined
the choice of the first, and Sir Roger, as the better
man, took the lady by the hand, leading, through all
the shower covering her with his hat, and gallanting
a familiar acquaintance, through rows of young fellows who winked at Sukey in the state she marched
off, Will Honeycomb bringing up the rear.

Much importunity prevailed upon the fair one to
admit of a collation, where, after declaring she had
no stomach, and eaten a couple of chickens, devoured
a truffle of salad, and drunk a full bottle to her share,
she sung ' The Old Man's Wish ' [1] to Sir Roger.  The
knight left the room for some time after supper, and
writ the following billet, which he conveyed to Sukey,

[1] In a song with this title by W. Pope, printed early in the eighteenth
century, and beginning :

If I live to grow old, for I find I go down,

the writer prayed that his fate might be to have a warm country
house, an easy nag, a dish of roast mutton, with pudding on Sundays,
and stout, and a reserve of Burgundy wine for the vicar.  He hoped it
might be said of him :

He governed his passion with an absolute sway,
And grew wiser and better as his strength wore away.

and Sukey to her friend Will Honeycomb. Will has given it to Sir Andrew Freeport, who read it last night to the club.

MADAM,—I am not so mere a country gentleman, but I can guess at the law business you had at the Temple. If you would go down to the country and leave off all your vanities but your singing, let me know at my lodgings in Bow Street, Covent Garden, and you shall be encouraged by,
Your humble Servant,
ROGER DE COVERLEY

My good friend could not well stand the raillery which was rising upon him; but to put a stop to it I delivered Will Honeycomb the following letter, and desired him to read it to the board :

MR. SPECTATOR,—Having seen a translation of one of the chapters in the Canticles into English verse, inserted among your late papers [1], I have ventured to send you the 7th chapter of the Proverbs in a poetical dress. If you think it worthy appearing among your speculations, it will be a sufficient reward for the trouble of
Your constant Reader,

A. B.

My son, th' instruction that my words impart,
Grave on the living tablet of thy heart ;
And all the wholesome precepts that I give,
Observe with strictest reverence, and live.

Let all thy homage be to wisdom paid.
Seek her protection, and implore her aid ;
That she may keep thy soul from harm secure,
And turn thy footsteps from the harlot's door.
Who with cursed charms lures the unwary in,
And soothes with flattery their souls to sin.

Once from my window as I cast mine eye
On those that passed in giddy numbers by,
A youth among the foolish youths I spied,
Who took not sacred wisdom for his guide.

---

[1] See No. 388.

Just as the sun withdrew his cooler light,
And evening soft led on the shades of night
He stole in covert twilight to his fate,
And passed the corner near the harlot's gate;
When, lo, a woman comes!
Loose her attire, and such her glaring dress
As aptly did the harlot's mind express:

Subtle she is, and practised in the arts
By which the wanton conquer heedless hearts:
Stubborn and loud she is; she hates her home,
Varying her place and form, she loves to roam;
Now she's within, now in the street does stray,
Now at each corner stands, and waits her prey.
The youth she seized, and laying now aside
All modesty, the female's justest pride,
She said, with an embrace, 'Here at my house
Peace-offerings are, this day I paid my vows.
I therefore came abroad to meet my dear,
And, lo, in happy hour I find thee here.

'My chamber I've adorned, and o'er my bed
Are coverings of the richest tap'stry spread,
With linen it is decked from Egypt brought,
And carvings by the curious artist wrought;
It wants no glad perfume Arabia yields
In all her citron groves, and spicy fields:
Here all her store of richest odours meets,
I'll lay thee in a wilderness of sweets.
Whatever to the sense can grateful be
I have collected there—I want but thee.
My husband's gone a journey far away,
Much gold he took abroad, and long will stay,
He named for his return a distant day.'

Upon her tongue did such smooth mischief dwell,
And from her lips such welcome flattery fell.
Th' unguarded youth, in silken fetters tied,
Resigned his reason, and with ease complied.
Thus does the ox to his own slaughter go,
And thus is senseless of th' impending blow.
Thus flies the simple bird into the snare
That skilful fowlers for his life prepare.
But let my sons attend, attend may they
Whom youthful vigour may to sin betray;
Let them false charmers fly, and guard their hearts
Against the wily wanton's pleasing arts.
With care direct their steps, nor turn astray
To tread the paths of her deceitful way;
Lest they too late of her fell power complain,
And fall, where many mightier have been slain.

T.

No. 411.  *Saturday, June 21, 1712*  [ADDISON

*Avia Pieridum peragro loca, nullius ante
Trita solo; juvat integros accedere fonteis;
Atque haurire.*  LUCR. i, 925

OUR sight is the most perfect and most delightful
of all our senses.  It fills the mind with the largest
variety of ideas, converses with its objects at the
greatest distance, and continues the longest in action
without being tired or satiated with its proper enjoyments.  The sense of feeling can indeed give us a
notion of extension, shape, and all other ideas that
enter at the eye, except colours; but at the same
time it is very much straitened and confined in its
operations, to the number, bulk, and distance of its
particular objects.  Our sight seems designed to supply all these defects, and may be considered as a
more delicate and diffusive kind of touch, that spreads
itself over an infinite multitude of bodies, comprehends the largest figures, and brings into our reach
some of the most remote parts of the universe.

It is this sense which furnishes the imagination
with its ideas; so that by the pleasures of the imagination or fancy (which I shall use promiscuously) I
here mean such as arise from visible objects, either
when we have them actually in our view, or when
we call up their ideas into our minds by paintings,
statues, descriptions, or any the like occasion.  We
cannot indeed have a single image in the fancy that
did not make its first entrance through the sight;
but we have the power of retaining, altering, and
compounding those images which we have once received into all the varieties of picture and vision that
are most agreeable to the imagination; for by this
faculty a man in a dungeon is capable of entertaining
himself with scenes and landscapes more beautiful
than any that can be found in the whole compass of
nature.

There are few words in the English language which
are employed in a more loose and uncircumscribed

sense than those of the fancy and the imagination [1].
I therefore thought it necessary to fix and determine the notion of these two words, as I intend to
make use of them in the thread of my following
speculations, that the reader may conceive rightly
what is the subject which I proceed upon.  I must
therefore desire him to remember, that by the pleasures of the imagination I mean only such pleasures
as arise originally from sight, and that I divide
these pleasures in two kinds : my design being first
of all to discourse of those primary pleasures of the
imagination which entirely proceed from such objects
as are before our eyes [2]; and in the next place, to
speak of those secondary pleasures of the imagination
which flow from the ideas of visible objects, when the
objects are not actually before the eye, but are called
up into our memories, or formed into agreeable
visions of things that are either absent or fictitious.

The pleasures of the imagination, taken in their
full extent, are not so gross as those of sense, nor
so refined as those of the understanding.  The last
are, indeed, more preferable, because they are founded
on some new knowledge or improvement in the mind
of man; yet it must be confessed, that those of the
imagination are as great and as transporting as the
other.  A beautiful prospect delights the soul, as
much as a demonstration; and a description in Homer
has charmed more readers than a chapter in Aristotle [3].  Besides, the pleasures of the imagination

[1] Akenside's poem on *The Pleasures of the Imagination* was suggested
by these papers of Addison's.  Blair, in his *Rhetoric*, devoted four
lectures to a 'critical examination of the style of Mr Addison in
Nos. 411, 412, 413, and 414 of the *Spectator*'.  The MS. Note-Book
already referred to (see No. 170) shows with how much care these
papers were written.

[2] 'Are present to the eye' (folio).

[3] The MS. Note-Book already mentioned (see No. 170) has lost
several of the first leaves, and opens with this sentence of the first of
Addison's papers on the Imagination.  The book contains also the first
draughts of Nos. 412, 413, 414, 416, 417, 418, 420, and 421, but many
additions were made before publication.  Of No. 411 the MS. contains
only the remainder of this paragraph, and the sentence about Bacon on
p. 39 below.

have this advantage, above those of the understanding, that they are more obvious, and more easy to be acquired. It is but opening the eye, and the scene enters. The colours paint themselves on the fancy, with very little attention of thought or application of mind in the beholder. We are struck, we know not how, with the symmetry of anything we see, and immediately assent to the beauty of an object, without inquiring into the particular causes and occasions of it [1].

A man of a polite imagination is let into a great many pleasures that the vulgar are not capable of receiving. He can converse with a picture, and find an agreeable companion in a statue. He meets with a secret refreshment in a description, and often feels a greater satisfaction in the prospect of fields and meadows, than another does in the possession. It gives him, indeed, a kind of property in everything he sees, and makes the most rude uncultivated parts of nature administer to his pleasures. So that he looks upon the world, as it were, in another light, and discovers in it a multitude of charms that conceal themselves from the generality of mankind.

There are, indeed, but very few who know how to be idle and innocent, or have a relish of any pleasures that are not criminal; every diversion they take is at the expense of some one virtue or another, and their very first step out of business is into vice or folly. A man should endeavour, therefore, to make the sphere of his innocent pleasures as wide as possible, that he may retire into them with safety, and find in them such a satisfaction as a wise man would not blush to take. Of this nature are those of the imagination, which do not require such a bent of thought as is necessary to our more serious employments, nor, at the same time, suffer the mind to sink into that negligence and remissness which are apt to accompany our more sensual delights, but, like a gentle exercise to the faculties, awaken them

[1] 'Without being able to give a reason for it' (MS.).

from sloth and idleness, without putting them upon any labour or difficulty.

We might here add, that the pleasures of the fancy are more conducive to health than those of the understanding, which are worked out by dint of thinking, and attended with too violent a labour of the brain. Delightful scenes, whether in nature, painting, or poetry, have a kindly influence on the body as well as the mind, and not only serve to clear and brighten the imagination, but are able to disperse grief and melancholy, and to set the animal spirits in pleasing and agreeable motions. For this reason Sir Francis Bacon, in his *Essay upon Health*, has not thought it improper to prescribe to his reader a poem or a prophet, where he particularly dissuades him from knotty and subtle disquisitions, and advises him to pursue studies that fill the mind with splendid and illustrious objects, as histories, fables, and contemplations of nature.

I have in this paper, by way of introduction, settled the notion of those pleasures of the imagination which are the subject of my present undertaking, and endeavoured, by several considerations, to recommend to my reader the pursuit of those pleasures. I shall, in my next paper, examine the several sources from whence these pleasures are derived.　　　　O.

No. 412.　　*Monday, June 23, 1712*　　[ADDISON

*Divisum sic breve fiet opus.* MART., *Epig.* iv, 83

I SHALL first consider those pleasures of the imagination which arise from the actual view and survey of outward objects. And these, I think, all proceed from the sight of what is great, uncommon, or beautiful. There may, indeed, be something so terrible or offensive, that the horror or loathsomeness of an object may overbear the pleasure which results from its greatness, novelty, or beauty; but still there will be such a mixture of delight in the very disgust it

gives us, as any of these three qualifications are most
conspicuous and prevailing.

By greatness, I do not only mean the bulk of any
single object, but the largeness of a whole view, considered as one entire piece.  Such are the prospects
of an open champian[1] country, a vast uncultivated
desert, of huge heaps of mountains, high rocks and
precipices, or a wide expanse of waters, where we
are not struck with the novelty or beauty of the sight,
but with that rude kind of magnificence which appears in many of these stupendous works of Nature.
Our imagination loves to be filled with an object, or
to grasp at anything that is too big for its capacity.
We are flung into a pleasing astonishment at such
unbounded views, and feel a delightful stillness and
amazement in the soul at the apprehension of them.
The mind[2] of man naturally hates everything that
looks like a restraint upon it, and is apt to fancy
itself under a sort of confinement, when the sight is
pent up in a narrow compass, and shortened on every
side by the neighbourhood of walls or mountains.  On
the contrary, a spacious horizon is an image of liberty,
where the eye has room to range abroad, to expatiate
at large on the immensity of its views, and to lose
itself amidst the variety of objects that offer themselves to its observation.  Such wide and undetermined prospects are as pleasing to the fancy, as the
speculations of eternity or infinitude are to the understanding.  But if there be a beauty or uncommonness
joined with this grandeur, as in a troubled ocean, a
heaven adorned with stars and meteors, or a spacious
landscape cut out into rivers, woods, rocks, and
meadows, the pleasure still grows upon us, as it
arises from more than a single principle.

Everything that is new or uncommon raises a
pleasure in the imagination, because it fills the soul
with an agreeable surprise, gratifies its curiosity, and
gives it an idea of which it was not before possessed.

[1] Champaign, flat.
[2] This, with the two following sentences, is among the additions in
the MS. in Addison's own writing.

We are, indeed, so often conversant with one set of objects, and tired out with so many repeated shows of the same things, that whatever is new or uncommon contributes a little to vary human life, and to divert our minds, for a while, with the strangeness of its appearance : it serves us for a kind of refreshment, and takes off from that satiety we are apt to complain of in our usual and ordinary entertainments. It is this that bestows charms on a monster, and makes even the imperfections of nature please us. It is this that recommends variety, where the mind is every instant called off to something new, and the attention not suffered to dwell too long, and waste itself on any particular object. It is this, likewise, that improves what is great or beautiful, and makes it afford the mind a double entertainment. Groves, fields, and meadows are at any season of the year pleasant to look upon, but never so much as in the opening of the spring, when they are all new and fresh with their first gloss upon them, and not yet too much accustomed and familiar to the eye. For this reason there is nothing that more enlivens a prospect than rivers, jetteaus, or falls of water, where the scene is perpetually shifting, and entertaining the sight every moment with something that is new. We are quickly tired with looking upon hills and valleys, where everything continues fixed and settled in the same place and posture, but find our thoughts a little agitated and relieved at the sight of such objects as are ever in motion, and sliding away from beneath the eye of the beholder.

But there is nothing that makes its way more directly to the soul than beauty, which immediately diffuses a secret satisfaction and complacency through the imagination, and gives a finishing to anything that is great or uncommon. The very first discovery of it strikes the mind with an inward joy, and spreads a cheerfulness and delight through all its faculties. There is not, perhaps, any real beauty or deformity more in one piece of matter than another, because we might have been so made that whatsoever now appears loathsome to us might have shown itself agreeable; but we find by experience that there are several modifications of matter which the mind, without any previous consideration, pronounces at first sight beautiful or deformed. Thus [1] we see that every different species of sensible creatures has its different notions of beauty, and that each of them is most affected with the beauties of its own kind. This is nowhere more remarkable than in birds of the same shape and proportion, where we often see the male determined in his courtship by the single grain or tincture of a feather, and never discovering any charms but in the colour of its species.

> Scit thalamo servare fidem, sanctasque veretur
> Connubii leges, non illum in pectore candor
> Sollicitat niveus; neque pravum accendit amorem
> Splendida lanugo, vel honesta in vertice crista,
> Purpureusve nitor pennarum; ast agmina latè
> Fæmineá explorat cautus, maculasque requirit
> Cognatas, paribusque interlita corpora guttis:
> Ni faceret, pictis sylvam circum undique monstris
> Confusam aspiceres vulgò, partusque biformes,
> Et genus ambiguum, et veneris monumenta nefandæ.
> Hinc Merula in nigro se oblectat nigra marito,
> Hinc socium lasciva petit Philomela canorum,
> Agnoscitque pares sonitus, hinc Noctua tetram
> Canitiem alarum, et glaucos miratur ocellos.
> Nempe sibi semper constat, crescitque quotannis
> Lucida progenies, castos confessa parentes;
> Dum virides inter saltus locosque sonoros
> Vere novo exultat, plumasque decora juventus
> Explicat ad solem, patriisque coloribus ardet [2].

There is a second kind of beauty that we find in the several products of art and nature which does not work in the imagination with that warmth and violence as the beauty that appears in our proper species, but is apt, however, to raise in us a secret

[1] Most of the remainder of this paper was added to the MS. in Addison's writing.

[2] Addison's MS. shows, by corrections in his handwriting of four or five lines in this piece of Latin verse, that he was himself its author. Thus in the last line he had begun with 'Scintillat solitis', altered that to 'Ostentat solitas', struck out that also, and finally wrote as above, 'Explicat ad solem'.

delight, and a kind of fondness for the places or objects in which we discover it. This consists either in the gaiety or variety of colours, in the symmetry and proportion of parts, in the arrangement and disposition of bodies, or in a just mixture and concurrence of all together. Among these several kinds of beauty the eye takes most delight in colours. We nowhere meet with a more glorious or pleasing show in nature than what appears in the heavens at the rising and setting of the sun, which is wholly made up of those different stains of light that show themselves in clouds of a different situation. For this reason we find the poets, who are always addressing themselves to the imagination, borrowing more of their epithets from colours than from any other topic.

As the fancy delights in everything that is great, strange, or beautiful, and is still more pleased the more it finds of these perfections in the same object, so it is capable of receiving a new satisfaction by the assistance of another sense. Thus any continued sound, as the music of birds, or a fall of water, awakens every moment the mind of the beholder, and makes him more attentive to the several beauties of the place that lie before him. Thus if there arises a fragrancy of smells or perfumes, they heighten the pleasures of the imagination, and make even the colours and verdure of the landscape appear more agreeable; for the ideas of both senses recommend each other, and are pleasanter together than when they enter the mind separately. As the different colours of a picture, when they are well disposed, set off one another, and receive an additional beauty from the advantage of their situation.          O.

No. 413.          *Tuesday*, June 24, 1712          [ADDISON

*Causa latet, vis est notissima.*  OVID, *Met.*

THOUGH in yesterday's paper we considered how everything that is great, new, or beautiful, is apt to affect the imagination with pleasure, we must own that it is impossible for us to assign the necessary cause of this pleasure, because we know neither the nature of an idea, nor the substance of a human soul, which might help us to discover the conformity or disagreeableness of the one to the other; and therefore, for want of such a light, all that we can do in speculations of this kind, is to reflect on those operations of the soul that are most agreeable, and to range, under their proper heads, what is pleasing or displeasing to the mind, without being able to trace out the several necessary and efficient causes from whence the pleasure or displeasure arises.

Final causes lie more bare and open to our observation, as there are often a great variety that belong to the same effect; and these, though they are not altogether so satisfactory, are generally more useful than the other, as they give us greater occasion of admiring the goodness and wisdom of the first Contriver.

One of the final causes of our delight, in anything that is great, may be this. The Supreme Author of our being has so formed the soul of man, that nothing but Himself can be its last, adequate, and proper happiness. Because, therefore, a great part of our happiness must arise from the contemplation of His Being, that he might give our souls a just relish of such a contemplation, He has made them naturally delight in the apprehension of what is great or unlimited. Our admiration, which is a very pleasing motion of the mind, immediately rises at the consideration of any object that takes up a great deal of room in the fancy, and, by consequence, will improve into the highest pitch of astonishment and devotion when we contemplate His nature, that is neither circumscribed by time nor place, nor to be comprehended by the largest capacity of a created being.

He has annexed a secret pleasure to the idea of anything that is new or uncommon, that He might encourage us in the pursuit after knowledge, and

engage us to search into the wonders of His creation;
for every new idea brings such a pleasure along with
it, as rewards any pains we have taken in its acquisition, and consequently serves as a motive to put us
upon fresh discoveries.

He has made everything that is beautiful in our
own species pleasant, that all creatures might be
tempted to multiply their kind, and fill the world
with inhabitants; for 'tis very remarkable that wherever Nature is crossed in the production of a monster
(the result of any unnatural mixture) the breed is
incapable of propagating its likeness, and of founding
a new order of creatures; so that unless all animals
were allured by the beauty of their own species,
generation would be at an end, and the earth unpeopled.

In the last place, He has made everything that is
beautiful in all other objects pleasant, or rather has
made so many objects appear beautiful, that He
might render the whole creation more gay and delightful.  He has given almost everything about us
the power of raising an agreeable idea in the imagination; so that it is impossible for us to behold His
works with coldness or indifference, and to survey so
many beauties without a secret satisfaction and complacency.  Things would make but a poor appearance
to the eye, if we saw them only in their proper figures
and motions.  And what reason can we assign for
their exciting in us many of those ideas which are
different from anything that exists in the objects
themselves (for such are light and colours), were it
not to add supernumerary ornaments to the universe,
and make it more agreeable to the imagination?  We
are everywhere entertained with pleasing shows and
apparitions, we discover imaginary glories in the
heavens, and in the earth, and see some of this
visionary beauty poured out upon the whole creation;
but what a rough unsightly sketch of Nature should
we be entertained with, did all her colouring disappear, and the several distinctions of light and shade

vanish? In short, our souls are at present delightfully lost and bewildered in a pleasing delusion, and we walk about like the enchanted hero of a romance, who sees beautiful castles, woods, and meadows; and at the same time hears the warbling of birds, and the purling of streams; but upon the finishing of some secret spell, the fantastic scene breaks up, and the disconsolate knight finds himself on a barren heath, or in a solitary desert. It is not improbable that something like this may be the state of the soul after its first separation, in respect of the images it will receive from matter; though indeed the ideas of colours are so pleasing and beautiful in the imagination, that it is possible the soul will not be deprived of them, but perhaps find them excited by some other occasional cause, as they are at present by the different impressions of the subtle matter on the organ of sight.

I have here supposed that my reader is acquainted with that great modern discovery, which is at present universally acknowledged by all the inquirers into natural philosophy, namely, that light and colours, as apprehended by the imagination, are only ideas in the mind, and not qualities that have any existence in matter. As this is a truth which has been proved incontestably by many modern philosophers, and is indeed one of the finest speculations in that science, if the English reader would see the notion explained at large, he may find it in the eighth chapter of the second book of Mr Locke's *Essay on Human Understanding*. O.

*June 24, 1712*

Mr Spectator [1],—I would not divert the course of your discourses when you seem bent upon obliging the world with a train of thinking, which, rightly attended

---

[1] This letter was not reprinted in the collected edition of the *Spectator*. In No. 417 the following advertisement appeared : ' Whereas the proposal called the Multiplication Table is under an Information from the Attorney-General, in Humble Submission and Duty to Her

to, may render the life of every man who reads it
more easy and happy for the future. The pleasures
of the imagination are what bewilder life when reason
and judgment do not interpose; it is therefore a
worthy action in you to look carefully into the powers
of fancy, that other men, from the knowledge of them,
may improve their joys and allay their griefs by a
just use of that faculty. I say, sir, I would not interrupt you in the progress of this discourse; but if you
will do me the favour of inserting this letter in your
next paper you will do some service to the public,
though not in so noble a way of obliging as that of
improving their minds. Allow me, sir, to acquaint you
with a design (of which I am partly author), though it
tends to no greater a good than that of getting money.
I should not hope for the favour of a philosopher in
this matter, if it were not attempted under all the restrictions which you sages put upon private acquisitions.

The first purpose which every good man is to propose to himself, is the service of his prince and
country; after that is done, he cannot add to himself, but he must also be beneficial to them. This
scheme of gain is not only consistent with that end,
but has its very being in subordination to it; for no
man can be a gainer here but at the same time he
himself, or some other, must succeed in their dealings
with the government. It is called the *Multiplication
Table*, and is so far calculated for the immediate
service of her majesty, that the same person who is
fortunate in the lottery of the State may receive yet
further advantage in this table. And I am sure nothing can be more pleasing to her gracious temper
than to find out additional methods of increasing their
good fortune who adventure anything in her service,
or laying occasions for others to become capable of

Majesty the said Undertaking is laid down, and attendance is this day
given at the last house on the left hand in Ship Yard in Bartholomew
Lane, in order to repay such sums as have been paid into the said
Table without deduction.' An Act against illicit lotteries came into
operation on June 24, the very day on which Steele's letter appeared in
the *Spectator*. Swift, writing on July 1, says, 'Steele was arrested
the other day for making a lottery directly against an Act of Parliament. He is now under prosecution, but they think it will be dropped
out of pity.' Probably this story of an arrest was based on a false
report; Steele wrote to his wife on June 28 that all was safe and well.

serving their country, who are at present in too low circumstances to exert themselves. The manner of executing the design is, by giving out receipts for half-guineas received, which shall entitle the fortunate bearer to certain sums in the table, as is set forth at large in the proposals printed the 23rd instant. There is another circumstance in this design which gives me hopes of your favour to it, and that is what Tully advises, to wit, that the benefit is made as diffusive as possible. Every one that has half-a-guinea is put into a possibility, from that small sum, to raise himself an easy fortune; when these little parcels of wealth are, as it were, thus thrown back again into the re-donation of Providence, we are to expect that some who live under hardship or obscurity may be produced to the world in the figure they deserve by this means. I doubt not but this last argument will have force with you, and I cannot add another to it, but what your severity will, I fear, very little regard; which is, that                          I am, Sir,
Your greatest Admirer,
RICHARD STEELE

No. 414.    *Wednesday, June 25, 1712*    [ADDISON

*Alterius sic*
*Altera poscit opem res, et conjurat amice.*
HOR., *Ars Poet.* 410

IF we consider the works of Nature and art, as they are qualified to entertain the imagination, we shall find the last very defective, in comparison of the former; for though they may sometimes appear as beautiful or strange, they can have nothing in them of the vastness and immensity which afford so great an entertainment to the mind of the beholder. The one may be as polite and delicate as the other, but can never show herself so august and magnificent in the design. There is something more bold and masterly in the rough, careless strokes of Nature, than in the nice touches and embellishments of art. The beauties of the most stately garden or palace lie in a narrow compass, the imagination immediately

runs them over, and requires something else to
gratify her; but, in the wide fields of Nature, the
sight wanders up and down without confinement,
and is fed with an infinite variety of images, without
any certain stint or number.  For this reason we
always find the poet in love with a country life,
where Nature appears in the greatest perfection, and
furnishes out all those scenes that are most apt to
delight the imagination [1].

Scriptorum chorus omnis amat nemus et fugit urbes.
                                                HOR.[2]

Hic secura quies, et nescia fallere vita,
Dives opum variarum ; hic latis otia fundis,
Speluncæ, vivique lacus, hic frigida Tempe,
Mugitusque boum, mollesque sub arbore somni.
                                                VIR.[3]

But though there are several of these wild scenes
that are more delightful than any artificial shows,
yet we find the works of Nature still more pleasant,
the more they resemble those of art : for in this
case our pleasure rises from a double principle;
from the agreeableness of the objects to the eye, and
from their similitude to other objects : we are pleased
as well with comparing their beauties as with surveying them, and can represent them to our minds,
either as copies or originals.  Hence it is that we
take delight in a prospect which is well laid out,
and diversified with fields and meadows, woods and
rivers: in those accidental landscapes of trees, clouds,
and cities, that are sometimes found in the veins
of marble, in the curious fretwork of rocks and
grottoes; and, in a word, in anything that hath such
a variety or regularity as may seem the effect of
design, in what we call the works of chance.

[1] This sentence (in Addison's writing in the MS.) was first written
thus: 'For this reason we find the poets always crying up a country
life where Nature is left to herself, and appears to the best advantage.'
This was altered as follows: 'For this reason we find all fanciful men,
and the poets in particular, still in love with a country life, where
Nature is left to herself, and furnishes out all the variety of scenes
that are most delightful to the imagination.'
[2] Ep. ii, 77.                          [3] Georg. ii, 476.

If the products of Nature rise in value, according
as they more or less resemble those of art, we may
be sure that artificial works receive a greater advantage from their resemblance of such as are natural;
because here the similitude is not only pleasant, but
the pattern more perfect.    The prettiest landscape
I ever saw was one drawn on the walls of a dark
room,   which   stood   opposite   on   one   side   to   a
navigable river, and on the other to a park[1].    The
experiment is very common in optics.    Here you
might discover the waves and fluctuations of the
water in strong and proper colours, with the picture
of a ship entering at one end and failing by degrees
through the whole piece.    On another there appeared
the green shadows of trees waving to and fro with
the wind, and herds of deer among them in minia-
ture, leaping about upon the wall.    I must confess,
the novelty of such a sight may be one occasion of
its pleasantness to the imagination;    but certainly
the chief reason is its near resemblance to Nature,
as it does not only, like other pictures, give the
colour and figure, but the motion of the things it
represents.

We have before observed, that there is generally
in Nature something more grand and august than
what we meet with in the curiosities of art.    When,
therefore, we see this imitated in any measure, it
gives us a nobler and more exalted kind of pleasure
than what we receive from the nicer and more
accurate productions of art.    On this account our
English gardens are not so entertaining to the fancy
as those in France and Italy, where we see a large
extent of ground covered over with an agreeable
mixture of garden and forest, which represent everywhere an artificial rudeness, much more charming
than that neatness and elegancy which we meet with
in those of our own country.    It might, indeed, be
of ill consequence to the public, as well as unprofitable to private persons, to alienate so much ground

[1] The Camera Obscura at Greenwich.

from pasturage, and the plough, in many parts of a country that is so well peopled, and cultivated to a far greater advantage. But why may not a whole estate be thrown into a kind of garden by frequent plantations, that may turn as much to the profit as the pleasure of the owner? A marsh overgrown with willows, or a mountain shaded with oaks, are not only more beautiful, but more beneficial, than when they lie bare and unadorned. Fields of corn make a pleasant prospect, and if the walks were a little taken care of that lie between them, if the natural embroidery of the meadows were helped and improved by some small additions of art, and the several rows of hedges set off by trees and flowers, that the soil was capable of receiving, a man might make a pretty landscape of his own possessions.

Writers who have given us an account of China tell us, the inhabitants of that country laugh at the plantations of our Europeans, which are laid by the rule and line; because, they say, any one may place trees in equal rows and uniform figures. They choose rather to show a genius in works of this nature, and therefore always conceal the art by which they direct themselves. They have a word, it seems, in their language by which they express the particular beauty of a plantation that thus strikes the imagination at first sight, without discovering what it is that has so agreeable an effect. Our British gardeners, on the contrary, instead of humouring Nature, love to deviate from it as much as possible. Our trees rise in cones, globes, and pyramids. We see the marks of the scissors upon every plant and bush. I do not know whether I am singular in my opinion, but, for my own part, I would rather look upon a tree in all its luxuriancy and diffusion of boughs and branches, than when it is thus cut and trimmed into a mathematical figure; and cannot but fancy that an orchard in flower looks infinitely more delightful than all the little labyrinths of the most finished parterre. But as our great modellers of gardens

have their magazines of plants to dispose of, it is
very natural for them to tear up all the beautiful
plantations of fruit trees, and contrive a plan that
may most turn to their own profit, in taking off
their evergreens, and the like movable plants, with
which their shops are plentifully stocked.          O.

No. 415.     *Thursday, June 26, 1712*     [ADDISON

*Adde tot egregias urbes, operumque laborem.*
VIRG., *Georg.* ii, 155

HAVING already shown how the fancy is affected
by the works of Nature, and afterwards considered
in general both the works of Nature and of art, how
they mutually assist and complete each other, in
forming such scenes and prospects as are most apt
to delight the mind of the beholder, I shall in this
paper throw together some reflections on that particular art which has a more immediate tendency
than any other to produce those primary pleasures
of the imagination which have hitherto been the
subject of this discourse.  The art I mean is that
of architecture, which I shall consider only with
regard to the light in which the foregoing speculations have placed it, without entering into those
rules and maxims which the great masters of architecture have laid down, and explained at large in
numberless treatises upon that subject.
   Greatness, in the works of architecture, may be
considered as relating to the bulk and body of the
structure, or to the manner in which it is built.  As
for the first, we find the ancients, especially among
the Eastern nations of the world, infinitely superior
to the moderns.
   Not to mention the Tower of Babel, of which an
old author says there were the foundations to be
seen in his time, which looked like a spacious mountain, what could be more noble than the walls of
Babylon, its hanging gardens, and its temple to
Jupiter Belus, that rose a mile high by eight several

storeys, each storey a furlong in height, and on the
top of which was the Babylonian observatory? I
might here likewise take notice of the huge rock
that was cut into the figure of Semiramis, with the
smaller rocks that lay by it in the shape of tributary
kings; the prodigious basin, or artificial lake, which
took in the whole Euphrates, until such time as a
new canal was formed for its reception, with the
several trenches through which that river was conveyed. I know there are persons who look upon
some of these wonders of art as fabulous, but I cannot find any grounds for such a suspicion, unless it
be that we have no such works among us at present :
there were indeed many greater advantages for building in those times, and in that part of the world,
than have been met with ever since. The earth was
extremely fruitful, men lived generally on pasturage,
which requires a much smaller number of hands than
agriculture : there were few trades to employ the
busy part of mankind, and fewer arts and sciences to
give work to men of speculative tempers; and what
is more than all the rest, the prince was absolute;
so that when he went to war, he put himself at the
head of a whole people. As we find Semiramis
leading her three [1] millions to the field, and yet
overpowered by the number of her enemies. 'Tis
no wonder, therefore, when she was at peace, and
turned her thoughts on building, that she could
accomplish so great works, with such a prodigious
multitude of labourers : besides that in her climate
there was small interruption of frosts and winters,
which make the Northern workmen lie half the year
idle. I might mention, too, among the benefits of
the climate, what historians say of the earth, that it
sweated out a bitumen or natural kind of mortar,
which is doubtless the same with that mentioned in
Holy Writ as contributing to the structure of Babel :
' Slime they used instead of mortar [2].'

In Egypt we still see their pyramids, which answer

· [1] 'Two' (folio).　　[2] *Gen.* xi, 3 ('Slime had they for mortar ').

to the descriptions that have been made of them; and I question not but a traveller might find out some remains of the labyrinth that covered a whole province, and had a hundred temples disposed among its several quarters and divisions.

The wall of China is one of these Eastern pieces of magnificence, which makes a figure even in the map of the world, although an account of it would have been thought fabulous, were not the wall itself still extant.

We are obliged to devotion for the noblest buildings that have adorned the several countries of the world. It is this which has set men at work on temples and public places of worship, not only that they might, by the magnificence of the building, invite the Deity to reside within it, but that such stupendous works might, at the same time, open the mind to vast conceptions, and fit it to converse with the divinity of the place. For everything that is majestic imprints an awfulness and reverence on the mind of the beholder, and strikes in with the natural greatness of the soul.

In the second place we are to consider greatness of manner in architecture, which has such force upon the imagination, that a small building, where it appears, shall give the mind nobler ideas than one of twenty times the bulk, where the manner is ordinary or little. Thus, perhaps, a man would have been more astonished with the majestic air that appeared in one of Lysippus's [1] statues of Alexandria, though no bigger than the life, than he might have been with Mount Athos, had it been cut into the figure of the hero, according to the proposal of Phidias [2], with a river in one hand and a city in the other.

Let any one reflect on the disposition of mind he finds in himself, at his first entrance into the Pantheon at Rome, and how his imagination is filled

1 ʻProtogenes'sʼ (folio).
2 Not Phidias, but Dinocrates, the famous architect of Macedonia.

with something great and amazing; and at the same time consider how little, in proportion, he is affected with the inside of a Gothic cathedral, though it be five times larger than the other; which can arise from nothing else, but the greatness of the manner in the one, and the meanness in the other.

I have seen an observation upon this subject in a French author, which very much pleased me. It is in Monsieur Fréard's *Parallel of the Ancient and Modern Architecture* [1]. I shall give it the reader with the same terms of art which he has made use of: ' I am observing ', says he, ' a thing which in my opinion is very curious, whence it proceeds, that in the same quantity of superficies, the one manner seems great and magnificent, and the other poor and trifling; the reason is fine and uncommon. I say then, that to introduce into architecture this grandeur of manner, we ought so to proceed, that the division of the principal members of the order may consist but of few parts, that they be all great and of a bold and ample relievo, and swelling; and that the eye, beholding nothing little and mean, the imagination may be more vigorously touched and affected with the work that stands before it. For example, in a cornice, if the gola or cynatium of the corona, the coping, the modillions or dentelli, make a noble show by their graceful projections, if we see none of that ordinary confusion which is the result of those little cavities, quarter rounds of the astragal, and I know not how many other intermingled particulars, which produce no effect in great and massy works, and which very unprofitably take up place to the prejudice of the principal member, it is most certain that this manner will appear solemn and great; as, on the contrary, that will have but a poor and mean effect where there is a redundancy of those smaller ornaments, which

---

[1] An English translation of Roland Fréard de Chambray's *Parallèle de l'Architecture antique et de la moderne* (1650) was published by John Evelyn in 1664.

divide and scatter the angles of the sight into such a multitude of rays, so pressed together that the whole will appear but a confusion.'

Among all the figures in architecture, there are none that have a greater air than the concave and the convex; and we find in all the ancient and modern architecture, as well in the remote parts of China as in countries nearer home, that round pillars and vaulted roofs make a great part of those buildings which are designed for pomp and magnificence. The reason I take to be, because in these figures we generally see more of the body than in those of other kinds. There are, indeed, figures of bodies where the eye may take in two-thirds of the surface; but as in such bodies the sight must split upon several angles, it does not take in one uniform idea, but several ideas of the same kind. Look upon the outside of a dome, your eye half surrounds it; look up into the inside, and at one glance you have all the prospect of it; the entire concavity falls into your eye at once, the sight being as the centre that collects and gathers into it the lines of the whole circumference. In a square pillar, the sight often takes in but a fourth part of the surface, and, in a square concave, must move up and down to the different sides, before it is master of all the inward surface. For this reason, the fancy is infinitely more struck with the view of the open air, and skies, that passes through an arch, than what comes through a square, or any other figure. The figure of the rainbow does not contribute less to its magnificence, than the colours to its beauty, as it is very poetically described by the son of Sirach: 'Look upon the rainbow, and praise Him that made it; very beautiful it is in its brightness; it encompasses the heavens with a glorious circle, and the hands of the Most High have bended it [1].'

Having thus spoken of that greatness which affects the mind in architecture, I might next show the

---

[1] *Ecclesiasticus*, xliii, 11.

pleasure that rises in the imagination from what
appears new and beautiful in this art; but as every
beholder has naturally a greater taste of these two
perfections in every building which offers itself to
his view than of that which I have hitherto considered, I shall not trouble my reader with any
reflections upon it. It is sufficient for my present
purpose to observe that there is nothing in this whole
art which pleases the imagination, but as it is great,
uncommon, or beautiful.                           O.

## No. 416.      *Friday, June 27, 1712*      [ADDISON

*Quatenus hoc simile est oculis, quod mente videmus.*
LUCR. iv, 750-1

I AT first divided the pleasures of the imagination
into such as arise from objects that are actually
before our eyes, or that once entered in at our eyes,
and are afterwards called up into the mind, either
barely by its own operations, or on occasion of something without us, as statues or descriptions. We
have already considered the first division, and shall
therefore enter on the other, which, for distinction
sake, I have called the secondary pleasures of the
imagination. When I say the ideas we receive from
statues, descriptions, or such like occasions, are the
same that were once actually in our view, it must
not be understood that we had once seen the very
place, action, or person which are carved or described. It is sufficient that we have seen places,
persons, or actions, in general, which bear a resemblance, or at least some remote analogy with what
we find represented. Since it is in the power of the
imagination, when it is once stocked with particular
ideas, to enlarge, compound, and vary them at her
own pleasure.

Among the different kinds of representation, statuary is the most natural, and shows us something
likest the object that is represented. To make u~
of a common instance, let one who is born blii

take an image in his hands, and trace out with his
fingers the different furrows and impressions of the
chisel, and he will easily conceive how the shape of
a man, or beast, may be represented by it; but
should he draw his hand over a picture, where all
is smooth and uniform, he would never be able to
imagine how the several prominences and depres-
sions of a human body could be shown on a plain
piece of canvas that has in it no unevenness or irregularity. Description runs yet further from the
things it represents than painting; for a picture
bears a real resemblance to its original, which letters
and syllables are wholly void of. Colours speak all
languages, but words are understood only by such a
people or nation. For this reason, though men's
necessities quickly put them on finding out speech,
writing is probably of a later invention than painting;
particularly we are told that in America, when the
Spaniards first arrived there, expresses were sent
to the Emperor of Mexico in paint, and the news
of his country delineated by the strokes of a pencil,
which was a more natural way than that of writing,
though at the same time much more imperfect,
because it is impossible to draw the little connec-
tions of speech, or to give the picture of a conjunction or an adverb. It would be yet more strange to
represent visible objects by sounds that have no ideas
annexed to them, and to make something like description in music. Yet it is certain there may be
confused, imperfect notions of this nature raised in
the imagination by an artificial composition of notes;
and we find that great masters in the art are able,
sometimes, to set their hearers in the heat and hurry
of a battle, to overcast their minds with melancholy
scenes and apprehensions of deaths and funerals, or
to lull them into pleasing dreams of groves and
elysiums.

In all these instances this secondary pleasure of
the imagination proceeds from that action of the
mind which compares the ideas arising from the

original objects, with the ideas we receive from the statue, picture, description, or sound that represents them. It is impossible for us to give the necessary reason why this operation of the mind is attended with so much pleasure, as I have before observed on the same occasion; but we find a great variety of entertainments derived from this single principle : for it is this that not only gives us a relish of statuary, painting, and description, but makes us delight in all the actions and arts of mimicry. It is this that makes the several kinds of wit pleasant, which consists, as I have formerly shown, in the affinity of ideas : and we may add, it is this also that raises the little satisfaction we sometimes find in the different sorts of false wit; whether it consist in the affinity of letters, as in anagram, acrostic; or of syllables, as in doggerel rhymes, echoes; or of words, as in puns, quibbles; or of a whole sentence or poem, to wings, and altars. The final cause, probably, of annexing pleasure to this operation of the mind was to quicken and encourage us in our searches after truth, since the distinguishing one thing from another, and the right discerning betwixt our ideas, depends wholly upon our comparing them together, and observing the congruity or disagreement that appears among the several works of Nature.

But I shall here confine myself to those pleasures of the imagination which proceed from ideas raised by words, because most of the observations that agree with descriptions are equally applicable to painting and statuary.

Words, when well chosen, have so great a force in them, that a description often gives us more lively ideas than the sight of things themselves. The reader finds a scene drawn in stronger colours, and painted more to the life in his imagination by the help of words, than by an actual survey of the scene which they describe. In this case the poet seems to get the better of Nature; he takes, indeed,

the landscape after her, but gives it more vigorous
touches, heightens its beauty, and so enlivens the
whole piece that the images which flow from the
objects themselves appear weak and faint in comparison of those that come from the expressions.
The reason probably may be, because in the survey
of any object we have only so much of it painted
on the imagination as comes in at the eye; but in
its description the poet gives us as free a view of it
as he pleases, and discovers to us several parts that
either we did not attend to, or that lay out of our
sight when we first beheld it. As we look on any
object our idea of it is, perhaps, made up of two or
three simple ideas; but when the poet represents
it, he may either give us a more complex idea of it,
or only raise in us such ideas as are most apt to
affect the imagination.

It may be here worth our while to examine how
it comes to pass that several readers, who are all
acquainted with the same language, and know the
meaning of the words they read, should nevertheless
have a different relish of the same descriptions.
We find one transported with a passage which
another runs over with coldness and indifference, or
finding the representation extremely natural, where
another can perceive nothing of likeness and conformity. This different taste must proceed either
from the perfection of imagination in one more than
in another, or from the different ideas that several
readers affix to the same words. For to have a true
relish and form a right judgment of a description
a man should be born with a good imagination, and
must have well weighed the force and energy that
lie in the several words of a language, so as to be
able to distinguish which are most significant and
expressive of their proper ideas, and what additional
strength and beauty they are capable of receiving
from conjunction with others. The fancy must be
warm to retain the print of those images it hath
received from outward objects; and the judgment

discerning, to know what expressions are most proper to clothe and adorn them to the best advantage. A man who is deficient in either of these respects, though he may receive the general notion of a description, can never see distinctly all its particular beauties; as a person with a weak sight may have the confused prospect of a place that lies before him, without entering into its several parts, or discerning the variety of its colours in their full glory and perfection.                                         O.

No. 417.       *Saturday, June* 28, 1712       [ADDISON

*Quem tu Melpomene semel*
  *Nascentem placido lumine videris,*
*Illum non labor Isthmius*
  *Clarabit pugilem, non equus impiger, &c.*
  *Sed quæ Tibur aquæ fertile perfluunt,*
*Et spissæ nemorum comæ*
  *Fingent Æolio carmine nobilem.*

                                         HOR., 4, *Od.* iii, 1

WE may observe, that any single circumstance of what we have formerly seen often raises up a whole scene of imagery, and awakens numberless [1] ideas that before slept in the imagination; such a particular smell or colour is able to fill the mind, on a sudden, with the picture of the fields or gardens where we first met with it, and to bring up into view all the variety of images that once attended it. Our imagination takes the hint, and leads us unexpectedly into cities or theatres, plains or meadows. We may further observe, when the fancy thus reflects on the scenes that have passed in it formerly, those which were at first pleasant to behold appear more so upon reflection, and that the memory heightens the delightfulness of the original. A Cartesian would account for both these instances in the following manner :

The set of ideas, which we received from such a prospect or garden, having entered the mind at the

---

[1] 'A thousand' (folio).

same time, have a set of traces belonging to them in the brain, bordering very near upon one another; when, therefore, any one of these ideas arises in the imagination, and consequently despatches a flow of animal spirits to its proper trace, these spirits, in the violence of their motion, run not only into the trace to which they were more particularly directed, but into several of those that lie about it : by this means they awaken other ideas of the same set, which immediately determine .a new despatch of spirits that in the same manner open other neighbouring traces, till at last the whole set of them is blown up, and the whole prospect or garden flourishes in the imagination.  But because the pleasure we received from these places far surmounted and overcame the little disagreeableness we found in them, for this reason there was at first a wider passage worn in the pleasure traces, and, on the contrary, so narrow a one in those which belonged to the disagreeable ideas, that they were quickly stopped up, and rendered incapable of receiving any animal spirits, and consequently of exciting any unpleasant ideas in the memory.

It would be in vain to inquire whether the power of imagining things strongly proceeds from any greater perfection in the soul, or from any nicer texture in the brain of one man than of another. But this is certain, that a noble writer should be born with this faculty in its full strength and vigour, so as to be able to receive lively ideas from outward objects, to retain them long, and to range them together, upon occasion, in such figures and representations as are most likely to hit the fancy of the reader.  A poet should take as much pains in forming his imagination as a philosopher in cultivating his understanding. He must gain a due relish of the works of Nature, and be thoroughly conversant in the various scenery of a country life [1].

---

[1] This paragraph (in Addison's writing) concludes thus in the MS.: ' He must love to hide himself in woods and to haunt the springs and meadows.  "Quem tu", &c. [see motto]. His head must be full of the humming of bees, the bleating of flocks, and the melody of birds.

When he is stored with country images, if he would go beyond pastoral and the lower kinds of poetry, he ought to acquaint himself with the pomp and magnificence of courts. He should be very well versed in everything that is noble and stately in the productions of art, whether it appear in painting or statuary, in the great works of architecture which are in their present glory, or in the ruins of those which flourished in former ages [1].

Such advantages as these help to open a man's thoughts, and to enlarge his imagination, and will therefore have their influence on all kinds of writing, if the author knows how to make right use of them. And among those of the learned languages who excel in this talent, the most perfect in their several kinds are, perhaps, Homer, Virgil, and Ovid. The first strikes the imagination wonderfully with what is great, the second with what is beautiful, and the last with what is strange. Reading the *Iliad* is like travelling through a country uninhabited, where the fancy is entertained with a thousand savage prospects of vast deserts, wide uncultivated marshes, huge forests, misshapen rocks, and precipices. On the contrary, the *Æneid* is like a well-ordered garden, where it is impossible to find out any part unadorned, or to cast our eyes upon a single spot that does not produce some beautiful plant or flower. But when we are in the *Metamorphoses*, we are walking on enchanted ground, and see nothing but scenes of magic lying round us [2].

Homer is in his province when he is describing a battle or a multitude, a hero or a god. Virgil is never better pleased than when he is in his elysium,

---

The verdure of the grass, the embroidery of the flowers, and the glistening of the dew must be painted strong on his imagination.'

[1] 'Milton would never have been able to have built his Pandemonium, or to have laid out his Paradise, had not he seen the palaces and gardens of Italy; and it would be easy to show several descriptions out of the old poets that probably owed their original to pictures and statues that were then in vogue' (Addison's MS.).

[2] This paragraph, together with the one that follows, was added to the MS. in Addison's writing.

or copying out an entertaining picture. Homer's epithets generally mark out what is great, Virgil's what is agreeable. Nothing can be more magnificent than the figure Jupiter makes in the first *Iliad*, nor more charming than that of Venus in the first *Æneid* :

'Η, καὶ κυανέῃσιν ἐπ' ὀφρύσι νεῦσε Κρονίων·
'Αυβρόσιαι δ' ἄρα χαῖται ἐπερρώσαντο ἄνακτος,
Κρατὸς ἀπ' ἀθανάτοιο· μέγαν δ' ἐλέλιξεν Ὄλυμπον[1].

Dixit, et avertens roseâ cervice refulsit :
Ambrosiæque comæ divinum vertice odorem
Spiravere : pedes vestis defluxit ad imos :
Et vera incessu patuit dea[2].

Homer's persons are most of them godlike and terrible : Virgil has scarce admitted any into his poem who are not beautiful, and has taken particular care to make his hero so.

Lumenque juventæ
Purpureum, et lætos oculis afflarat honores[3].

In a word, Homer fills his readers with sublime ideas, and, I believe, has raised the imagination of all the good poets that have come after him. I shall only instance Horace, who immediately takes fire at the first hint of any passage in the *Iliad* or *Odyssey*, and always rises above himself when he has Homer in his view. Virgil has drawn together into his *Æneid* all the pleasing scenes his subject is capable of admitting, and in his *Georgics* has given us a collection of the most delightful landscapes that can be made out of fields and woods, herds of cattle, and swarms of bees.

Ovid, in his *Metamorphoses*, has shown us how the imagination may be affected by what is strange. He describes a miracle in every story, and always gives us the sight of some new creature at the end of it. His art consists chiefly in well-timing his description before the first shape is quite worn off, and the new one perfectly finished ; so that he every-

---

[1] *Iliad*, i, 528.    [2] *Æneid*, i, 402.    [3] *Ibid.*, i, 590.

where entertains us with something we never saw before, and shows monster after monster to the end of the *Metamorphoses*.

If I were to name a poet that is a perfect master in all these arts of working on the imagination, I think Milton may pass for one : and if his *Paradise Lost* falls short of the *Æneid* or *Iliad* in this respect, it proceeds rather from the fault of the language in which it is written than from any defect of genius in the author.  So divine a poem in English is like a stately palace built of brick, where one may see architecture in as great a perfection as in one of marble, though the materials are of a coarser nature. But to consider it only as it regards our present subject : what can be conceived greater than the battle of angels, the majesty of Messiah, the stature and behaviour of Satan and his peers?  What more beautiful than pandemonium, paradise, heaven, angels, Adam and Eve?  What more strange than the creation of the world, the several metamorphoses of the fallen angels, and the surprising adventures their leader meets with in his search after paradise? No other subject could have furnished a poet with scenes so proper to strike the imagination, as no other poet could have painted those scenes in more strong and lively colours.                                    O.

No. 418.     *Monday, June 30, 1712*     [ADDISON

*Ferat et rubus asper amomum.*  VIRG., *Eclog.* iii, 89

THE pleasures of these secondary views of the imagination, are of a wider and more universal nature than those it has when joined with sight; for not only what is great, strange, or beautiful, but anything that is disagreeable when looked upon, pleases us in an apt description.  Here, therefore, we must inquire after a new principle of pleasure, which is nothing else but the action of the mind, which compares the ideas that arise from words, with the ideas that arise from the objects themselves; and why this operation of the mind is attended with so much pleasure, we have before considered. For this reason, therefore, the description of a dunghill is pleasing to the imagination, if the image be represented to our minds by suitable expressions; though, perhaps, this may be more properly called the pleasure of the understanding than of the fancy, because we are not so much delighted with the image that is contained in the description, as with the aptness of the description to excite the image.

But if the description of what is little, common, or deformed, be acceptable to the imagination, the description of what is great, surprising, or beautiful, is much more so; because here we are not only delighted with comparing the representation with the original, but are highly pleased with the original itself. Most readers, I believe, are more charmed with Milton's description of paradise, than of hell; they are both, perhaps, equally perfect in their kind, but in the one the brimstone and sulphur are not so refreshing to the imagination, as the beds of flowers and the wilderness of sweets in the other.

There is yet another circumstance which recommends a description more than all the rest, and that is, if it represents to us such objects as are apt to raise a secret ferment in the mind of the reader, and to work with violence upon his passions. For, in this case, we are at once warmed and enlightened, so that the pleasure becomes more universal, and is several ways qualified to entertain us. Thus, in painting, it is pleasant to look on the picture of any face, where the resemblance is hit, but the pleasure increases, if it be the picture of a face that is beautiful, and is still greater, if the beauty be softened with an air of melancholy or sorrow. The two leading passions which the more serious parts of poetry endeavour to stir up in us, are terror and pity. And here, by the way, one would wonder how it comes to pass, that such passions as are very unpleasant at all other times, are very agreeable when excited by proper descriptions. It is not strange that we should take delight in such passages as are apt to produce hope, joy, admiration, love, or the like emotions in us, because they never rise in the mind without an inward pleasure which attends them. But how comes it to pass, that we should take delight in being terrified or dejected by a description, when we find so much uneasiness in the fear or grief which we receive from any other occasion?

If we consider, therefore, the nature of this pleasure, we shall find that it does not arise so properly from the description of what is terrible, as from the reflection we make on ourselves at the time of reading it. When we look on such hideous objects, we are not a little pleased to think we are in no danger of them. We consider them, at the same time, as dreadful and harmless; so that the more frightful appearance they make, the greater is the pleasure we receive from the sense of our own safety. In short, we look upon the terrors of a description, with the same curiosity and satisfaction that we survey a dead monster :

> Informe cadaver
> Protrahitur ; nequeunt expleri corda tuendo
> Terribiles oculos : vultum, villosaque sætis
> Pectora semiferi, atque extinctos faucibus ignes.
>
> VIRG.[1]

It is for the same reason that we are delighted with the reflecting upon dangers that are past, or in looking on a precipice at a distance, which would fill us with a different kind of horror, if we saw it hanging over our heads.

In the like manner, when we read of torments, wounds, deaths, and the like dismal accidents, our pleasure does not flow so properly from the grief which such melancholy descriptions give us, as from the secret comparison which we make between ourselves and the person who suffers. Such repre-

[1] *Æneid*, viii, 264.

sentations teach us to set a just value upon our
own condition, and make us prize our good fortune
which exempts us from the like calamities.  This
is, however, such a kind of pleasure as we are not
capable of receiving, when we see a person actually
lying under the tortures that we meet with in a description; because, in this case, the object presses
too close upon our senses, and bears so hard upon
us, that it does not give us time or leisure to reflect
on ourselves.  Our thoughts are so intent upon the
miseries of the sufferer, that we cannot turn them
upon our own happiness.  Whereas, on the contrary,
we consider the misfortunes we read in history or
poetry, either as past, or as fictitious, so that the
reflection upon ourselves rises in us insensibly, and
overbears the sorrow we conceive for the sufferings
of the afflicted.

But because the mind of man requires something
more perfect in matter, than what it finds there, and
can never meet with any sight in Nature which sufficiently answers its highest ideas of pleasantness; or,
in other words, because the imagination can fancy to
itself things more great, strange, or beautiful, than
the eye ever saw, and is still sensible of some defect
in what it has seen; on this account it is the part
of a poet to humour the imagination in its own
notions, by mending and perfecting Nature where he
describes a reality, and by adding greater beauties
than are put together in Nature, where he describes
a fiction.

He is not obliged to attend her in the slow advances which she makes from one season to another,
or to observe her conduct, in the successive production of plants and flowers.  He may draw into his
description all the beauties of the spring and autumn,
and make the whole year contribute something to
render it the more agreeable.  His rose-trees, wood-
bines, and jessamines may flower together, and his
beds be covered at the same time with lilies, violets,
and amaranths.  His soil is not restrained to any

particular set of plants, but is proper either for oaks or myrtles, and adapts itself to the products of every climate.  Oranges may grow wild in it; myrrh may be met with in every hedge, and if he thinks it proper to have a grove of spices, he can quickly command sun enough to raise it.  If all this will not furnish out an agreeable scene, he can make several new species of flowers, with richer scents and higher colours, than any that grow in the gardens of Nature.  His consorts of birds may be as full and harmonious, and his woods as thick and gloomy as he pleases.  He is at no more expense in a long vista than a short one, and can as easily throw his cascades from a precipice of half a mile high, as from one of twenty yards.  He has his choice of the winds, and can turn the course of his rivers in all the variety of meanders that are most delightful to the reader's imagination.  In a word, he has the modelling of Nature in his own hands, and may give her what charms he pleases, provided he does not reform her too much, and run into absurdities, by endeavouring to excel [1].                       O.


No. 419.        *Tuesday, July 1, 1712*        [ADDISON

*Mentis gratissimus error.*    HOR., 2 *Ep.* ii, 140

THERE is a kind of writing wherein the poet quite loses sight of Nature, and entertains his reader's imagination with the characters and actions of such persons as have many of them no existence but what he bestows on them; such are fairies, witches, magicians, demons, and departed spirits.  This Mr Dryden calls the fairy way of writing, which is, indeed, more difficult than any other that depends on the poet's fancy, because he has no pattern to follow in it, and must work altogether out of his own invention.

There is a very odd turn of thought required for

[1] This paragraph was added to the MS. in Addison's writing.

this sort of writing, and it is impossible for a poet to succeed in it, who has not a particular cast of fancy, and an imagination naturally fruitful and superstitious. Besides this, he ought to be very well versed in legends and fables, antiquated romances, and the traditions of nurses and old women, that he may fall in with our natural prejudices, and humour those notions which we have imbibed in our infancy. For, otherwise, he will be apt to make his fairies talk like people of his own species, and not like other sets of beings, who converse with different objects, and think in a different manner from that of mankind.

> Sylvis deducti caveant, me judice, Fauni,
> Ne velut innati triviis ac pæne forenses,
> Aut nimium teneris juvenentur versibus.        Hor.[1]

I do not say with Mr Bayes, in the *Rehearsal*, that spirits must not be confined to speak sense, but it is certain their sense ought to be a little discoloured, that it may seem particular, and proper to the person and the condition of the speaker.

These descriptions raise a pleasing kind of horror in the mind of the reader, and amuse his imagination with the strangeness and novelty of the persons who are represented in them. They bring up into our memory the stories we have heard in our childhood, and favour those secret terrors and apprehensions to which the mind of man is naturally subject. We are pleased with surveying the different habits and behaviours of foreign countries, how much more must we be delighted and surprised when we are led, as it were, into a new creation, and see the persons and manners of another species? Men of cold fancies, and philosophical dispositions, object to this kind of poetry, that it has not probability enough to affect the imagination. But to this it may be answered, that we are sure, in general, there are many intellectual beings in the world besides ourselves, and several species of spirits, who are subject to different

---

[1] *Ars Poet.* 244.

laws and economies from those of mankind; when we see, therefore, any of these represented naturally, we cannot look upon the representation as altogether impossible; nay, many are prepossessed with such false opinions, as dispose them to believe these particular delusions; at least, we have all heard so many pleasing relations in favour of them, that we do not care for seeing through the falsehood, and willingly give ourselves up to so agreeable an imposture.

The ancients have not much of this poetry among them, for, indeed, almost the whole substance of it owes its original to the darkness and superstition of later ages, when pious frauds were made use of to amuse mankind, and frighten them into a sense of their duty.  Our forefathers looked upon nature with more reverence and horror, before the world was enlightened by learning and philosophy, and loved to astonish themselves with the apprehensions of witchcraft, prodigies, charms, and enchantments. There was not a village in England that had not a ghost in it, the churchyards were all haunted, every large common had a circle of fairies belonging to it, and there was scarce a shepherd to be met with who had not seen a spirit.

Among all the poets of this kind our English are much the best, by what I have yet seen, whether it be that we abound with more stories of this nature, or that the genius of our country is fitter for this sort of poetry.  For the English are naturally fanciful, and very often disposed by that gloominess and melancholy of temper, which is so frequent in our nation, to many wild notions and visions, to which others are not so liable.

Among the English, Shakespeare has incomparably excelled all others.  That noble extravagance of fancy, which he had in so great perfection, throughly qualified him to touch this weak superstitious part of his reader's imagination, and made him capable of succeeding, where he had nothing to support him besides the strength of his own genius.  There is something so wild and yet so solemn in the speeches of his ghosts, fairies, witches, and the like imaginary persons, that we cannot forbear thinking them natural, though we have no rule by which to judge of them, and must confess, if there are such beings in the world, it looks highly probable they should talk and act as he has represented them.

There is another sort of imaginary beings that we sometimes meet with among the poets, when the author represents any passion, appetite, virtue, or vice, under a visible shape, and makes it a person or an actor in his poem. Of this nature are the descriptions of Hunger and Envy in Ovid, of Fame in Virgil, and of Sin and Death in Milton. We find a whole creation of the like shadowy persons in Spenser, who had an admirable talent in representations of this kind. I have discoursed of these emblematical persons in former papers [1], and shall therefore only mention them in this place. Thus we see how many ways poetry addresses itself to the imagination, as it has not only the whole circle of nature for its province, but makes new worlds of its own, shows us persons who are not to be found in being, and represents even the faculties of the soul, with her several virtues and vices, in a sensible shape and character.

I shall, in my two following papers, consider in general how other kinds of writing are qualified to please the imagination, with which I intend to conclude this essay.                    O.

[1] See No. 273.

No. 420.          *Wednesday, July 2, 1712*          [ADDISON

*Quocunque volent animum auditoris agunto.*
HOR., *Ars Poet.* 100

As [1] the writers in poetry and fiction borrow their several materials from outward objects, and join them together at their own pleasure, there are others who are obliged to follow Nature more closely, and to take entire scenes out of her. Such are historians, natural philosophers, travellers, geographers, and, in a word, all who describe visible objects of a real existence.

It is the most agreeable talent of an historian, to be able to draw up his armies and fight his battles in proper expressions, to set before our eyes the divisions, cabals, and jealousies of great men, and to lead us step by step into the several actions and events of his history. We love to see the subject unfolding itself by just degrees, and breaking upon us insensibly, that so we may be kept in a pleasing suspense, and have time given us to raise our expectations, and to side with one of the parties concerned in the relation. I confess this shows more the art than the veracity of the historian, but I am only to speak of him as he is qualified to please the imagination. And in this respect Livy has perhaps excelled all who went before him, or have written since his time. He describes everything in so lively a manner, that his whole history is an admirable picture, and touches on such proper circumstances in every story, that his reader becomes a kind of spectator, and feels in himself all the variety of passions which are correspondent to the several parts of the relation.

But among this set of writers there are none who more gratify and enlarge the imagination than the authors of the new philosophy, whether we consider their theories of the earth or heavens, the discoveries

1 The only portions of this paper that are in Addison's MS. Note-Book (see No. 411) are this paragraph and the first sentence of the third paragraph.

they have made by glasses, or any other of their contemplations on nature. We are not a little pleased to find every green leaf swarm with millions of animals that at their largest growth are not visible to the naked eye. There is something very engaging to the fancy, as well as to our reason, in the treatises of metals, minerals, plants, and meteors; but when we survey the whole earth at once, and the several planets that lie within its neighbourhood, we are filled with a pleasing astonishment, to see so many worlds hanging one above another, and sliding round their axles in such an amazing pomp and solemnity. If after this we contemplate those wide fields of ether, that reach in height as far as from Saturn to the fixed stars, and run abroad almost to an infinitude, our imagination finds its capacity filled with so immense a prospect, and puts itself upon the stretch to comprehend it. But if we yet rise higher, and consider the fixed stars as so many vast oceans of flame, that are each of them attended with a different set of planets, and still discover new firmaments and new lights, that are sunk farther in those unfathomable depths of ether, so as not to be seen by the strongest of our telescopes, we are lost in such a labyrinth of suns and worlds, and confounded with the immensity and magnificence of Nature.

Nothing is more pleasant to the fancy, than to enlarge itself, by degrees, in its contemplation of the various proportions which its several objects bear to each other, when it compares the body of man to the bulk of the whole earth, the earth to the circle it describes round the sun, that circle to the sphere of the fixed stars, the sphere of the fixed stars to the circuit of the whole creation, the whole creation itself to the infinite space that is everywhere diffused about it; or when the imagination works downward, and considers the bulk of a human body, in respect of an animal a hundred times less than a mite, the particular limbs of such an animal, the different springs which actuate the limbs, the spirits which set these springs a-going, and the proportionable minuteness of these several parts, before they have arrived at their full growth and perfection. But if, after all this, we take the least particle of these animal spirits, and consider its capacity of being wrought into a world, that shall contain within those narrow dimensions a heaven and earth, stars and planets, and every different species of living creatures, in the same analogy and proportion they bear to each other in our own universe; such a speculation, by reason of its nicety, appears ridiculous to those who have not turned their thoughts that way, though, at the same time, it is founded on no less than the evidence of a demonstration. Nay, we might yet carry it farther, and discover in the smallest particle of this little world, a new inexhausted fund of matter, capable of being spun out into another universe.

I have dwelt the longer on this subject, because I think it may show us the proper limits, as well as the defectiveness, of our imagination; how it is confined to a very small quantity of space, and immediately stopped in its operations, when it endeavours to take in anything that is very great, or very little. Let a man try to conceive the different bulk of an animal which is twenty, from another which is a hundred times less than a mite, or to compare, in his thoughts, a length of a thousand diameters of the earth with that of a million, and he will quickly find that he has no different measures in his mind, adjusted to such extraordinary degrees of grandeur or minuteness. The understanding, indeed, opens an infinite space on every side of us, but the imagination, after a few faint efforts, is immediately at a stand, and finds herself swallowed up in the immensity of the void that surrounds it. Our reason can pursue a particle of matter through an infinite variety of divisions, but the fancy soon loses sight of it, and feels in itself a kind of chasm, that wants to be filled with matter of a more sensible bulk. We can neither widen nor contract the faculty to the dimensions of either extreme. The object is too big for our capacity, when we would comprehend the circumference of a world, and dwindles into nothing, when we endeavour after the idea of an atom.

It is possible this defect of imagination may not be in the soul itself, but as it acts in conjunction with the body. Perhaps there may not be room in the brain for such a variety of impressions, or the animal spirits may be incapable of figuring them in such a manner, as is necessary to excite so very large or very minute ideas. However it be, we may well suppose that beings of a higher nature very much excel us in this respect, as it is probable the soul of man will be infinitely more perfect hereafter in this faculty, as well as in all the rest; insomuch that, perhaps, the imagination will be able to keep pace with the understanding, and to form in itself distinct ideas of all the different modes and quantities of space.

No. 421.        *Thursday, July 3, 1712*        [ADDISON

*Ignotis errare locis, ignota videre*
*Flumina gaudebat; studio minuente laborem.*
                                OVID, *Met.* iv, 204

THE pleasures of the imagination are not wholly confined to such particular authors as are conversant in material objects, but are often to be met with among the polite masters of morality, criticism, and other speculations abstracted from matter, who, though they do not directly treat of the visible parts of Nature, often draw from them their similitudes, metaphors, and allegories. By these allusions a truth in the understanding is as it were reflected by the imagination; we are able to see something like colour and shape in a notion, and to discover a scheme of thoughts traced out upon matter. And here the mind receives a great deal of satisfaction, and has two of its faculties gratified at the same time, while the fancy is busy in copying after the understanding, and transcribing ideas out of the intellectual world into the material.

The great art of a writer shows itself in the choice of pleasing allusions, which are generally to be taken from the great or beautiful works of art or Nature; for though whatever is new or uncommon is apt to delight the imagination, the chief design of an allusion being to illustrate and explain the passages of an author, it should be always borrowed from what is more known and common, than the passages which are to be explained.

Allegories, when well chosen, are like so many tracks of light in a discourse, that make everything about them clear and beautiful. A noble metaphor, when it is placed to an advantage, casts a kind of glory round it, and darts a lustre through a whole sentence. These different kinds of allusion are but so many different manners of similitude, and, that they may please the imagination, the likeness ought to be very exact, or very agreeable, as we love to see a picture where the resemblance is just, or the posture and air graceful. But we often find eminent writers very faulty in this respect; great scholars are apt to fetch their comparisons and allusions from the sciences in which they are most conversant, so that a man may see the compass of their learning in a treatise on the most indifferent subject. I have read a discourse upon love, which none but a profound chymist could understand, and have heard many a sermon that should only have been preached before a congregation of Cartesians. On the contrary, your men of business usually have recourse to such instances as are too mean and familiar. They are for drawing the reader into a game of chess or tennis, or for leading him from shop to shop, in the cant of particular trades and employments. It is certain, there may be found an infinite variety of very agreeable allusions in both these kinds, but, for the generality, the most entertaining ones lie in the works of Nature, which are obvious to all capacities, and more delightful than what is to be found in arts and sciences [1].

It is this talent of affecting the imagination, that gives an embellishment to good sense, and makes one man's compositions more agreeable than another's. It sets off all writings in general, but is the very life and highest perfection of poetry. Where it shines in an eminent degree, it has preserved several poems for many ages, that have nothing else to recommend them; and where all the other beauties are present, the work appears dry and insipid, if this single one be wanting. It has something in it like creation; it bestows a kind of existence, and draws up to the reader's view several objects which are not to be found in being. It makes additions to nature, and gives a greater variety to God's works. In a word, it is able to beautify and adorn the most illustrious scenes in the universe, or to fill the mind with more glorious shows and apparitions [2], than can be found in any part of it.

We have now discovered the several originals of those pleasures that gratify the fancy; and here, perhaps, it would not be very difficult to cast under their proper heads those contrary objects, which are apt to fill it with distaste and terror; for the imagination is as liable to pain as pleasure. When the brain is hurt by any accident, or the mind disordered by dreams or sickness, the fancy is overrun with wild dismal ideas, and terrified with a thousand hideous monsters of its own framing.

> Eumenidum veluti demens videt agmina Pentheus,
> Et solem geminum, et duplices se ostendere Thebas.
> Aut Agamemnonius scenis agitatus Orestes.
> Armatam facibus matrem et serpentibus atris
> Quum videt, ultricesque sedent in limine Diræ.          VIRG.[3]

---

[1] This paragraph was added to the MS. in Addison's writing.

[2] 'Glorious scenes' (MS.). As first written, the sentence ran, 'fill the mind with such glorious scenes as are not to be paralleled by any part of the whole six days' productions'.

[3] Æn. iv, 469.

There is not a sight in Nature so mortifying as that of a distracted person, when his imagination is troubled, and his whole soul disordered and confused. Babylon in ruins is not so melancholy a spectacle. But to quit so disagreeable a subject, I shall only consider, by way of conclusion, what an infinite advantage this faculty gives an Almighty Being over the soul of man, and how great a measure of happiness or misery we are capable of receiving from the imagination only.

We have already seen the influence that one man has over the fancy of another, and with what ease he conveys into it a variety of imagery; how great a power then may we suppose lodged in Him, who knows all the ways of affecting the imagination, who can infuse what ideas He pleases, and fill those ideas with terror and delight to what degree He thinks fit? He can excite images in the mind, without the help of words, and make scenes rise up before us and seem present to the eye, without the assistance of bodies or exterior objects. He can transport the imagination with such beautiful and glorious visions as cannot possibly enter into our present conceptions, or haunt it with such ghastly spectres and apparitions as would make us hope for annihilation, and think existence no better than a curse. In short, He can so exquisitely ravish or torture the soul through this single faculty, as might suffice to make up the whole heaven or hell of any finite being.

This essay on the Pleasures of the Imagination having been published in separate papers; I shall conclude it with a Table of the principal Contents in each paper.

# THE CONTENTS

## PAPER I

The perfection of our sight above our other senses
—The pleasures of the imagination arise originally
from sight—The pleasures of the imagination divided
under two heads—The pleasures of the imagination
in some respects equal to those of the understanding
—The extent of the pleasures of the imagination—
The advantages a man receives from a relish of these
pleasures—In what respect they are preferable to
those of the understanding.

## PAPER II

Three sources of all the pleasures of the imagination, in our survey of outward objects—How what
is great pleases the imagination—How what is new
pleases the imagination—How what is beautiful in
our own species pleases the imagination—How what
is beautiful in general pleases the imagination—What
other accidental causes may contribute to the height-
ening of these pleasures.

## PAPER III

Why the necessary cause of our being pleased with
what is great, new, or beautiful, unknown—Why the
final cause more known and more useful—The final
cause of our being pleased with what is great—The
final cause of our being pleased with what is new—
The final cause of our being pleased with what is
beautiful in our own species—The final cause of our
being pleased with what is beautiful in general.

## PAPER IV

The works of Nature more pleasant to the imagination than those of art—The works of Nature
still more pleasant, the more they resemble those of

art—The works of art more pleasant, the more they resemble those of Nature—Our English plantations and gardens considered in the foregoing light.

## Paper V

Of architecture as it affects the imagination—Greatness in architecture relates either to the bulk or to the manner—Greatness of bulk in the ancient Oriental buildings—The ancient accounts of these buildings confirmed: 1. From the advantages for raising such works in the first ages of the world and in the Eastern climates; 2. From several of them which are still extant—Instances how greatness of manner affects the imagination—A French author's observation on this subject—Why concave and convex figures give a greatness of manner to works of architecture—Everything that pleases the imagination in architecture either great, beautiful, or new.

## Paper VI

The secondary pleasures of the imagination—The several sources of these pleasures (statuary, painting, description, and music) compared together—The final cause of our receiving pleasure from these several sources—Of descriptions in particular—The power of words over the imagination—Why one reader more pleased with descriptions than another.

## Paper VII

How a whole set of ideas hang together, &c.: a natural cause assigned for it—How to perfect the imagination of a writer: who among the ancient poets had this faculty in its greatest perfection—Homer excelled in imagining what is great; Virgil in imagining what is beautiful; Ovid in imagining what is new—Our own countryman, Milton, very perfect in all three respects.

### Paper VIII

Why anything that is unpleasant to behold pleases the imagination when well described—Why the imagination receives a more exquisite pleasure from the description of what is great, new, or beautiful—The pleasure still heightened, if what is described raises passion in the mind—Disagreeable passions pleasing when raised by apt descriptions—Why terror and grief are pleasing to the mind, when excited by descriptions—A particular advantage the writers in poetry and fiction have to please the imagination—What liberties are allowed them.

### Paper IX

Of that kind of poetry which Mr Dryden calls the fairy-way of writing—How a poet should be qualified for it—The pleasures of the imagination that arise from it—In this respect, why the moderns excel the ancients—Why the English excel the moderns—Who the best among the English—Of emblematical persons.

### Paper X

What authors please the imagination who have nothing to do with fiction—How history pleases the imagination—How the authors of the new philosophy please the imagination—The bounds and defects of the imagination—Whether these defects are essential to the imagination.

### Paper XI

How those please the imagination who treat of subjects abstracted from matter, by allusions taken from it—What allusions most pleasing to the imagination—Great writers how faulty in this respect—Of the art of imagining in general—The imagination capable of pain as well as pleasure—In what degree the imagination is capable either of pain or pleasure.

O.

No. 422.        *Friday, July 4, 1712*        [STEELE

*Hæc scripsi non otii abundantia, sed amoris erga te.*
                                        TULL., *Epis.*

I DO not know anything which gives greater disturbance to conversation than the false notion some
people have of raillery.   It ought certainly to be the
first point to be aimed at in society, to gain the
good will of those with whom you converse.   The
way to that is to show you are well inclined towards
them.   What then can be more absurd than to set
up for being extremely sharp and biting, as the term
is, in your expressions to your familiars?   A man
who has no good quality but courage is in a very ill
way towards making an agreeable figure in the world,
because that which he has superior to other people
cannot be exerted without raising himself an enemy.
Your gentleman of a satirical vein is in the like condition.   To say a thing which perplexes the heart of
him you speak to, or brings blushes into his face, is
a degree of murder; and it is, I think, an unpardonable offence to show a man you do not care whether
he is pleased or displeased.   But won't you then take
a jest?   Yes, but pray let it be a jest.   It is no jest
to put me, who am so unhappy as to have an utter
aversion to speaking to more than one man at a time,
under a necessity to explain myself in much company,
and reducing me to shame and derision, except I
perform what my infirmity of silence disables me
to do.

Callisthenes has great wit accompanied with that
quality (without which a man can have no wit at all),
a sound judgment.   This gentleman rallies the best
of any man I know, for he forms his ridicule upon a
circumstance which you are in your heart not unwilling to grant him, to wit, that you are guilty of
an excess in something which is in itself laudable.
He very well understands what you would be, and
needs not fear your anger for declaring you are a

little too much that thing. The generous will bear being reproached as lavish, and the valiant rash, without being provoked to resentment against their monitor. What has been said to be a mark of a good writer will fall in with the character of a good companion. The good writer makes his reader better pleased with himself, and the agreeable man makes his friends enjoy themselves, rather than him, while he is in their company. Callisthenes does this with inimitable pleasantry. He whispered a friend the other day, so as to be overheard by a young officer who gave symptoms of cocking upon the company, 'That gentleman has very much the air of a general officer.' The youth immediately put on a composed behaviour, and behaved himself suitably to the conceptions he believed the company had of him. It is to be allowed that Callisthenes will make a man run into impertinent relations to his own advantage, and express the satisfaction he has in his own dear self till he is very ridiculous; but in this case the man is made a fool by his own consent, and not exposed as such whether he will or no[1]. I take it therefore, that to make raillery agreeable a man must either not know he is rallied, or think never the worse of himself if he sees he is.

[1] In his *Character of Mrs Johnson* Swift says: 'She was never positive in arguing, and she usually treated those who were so in a manner which well enough gratified that unhappy disposition; yet in such a sort as made it very contemptible, and at the same time did some hurt to the owners. Whether this proceeded from her answers in general, or from her indifference to persons, or from her despair of mending them, or from the same practice which she much liked in Mr Addison, I cannot determine; but when she saw any of the company very warm in a wrong opinion, she was more inclined to confirm them in it than oppose them.' Mr Dobson, who quotes this passage, says that 'it almost reads as if Callisthenes were modelled on Addison'. If this be so, we may be sure that it was unintentional on Steele's part. According to Pope (*Prologue to the Satires*, 201, 202), Addison would

> Assent with civil leer,
> And without sneering, teach the rest to sneer.

In No. 163 of the *Tatler* Addison gives a description of Bickerstaff diverting himself—but not before others—at the expense of Ned Softly and his verses.

Acetus is of a quite contrary genius, and is more generally admired than Callisthenes, but not with justice. Acetus has no regard to the modesty or weakness of the person he rallies; but if his quality or humility gives him any superiority to the man he would fall upon, he has no mercy in making the onset. He can be pleased to see his best friend out of countenance, while the laugh is loud in his own applause. His raillery always puts the company into little divisions and separate interests, while that of Callisthenes cements it, and makes every man not only better pleased with himself, but also with all the rest in the conversation.

To rally well, it is absolutely necessary that kindness must run through all you say, and you must ever preserve the character of a friend to support your pretensions to be free with a man. Acetus ought to be banished human society, because he raises his mirth upon giving pain to the person upon whom he is pleasant. Nothing but the malevolence, which is too general towards those who excel, could make his company tolerated; but they with whom he converses are sure to see some man sacrificed wherever he is admitted, and all the credit he has for wit is owing to the gratification it gives to other men's ill-nature.

Minutius has a wit that conciliates a man's love, at the same time that it is exerted against his faults. He has an art of keeping the person he rallies in countenance, by insinuating that he himself is guilty of the same imperfection. This he does with so much address, that he seems rather to bewail himself than fall upon his friend.

It is really monstrous to see how unaccountably it prevails among men, to take the liberty of displeasing each other. One would think sometimes that the contention is, who shall be most disagreeable? Allusions to past follies, hints which revive what a man has a mind to forget for ever, and deserves that all the rest of the world should, are commonly brought forth even in company of men of distinction. They do not thrust with the skill of fencers, but cut up with the barbarity of butchers. It is, methinks, below the character of men of humanity and good manners to be capable of mirth while there is any one of the company in pain and disorder. They who have the true taste of conversation enjoy themselves in a communication of each other's excellences, and not in a triumph over their imperfections. Fortius would have been reckoned a wit if there had never been a fool in the world : he wants not foils to be a beauty, but has that natural pleasure in observing perfection in others, that his own faults are overlooked out of gratitude by all his acquaintance.

After these several characters of men who succeed or fail in raillery, it may not be amiss to reflect a little further what one takes to be the most agreeable kind of it; and that to me appears when the satire is directed against vice, with an air of contempt of the fault, but no ill-will to the criminal. Mr Congreve's 'Doris' is a masterpiece in this kind [1]. It is the character of a woman utterly abandoned, but her impudence, by the finest piece of raillery, is made only generosity.

> Peculiar therefore is her way,
> Whether by Nature taught,
> I shall not undertake to say,
> Or by experience bought.

> For who o'er night obtained her grace,
> She can next day disown,
> And stare upon the strange man's face,
> As one she ne'er had known.

---

[1] In the Dedication to Congreve of the *Poetical Miscellanies*, which Steele published in 1714, he spoke of the 'inimitable "Doris," which excels, for politeness, fine raillery, and courtly satire, anything we can meet with in any language.' And again, ' I cannot leave my favourite "Doris" without taking notice how much that short performance discovers a true knowledge of life. Doris is the character of a libertine woman of condition, and the satire is worked up accordingly ; for people of quality are seldom touched with any representation of their vices but in a light which makes them ridiculous.'

So well she can the truth disguise,
  Such artful wonder frame,
The lover or distrusts his eyes,
  Or thinks 'twas all a dream

Some censure this as lewd or low,
  Who are to bounty blind ;
For to forget what we bestow,
  Bespeaks a noble mind.

No. 423.          *Saturday, July 5, 1712*          [STEELE

*Nuper idoneus.* HOR., 3 *Od.* xxvi, 1

I LOOK upon myself as a kind of guardian of the
fair, and am always watchful to observe anything
which concerns their interest.  The present paper
shall be employed in the service of a very fine young
woman, and the admonitions I give her may not be
unuseful to the rest of the sex.  Gloriana shall be
the name of the heroine in to-day's entertainment;
and when I have told you that she is rich, witty,
young, and beautiful, you will believe she does not
want admirers.  She has had since she came to town
about twenty-five of those lovers who make their
addresses by way of jointure and settlement.  These
come and go, with great indifference on both sides;
and as beauteous as she is, a line in a deed has had
exception enough against it, to outweigh the lustre
of her eyes, the readiness of her understanding, and
the merit of her general character.  But among the
crowd of such cool adorers, she has two who are very
assiduous in their attendance.  There is something
so extraordinary and artful in their manner of application, that I think it but common justice to alarm
her in it.  I have done it in the following letter :

MADAM,—I have for some time taken notice of two
gentlemen who attend you in all public places, both of
whom have also easy access to you at your own house.
But the matter is adjusted between them, and Damon,
who so passionately addresses you, has no design upon
you; but Strephon, who seems to be indifferent to

you, is the man who is, as they have settled it, to have
you. The plot was laid over a bottle of wine; and
Strephon, when he first thought of you, proposed to
Damon to be his rival. The manner of his breaking
of it to him, I was so placed at a tavern that I could
not avoid hearing. 'Damon', said he, with a deep
sigh, 'I have long languished for that miracle of beauty
Gloriana; and if you will be very steadfastly my
rival, I shall certainly obtain her. Do not', continued
he, 'be offended at this overture; for I go upon the
knowledge of the temper of the woman, rather than
any vanity that I should profit by an opposition of
your pretensions to those of your humble servant.
Gloriana has very good sense, a quick relish of the
satisfactions of life, and will not give herself, as the
crowd of women do, to the arms of a man to whom
she is indifferent. As she is a sensible woman, expressions of rapture and adoration will not move her
neither; but he that has her must be the object of
her desire, not her pity. The way to this end I take
to be, that a man's general conduct should be agreeable,
without addressing in particular to the woman he loves.
Now, sir, if you will be so kind as to sigh and die
for Gloriana, I will carry it with great respect towards
her, but seem void of any thoughts as a lover. By
this means I shall be in the most amiable light of
which I am capable; I shall be received with freedom, you with reserve.' Damon, who has himself no
designs of marriage at all, easily fell into a scheme;
and you may observe, that wherever you are Damon
appears also. You see he carries on an unaffecting
exactness in his dress and manner, and strives always
to be the very contrary of Strephon. They have
already succeeded so far, that your eyes are ever in
search of Strephon, and turn themselves of course
from Damon. They meet and compare notes upon
your carriage; and the letter which was brought to
you the other day, was a contrivance to remark your
resentment. When you saw the billet subscribed
'Strephon', and turned away with a scornful air, and
cried 'Impertinence!' you gave hopes to him that
shuns you, without mortifying him that languishes
for you.

What I am concerned for, madam, is that in the

disposal of your heart you should know what you are doing, and examine it before it is lost. Strephon contradicts you in discourse with the civility of one who has a value for you, but gives up nothing like one that loves you. This seeming unconcern gives this behaviour the advantage of sincerity, and insensibly obtains your good opinion, by appearing disinterested in the purchase of it. If you watch these correspondents hereafter, you will find that Strephon makes his visit of civility immediately after Damon has tired you with one of love. Though you are very discreet, you will find it no easy matter to escape the toils so well laid, as when one studies to be disagreeable in passion, the other to be pleasing without it. All the turns of your temper are carefully watched, and their quick and faithful intelligence gives your lovers irresistible advantage. You will please, madam, to be upon your guard, and take all the necessary precautions against one who is amiable to you before he is enamoured.          I am, Madam,

Your most obedient Servant

Strephon makes great progress in this lady's good graces; for most women being actuated by some little spirit of pride and contradiction, he has the good effects of both those motives by this covert way of courtship. He received a message yesterday from Damon in the following words, superscribed ' With speed '.

All goes well; she is very angry at me, and I daresay hates me in earnest. It is a good time to visit.                                                    Yours

The comparison of Strephon's gaiety to Damon's languishment, strikes her imagination with a prospect of very agreeable hours with such a man as the former, and abhorrence of the insipid prospect with one like the latter. To know when a lady is displeased with another, is to know the best time of advancing yourself. This method of two persons

playing into each other's hand is so dangerous, that
I cannot tell how a woman could be able to with-
stand such a siege. The condition of Gloriana, I am
afraid, is irretrievable, for Strephon has had so many
opportunities of pleasing without suspicion, that all
which is left for her to do is to bring him, now she
is advised, to an explanation of his passion, and
beginning again, if she can conquer the kind sentiments she has already conceived for him. When
one shows himself a creature to be avoided, the
other proper to be fled to for succour, they have the
whole woman between them, and can occasionally
rebound her love and hatred from one to the other,
in such a manner as to keep her at a distance from
all the rest of the world, and cast lots for the
conquest.

*N.B.*—I have many other secrets which concern
the empire of Love, but I consider that while I alarm
my women, I instruct my men.                    T.


No. 424.        *Monday, July 7, 1712*        [STEELE

*Est Ulubris, animus si te non deficit.* HOR., 1 *Ep.* xi, 30

LONDON, *June* 24

MR SPECTATOR,—A man who has it in his power
to choose his own company, would certainly be much
to blame should he not, to the best of his judgment,
take such as are of a temper most suitable to his own;
and where that choice is wanting, or where a man
is mistaken in his choice, and yet under a necessity
of continuing in the same company, it will certainly
be his interest to carry himself as easily as possible.
In this I am sensible I do but repeat what has been
said a thousand times, at which, however, I think
nobody has any title to take exception, but they who
never failed to put this in practice. Not to use any
longer preface, this being the season of the year in
which great numbers of all sorts of people retire from

this place of business and pleasure to country solitude, I think it not improper to advise them to take with them as great a stock of good humour as they can; for though a country life is described as the most pleasant of all others, and though it may in truth be so, yet it is so only to those who know how to enjoy leisure and retirement.

As for those who can't live without the constant helps of business or company, let them consider, that in the country there is no Exchange, there are no playhouses, no variety of coffee-houses, nor many of those other amusements which serve here as so many reliefs from the repeated occurrences in their own families; but that there the greatest part of their time must be spent within themselves, and consequently it behoves them to consider how agreeable it will be to them before they leave this dear town.

I remember, Mr Spectator, we were very well entertained last year with the advices you gave us from Sir Roger's country seat; which I the rather mention because 'tis almost impossible not to live pleasantly where the master of a family is such a one as you there describe your friend, who cannot, therefore (I mean as to his domestic character), be too often recommended to the imitation of others. How amiable is that affability and benevolence with which he treats his neighbours and every one, even the meanest of his own family! And yet how seldom imitated? Instead of which we commonly meet with ill-natured expostulations, noise, and chidings. And this I hinted, because the humour and disposition of the head is what chiefly influences all the other parts of a family.

An agreement and kind correspondence between friends and acquaintance is the greatest pleasure of life. This is an undoubted truth, and yet any man who judges from the practice of the world will be almost persuaded to believe the contrary; for how can we suppose people should be so industrious to make themselves uneasy? what can engage them to entertain and foment jealousies of one another upon every the least occasion? Yet so it is, there are people who, as it should seem, delight in being troublesome and vexatious, who, as Tully speaks, 'Mira sunt alacritate ad litigandum' (Have a certain cheerfulness in wrangling). And thus it happens that there are very few families in which there are not feuds and animosities, though 'tis every one's interest, there more particularly, to avoid 'em, because there (as I would willingly hope) no one gives another uneasiness without feeling some share of it. But I am gone beyond what I designed, and had almost forgot what I chiefly proposed; which was barely to tell you how hardly we who pass most of our time in town dispense with a long vacation in the country, how uneasy we grow to ourselves and to one another when our conversation is confined, insomuch that by Michaelmas 'tis odds but we come to downright squabbling, and make as free with one another to our faces as we do with the rest of the world behind their backs. After I have told you this, I am to desire that you would now and then give us a lesson of good humour, a family piece; which, since we are all very fond of you, I hope may have some influence upon us.

After these plain observations, give me leave to give you an hint of what a set of company of my acquaintance, who are now gone into the country, and have the use of an absent nobleman's seat, have settled among themselves to avoid the inconveniences above mentioned. They are a collection of ten or twelve, of the same good inclination towards each other, but of very different talents and inclinations: from hence they hope that the variety of their tempers will only create variety of pleasures. But as there always will arise among the same people, either for want of diversity of objects, or the like causes, a certain satiety, which may grow into ill humour or discontent, there is a large wing of the house which they design to employ in the nature of an infirmary. Whoever says a peevish thing, or acts anything which betrays a sourness or indisposition to company, is immediately to be conveyed to his chambers in the infirmary, from whence he is not to be relieved until by his manner of submission, and the sentiments expressed in his petition for that purpose, he appears to the majority of the company to be again fit for society. You are to understand that all ill-natured words or uneasy gestures are sufficient cause for banishment; speaking impatiently to servants, making a man

repeat what he says, or anything that betrays inattention or dishumour, are also criminal without reprieve :
but it is provided that whoever observes the ill-natured
fit coming upon himself, and voluntarily retires, shall
be received at his return from the infirmary with the
highest marks of esteem. By these and other wholesome methods it is expected that, if they cannot cure
one another, yet at least they have taken care that
the ill humour of one shall not be troublesome to
the rest of the company. There are many other rules
which the society have established for the preserva-
tion of their ease and tranquillity, the effects of which,
with the incidents that arise among them, shall be
communicated to you from time to time for the public
good [1] by,

Sir,

Your most humble Servant,

T.                                                     R. O.

---

No. 425.     *Tuesday, July 8, 1712*     [BUDGELL [2]

> *Frigora mitescunt Zephyris, ver proterit æstas*
> *Interitura, simul*
> *Pomifer Auctumnus fruges effuderit, et mox*
> *Bruma recurrit iners.*          HOR., 4 Od. vii, 9

MR SPECTATOR,—There is hardly anything gives me
a more sensible delight than the enjoyment of a cool
still evening, after the uneasiness of a hot sultry day.
Such a one I passed not long ago, which made me
rejoice when the hour was come for the sun to set,
that I might enjoy the freshness of the evening in
my garden, which then affords me the pleasantest hours
I pass in the whole four-and-twenty. I immediately
rose from my couch, and went down into it. You
descend at first by twelve stone steps into a large
square divided into four grass plots, in each of which
is a statue of white marble. This is separated from a
large parterre by a low wall, and from thence, through
a pair of iron gates, you are led into a long broad
walk of the finest turf, set on each side with tall
yews, and on either hand bordered by a canal, which

---

1 See No. 429.          2 Or Pope. See No. 404.

on the right divides the walk from a wilderness parted
into variety of alleys and arbours, and on the left
from a kind of amphitheatre, which is the receptacle
of a great number of oranges and myrtles.  The moon
shone bright, and seemed then most agreeably to
supply the place of the sun, obliging me with as much
light as was necessary to discover a thousand pleasing
objects, and at the same time divested of all power
of heat.  The reflection of it in the water, the fanning
of the wind rustling on the leaves, the singing of the
thrush and nightingale, and the coolness of the walks,
all conspired to make me lay aside all displeasing
thoughts, and brought me into such a tranquillity of
mind as is, I believe, the next happiness to that of
hereafter.  In this sweet retirement I naturally fell
into the repetition of some lines out of a poem of
Milton's, which he entitles *Il Penseroso*, the ideas of
which were exquisitely suited to my present wander-
ings of thought :

> Sweet bird ! that shun'st the noise of folly,
> Most musical ! most melancholy !
> Thee, chauntress, of the woods among,
> I woo to hear thy evening song :
> And missing thee, I walk unseen
> On the dry, smooth-shaven green,
> To behold the wandering moon,
> Riding near her highest noon,
> Like one that hath been led astray,
> Through the heaven's wide pathless way,
> And oft, as if her head she bowed,
> Stooping through a fleecy cloud.
>
> Then let some strange mysterious dream
> Wave with his wings in airy stream,
> Of lively portraiture displayed,
> Softly on my eyelids laid ;
> And as I wake, sweet music breathe
> Above, about, or underneath,
> Sent by spirits to mortals good,
> Or th' unseen genius of the wood.

I reflected then upon the sweet vicissitudes of
night and day, on the charming disposition of the
seasons, and their return again in a perpetual circle;
' And oh !' said I, ' that I could from these my declining years, return again to my first spring of youth
and vigour; but that, alas ! is impossible. All that
remains within my power, is to soften the incon-

veniences I feel, with an easy contented mind, and
the enjoyment of such delights as this solitude affords
me.' In this thought I sate me down on a bank of
flowers and dropped into a slumber, which, whether it
were the effect of fumes and vapours, or my present
thoughts, I know not; but methought the genius of
the garden stood before me, and introduced into the
walk where I lay this drama and different scenes of
the revolution of the year, which, whilst I then saw,
even in my dream, I resolved to write down and
send to the *Spectator*.

The first person whom I saw advancing towards
me, was a youth of a most beautiful air and shape,
though he seemed not yet arrived at that exact proportion and symmetry of parts which a little more
time would have given him; but, however, there was
such a bloom in his countenance, such satisfaction
and joy, that I thought it the most desirable form
that I had ever seen. He was clothed in a flowing
mantle of green silk, interwoven with flowers; he had
a chaplet of roses on his head, and a narcissus in
his hand; primroses and violets sprang up under his
feet, and all Nature was cheered at his approach.
Flora was on one hand and Vertumnus on the other,
in a robe of changeable silk. After this I was surprised to see the moonbeams reflected with a sudden
glare from armour, and to see a man completely armed
advancing with his sword drawn. I was soon informed
by the genius it was Mars, who had long usurped a
place among the attendants of the Spring. He made
way for a softer appearance; it was Venus, without
any ornament but her own beauties, not so much as
her own cestus, with which she had encompassed a
globe, which she held in her right hand, and in her
left she had a sceptre of gold. After her followed
the Graces with their arms entwined within one
another; their girdles were loosed, and they moved
to the sound of soft music, striking the ground alternately with their feet. Then came up the three months
which belong to this season. As March advanced towards me, there was methought in his look a lowering
roughness, which ill befitted a month which was ranked
in so soft a season; but as he came forward his
features became insensibly more mild and gentle. He

smoothed his brow, and looked with so sweet a countenance that I could not but lament his departure,
though he made way for April. He appeared in the
greatest gaiety imaginable, and had a thousand pleasures to attend him. His look was frequently clouded,
but immediately returned to its first composure, and
remained fixed in a smile. Then came May, attended
by Cupid with his bow strung, and in a posture to let
fly an arrow. As he passed by methought I heard a
confused noise of soft complaints, gentle ecstasies, and
tender sighs of lovers; vows of constancy, and as many
complainings of perfidiousness; all which the winds
wafted away as soon as they had reached my hearing.
After these I saw a man advance in the full prime and
vigour of his age, his complexion was sanguine and
ruddy, his hair black, and fell down in beautiful ring-
lets beneath his shoulders; a mantle of hair-coloured
silk hung loosely upon him. He advanced with a hasty
step after the Spring, and sought out the shade and
cool fountains which played in the garden. He was
particularly well pleased when a troop of zephyrs
fanned him with their wings. He had two companions
who walked on each side, that made him appear the
most agreeable : the one was Aurora, with fingers
of roses, and her feet dewy, attired in grey; the
other was Vesper, in a robe of azure beset with drops
of gold, whose breath he caught whilst it passed over
a bundle of honeysuckles and tuberoses which he held
in his hand. Pan and Ceres followed them with four
reapers, who danced a morris to the sound of oaten
pipes and cymbals. Then came the attendant months :
June retained still some small likeness of the Spring;
but the other two seemed to step with a less vigorous
tread, especially August, who seemed almost to faint,
whilst for half the steps he took the dog-star levelled
his rays full at his head. They passed on and made
way for a person that seemed to bend a little under
the weight of years; his beard and hair, which were
full grown, were composed of an equal number of black
and grey; he wore a robe which he had girt round
him of a yellowish caste, not unlike the colour of fallen
leaves which he walked upon. I thought he hardly
made amends for expelling the foregoing scene by the
large quantity of fruits which he bore in his hands.

Plenty walked by his side with an healthy, fresh countenance, pouring out from an horn all the various product of the year. Pomona followed with a glass of cider in her hand, with Bacchus in a chariot drawn by tigers, accompanied by a whole troop of satyrs, fauns, and sylvans. September, who came next, seemed in his looks to promise a new Spring, and wore the livery of those months. The succeeding month was all soiled with the juice of grapes, as if he had just come from the wine-press. November, though he was in this division, yet by the many stops he made, seemed rather inclined to the Winter, which followed close at his heels. He advanced in the shape of an old man in the extremity of age : the hair he had was so very white it seemed a real snow ; his eyes were red and piercing, and his beard hung with a great quantity of icicles ; he was wrapped up in furs, but yet so pinched with excess of cold that his limbs were all contracted and his body bent to the ground, so that he could not have supported himself had it not been for Comus, the god of revels, and Necessity, the mother of Fate, who sustained him on each side. The shape and mantle of Comus was one of the things that most surprised me ; as he advanced towards me his countenance seemed the most desirable I had ever seen : on the fore part of his mantle was pictured Joy, Delight, and Satisfaction, with a thousand emblems of merriment, and jests with faces looking two ways at once ; but as he passed from me I was amazed at a shape so little correspondent to his face : his head was bald, and all the rest of his limbs appeared old and deformed. On the hinder part of his mantle was represented Murder, with dishevelled hair and a dagger all bloody, Anger in a robe of scarlet, and Suspicion squinting with both eyes ; but above all the most conspicuous was the battle of the Lapithæ and the Centaurs. I detested so hideous a shape, and turned my eyes upon Saturn, who was stealing away behind him, with a scythe in one hand and an hour-glass in t'other, unobserved. Behind Necessity was Vesta, the goddess of fire, with a lamp which was perpetually supplied with oil, and whose flame was eternal. She cheered the rugged brow of Necessity, and warmed her so far as almost to make her assume the features

and likeness of Choice. December, January, and
February passed on after the rest, all in furs; there
was little distinction to be made amongst them, and
they were only more or less displeasing as they discovered more or less haste towards the grateful return
of Spring.                                            Z.


No. 426.     *Wednesday, July 9, 1712*     [STEELE

*Quid non mortalia pectora cogis,*
*Auri sacra fames.*                    VIRG., *Æn.* iii, 56

A VERY agreeable friend of mine, the other day,
carrying me in his coach into the country to dinner,
fell into discourse concerning the care of parents
due to their children, and the piety of children
towards their parents. He was reflecting upon the
succession of particular virtues and qualities there
might be preserved from one generation to another,
if these regards were reciprocally held in veneration.
But as he never fails to mix an air of mirth and
good humour with his good sense and reasoning, he
entered into the following relation:

I will not be confident in what century or under
what reign it happened, that this want of mutual confidence and right understanding between father and
son was fatal to the family of the Valentines in
Germany. Basilius Valentinus was a person who had
arrived at the utmost perfection in the hermetic art,
and initiated his son Alexandrinus in the same mysteries: but as you know they are not to be attained
but by the painful, the pious, the chaste and pure of
heart, Basilius did not open to him, because of his
youth and the deviations too natural to it, the greatest
secrets of which he was master, as well knowing that
the operation would fail in the hands of a man so
liable to errors in life as Alexandrinus. But believing, from a certain indisposition of mind as well as
body, his dissolution was drawing nigh, he called
Alexandrinus to him, and as he lay on a couch, over

against which his son was seated, and prepared by sending out servants one after another, and admonition to examine that no one overheard them, he revealed the most important of his secrets with the solemnity and language of an adept. 'My son', said he, 'many have been the watchings, long the lucubrations, constant the labours of thy father, not only to gain a great and plentiful estate to his posterity, but also to take care that he should have no posterity. Be not amazed, my child; I do not mean that thou shalt be taken from me, but that I will never leave thee, and consequently cannot be said to have posterity. Behold, my dearest Alexandrinus, the effect of what was propagated in nine months. We are not to contradict Nature, but to follow and to help her; just as long as an infant is in the womb of its parent, so long are these medicines of revivification in preparing. Observe this small phial and this little gallipot, in this an unguent, in the other a liquor. In these, my child, are collected such powers as shall revive the springs of life when they are yet but just ceased, and give new strength, new spirits, and, in a word, wholly restore all the organs and senses of the human body to as great a duration as it had before enjoyed from its birth, to the day of the application of these my medicines. But, my beloved son, care must be taken to apply them within ten hours after the breath is out of the body, while yet the clay is warm with its late life, and yet capable of resuscitation. I find my frame grown crazy with perpetual toil and meditation; and I conjure you, as soon as I am dead, to anoint me with this unguent; and when you see me begin to move, pour into my lips this inestimable liquor, else the force of the ointment will be ineffectual. By this means you will give me life as I have you, and we will from that hour mutually lay aside the authority of having bestowed life on each other, but live as brethren, and prepare new medicines against such another period of time as will demand another application of the same restoratives.' In a few days after these wonderful ingredients were delivered to Alexandrinus, Basilius departed this life. But such was the pious sorrow of the son at the loss of so excellent a father, and the first transports of grief had so

wholly disabled him from all manner of business, that
he never thought of the medicines till the time to
which his father had limited their efficacy was expired.
To tell the truth, Alexandrinus was a man of wit and
pleasure, and considered his father had lived out his
natural time, his life was long and uniform, suitable
to the regularity of it; but that he himself, poor
sinner, wanted a new life, to repent of a very bad
one hitherto; and in the examination of his heart,
resolved to go on as he did with this natural being
of his, but repent very faithfully, and spend very
piously the life to which he should be restored by
application of these rarities, when time should come,
to his own person.

It has been observed, that Providence frequently
punishes the self-love of men who would do immoder-
ately for their own offspring, with children very much
below their characters and qualifications, insomuch
that they only transmit their names to be borne by
those who give daily proofs of the vanity of the labour
and ambition of their progenitors.

It happened thus in the family of Basilius; for
Alexandrinus began to enjoy his ample fortune in
all the extremities of household expense, furniture,
and insolent equipage; and this he pursued till the
day of his own departure began, as he grew sensible,
to approach. As Basilius was punished with a son
very unlike him, Alexandrinus was visited with one of
his own disposition. It is natural that ill men should
be suspicious, and Alexandrinus, besides that jealousy,
had proofs of the vicious disposition of his son
Renatus, for that was his name.

Alexandrinus, as I observed, having very good
reasons for thinking it unsafe to trust the real secret
of his phial and gallipot to any man living, pro-
jected to make sure work, and hope for his success
depending from the avarice, not the bounty of his
benefactor.

With this thought he called Renatus to his bed-
side, and bespoke him in the most pathetic gesture and
accent. 'As much, my son, as you have been addicted
to vanity and pleasure, as I also have been before
you, [neither] you nor I could escape the fame, or
the good effects of the profound knowledge of our

progenitor, the renowned Basilius. His symbol is very well known in the philosophic world, and I shall never forget the venerable air of his countenance, when he let me into the profound mysteries of the Smaragdine Table of Hermes. "It is true", said he, "and far removed from all colour of deceit, That which is inferior is like that which is superior, by which are acquired and perfected all the miracles of a certain work. The father is the sun, the mother the moon, the wind is in the womb, the earth is the nurse of it, and mother of all perfection. All this must be received with modesty and wisdom." The cynical people carry in all their jargon a whimsical sort of piety, which is ordinary with great lovers of money, and is no more but deceiving themselves that their regularity and strictness of manners, for the ends of this world, has some affinity to the innocence of heart which must recommend them to the next.' Renatus wondered to hear his father talk so like an adept, and with such a mixture of piety; while Alexandrinus, observing his attention fixed, proceeded. 'This phial, child, and this little earthen pot will add to thy estate so much, as to make thee the richest man in the German Empire. I am going to my long home, but shall not return to common dust.' Then he resumed a countenance of alacrity, and told him that if within an hour after his death he anointed his whole body, and poured down his throat that liquor which he had from old Basilius, the corpse would be converted into pure gold. I will not pretend to express to you the unfeigned tenderness that passed between these two extraordinary persons; but if the father recommended the care of his remains with vehemence and affection, the son was not behindhand in professing that he would not cut the least bit off him, but upon the utmost extremity, or to provide for his younger brothers and sisters.

Well, Alexandrinus died, and the heir of his body (as our term is) could not forbear, in the wantonness of his heart, to measure the length and breadth of his beloved father, and cast up the ensuing value of him before he proceeded to operation. When he knew the immense reward of his pains, he began the work : but lo ! when he had anointed the corpse all over, and

began to apply the liquor, the body stirred, and
Renatus, in a fright, broke the phial[1].

                                             T.


No. 427.     *Thursday, July 10, 1712*          [STEELE

*Quantum a rerum turpitudine abes, tantum te a verborum libertate
sejungas.* TULL.

IT is a certain sign of an ill heart to be inclined
to defamation. They who are harmless and innocent
can have no gratification that way; but it ever rises
from a neglect of what is laudable in a man's self,
and an impatience of seeing it in another, else why
should virtue provoke? Why should beauty displease
in such a degree, that a man given to scandal never
lets the mention of either pass by him without offering something to the diminution of it? A lady the
other day at a visit, being attacked somewhat rudely
by one whose own character has been very roughly
treated, answered a great deal of heat and intemperance very calmly : ' Good madam, spare me, who am
none of your match; I speak ill of nobody, and it is
a new thing to me to be spoken ill of.' Little minds
think fame consists in the number of votes they
have on their side among the multitude, whereas it
is really the inseparable follower of good and worthy
actions. Fame is as natural a follower of merit as
a shadow is of a body. It is true, when crowds
press upon you this shadow cannot be seen, but
when they separate from around you it will again
appear. The lazy, the idle, and the froward are the
persons who are most pleased with the little tales
which pass about the town to the disadvantage of

[1] This tale is from the *Description of the memorable Sea and Land
Travels through Persia to the East Indies,* by Johann Albrecht von
Mandelslo, translated from the German of Olearius, by J. B. B.,
Book v, p. 189. Basil Valentine, whom it makes the hero of a story
after the manner of the romances of Virgil the Enchanter, was an
alchemist of the sixteenth century, who is believed to have been a
Benedictine monk of Erfurth, and is not known to have had any
children. He was the author of the *Currus Triumphalis Antimonii*
(Morley).

the rest of the world. Were it not for the pleasure of speaking ill, there are numbers of people who are too lazy to go out of their own houses, and too ill-natured to open their lips in conversation. It was not a little diverting the other day to observe a lady reading a post letter, and at these words, ' After all her airs, he has heard some story or other, and the match is broke off ', give orders in the midst of her reading, ' Put to the horses '. That a young woman of merit has missed an advantageous settlement was news not to be delayed, lest somebody else should have given her malicious acquaintance that satisfaction before her. The unwillingness to receive good tidings is a quality as inseparable from a scandal-bearer as the readiness to divulge bad. But, alas, how wretchedly low and contemptible is that state of mind that cannot be pleased but by what is the subject of lamentation! This temper has ever been in the highest degree odious to gallant spirits. The Persian soldier, who was heard reviling Alexander the Great, was well admonished by his officer : ' Sir, you are paid to fight against Alexander, and not to rail at him.'

Cicero in one of his pleadings [1], defending his client from general scandal, says very handsomely, and with much reason, ' There are many who have particular engagements to the prosecutor; there are many who are known to have ill-will to him for whom I appear; there are many who are naturally addicted to defamation, and envious of any good to any man, who may have contributed to spread reports of this kind : for nothing is so swift as scandal, nothing is more easy sent abroad, nothing received with more welcome, nothing diffuses itself so universally. I shall not desire that if any report to our disadvantage has any ground for it, you would overlook or extenuate it : but if there be anything advanced without a person who can say whence he had it, or which is attested by one who forgot who

---

[1] *Oratio pro Cn. Plancio.*

told him it, or who had it from one of so little consideration that he did not think it worth his notice,
all such testimonies as these, I know, you will think
too slight to have any credit against the innocence and
honour of your fellow-citizen.' When an ill-report
is traced, it very often vanishes among such as the
orator has here recited. And how despicable a creature must that be, who is in pain for what passes
among so frivolous a people? There is a town in
Warwickshire of good note, and formerly pretty
famous for much animosity and dissension, the chief
families of which have now turned all their whispers,
backbitings, envies, and private malices into mirth
and entertainment, by means of a peevish old gentlewoman, known by the title of the Lady Bluemantle.
This heroine has for many years together outdone
the whole sisterhood of gossips in invention, quick
utterance, and unprovoked malice. This good body
is of a lasting constitution, though extremely de-
cayed in her eyes, and decrepit in her feet. The
two circumstances of being always at home from her
lameness, and very attentive from her blindness,
make her lodgings the receptacle of all that passes
in town, good or bad; but for the latter, she seems
to have the better memory. There is another thing
to be noted of her, which is, that as it is usual with
old people, she has a livelier memory of things which
passed when she was very young, than of late years.
Add to all this, that she does not only not love anybody, but she hates everybody. The statue in
Rome [1] does not serve to vent malice half so well,
as this old lady does to disappoint it. She does not
know the author of anything that is told her, but can
readily repeat the matter itself; therefore, though
she exposes all the whole town, she offends no one
body in it. She is so exquisitely restless and peevish,
that she quarrels with all about her, and sometimes
in a freak will instantly change her habitation. To

---

[1] See No. 23. Steele printed several letters from Pasquin of Rome
to Isaac Bickerstaff of Great Britain in the *Tatler* (Nos. 129, 140, 187).

indulge this humour, she is led about the grounds belonging to the same house she is in, and the persons to whom she is to remove, being in the plot, are ready to receive her at her own chamber again. At stated times, the gentlewoman at whose house she supposes she is at the time, is sent for to quarrel with, according to her common custom. When they have a mind to drive the jest, she is immediately urged to that degree, that she will board in a family with which she has never yet been; and away she will go this instant, and tell them all that the rest have been saying of them. By this means she has been an inhabitant of every house in the place without stirring from the same habitation; and the many stories which everybody furnishes her with to favour that deceit, make her the general intelligencer of the town of all that can be said by one woman against another. Thus groundless stories die away, and sometimes truths are smothered under the general word. When they have a mind to discountenance a thing, 'Oh! that is in my Lady Bluemantle's memoirs.'

Whoever receives impressions to the disadvantage of others without examination, is to be had in no other credit for intelligence than this good Lady Bluemantle, who is subjected to have her ears imposed upon for want of other helps to better information. Add to this, that other scandal-bearers suspend the use of these faculties which she has lost, rather than apply them to do justice to their neighbours; and I think, for the service of my fair readers, to acquaint them that there is a voluntary Lady Bluemantle at every visit in town.                T.


No. 428.      *Friday, July 11, 1712*     [STEELE

*Occupet extremum scabies.* HOR., *Ars Poet.* 417

IT is an impertinent and unreasonable fault in conversation, for one man to take up all the discourse. It may possibly be objected to me myself, that I am guilty in this kind, in entertaining the town every day, and not giving so many able persons who have it more in their power, and as much in their inclination, an opportunity to oblige mankind with their thoughts. 'Besides', said one whom I overheard the other day, ' why must this paper turn altogether upon topics of learning and morality? Why should it pretend only to wit, humour, or the like, things which are useful only to amuse men of literature and superior education? I would have it consist also of all things which may be necessary or useful to any part of society, and the mechanic arts should have their place as well as the liberal. The ways of gain, husbandry, and thrift, will serve a greater number of people, than discourses upon what was well said or done by such a philosopher, hero, general, or poet.' I no sooner heard this critic talk of my works, but I minuted what he had said; and from that instant resolved to enlarge the plan of my speculations, by giving notice to all persons of all orders, and each sex, that if they are pleased to send me discourses, with their names and places of abode to them, so that I can be satisfied the writings are authentic, such their labours shall be faithfully inserted in this paper. It will be of much more consequence to a youth in his apprenticeship, to know by what rules and arts such a one became sheriff of the city of London, than to see the sign of one of his own quality with a lion's heart in each hand. The world indeed is enchanted with romantic and improbable achievements, when the plain path to respective greatness and success in the way of life a man is in, is wholly overlooked. Is it possible that a young man at present could pass his time better, than in reading the history of stocks, and knowing by what secret springs they have such sudden ascents and falls in the same day? Could he be better conducted in his way to wealth, which is the great article of life, than in a treatise dated from Change Alley by

an able proficient there? Nothing certainly could
be more useful, than to be well instructed in his
hopes and fears; to be diffident when others exult
and, with a secret joy, buy when others think it their
interest to sell. I invite all persons who have anything to say for the profitable information of the
public, to take their turns in my paper. They are
welcome, from the late noble inventor of the longitude [1], to the humble author of 'Strops for
Razors [2]'. If to carry ships in safety, to give help
to people tossed in a troubled sea, without knowing
to what shore they bear, what rocks to avoid, or
what coast to pray for in their extremity, be a
worthy labour, and an invention that deserves a
statue; at the same time, he who has found a means
to let the instrument which is to make your visage
less horrid, and your person more smug, easy in the
operation, is worthy of some kind of good reception.
If things of high moment meet with renown, those
of little consideration, since of any consideration,

[1] If this mean the Marquis of Worcester, the exact ascertainment of
the longitude was not one of his century of inventions. The sextant
had its origin in the mind of Sir Isaac Newton, who was knighted in
1705, and living at this time, but its practical inventor was Thomas
Godfrey, a glazier at Philadelphia. Godfrey's instrument is said to
have been seen by John Hadley, or that English philosopher, after
whom the instrument is named, invented it at the same time, about
1730 (Morley).
[2] In No. 428 was an advertisement of ' the famous original Venetian
Strops, neatly fixed on boards, now brought to the highest perfection,
so as vastly to exceed all others, and for polishing and setting razors,
penknives, lances, &c., are not to be paralleled. . . . Price 1s. each. . . .
Sold only at Mr Allcroft's, a Toy-shop, at the Bluecoat Boy, against
the Royal Exchange in Cornhill; Mr Paiston's, a Stationer, at the
May Pole in the Strand; and at Mr Cooper's, a Toy-shop, the corner
of Charles Court, near York Buildings, in the Strand'. A controversy
about razor-strops was carried on in advertisements in 1710, and was
continued after the cessation of the Tatler. On January 13, 1710–11,
Swift told Esther Johnson that several imitations of that paper had
appeared; 'and one of them holds on still, and to-day it advertised
against Harrison's; and so there must be disputes which are genuine,
like the strops for razors'. In No. 509 of the Spectator, Steele again
refers to 'the author of the true strops for razors'. In a paper on
advertisements in the Tatler (No. 224), Addison says, ' Above half the
advertisements one meets with nowadays are purely polemical. The
inventors of "Strops for razors" have written against one another this
way for several years, and that with great bitterness.'

are not to be despised.  In order that no merit may
lie hid, and no art unimproved, I repeat it, that I
call artificers, as well as philosophers, to my assistance in the public service.  It would be of great use,
if we had an exact history of the successes of every
great shop within the city walls, what tracts of land
have been purchased by a constant attendance within
a walk of thirty feet.  If it could also be noted in the
equipage of those who are ascended from the successful trade of their ancestors into figure and equipage,
such accounts would quicken industry in the pursuit
of such acquisitions, and discountenance luxury in
the enjoyment of them.

To diversify these kind of informations, the industry of the female world is not to be unobserved :
she to whose household virtues it is owing that men
do honour to her husband, should be recorded with
veneration; she who has wasted his labours, with
infamy.  When we are come into domestic life in
this manner, to awaken caution and attendance to
the main point, it would not be amiss to give now
and then a touch of tragedy, and describe that most
dreadful of all human conditions, the case of bankruptcy; how plenty, credit, cheerfulness, full hopes,
and easy possessions are in an instant turned into
penury, faint aspects, diffidence, sorrow, and misery;
how the man, who with an open hand the day before
could administer to the extremities of others, is
shunned to-day by the friend of his bosom.  It would
be useful to show how just this is on the negligent,
how lamentable on the industrious.  A paper written
by a merchant might give this island a true sense
of the worth and importance of his character : it
might be visible from what he could say that no
soldier entering a breach adventures more for honour
than the trader does for wealth to his country.  In
both cases the adventurers have their own advantage,
but I know no cases wherein everybody else is a
sharer in the success.

It is objected by readers of history that the battles

in those narrations are scarce ever to be understood. This misfortune is to be ascribed to the ignorance of historians in the methods of drawing up, changing the forms of a battalia, and the enemy retreating from, as well as approaching to, the charge. But in the discourses from the correspondents whom I now invite, the danger will be of another kind; and it is necessary to caution them only against using terms of art, and describing things that are familiar to them in words unknown to their readers. I promise myself a great harvest of new circumstances, persons, and things from this proposal; and a world which many think they are well acquainted with discovered as wholly new. This sort of intelligence will give a lively image of the chain and mutual dependence of human society, take off impertinent prejudices, enlarge the minds of those whose views are confined to their own circumstances; and, in short, if the knowing in several arts, professions, and trades will exert themselves, it cannot but produce a new field of diversion, an instruction more agreeable than has yet appeared.        T.


No. 429.        *Saturday, July* 12, 1712        [STEELE

*Populumque falsis*
*Dedocet uti*
*Vocibus.*        HOR., 2 *Od.* ii, 19

MR. SPECTATOR,—Since I gave an account of an agreeable set of company which were gone down into the country [1], I have received advices from thence that the institution of an infirmary for those who should be out of humour has had very good effects. My letters mention particular circumstances of two or three persons who had the good sense to retire of their own accord, and notified that they were withdrawn, with the reasons of it, to the company, in their respective memorials.

1 See No. 424.

' *The Memorial of* MRS MARY DAINTY, *Spinster,*

' Humbly sheweth,

' That conscious of her own want of merit, accompanied with a vanity of being admired, she had gone into exile of her own accord.

' She is sensible that a vain person is the most insufferable creature living in a well-bred assembly.

' That she desired, before she appeared in public again, she might have assurances that, though she might be thought handsome, there might not more address or compliment be paid to her than to the rest of the company.

' That she conceived it a kind of superiority that one person should take upon him to commend another.

' Lastly, that she went into the infirmary to avoid a particular person who took upon him to profess an admiration of her.

' She therefore prayed that to applaud out of due place might be declared an offence, and punished in the same manner with detraction, in that the latter did but report persons defective, and the former made them so.

' All which is submitted, &c.'

There appeared a delicacy and sincerity in this memorial very uncommon, but my friend informs me that the allegations of it were groundless, insomuch that this declaration of an aversion to being praised was understood to be no other than a secret trap to purchase it, for which reason it lies still on the table unanswered.

' *The Humble Memorial of the* LADY LYDIA LOLLER,

' Sheweth,

' That the Lady Lydia is a woman of quality married to a private gentleman.

' That she finds herself neither well nor ill.

' That her husband is a clown.

' That Lady Lydia cannot see company.

'That she desires the infirmary may be her apartment during her stay in the country.

'That they would please to make merry with their equals.

'That Mr Loller might stay with them if he thought fit.'

It was immediately resolved that Lady Lydia was still at London.

'*The Humble Memorial of* THOMAS SUDDEN, Esq., *of the Inner Temple,*

'Sheweth,

'That Mr Sudden is conscious that he is too much given to argumentation.

'That he talks loud.

'That he is apt to think all things matter of debate.

'That he stayed behind in Westminster Hall when the late shake of the roof happened, only because a counsel of the other side asserted it was coming down.

'That he cannot for his life consent to anything.

'That he stays in the infirmary to forget himself.

'That as soon as he has forgot himself he will wait on the company.'

His indisposition was allowed to be sufficient to require a cessation from company.

'*The Memorial of* FRANK JOLLY,

'Sheweth,

'That he hath put himself into the infirmary, in regard he is sensible of a certain rustic mirth, which renders him unfit for polite conversation.

'That he intends to prepare himself by abstinence and thin diet to be one of the company.

'That at present he comes into a room as if he were an express from abroad.

'That he has chosen an apartment with a matted ante-chamber, to practise motion without being heard.

'That he bows, talks, drinks, eats, and helps himself before a glass, to learn to act with moderation.

'That by reason of his luxuriant health he is oppressive to persons of composed behaviour.

'That he is endeavouring to forget the word "Pshaw, pshaw".

'That he is also weaning himself from his cane.

'That when he has learnt to live without his said cane, he will wait on the company', &c.

'The Memorial of JOHN RHUBARB, Esq.,

'Sheweth,

'That your petitioner has retired to the infirmary, but that he is in perfect good health, except that he has by long use, and for want of discourse, contracted an habit of complaint that he is sick.

'That he wants for nothing under the sun, but what to say; and therefore has fallen into this unhappy malady of complaining that he is sick.

'That this custom of his makes him, by his own confession, fit only for the infirmary, and therefore he has not waited for being sentenced to it.

'That he is conscious there is nothing more improper than such a complaint in good company, in that they must pity, whether they think the lamenter ill or not; and that the complainant must make a silly figure, whether he is pitied or not.

'Your petitioner humbly prays, that he may have time to know how he does, and he will make his appearance.'

The Valetudinarian was likewise easily excused; and this society being resolved not only to make it their business to pass their time agreeably for the present season, but also to commence such habits in themselves as may be of use in their future conduct in general, are very ready to give in to a fancied or real incapacity to join with their measures, in order to have no humorist, proud man, impertinent or sufficient fellow, break in upon their happiness. Great evils seldom happen to disturb company, but indulgence in particularities of humour is the seed of making half our time hang in suspense, or waste away under real discomposures.

Among other things it is carefully provided, that there may not be disagreeable familiarities. No one is to appear in the public rooms undressed, or enter abruptly into each other's apartment without intimation. Every one has hitherto been so careful in his behaviour, that there has but one offender in ten days' time been sent into the infirmary, and that was for throwing away his cards at whist.

He has offered his submission in the following terms :

'*The Humble Petition of* JEOFFRY HOTSPUR, Esq.,
'Sheweth,

'Though the petitioner swore, stamped, and threw down his cards, he has all imaginable respect for the ladies and the whole company.

'That he humbly desires it may be considered in the case of gaming, there are many motives which provoke to disorder.

'That the desire of gain, and the desire of victory, are both thwarted in losing.

'That all conversations in the world have indulged human infirmity in this case.

'Your petitioner therefore most humbly prays, that he may be restored to the company, and he hopes to bear ill fortune with a good grace for the future, and to demean himself so as to be no more cheerful when he wins, than grave when he loses.'                   T.


No. 430.        *Monday, July 14, 1712*        [STEELE

*Quære peregrinum, vicinia rauca reclamat.*
                                    HOR., 1 *Ep.* xvii, 62

SIR,—As you are Spectator-General, you may with authority censure whatsoever looks ill and is offensive to the sight, the worst nuisance of which kind methinks is the scandalous appearance of poor in all parts of this wealthy city. Such miserable objects affect the compassionate beholder with dismal ideas, discompose the cheerfulness of his mind, and deprive him of the pleasure that he might otherwise take in surveying the grandeur of our metropolis. Who can without remorse see a disabled sailor, the purveyor of our luxury, destitute of necessaries? Who can behold an honest soldier that bravely withstood the enemy, prostrate and in want amongst his friends? It were endless to mention all the variety of wretchedness, and the numberless poor, that not only singly, but in companies, implore your charity. Spectacles of this nature everywhere occur; and it is unaccountable, that amongst the many lamentable cries that infest this town, your Comptroller-General[1] should not take notice of the most shocking, viz. those of the needy and afflicted. I can't but think he waived it merely out of good breeding, choosing rather to stifle his resentment than upbraid his countrymen with inhumanity; however, let not charity be sacrificed to popularity, and if his ears were deaf to their complaints, let not your eyes overlook their persons. There are, I know, many impostors among them. Lameness and blindness are certainly very often acted; but can those that have their sight and limbs employ them better than in knowing whether they are counterfeited or not? I know not which of the two misapplies his senses most, he who pretends himself blind to move compassion, or he who beholds a miserable object without pitying it. But in order to remove such impediments, I wish, Mr Spectator, you would give us a discourse upon beggars, that we may not pass by true objects of charity or give to impostors. I looked out of my window the other morning earlier than ordinary, and saw a blind beggar, an hour before the passage he stands in is frequented, with a needle and thread, thriftily mending his stockings: my astonishment was still greater when I beheld a lame fellow, whose legs were too big to walk with in an hour after, bring him a pot of ale. I will not mention the shakings, distortions, and convulsions which many of them practise to gain an alms; but sure I am, they ought to be taken care of in this condition, either by the beadle or the magistrate. They, it seems, relieve their posts according to their talents: there is the voice of an old woman never begins to beg till nine in the evening, and then she is destitute of lodging, turned out for want of rent, and has the same ill

1 See No. 251.

fortune every night in the year. You should employ an officer to hear the distress of each beggar that is constant at a particular place, who is ever in the same tone, and succeeds because his audience is continually changing, though he does not alter his lamentation. If we have nothing else for our money, let us have more invention to be cheated with. All which is submitted to your Spectatorial vigilance; and I am,

Sir,

Your most humble Servant

SIR,—I was last Sunday highly transported at our parish church; the gentleman in the pulpit pleaded movingly in behalf of the poor children, and they for themselves much more forcibly by singing an hymn; and I had the happiness to be a contributor to this little religious institution of innocents, and I am sure I never disposed of money more to my satisfaction and advantage. The inward joy I find in myself, and the goodwill I bear to mankind, make me heartily wish these pious works may be encouraged, that the present promoters may reap the delight and posterity the benefit of them. But whilst we are building this beautiful edifice, let not the old ruins remain in view to sully the prospect : whilst we are cultivating and improving this young hopeful offspring, let not the ancient and helpless creatures be shamefully neglected. The crowds of poor, or pretended poor, in every place are a great reproach to us, and eclipse the glory of all other charity. It is the utmost reproach to society that there should be a poor man unrelieved or a poor rogue unpunished. I hope you will think no part of human life out of your consideration, but will, at your leisure, give us the history of plenty and want, and the natural gradations towards them, calculated for the cities of London and Westminster.

I am, Sir,

Your most humble Servant,

T. D.

MR SPECTATOR,—I beg you would be pleased to take notice of a very great indecency which is extremely common, though, I think, never yet under your censure.

It is, sir, the strange freedoms some ill-bred married
people take in company : the unseasonable fondness of
some husbands, and the ill-timed tenderness of some
wives. They talk and act as if modesty was only fit
for maids and bachelors, and that too before both. I
was once, Mr Spectator, where the fault I speak of
was so very flagrant, that (being, you must know, a
very bashful fellow, and several young ladies in the
room), I protest, I was quite out of countenance.
Lucina, it seems, was breeding, and she did nothing
but entertain the company with a discourse upon the
difficulty of reckoning to a day, and said she knew
those who were certain to an hour ; then fell a-laugh-
ing at a silly inexperienced creature, who was a month
above her time. Upon her husband's coming in, she
put several questions to him, which he not caring to
resolve, 'Well', cries Lucina, 'I shall have them all
at night.' But, lest I should seem guilty of the very
fault I write against, I shall only entreat Mr Spectator to correct such misdemeanours.

For higher of the genial bed by far,
And with mysterious reverence I deem [1].

I am, Sir,
Your humble Servant,
T.                         T. MEANWELL

No. 431.     *Tuesday, July 15, 1712*     [STEELE

*Quid dulcius hominum generi a natura datum est, quam sui cuique
liberi ?* TULL.

I HAVE lately been casting in my thoughts the
several unhappinesses of life, and comparing the
infelicities of old age to those of infancy. The
calamities of children are due to the negligence or
misconduct of parents, those of age to the past life
which led to it. I have here the history of a boy
and girl to their wedding-day, and think I cannot
give the reader a livelier image of the insipid way
which time uncultivated passes, than by entertaining

[1] *Paradise Lost*, viii, 598, 599.

him with their authentic epistles, expressing all that was remarkable in their lives until the period of their life above mentioned. The sentence at the head of this paper, which is only a warm interrogation, ' What is there in nature so dear as a man's own children to him?' is all the reflection I shall at present make on those who are negligent or cruel in the education of them.

Mr Spectator,—I am now entering into my one and twentieth year, and do not know that I had one day's thorough satisfaction since I came to years of any reflection, until the time they say others lose their liberty, the day of my marriage. I am son to a gentleman of a very great estate, who resolved to keep me out of the vices of the age; and in order to it, never let me see anything that he thought could give me the least pleasure. At ten years old I was put to a grammar school, where my master received orders every post to use me very severely, and have no regard to my having a great estate. At fifteen I was removed to the university, where I lived, out of my father's great discretion, in scandalous poverty and want, until I was big enough to be married, and I was sent for to see the lady who sends you the underwritten. When we were put together, we both considered that we could not be worse than we were in taking one another, and out of a desire of liberty entered into wedlock. My father says I am now a man, and may speak to him like another gentleman.

> I am, Sir,
> Your most humble Servant,
> RICHARD RENTFREE

Mr Spec.,—I grew tall and wild at my mother's, who is a gay widow, and did not care for showing me until about two years and a half ago; at which time my guardian uncle sent me to a boarding-school, with orders to contradict me in nothing, for I had been misused enough already. I had not been there above a month, when, being in the kitchen, I saw some oatmeal on the dresser; I put two or three corns in my mouth, liked it, stole a handful, went into my chamber, chewed it, and for two months after never failed taking toll of every pennyworth of oatmeal that came into the house. But one day playing with a tobacco-pipe between my teeth, it happened to break in my mouth, and the spitting out the pieces left such a delicious roughness on my tongue, that I could not be satisfied until I had champed up the remaining part of the pipe. I forsook the oatmeal, and stuck to the pipes three months, in which time I had dispensed with thirty-seven foul pipes, all to the boles : they belonged to an old gentleman, father to my governess—he locked up the clean ones. I left off eating of pipes, and fell to licking of chalk. I was soon tired of this; I then nibbled all the red wax of our last ball-tickets, and three weeks after the black wax from the burying-tickets of the old gentleman. Two months after this I lived upon thunderbolts, a certain long, round, bluish stone, which I found among the gravel in our garden. I was wonderfully delighted with this; but thunderbolts growing scarce, I fastened tooth and nail upon our garden wall, which I stuck to almost a twelvemonth, and had in that time peeled and devoured half a foot towards our neighbour's yard. I now thought myself the happiest creature in the world, and I believe in my conscience, I had eaten quite through, had I had it in my chamber; but now I became lazy, and unwilling to stir, and was obliged to seek food nearer home. I then took a strange hankering to coals; I fell to scranching them, and had already consumed, I am certain, as much as would have dressed my wedding-dinner, when my uncle came for me home. He was in the parlour with my governess when I was called down. I went in, fell on my knees, for he made me call him father; and when I expected the blessing I asked, the good gentleman, in a surprise, turns himself to my governess, and asks whether this (pointing to me) was his daughter? 'This', added he, 'is the very picture of death. My child was a plump-faced, hale, fresh-coloured girl; but this looks as if she were half starved, a mere skeleton.' My governess, who is really a good woman, assured my father I had wanted for nothing; and withal told him I was continually eating some trash or other, and that I was almost eaten up with the green-sickness, her

orders being never to cross me. But this magnified[1]
but little with my father, who presently, in a kind of
pet, paying for my board, took me home with him. I
had not been long at home, but one Sunday at church
(I shall never forget it) I saw a young neighbouring
gentleman that pleased me hugely; I liked him of all
men I ever saw in my life; and began to wish I could
be as pleasing to him. The very next day he came,
with his father, a-visiting to our house. We were left
alone together, with directions on both sides to be in
love with one another, and in three weeks' time we were
married. I regained my former health and complexion,
and am now as happy as the day is long. Now, Mr
Spec., I desire you would find out some name for these
craving damsels, whether dignified or distinguished
under some or all of the following denominations, to
wit: trash-eaters, oatmeal-chewers, pipe-champers,
chalk-lickers, wax-nibblers, coal-scranchers, wall-
peelers, or gravel-diggers. And, good sir, do your
utmost endeavour to prevent (by exposing) this
unaccountable folly, so prevailing among the young ones
of our sex, who may not meet with such sudden good
luck as,                Sir,
              Your constant Reader,
                and very humble Servant,
                        SABINA GREEN,
                  NOW SABINA RENTFREE.


No. 432.     *Wednesday, July 16, 1712*     [STEELE

*Inter strepit anser olores.* VIRG., *Eclog.* ix, 36

                              OXFORD, *July* 14

MR SPECTATOR,—According to a late invitation in one
of your papers[2] to every man who pleases to write, I
have sent you the following short dissertation against
the vice of being prejudiced.
                    Your most humble Servant


Man is a sociable creature, and a lover of glory;
whence it is, that when several persons are united in

---

1 Latham, who quotes this passage, suggests that 'magnified' is
here a voluntary metamorphosis of 'signified'.
2 No. 428.

the same society, they are studious to lessen the reputation of others, in order to raise their own.  The wise are content to guide the springs in silence, and rejoice in secret at their regular progress : to prate and triumph is the part allotted to the trifling and superficial.  The geese were providentially ordained to save the Capitol. Hence it is, that the invention of marks and devices to distinguish parties, is owing to the beaux and belles of this island[1].  Hats moulded into different cocks and pinches, have long bid mutual defiance; patches have been set against patches in battle array; stocks have risen or fallen in proportion to head-dresses; and peace or war been expected, as the white or the red hood hath prevailed.  These are the standard-bearers in our contending armies, the dwarfs and squires who carry the impresses of the giants or knights, not born to fight themselves, but to prepare the way for the ensuing combat.

It is matter of wonder to reflect how far men of weak understanding and strong fancy are hurried by their prejudices, even to the believing that the whole body of the adverse party are a band of villains and demons.  Foreigners complain that the English are the proudest nation under heaven.  Perhaps they too have their share ; but, be that as it will, general charges against bodies of men is the fault I am writing against. It must be owned, to our shame, that our common people, and most who have not travelled, have an irrational contempt for the language, dress, customs, and even the shape and minds of other nations.  Some men, otherwise of sense, have wondered that a great genius should spring out of Ireland ; and think you mad in affirming that fine odes have been written in Lapland[2].

This spirit of rivalship which heretofore reigned in the two universities is extinct, and almost over betwixt college and college : in parishes and schools the thirst of glory still obtains.  At the seasons of football and cock-fighting, these little republics re-assume their national hatred to each other.  My tenant in the country is verily persuaded that the parish of the enemy hath not one honest man in it.

I always hated satires against woman, and satires

1 See Nos. 81, 265, 319.          2 See Nos. 366, 406.

against man; I am apt to suspect a stranger who laughs at the religion of the Faculty : my spleen rises at a dull rogue, who is severe upon mayors and aldermen; and was never better pleased than with a piece of justice executed upon the body of a Templar, who was very arch upon parsons.

The necessities of mankind require various employments; and whoever excels in his province is worthy of praise. All men are not educated after the same manner, nor have all the same talents. Those who are deficient deserve our compassion, and have a title to our assistance. All cannot be bred in the same place; but in all places there arise, at different times, such persons as do honour to their society, which may raise envy in little souls, but are admired and cherished by generous spirits.

It is certainly a great happiness to be educated in societies of great and eminent men. Their instructions and examples are of extraordinary advantage. It is highly proper to instil such a reverence of the governing persons, and concern for the honour of the place, as may spur the growing members to worthy pursuits and honest emulation : but to swell young minds with vain thoughts of the dignity of their own brotherhood, by debasing and vilifying all others, doth them a real injury. By this means I have found that their efforts have become languid, and their prattle irksome, as thinking it sufficient praise that they are children of so illustrious and ample a family. I should think it a surer, as well as more generous method, to set before the eyes of youth such persons as have made a noble progress in fraternities less talked of; which seems tacitly to reproach their sloth, who loll so heavily in the seats of mighty improvement : active spirits hereby would enlarge their notions, whereas by a servile imitation of one, or perhaps two, admired men in their own body, they can only gain a secondary and derivative kind of fame. These copies of men, like those of authors or painters, run into affectations of some oddness, which perhaps was not disagreeable in the original, but sits ungracefully on the narrow-souled transcriber.

By such early corrections of vanity, while boys are growing into men, they will gradually learn not to censure superficially; but imbibe those principles of general kindness and humanity which alone can make them easy to themselves, and beloved by others.

Reflections of this nature have expunged all prejudices out of my heart, insomuch that though I am a firm Protestant I hope to see the Pope and Cardinals without violent emotions; and though I am naturally grave, I expect to meet good company at Paris.

I am, Sir,
Your obedient Servant


Mr Spectator,—I find you are a general undertaker, and have by your correspondents or self an insight into most things; which makes me apply myself to you at present in the sorest calamity that ever befell man. My wife has taken something ill of me, and has not spoke one word, good or bad, to me or anybody in the family since Friday was sevennight. What must a man do in that case? Your advice would be a great obligation to,

Sir,
Your most humble Servant,
Ralph Thimbleton


Mr Spectator,—When you want a trifle to fill up a paper, in inserting this you will lay an obligation on,
Your humble Servant,

*July* 15, 1712                                    Olivio


'Dear Olivia,—It is but this moment I have had the happiness of knowing to whom I am obliged for the present I received the second of April. I am heartily sorry it did not come to hand the day before; for I can't but think it very hard upon people to lose their jest, that offer at one but once a year. I congratulate myself however upon the earnest given me of something further intended in my favour, for I am told, that the man who is thought worthy by a lady to make a fool of, stands fair enough in her opinion to become one day her husband. Until such time as I have the honour of being sworn, I take leave to subscribe myself,

Dear Olivia,
Your fool Elect,

T.                                              Nicodemuncio

No. 433.        *Thursday, July 17, 1712*        [ADDISON

*Perlege Mæonio cantatas carmine ranas,*
*Et frontem nugis solvere disce meis.*

MART., *Epig.* xiv, 183

THE moral world, as consisting of males and females, is of a mixed nature, and filled with several customs, fashions, and ceremonies, which would have no place in it, were there but one sex. Had our species no females in it, men would be quite different creatures from what they are at present; their endeavours to please the opposite sex polishes and refines them out of those manners which are most natural to them, and often sets them upon modelling themselves, not according to the plans which they approve in their own opinions, but according to those plans which they think are most agreeable to the female world. In a word, man would not only be an unhappy, but a rude unfinished creature, were he conversant with none but those of his own make.

Women, on the other side, are apt to form themselves in everything with regard to that other half of reasonable creatures, with whom they are here blended and confused; their thoughts are ever turned upon appearing amiable to the other sex; they talk, and move, and smile with a design upon us; every feature of their faces, every part of their dress is filled with snares and allurements. There would be no such animals as prudes or coquettes in the world, were there not such an animal as man. In short, it is the male that gives charms to womankind, that produces an air in their faces, a grace in their motions, a softness in their voices, and a delicacy in their complexions.

As this mutual regard between the two sexes tends to the improvement of each of them, we may observe that men are apt to degenerate into rough and brutal natures, who live as if there were no such things as women in the world; as, on the contrary, women who have an indifference or aversion for their counterparts in human nature are generally sour and unamiable, sluttish and censorious.

I am led into this train of thoughts by a little manuscript which is lately fallen into my hands, and which I shall communicate to the reader, as I have done some other curious pieces of the same nature, without troubling him with any inquiries about the author of it. It contains a summary account of two different states which bordered upon one another. The one was a commonwealth of Amazons, or women without men; the other was a republic of males that had not a woman in their whole community. As these two states bordered upon one another, it was their way, it seems, to meet upon their frontiers at a certain season of the year, where those among the men who had not made their choice in any former meeting, associated themselves with particular women, whom they were afterwards obliged to look upon as their wives in every one of these yearly rencounters. The children that sprung from this alliance, if males, were sent to their respective fathers; if females, continued with their mothers. By means of this anniversary carnival, which lasted about a week, the commonwealths were recruited from time to time, and supplied with their respective subjects.

These two states were engaged together in a perpetual league, offensive and defensive, so that if any foreign potentate offered to attack either of them, both the sexes fell upon him at once, and quickly brought him to reason. It was remarkable that for many ages this agreement continued inviolable between the two states, notwithstanding, as was said before, they were husbands and wives; but this will not appear so wonderful if we consider that they did not live together above a week in a year.

In the account which my author gives of the male republic, there were several customs very remarkable. The men never shaved their beards, or pared their nails above once in a twelvemonth, which was probably about the time of the great annual meeting upon their frontiers. I find the name of a minister of state in one part of their history, who was fined for appearing too frequently in clean linen; and of a certain great general who was turned out of his post for effeminacy, it having been proved upon him by several credible witnesses that he washed his face every morning. If any member of the commonwealth had a soft voice, a smooth face, or a supple behaviour, he was banished into the commonwealth of females, where he was treated as a slave, dressed in petticoats, and set a spinning. They had no titles of honour among them, but such as denoted some bodily strength or perfection, as such an one ' the tall ', such an one ' the stocky [1] ', such an one ' the gruff '. Their public debates were generally managed with kicks and cuffs, insomuch that they often came from the council table with broken shins, black eyes, and bloody noses. When they would reproach a man in the most bitter terms, they would tell him his teeth were white, or that he had a fair skin, and a soft hand. The greatest man I meet with in their history, was one who could lift five hundredweight, and wore such a prodigious pair of whiskers as had never been seen in the commonwealth before his time. These accomplishments it seems had rendered him so popular, that if he had not died very seasonably it is thought he might have enslaved the republic. Having made this short extract out of the history of the male commonwealth, I shall look into the history of the neighbouring state which consisted of females, and if I find anything in it, will not fail to communicate it to the public.　　　C.

---

[1] Stout ; an unusual word.

No. 434.　　*Friday, July 18, 1712*　　[ADDISON

*Quales Threiciæ quum flumina Thermodontis*
*Pulsant, et pictis bellantur Amazones armis:*
*Seu circum Hippolyten, seu quum se Martia curru*
*Penthesilea refert, magnoque ululante tumultu*
*Feminea exultant lunatis agmina peltis.*

VIRG., *Æn.* xi, 650

HAVING carefully perused the manuscript I mentioned in my yesterday's paper, so far as it relates to the republic of women, I find in it several particulars which may very well deserve the reader's attention.

The girls of quality, from six to twelve years old, were put to public schools, where they learned to box and play at cudgels, with several other accomplishments of the same nature; so that nothing was more usual than to see a little miss returning home at night with a broken pate, or two or three teeth knocked out of her head. They were afterwards taught to ride the great horse, to shoot, dart, or sling, and enlisted into several companies, in order to perfect themselves in military exercises. No woman was to be married until she had killed her man. The ladies of fashion used to play with young lions instead of lapdogs, and when they made any parties of diversion, instead of entertaining themselves at ombre or piquet, they would wrestle and pitch the bar for a whole afternoon together. There was never any such thing as a blush seen, or a sigh heard in the commonwealth. The women never dressed but to look terrible, to which end they would sometimes after a battle paint their cheeks with the blood of their enemies. For this reason likewise the face which had the most scars was looked upon as the most beautiful. If they found lace, jewels, ribbons, or any ornaments in silver or gold among the booty which they had taken, they used to dress their horses with it, but never entertained a thought of wearing it themselves. There were particular rights and privileges allowed to any member of the common-

wealth who was a mother of three daughters. The
senate was made up of old women; for by the laws
of the country none was to be a councillor of state
that was not past child-bearing. They used to boast
their republic had continued four thousand years,
which is altogether improbable, unless we may suppose, what I am very apt to think, that they measured
their time by lunar years.

There was a great revolution brought about in
this female republic by means of a neighbouring king,
who had made war upon them several years with
various success, and at length overthrew them in a
very great battle. This defeat they ascribe to several
causes; some say that the secretary of state having
been troubled with the vapours, had committed some
fatal mistakes in several despatches about that time.
Others pretend that the first minister, being big with
child, could not attend the public affairs, as so great
an exigency of state required; but this I can give no
manner of credit to, since it seems to contradict a
fundamental maxim in their government which I
have before mentioned. My author gives the most
probable reason of this great disaster; for he affirms,
that the general was brought to bed, or (as others
say) miscarried the very night before the battle.
However it was, this signal overthrow obliged them
to call in the male republic to their assistance; but
notwithstanding their common efforts to repulse the
victorious enemy, the war continued for many years
before they could entirely bring it to a happy conclusion.

The campaigns which both sexes passed together
made them so well acquainted with one another that
at the end of the war they did not care for parting.
In the beginning of it they lodged in separate camps,
but afterwards, as they grew more familiar, they
pitched their tents promiscuously.

From this time, the armies being chequered with
both sexes, they polished apace. The men used to
invite their fellow-soldiers into their quarters, and

would dress their tents with flowers and boughs for their reception. If they chanced to like one more than another, they would be cutting her name in the table, or chalking out her figure upon a wall, or talking of her in a kind of rapturous language, which by degrees improved into verse and sonnet. These were as the first rudiments of architecture, painting, and poetry among this savage people. After any advantage over the enemy, both sexes used to jump together and make a clattering with their swords and shields for joy, which in a few years produced several regular tunes and set dances.

As the two armies romped on these occasions, the women complained of the thick bushy beards and long nails of their confederates, who thereupon took care to prune themselves into such figures as were most pleasing to their female friends and allies.

When they had taken any spoils from the enemy, the men would make a present of everything that was rich and showy to the women whom they most admired, and would frequently dress the necks, or heads, or arms of their mistresses with anything which they thought appeared gay or pretty. The women, observing that the men took delight in looking upon 'em when they were adorned with such trappings and gewgaws, set their heads at work to find out new inventions, and to outshine one another in all councils of war or the like solemn meetings. On the other hand, the men observing how the women's hearts were set upon finery, begun to embellish themselves and look as agreeably as they could in the eyes of their associates. In short, after a few years conversing together, the women had learnt to smile and the men to ogle, the women grew soft and the men lively.

When they had thus insensibly formed one another, upon the finishing of the war, which concluded with an entire conquest of their common enemy, the colonels in one army married the colonels in the other; the captains in the same manner took the captains to their wives; the whole body of common soldiers were matched, after the example of their leaders. By this means the two republics incorporated with one another, and became the most flourishing and polite government in the part of the world which they inhabited.

C.

No. 435.     *Saturday, July 19, 1712*     [ADDISON

*Nec duo sunt at forma duplex, nec femina dici*
*Nec puer ut possit, neutrumque et utrumque videntur.*
OVID, *Met.* iv, 378

MOST of the papers I give the public are written on subjects that never vary, but are for ever fixed and immutable. Of this kind are all my more serious essays and discourses; but there is another sort of speculations which I consider as occasional papers, that take their rise from the folly, extravagance, and caprice of the present age. For I look upon myself as one set to watch the manners and behaviour of my countrymen and contemporaries, and to mark down every absurd fashion, ridiculous custom, or affected form of speech that makes its appearance in the world during the course of these my speculations. The petticoat no sooner began to swell, but I observed its motions. The party patches had not time to muster themselves before I detected them. I had intelligence of the coloured hood the very first time it appeared in a public assembly [1]. I might here mention several other the like contingent subjects upon which I have bestowed distinct papers. By this means I have so effectually quashed those irregularities which gave occasion to 'em, that I am afraid posterity will scarce have a sufficient idea of them to relish those discourses which were in no little vogue at the time when they were written. They will be apt to think that the fashions and customs I attacked were some fantastic

[1] See Nos. 81, 127, 265.

conceits of my own, and that their great-grandmothers could not be so whimsical as I have represented them.  For this reason, when I think on the
figure my several volumes of speculations will make
about a hundred years hence, I consider them as so
many pieces of old plate, where the weight will be
regarded but the fashion lost.

Among the several female extravagances I have
already taken notice of, there is one which still
keeps its ground.  I mean that of the ladies who
dress themselves in a hat and feather, a riding-coat
and a periwig; or at least tie up their hair in a bag
or ribbon, in imitation of the smart part of the
opposite sex.  As in my yesterday's paper I gave an
account of the mixture of the two sexes in one commonwealth, I shall here take notice of this mixture
of two sexes in one person.  I have already shown
my dislike of this immodest custom more than
once [1]; but in contempt of everything I have
hitherto said, I am informed that the highways
about this great city are still very much infested
with these female cavaliers.

I remember when I was at my friend Sir Roger
de Coverley's about this time twelvemonth, an
equestrian lady of this order appeared upon the
plains, which lay at a distance from his house.  I
was at that time walking in the fields with my old
friend; and as his tenants ran out on every side to
see so strange a sight, Sir Roger asked one of them
who came by us what it was?  To which the country
fellow replied, ''Tis a gentlewoman, saving your
worship's presence, in a coat and hat.'  This produced a great deal of mirth at the knight's house,
where we had a story at the same time of another
of his tenants, who, meeting this gentleman-like
lady on the highway, was asked by her whether that

[1] See Nos. 104, 331; also the 'Advertisement' to No. 485.  In No. 81
there was an advertisement of 'A complete Lady's Riding Habit, of
blue camblet, well laced with silver, being a coat, waistcoat, petticoat,
hat and feather, never worn but twice, to be sold at a very reasonable
rate at Mr Harford's, at the Acorn in York Street, Covent Garden'.

was Coverley Hall. The honest man, seeing only the male part of the querist, replied, ' Yes, sir '; but upon the second question, whether Sir Roger de Coverley was a married man, having dropped his eye upon the petticoat, he changed his note into ' No, madam '.

Had one of these hermaphrodites appeared in Juvenal's days, with what an indignation should we have seen her described by that excellent satirist. He would have represented her in her riding habit as a greater monster than the centaur. He would have called for sacrifices or purifying waters, to expiate the appearance of such a prodigy. He would have invoked the shades of Portia or Lucretia, to see into what the Roman ladies had transformed themselves.

For my own part, I am for treating the sex with greater tenderness, and have all along made use of the most gentle methods to bring them off from any little extravagance into which they are sometimes unwarily falling. I think it, however, absolutely necessary to keep up the partition between the two sexes, and to take notice of the smallest encroachments which the one makes upon the other. I hope, therefore, that I shall not hear any more complaints on this subject. I am sure my she-disciples who peruse these my daily lectures have profited but little by them, if they are capable of giving in to such an amphibious dress. This I should not have mentioned had not I lately met one of these, my female readers, in Hyde Park, who looked upon me with a masculine assurance, and cocked her hat full in my face.

For my part, I have one general key to the behaviour of the fair sex. When I see them singular in any part of their dress, I conclude it is not without some evil intention; and therefore question not but the design of this strange fashion is to smite more effectually their male beholders. Now, to set them right in this particular, I would fain have them consider with themselves whether we are not more likely to be struck by a figure entirely female, than with such an one as we may see every day in our glasses; or, if they please, let them reflect upon their own hearts, and think how they would be affected should they meet a man on horseback in his breeches and jack-boots, and at the same time dressed up in a commode and a night-raile [1].

I must observe that this fashion was first of all brought to us from France, a country which has infected all the nations of Europe with its levity. I speak not this in derogation of a whole people, having more than once found fault with those general reflections which strike at kingdoms or commonwealths in the gross; a piece of cruelty which an ingenious writer of our own compares to that of Caligula, who wished the Roman people had all but one neck, that he might behead them at a blow. I shall therefore only remark, that as liveliness and assurance are in a peculiar manner the qualifications of the French nation, the same habits and customs will not give the same offence to that people, which they produce among those of our own country. Modesty is our distinguishing character, as vivacity is theirs. And when this our national virtue appears in that female beauty, for which our British ladies are celebrated above all others in the universe, it makes up the most amiable object that the eye of man can possibly behold.      C.

No. 436.      *Monday, July 21, 1712*      [STEELE

*Verso pollice vulgi,*
*Quum libet, occidunt populariter.*

Juv., *Sat.* iii, 36

BEING a person of insatiable curiosity, I could not forbear going on Wednesday last to a place of no small renown for the gallantry of the lower order

---

[1] 'Raile' (A.S. *hrægl*) is a loose upper garment.

of Britons, namely, to the bear-garden at Hockley in the Hole [1], where (as a whitish brown paper, put into my hands in the street, informed me) there was to be a trial of skill to be exhibited between two masters of the noble science of defence, at two of the clock precisely. I was not a little charmed with the solemnity of the challenge, which ran thus :

I, James Miller, sergeant (lately come from the frontiers of Portugal), Master of the Noble Science of Defence, hearing in most places where I have been of the great fame of Timothy Buck of London, master of the said science, do invite him to meet me, and exercise at the several weapons following, viz. :

| | |
|---|---|
| Back-sword. | Single Falchion. |
| Sword and Dagger. | Case of Falchions. |
| Sword and Buckler. | Quarterstaff. |

If the generous ardour in James Miller to dispute the reputation of Timothy Buck had something resembling the old heroes of romance, Timothy Buck returned answer in the same paper with the like spirit, adding a little indignation at being challenged, and seeming to condescend to fight James Miller, not in regard to Miller himself, but in that, as the fame went out, he had fought Parkes of Coventry [2]. The acceptance of the combat ran in these words :

1 See No. 31.  Gay (*Trivia*, ii, 407–412) says :

When through the town, with slow and solemn air,
Led by the nostril, walks the muzzled bear,
Behind him moves, majestically dull,
The pride of Hockley-Hole, the surly bull ;
Learn hence the periods of the week to name :
Mondays and Thursdays are the days of game.

There are several references to the bear-garden in the *Tatler* (Nos. 28, 134), where Steele condemned the brutality of cock-fighting and fights by dogs, bulls, and bears.  In No. 630 of the *Spectator* there is an allusion to 'the gladiators of Hockley-in-the-Hole'.  In the *Beggar's Opera* Mrs Peachum says, 'You should to Hockley-in-the-Hole and to Marybone, child, to learn valour ; there are the schools that have bred so many brave men.

2 John Sparkes's tombstone at Coventry had this inscription : 'To

I, Timothy Buck, of Clare Market, Master of the Noble Science of Defence, hearing he did fight Mr Parkes of Coventry, will not fail (God willing) to meet this fair inviter at the time and place appointed, desiring a clear stage and no favour.

*Vivat Regina.*

I shall not here look back on the spectacles of the Greeks and Romans of this kind, but must believe this custom took its rise from the ages of knight-errantry : from those who loved one woman so well, that they hated all men and women else; from those who would fight you, whether you were or were not of their mind; from those who demanded the combat of their contemporaries, both for admiring their mistress or discommending her. I cannot therefore but lament that the terrible part of the ancient fight is preserved when the amorous side of it is forgotten. We have retained the barbarity, but lost the gallantry of the old combatants. I could wish, methinks, these gentlemen had consulted me in the promulgation of the conflict. I was obliged by a fair young maid, whom I understood to be called Elizabeth Preston, daughter of the keeper of the garden, with a glass of water; whom I imagined might have been, for form's sake, the general representative of the lady fought for, and from her beauty the proper Amarillis on these occasions. It would have ran better in the challenge : 'I, James Miller, sergeant, who have travelled parts abroad, and came last from the frontiers of Portugal, for the love of Elizabeth Preston, do assert, that the said Elizabeth is the fairest of women.' Then the answer : 'I, Timothy Buck, who have stayed in

---

the memory of Mr John Sparkes, a native of this city; he was a man of a mild disposition, a gladiator by profession, who, after having fought 350 battles in the principal parts of Europe with honour and applause, at length quitted the stage, sheathed his sword, and, with Christian resignation, submitted to the grand victor in the 52nd year of his age. *Anno salutis humanæ*, 1733.'

Sergeant James Miller afterwards became a captain, and fought in Scotland under the Duke of Cumberland in 1745.

Great Britain during all the war in foreign parts, for the sake of Susanna Page, do deny that Elizabeth Preston is so fair as the said Susanna Page. Let Susanna Page look on, and I desire of James Miller no favour.'

This would give the battle quite another turn; and a proper station for the ladies, whose complexion was disputed by the sword, would animate the disputants with a more gallant incentive than the expectation of money from the spectators; though I would not have that neglected, but thrown to that fair one whose lover was approved by the donor.

Yet, considering the thing wants such amendments, it was carried with great order. James Miller came on first, preceded by two disabled drummers, to show, I suppose, that the prospect of maimed bodies did not in the least deter him. There ascended with the daring Miller a gentleman, whose name I could not learn, with a dogged air, as unsatisfied that he was not principal. This son of anger lowered at the whole assembly, and weighing himself as he marched around from side to side, with a stiff knee and shoulder, he gave intimations of the purpose he smothered till he saw the issue of this encounter. Miller had a blue riband tied round the sword arm; which ornament I conceive to be the remain of that custom of wearing a mistress's favour on such occasions of old.

Miller is a man of six foot eight inches height, of a kind but bold aspect, well-fashioned, and ready of his limbs : and such a readiness as spoke his ease in them was obtained from a habit of motion in military exercise.

The expectation of the spectators was now almost at its height, and the crowd pressing in, several active persons thought they were placed rather according to their fortune than their merit, and took it in their heads to prefer themselves from the open area, or pit, to the galleries. This dispute between

desert and property brought many to the ground,
and raised others in proportion to the highest seats
by turns for the space of ten minutes, till Timothy
Buck came on, and the whole assembly giving up
their disputes, turned their eyes upon the champions.
Then it was that every man's affection turned to
one or the other irresistibly.  A judicious gentleman
near me said, ' I could, methinks, be Miller's second,
but I had rather have Buck for mine.'  Miller had
an audacious look, that took the eye; Buck a perfect
composure, that engaged the judgment.  Buck came
on in a plain coat, and kept all his air till the instant
of engaging; at which time he undressed to his shirt,
his arm adorned with a bandage of red riband.  No
one can describe the sudden concern in the whole
assembly; the most tumultuous crowd in Nature
was as still and as much engaged, as if all their lives
depended on the first blow.  The combatants met
in the middle of the stage, and shaking hands as
removing all malice, they retired with much grace
to the extremities of it; from whence they immediately faced about and approached each other, Miller
with an heart full of resolution, Buck with a watchful untroubled countenance; Buck regarding princi-
pally his own defence, Miller chiefly thoughtful of
annoying his opponent.  It is not easy to describe
the many escapes and imperceptible defences between two men of quick eyes and ready limbs; but
Miller's heat laid him open to the rebuke of the calm
Buck by a large cut on the forehead.  Much effusion
of blood covered his eyes in a moment, and the
huzzas of the crowd undoubtedly quickened the
anguish.  The assembly was divided into parties
upon their different ways of fighting; while a poor
nymph in one of the galleries apparently suffered
for Miller, and burst into a flood of tears.  As soon
as his wound was wrapped up, he came on again
with a little rage, which still disabled him further.
But what brave man can be wounded into more
patience and caution?  The next was a warm eager

onset, which ended in a decisive stroke on the left
leg of Miller. The lady in the gallery, during this
second strife, covered her face; and for my part I
could not keep my thoughts from being mostly employed on the consideration of her unhappy circumstance that moment, hearing the clash of swords and
apprehending life or victory concerned her lover in
every blow, but not daring to satisfy herself on whom
they fell. The wound was exposed to the view of
all who could delight in it, and sewed up on the
stage. The surly second of Miller declared at this
time, that he would that day fortnight fight Mr
Buck at the same weapons, declaring himself the
master of the renowned Gorman; but Buck denied
him the honour of that courageous disciple, and
asserting that he himself had taught that champion,
accepted the challenge.

There is something in Nature very unaccountable
on such occasions, when we see the people take a
certain painful gratification in beholding these en-
counters. Is it cruelty that administers this sort of
delight? or is it a pleasure which is taken in the
exercise of pity? It was methought pretty remarkable, that the business of the day being a trial of
skill, the popularity did not run so high as one
would have expected on the side of Buck. Is it that
people's passions have their rise in self-love, and
thought themselves (in spite of all the courage they
had) liable to the fate of Miller, but could not so
easily think of themselves qualified like Buck [1]?

Tully speaks of this custom with less horror than
one would expect, though he confesses it was much
abused in his time, and seems directly to approve of
it under its first regulations, when criminals only
fought before the people: ' Crudele gladiatorum
spectaculum et inhumanum nonnullis videri solet;
et haud scio annon ita sit ut nunc fit; quum vero
sontes ferro depugnabant, auribus fortasse multa,
oculis quidem nulla, poterat esse fortior contra dolor-

[1] See No. 449.

em et mortem disciplina[1]' (The shows of gladiators may be thought barbarous and inhuman, and
I know not but it is so as it is now practised; but in
those times, when only criminals were combatants,
the ear perhaps might receive many better instructions, but it is impossible that anything which affects
our eyes should fortify us so well against pain and
death).                                                  T.


No. 437.     *Tuesday, July 22, 1712*     [STEELE

*Tune Impune hæc facias ?    Tune hic homines adolescentulos
Imperitos rerum, eductos libere, in fraudem illicis ?
Sollicitando, et pollicitando eorum animos lactas ?
Ac meritricios amores nuptiis conglutinas ?*

TER., *And.* Act v, sc. 4

THE other day passed by me in her chariot a lady,
with that pale and wan complexion which we sometimes see in young people who are fallen into sorrow
and private anxiety of mind, which antedate age and
sickness. It is not three years ago since she was
gay, airy, and a little towards libertine in her carriage; but, methought, I easily forgave her that
little insolence, which she so severely pays for in
her present condition. Favilla, of whom I am
speaking, is married to a sullen fool with wealth;
her beauty and merit are lost upon the dolt, who is
insensible of perfection in anything. Their hours
together are either painful or insipid. The minutes
she has to herself in his absence, are not sufficient
to give vent at her eyes to the grief and torment of
his last conversation. This poor creature was sacrificed with a temper (which, under the cultivation
of a man of sense, would have made the most agreeable companion) into the arms of this loathsome
yoke-fellow by Sempronia. Sempronia is a good
lady, who supports herself in an affluent condition
by contracting friendship with rich young widows
and maids of plentiful fortunes at their own dis-

[1] Tuscul. Quæst., lib. ii, *De Tolerando Dolore.*

posal, and bestowing her friends upon worthless indigent fellows; on the other side, she ensnares inconsiderate and rash youths of great estates into the arms of vicious women. For this purpose she is accomplished in all the arts which can make her acceptable at impertinent visits; she knows all that passes in every quarter, and is well acquainted with all the favourite servants, busybodies, dependants, and poor relations of all persons of condition in the whole town. At the price of a good sum of money, Sempronia, by the instigation of Favilla's mother, brought about the match for the daughter, and the reputation of this which is apparently, in point of fortune, more than Favilla could expect, has gained her the visits and frequent attendance of the crowd of mothers, who had rather see their children miserable in great wealth, than the happiest of the race of mankind in a less conspicuous state of life. When Sempronia is so well acquainted with a woman's temper and circumstance, that she believes marriage would be acceptable to her, and advantageous to the man who shall get her, her next step is to look out for some one whose condition has some secret wound in it, and wants a sum, yet, in the eye of the world not unsuitable to her. If such is not easily had, she immediately adorns a worthless fellow with what estate she thinks convenient, and adds as great a share of good humour and sobriety as is requisite. After this is settled, no importunities, arts, and devices are omitted to hasten the lady to her happiness. In the general, indeed, she is a person of so strict justice that she marries a poor gallant to a rich wench, and a moneyless girl to a man of fortune. But then she has no manner of conscience in the disparity, when she has a mind to impose a poor rogue for one of an estate; she has no remorse in adding to it that he is illiterate, ignorant, and unfashioned, but makes those imperfections arguments of the truth of his wealth; and will, on such an occasion, with a very grave face, charge the people

of condition with negligence in the education of
their children. Exception being made t'other day
against an ignorant booby of her own clothing, whom
she was putting off for a rich heir, ' Madam ', said
she, ' you know there is no making children who
know they have estates attend their books.'

Sempronia by these arts is loaded with presents,
importuned for her acquaintance, and admired by
those who do not know the first taste of life, as a
woman of exemplary good breeding. But sure, to
murder and to rob are less iniquities than to raise
profit by abuses, as irreparable as taking away life;
but more grievous, as making it lastingly unhappy.
To rob a lady at play of half her fortune, is not so
ill as giving the whole and herself to an unworthy
husband. But Sempronia can administer consolation to an unhappy fair at home, by leading her to
an agreeable gallant elsewhere. She can then preach
the general condition of all the married world, and
tell an inexperienced young woman the methods of
softening her affliction, and laugh at her simplicity
and want of knowledge, with an ' Oh! my dear, you
will know better.'

The wickedness of Sempronia, one would think,
should be superlative, but I cannot but esteem that
of some parents equal to it; I mean such as sacrifice
the greatest endowments and qualifications to base
bargains. A parent who forces a child of a liberal
and ingenious[1] spirit into the arms of a clown or a
blockhead, obliges her to a crime too odious for a
name. It is in a degree the unnatural conjunction
of rational and brutal beings. Yet what is there
so common, as the bestowing an accomplished
woman with such a disparity. And I could name
crowds who lead miserable lives for want of knowledge in their parents of this maxim, that good sense
and good nature always go together. That which
is attributed to fools and called good nature, is only
an inability of observing what is faulty, which turns

[1] Ingenuous.

in marriage into a suspicion of everything as such, from a consciousness of that inability.

MR SPECTATOR,—I am entirely of your opinion[1] with relation to the equestrian females, who affect both the masculine and feminine air at the same time; and cannot forbear making a presentment against another order of them who grow very numerous and powerful; and since our language is not very capable of good compound words, I must be contented to call them only the 'Naked-shouldered'. These beauties are not contented to make lovers wherever they appear, but they must make rivals at the same time. Were you to see Gatty walk the Park at high Mall, you would expect those who followed her, and those who met her, could immediately draw their swords for her. I hope, sir, you will provide for the future, that women may stick to their faces for doing any future mischief, and not allow any but direct traders in beauty to expose more than the fore part of the neck, unless you please to allow this after-game to those who are very defective in the charms of the countenance. I can say, to my sorrow, the present practice is very unfair, when to look back is death; and it may be said of our beauties, as a great poet did of bullets,

> They kill and wound like Parthians as they fly.

I submit this to your animadversion; and am, for the little while I have left,
          Your humble Servant,
                The languishing PHILANTHUS

P.S. Suppose you mended my letter, and made a simile about the porcupine, but I submit that also.
                                        T.


No. 438.        *Wednesday, July 23, 1712*        [STEELE

> *Animum rege, qui nisi paret,*
> *Imperat.*                    HOR., 1 Ep. ii, 62

IT is a very common expression, that such a one is very good-natured but very passionate. The

---

[1] See No. 435.

expression indeed is very good-natured, to allow
passionate people so much quarter; but I think a
passionate man deserves the least indulgence imaginable. It is said, it is soon over; that is, all the
mischief he does is quickly despatched, which, I
think, is no great recommendation to favour. I have
known one of those good-natured passionate men
say in a mixed company, even to his own wife or
child, such things as the most inveterate enemy of
his family would not have spoke, even in imagination. It is certain that quick sensibility is inseparable from a ready understanding; but why should
not that good understanding call to itself all its
force on such occasions to master that sudden inclination to anger. One of the greatest souls now
in the world [1] is the most subject by nature to anger,
and yet so famous from a conquest of himself this
way, that he is the known example when you talk
of temper and command of a man's self. To contain the spirit of anger, is the worthiest discipline
we can put ourselves to. When a man has made any
progress this way, a frivolous fellow in a passion is
to him as contemptible as a froward child. It
ought to be the study of every man for his own quiet
and peace. When he stands combustible and ready
to flame upon everything that touches him, life is
as uneasy to himself as it is to all about him. Syncropius leads, of all men living, the most ridiculous
life; he is ever offending and begging pardon. If
his man enters the room without what he sent him
for, ' That blockhead ', begins he—— ' Gentlemen,
I ask your pardon; but servants nowadays——' The
wrong plates are laid, they are thrown into the middle
of the room; his wife stands by in pain for him,
which he sees in her face, and answers as if he had
heard all she was thinking; ' Why, what the devil!
why don't you take care to give orders in these
things?' His friends sit down to a tasteless plenty
of everything, every minute expecting new insults

[1] Somers. See Dedication to vol. i.

from his impertinent passions. In a word, to eat
with or visit Syncropius, is no other than going to
see him exercise his family, exercise their patience,
and his own anger.

It is monstrous that the shame and confusion in
which this good-natured angry man must needs behold his friends while he thus lays about him, does
not give him so much reflection as to create an
amendment. This is the most scandalous disuse of
reason imaginable; all the harmless part of him is
no more than that of a bulldog, they are tame no
longer than they are not offended. One of these
good-natured angry men shall, in an instant, as-
semble together so many allusions to secret circumstances as are enough to dissolve the peace of all
the families and friends he is acquainted with, in a
quarter of an hour, and yet the next moment be the
best natured man in the whole world. If you would
see passion in its purity, without mixture of reason,
behold it represented in a mad hero, drawn by a
mad poet. Nat. Lee makes his Alexander say
thus [1]:

> Away, begone, and give a whirlwind room,
> Or I will blow you up like dust!  Avaunt;
> Madness but meanly represents my toil,
> Eternal discord!
> Fury!  revenge!  disdain and indignation!
> Tear my swollen breast, make way for fire and tempest.
> My brain is burst, debate and reason quenched;
> The storm is up, and my hot bleeding heart
> Splits with the rack, while passions, like the wind,
> Rise up to heaven, and put out all the stars.

Every passionate fellow in town talks half the day
with as little consistency, and threatens things as
much out of his power.

The next disagreeable person to the outrageous
gentleman is one of a much lower order of anger,
and he is what we commonly call a peevish fellow.
A peevish fellow is one who has some reason in
himself for being out of humour, or has a natural

---

[1] *The Rival Queens*, Act iii, sc. 1.  See No. 39.

incapacity for delight, and therefore disturbs all who
are happier than himself with ' pishes ' and ' pshaws ',
or other well-bred interjections, at everything that
is said or done in his presence.   There should be
physic mixed in the food of all which these fellows
eat in good company.   This degree of anger passes,
forsooth, for a delicacy of judgment that won't admit
of being easily pleased : but none above the character
of wearing a peevish man's livery ought to bear with
his ill manners.   All things among men of sense and
condition should pass the censure, and have the protection, of the eye of reason.

No man ought to be tolerated in an habitual
humour, whim, or particularity of behaviour by any
who do not wait upon him for bread.   Next to the
peevish fellow is the snarler.   This gentleman deals
mightily in what we call the irony, and as these sort
of people exert themselves most against those below
them, you see their humour best in their talk to
their servants : ' That is so like you ', ' You are a
fine fellow ', ' Thou art the quickest head-piece ', and
the like.   One would think the hectoring, the storm-
ing, the sullen, and all the different species and
subordinations of the angry should be cured by knowing they live only as pardoned men, and how pitiful
is the condition of being only suffered?   But I am
interrupted by the pleasantest scene of anger and the
disappointment of it that I have ever known, which
happened while I was yet writing, and I overheard
as I sat in the back room of a French bookseller's [1].
There came into the shop a very learned man with
an erect solemn air, and though a person of great
parts otherwise, slow in understanding anything
which makes against himself.   The composure of the
faulty man, and the whimsical perplexity of him that
was justly angry, is perfectly new : after turning over
many volumes, said the seller to the buyer, ' Sir, you

[1] It is stated in the 1797 edition that this scene passed in the shop
of Mr Vaillant, and that the subject of it was a volume of Massillon's
Sermons.

know I have long asked you to send me back the
first volume of French Sermons I formerly lent you.'
—' Sir ', said the chapman [1], ' I have often looked
for it, but cannot find it; it is certainly lost, and I
know not to whom I lent it, it is so many years ago.'
—' Then, sir, here is the other volume; I'll send you
that, and please to pay for both.'—' My friend ', replied he, ' canst thou be so senseless as not to know
that one volume is as imperfect in my library as your
shop?'—' Yes, sir, but it is you have lost the first
volume, and to be short I will be paid.'—' Sir ', answered the chapman, ' you are a young man, your
book is lost, and learn by this little loss to bear much
greater adversities, which you must expect to meet
with.'—' Yes, sir, I'll bear when I must, but I have
not lost now, for I say you have it and shall pay me.'
—' Friend, you grow warm; I tell you the book is
lost, and I foresee, in the course even of a prosperous
life, that you will meet afflictions to make you mad
if you cannot bear this trifle.'—' Sir, there is in this
case no need of bearing, for you have the book.'—' I
say, sir, I have not the book, but your passion will
not let you hear enough to be informed that I have
it not.  Learn resignation of yourself to the distresses
of this life; nay, do not fret and fume : it is my duty
to tell you that you are of an impatient spirit, and an
impatient spirit is not without woe.'—' Was ever
anything like this?'—' Yes, sir, there have been many
things like this.  The loss is but a trifle, but your
temper is wanton and incapable of the least pain;
therefore let me advise you, be patient; the book is
lost, but do not you for that reason lose yourself.'

　　　　　　　　　　　　　　　　　　　　　T.

---

[1] Customer.  *Cf.* Swift's *Directions to Servants:* ' Your father sent a
cow to you to sell, and you could not find a *chapman* till nine at night.'

No. 439.     *Thursday, July 24, 1712*     [ADDISON

*Hi narrata ferunt alio, mensuraque ficti*
*Crescit : et auditis aliquid novus adjicit auctor.*
                                OVID, *Met.* xii, 57

OVID describes the Palace of Fame[1] as situated in the very centre of the universe, and perforated with so many windows and avenues as gave her the sight of everything that was done in the heavens, in the earth, and in the sea. The structure of it was contrived in so admirable a manner, that it echoed every word which was spoken in the whole compass of Nature; so that the palace, says the poet, was always filled with a confused hubbub of low-dying sounds, the voices being almost spent and worn out before they arrived at this general rendezvous of speeches and whispers.

I consider courts with the same regard to the governments which they superintend as Ovid's Palace of Fame, with regard to the universe. The eyes of a watchful minister run through the whole people. There is scarce a murmur or complaint that does not reach his ears. They have newsgatherers and intelligencers distributed into their several walks and quarters, who bring in their respective quotas, and make them acquainted with the discourse and conversation of the whole kingdom or commonwealth where they are employed. The wisest of kings, alluding to these invisible and unsuspected spies who are planted by kings and rulers over their fellow-citizens, as well as to those voluntary informers that are buzzing about the ears of a great man, and making their court by such secret methods of intelligence, has given us a very prudent caution : ' Curse not the king, no not in thy thought; and curse not the rich in thy bedchamber : for a bird of the air shall carry the voice, and that which hath wings shall tell the matter[2] '.

As it is absolutely necessary for rulers to make use

[1] *Metam.*, Book xii.          [2] *Eccl.* x, 20.

of other people's eyes and ears, they should take particular care to do it in such a manner that it may not bear too hard on the person whose life and conversation are inquired into. A man who is capable of so infamous a calling as that of a spy is not very much to be relied upon. He can have no great ties of honour or checks of conscience to restrain him in those covert evidences where the person accused has no opportunity of vindicating himself. He will be more industrious to carry that which is grateful than that which is true. There will be no occasion for him, if he does not hear and see things worth discovery; so that he naturally inflames every word and circumstance, aggravates what is faulty, perverts what is good, and misrepresents what is indifferent. Nor is it to be doubted but that such ignominious wretches let their private passions into these their clandestine informations, and often wreak their particular spite or malice against the person whom they are set to watch. It is a pleasant scene enough, which an Italian author describes between a spy and a cardinal who employed him. The cardinal is represented as minuting down everything that is told him. The spy begins with a low voice: ' Such an one, the advocate, whispered to one of his friends, within my hearing, that your eminence was a very great poltroon '; and after having given his patron time to take it down, adds, that another called him a mercenary rascal in a public conversation. The cardinal replies very well, and bids him go on. The spy proceeds, and loads him with reports of the same nature, till the cardinal rises in great wrath, calls him an impudent scoundrel, and kicks him out of the room.

It is observed of great and heroic minds, that they have not only shown a particular disregard to those unmerited reproaches which have been cast upon 'em, but have been altogether free from that impertinent curiosity of inquiring after them, or the poor revenge of resenting them. The histories of

Alexander and Cæsar are full of this kind of instances. Vulgar souls are of a quite contrary character. Dionysius, the tyrant of Sicily, had a dungeon which was a very curious piece of architecture; and of which, as I am informed, there are still to be seen some remains in that island. It was called ' Dionysius's Ear ', and built with several little windings and labyrinths in the form of a real ear. The structure of it made it a kind of whispering place, but such a one as gathered the voice of him who spoke into a funnel, which was placed at the very top of it. The tyrant used to lodge all his state criminals, or those whom he supposed to be engaged together in any evil designs upon him, in this dungeon. He had at the same time an apartment over it, where he used to apply himself to the funnel, and by that means overhear everything that was whispered in the dungeon. I believe one may venture to affirm, that a Cæsar or an Alexander would rather have died by the treason, than have used such disingenuous means for the detecting of it.

A man who in ordinary life is very inquisitive after everything which is spoken ill of him, passes his time but very indifferently. He is wounded by every arrow that is shot at him, and puts it in the power of every insignificant enemy to disquiet him. Nay, he will suffer from what has been said of him, when it is forgotten by those who said or heard it. For this reason I could never bear one of those officious friends that would be telling every malicious report, every idle censure that passed upon me. The tongue of man is so petulant, and his thoughts so variable, that one should not lay too great a stress upon any present speeches and opinions. Praise and obloquy proceed very frequently out of the same mouth upon the same person, and upon the same occasion. A generous enemy will sometimes bestow commendations, as the dearest friend cannot sometimes refrain from speaking ill. The man who is indifferent in either of these respects, gives his opinion at random, and praises or disapproves as he finds himself in humour.

I shall conclude this essay with part of a character, which is finely drawn by the Earl of Clarendon in the first book of his History, and which gives us the lively picture of a great man [1] teasing himself with an absurd curiosity:

He had not that application and submission, and reverence for the Queen, as might have been expected from his wisdom and breeding; and often crossed her pretences and desires with more rudeness than was natural to him. Yet he was impertinently solicitous to know what her majesty said of him in private, and what resentments she had towards him. And when by some confidants, who had their ends upon him from those offices, he was informed of some bitter expressions fallen from her majesty, he was so exceedingly afflicted and tormented with the sense of it, that sometimes by passionate complaints and representations to the King, sometimes by more dutiful addresses and expostulations with the Queen in bewailing his misfortune, he frequently exposed himself, and left his condition worse than it was before, and the eclaircissement commonly ended in the discovery of the persons from whom he had received his most secret intelligence.　　C.

No. 440.　　*Friday, July 25, 1712*　　[ADDISON

*Vivere si recte nescis, decede peritis.* HOR., 2 Ep. ii, 213

I HAVE already given my reader an account of a set of merry fellows who are passing their summer together in the country, being provided of a great house, where there is not only a convenient apartment for every particular person, but a large infirm-

---

1 Richard Weston, first Earl of Portland, who was made Lord Treasurer in 1628, and died in 1634. The honours and wealth that came to him left him dissatisfied, and he died unlamented, leaving a family which outlived the fortune he left behind him (*History of the Rebellion*, Book i, §§ 110–115).

ary for the reception of such of them as are any way
indisposed or out of humour[1]. Having lately received a letter from the secretary of this society, by
order of the whole fraternity, which acquaints me
with their behaviour during the last week, I shall
here make a present of it to the public :

MR. SPECTATOR,—We are glad to find that you
approve the establishment which we have here made
for the retrieving of good manners and agreeable conversation, and shall use our best endeavours so to
improve ourselves in this our summer retirement, that
we may next winter serve as patterns to the town.
But to the end that this our institution may be no
less advantageous to the public than to ourselves, we
shall communicate to you one week of our proceedings,
desiring you at the same time, if you see anything
faulty in them, to favour us with your admonitions.
For you must know, sir, that it has been proposed
among us to choose you for our visitor, to which I
must further add, that one of the college having
declared last week he did not like the *Spectator* of
the day, and not being able to assign any just reasons
for such his dislike, he was sent to the infirmary,
*nemine contradicente*.

On Monday the assembly was in very good humour,
having received some recruits of French claret that
morning; when unluckily, towards the middle of the
dinner, one of the company swore at his servant in a
very rough manner for having put too much water in
his wine.  Upon which the president of the day, who
is always the mouth of the company, after having
convinced him of the impertinence of his passion and
the insult it had made upon the company, ordered
his man to take him from the table and convey him to
the infirmary.  There was but one more sent away that
day ; this was a gentleman who is reckoned by some
persons one of the greatest wits, and by others one of
the greatest boobies about town.  This you will say is
a strange character, but what makes it stranger yet,
it is a very true one, for he is perpetually the reverse
of himself, being always merry or dull to excess.  We

[1] See Nos. 424, 429.

brought him hither to divert us, which he did very well upon the road, having lavished away as much wit and laughter upon the hackney coachman as might have served him during his whole stay here, had it been duly managed. He had been lumpish for two or three days, but was so far connived at, in hopes of recovery, that we despatched one of the briskest fellows among the brotherhood into the infirmary for having told him at table he was not merry. But our president observing that he indulged himself in this long fit of stupidity, and construing it as a contempt of the college, ordered him to retire into the place prepared for such companions. He was no sooner got into it, but his wit and mirth returned upon him in so violent a manner, that he shook the whole infirmary with the noise of it, and had so good an effect upon the rest of the patients, that he brought them all out to dinner with him the next day.

On Tuesday we were no sooner sat down, but one of the company complained that his head ached; upon which another asked him, in an insolent manner, what he did there then; this insensibly grew into some warm words, so that the president, in order to keep the peace, gave directions to take them both from the table and lodge them in the infirmary. Not long after, another of the company telling us he knew by a pain in his shoulder that we should have some rain, the president ordered him to be removed, and placed as a weather-glass in the apartment above mentioned.

On Wednesday a gentleman having received a letter written in a woman's hand, and changing colour twice or thrice as he read it, desired leave to retire into the infirmary. The president consented, but denied him the use of pen, ink, and paper till such time as he had slept upon it. One of the company being seated at the lower end of the table, and discovering his secret discontent, by finding fault with every dish that was served up, and refusing to laugh at anything that was said, the president told him, that he found he was in an uneasy seat, and desired him to accommodate himself better in the infirmary. After dinner a very honest fellow chancing to let a pun fall from him, his neighbour cried out, 'To the infirmary'; at the same time pretending to be sick at it, as having the same natural antipathy to a pun which some have to a cat. This produced a long debate. Upon the whole the punster was acquitted, and his neighbour sent off.

On Thursday there was but one delinquent. This was a gentleman of strong voice, but weak understanding. He had unluckily engaged himself in a dispute with a man of excellent sense, but of a modest elocution. The man of heat replied to every answer of his antagonist with a louder note than ordinary, and only raised his voice when he should have enforced his argument. Finding himself at length driven to an absurdity, he still reasoned in a more clamorous and confused manner, and to make the greater impression upon his hearers, concluded with a loud thump upon the table. The president immediately ordered him to be carried off, and dieted with watergruel, till such time as he should be sufficiently weakened for conversation.

On Friday there passed very little remarkable, saving only, that several petitions were read of the persons in custody, desiring to be released from their confinement, and vouching for one another's good behaviour for the future.

On Saturday we received many excuses from persons who had found themselves in an unsociable temper, and had voluntarily shut themselves up. The infirmary was indeed never so full as on this day, which I was at some loss to account for, till upon my going abroad I observed that it was an easterly wind. The retirement of most of my friends has given me opportunity and leisure of writing you this letter, which I must not conclude without assuring you, that all the members of our college, as well those who are under confinement as those who are at liberty, are your very humble Servants, though none more than, &c.     C.

No. 441.     *Saturday, July 26, 1712*     [ADDISON

*Si fractus illabatur orbis,*
*Impavidum ferient ruinæ.*

HOR., 3 *Od.* iii, 7

MAN, considered in himself, is a very helpless and a very wretched being. He is subject every moment to the greatest calamities and misfortunes. He is beset with dangers on all sides, and may become unhappy by numberless casualties, which he could not foresee, nor have prevented, had he foreseen them.

It is our comfort, while we are obnoxious to so many accidents, that we are under the care of One who directs contingencies, and has in His hands the management of everything that is capable of annoying or offending us; who knows the assistance we stand in need of, and is always ready to bestow it on those who ask it of Him.

The natural homage which such a creature bears to so infinitely wise and good a Being, is a firm reliance on Him for the blessings and conveniences of life, and an habitual trust in Him for deliverance out of all such dangers and difficulties as may befall us.

The man who always lives in this disposition of mind, has not the same dark and melancholy views of human nature as he who considers himself abstractedly from this relation to the Supreme Being. At the same time that he reflects upon his own weakness and imperfection, he comforts himself with the contemplation of those Divine attributes, which are employed for his safety and his welfare. He finds his want of foresight made up by the omniscience of Him who is his support. He is not sensible of his own want of strength, when he knows that his helper is Almighty. In short, the person who has a firm trust on the Supreme Being is powerful in His power, wise by His wisdom, happy by His happiness. He reaps the benefit of every Divine attribute, and

loses his own insufficiency in the fulness of Infinite
Perfection.

To make our lives more easy to us, we are commanded to put our trust in Him, who is thus able
to relieve and succour us; the Divine Goodness
having made such a reliance a duty, notwithstanding
we should have been miserable had it been forbidden
us.

Among several motives which might be made use
of to recommend this duty to us, I shall only take
notice of those that follow.

The first and strongest is, that we are promised,
'He will not fail those who put their trust in
Him'.

But without considering the supernatural blessing
which accompanies this duty, we may observe that
it has a natural tendency to its own reward, or in
other words, that this firm trust and confidence in
the great Disposer of all things contributes very much
to the getting clear of any affliction, or to the bearing
it manfully.  A person who believes he has his succour at hand, and that he acts in the sight of his
friend, often exerts himself beyond his abilities, and
does wonders that are not to be matched by one who
is not animated with such a confidence of success.  I
could produce instances from history, of generals,
who out of a belief that they were under the protection of some invisible assistant, did not only encourage their soldiers to do their utmost, but have
acted themselves beyond what they would have done,
had they not been inspired by such a belief.  I might
in the same manner show how such a trust in the
assistance of an Almighty Being naturally produces
patience, hope, cheerfulness, and all other dispositions of mind that alleviate those calamities which
we are not able to remove.

The practice of this virtue administers great comfort to the mind of man in times of poverty and
affliction, but most of all in the hour of death.  When
the soul is hovering in the last moments of its separa-

tion[1], when it is just entering on another state of existence, to converse with scenes and objects and companions that are altogether new, what can support her under such tremblings of thought, such fear, such anxiety, such apprehensions, but the casting of all her cares upon Him who first gave her being, who has conducted her through one stage of it, and will be always with her to guide and comfort her in her progress[2] through eternity?

David has very beautifully represented this steady reliance on God Almighty in his twenty-third Psalm, which is a kind of pastoral hymn, and filled with those allusions which are usual in that kind of writing. As the poetry is very exquisite, I shall present my reader with the following translation of it[3]:

I

The Lord my pasture shall prepare,
And feed me with a shepherd's care:
His presence shall my wants supply,
And guard me with a watchful eye;
My noon-day walks He shall attend,
And all my midnight hours defend.

II

When in the sultry glebe I faint,
Or on the thirsty mountain pant;
To fertile vales and dewy meads
My weary wandering steps He leads,
Where peaceful rivers soft and slow
Amid the verdant landscape flow.

III

Though in the paths of death I tread,
With gloomy horrors overspread;
My steadfast heart shall fear no ill,
For thou, O Lord, art with me still;
Thy friendly crook shall give me aid,
And guide me through the dreadful shade.

---

1 'Dissolution' (folio).          2 'Passage' (folio).
3 By Addison. Appended to No. 489 was the following 'Advertisement': 'The author of the *Spectator* having received the Pastoral Hymn in his 441st paper, set to music by one of the most eminent composers of our own country and by a foreigner, who has not put his name to his ingenious letter, thinks himself obliged to return his thanks to those gentlemen for the honour they have done him.'

IV

Though in a bare and rugged way,
Through devious lonely wilds I stray,
Thy bounty shall my pains beguile:
The barren wilderness shall smile
With sudden greens and herbage crowned,
And streams shall murmur all around.          C.

No. 442.          *Monday, July 28, 1712*          [STEELE

*Scribimus indocti doctique.*  HOR., 2 *Ep.* i, 117

I DO not know whether I enough explained myself
to the world, when I invited all men to be assistant
to me in this my work of speculation [1]; for I have
not yet acquainted my readers, that besides the
letters and valuable hints I have from time to time
received from my correspondents, I have by me
several curious and extraordinary papers sent with a
design (as no one will doubt when they are published)
that they might be printed entire, and without any
alteration, by way of *Spectator*. I must acknowledge
also, that I myself being the first projector of the
paper, thought I had a right to make them my own,
by dressing them in my own style, by leaving out
what would not appear like mine, and by adding
whatever might be proper to adapt them to the character and genius of my paper, with which it was
almost impossible these could exactly correspond, it
being certain that hardly two men think alike, and
therefore so many men so many *Spectators*. Besides, I must own my weakness for glory is such,
that if I consulted that only, I might be so far
swayed by it as almost to wish that no one could
write a *Spectator* besides myself; nor can I deny, but
upon the first perusal of those papers, I felt some
secret inclinations of ill-will towards the persons who
wrote them. This was the impression I had upon
the first reading them; but upon a late review (more
for the sake of entertainment than use) regarding
them with another eye than I had done at first (for

[1] No. 428.

by converting them as well as I could to my own use, I thought I had utterly disabled them from ever offending me again as *Spectators*), I found myself moved by a passion very different from that of envy; sensibly touched with pity, the softest and most generous of all passions, when I reflected what a cruel disappointment the neglect of those papers must needs have been to the writers, who impatiently longed to see them appear in print, and who, no doubt, triumphed to themselves in the hopes of having a share with me in the applause of the public; a pleasure so great that none but those who have experienced it can have a sense of it. In this manner of viewing those papers, I really found I had not done them justice, there being something so extremely natural and peculiarly good in some of them, that I will appeal to the world whether it was possible to alter a word in them without doing them a manifest hurt and violence; and whether they can ever appear rightly, and as they ought, but in their own native dress and colours. And therefore I think I should not only wrong them, but deprive the world of a considerable satisfaction, should I any longer delay the making them public.

After I have published a few of these *Spectators*, I doubt not but I shall find the success of them to equal, if not surpass, that of the best of my own. An author should take all methods to humble himself in the opinion he has of his own performances. When these papers appear to the world, I doubt not but they will be followed by many others; and I shall not repine, though I myself shall have left me but very few days to appear in public; but preferring the general weal and advantage to any considerations of myself, I am resolved for the future to publish any *Spectator* that deserves it, entire, and without any alteration; assuring the world (if there can be need of it) that it is none of mine; and if the authors think fit to subscribe their names, I will add them.

I think the best way of promoting this generous and useful design will be by giving out subjects or themes of all kinds whatsoever, on which (with a preamble of the extraordinary benefit and advantage that may accrue thereby to the public) I will invite all manner of persons, whether scholars, citizens, courtiers, gentlemen of the town or country, and all beaux, rakes, smarts, prudes, coquettes, housewives, and all sorts of wits, whether male or female, and however distinguished, whether they be true-wits, whole, or half-wits, or whether arch, dry, natural, acquired, genuine, or depraved wits; and persons of all sorts of tempers and complexions, whether the severe, the delightful, the impertinent, the agreeable, the thoughtful, busy, or careless; the serene or cloudy, jovial or melancholy, untowardly or easy; the cold, temperate, or sanguine; and of what manners or dispositions soever, whether the ambitious or humble-minded, the proud or pitiful, ingenuous or base-minded, good or ill-natured, public-spirited or selfish; and under what fortune or circumstance soever, whether the contented or miserable, happy or unfortunate, high or low, rich or poor (whether so through want of money or desire of more), healthy or sickly, married or single; nay, whether tall or short, fat or lean; and of what trade, occupation, profession, station, country, faction, party, persuasion, quality, age, or condition soever, who have ever made thinking a part of their business or diversion, and have anything worthy to impart on these subjects to the world; according to their several and respective talents or genius, and as the subject given out hits their tempers, humours, or circumstances, or may be made profitable to the public by their particular knowledge or experience in the matter proposed, to do their utmost on them by such a time; to the end they may receive the inexpressible and irresistible pleasure of seeing their essay allowed of and relished by the rest of mankind.

I will not prepossess the reader with too great

expectation of the extraordinary advantages which must redound to the public by these essays when the different thoughts and observations of all sorts of persons, according to their quality, age, sex, education, professions, humours, manners and conditions, &c., shall be set out by themselves in the clearest and most genuine light, and as they themselves would wish to have them appear to the world.

The thesis proposed for the present exercise of the adventurers to write *Spectators* is Money, on which subject all persons are desired to send in their thoughts within ten days after the date hereof.   T.

No. 443.    *Tuesday, July 29, 1712*    [STEELE

*Sublatam ex oculis quærimus invidi.*   HOR., 3 *Od.* xxiv, 32

CAMILLA [1] *to the* SPECTATOR

VENICE, *July* 10, N. S.

MR. SPECTATOR,—I take it extremely ill that you do not reckon conspicuous persons of your nation are within your cognisance, though out of the dominions of Great Britain. I little thought in the green years of my life that I should ever call it an happiness to be out of dear England; but as I grew to woman I found myself less acceptable in proportion to the increase of my merit. Their ears in Italy are so differently formed from the make of yours in England, that I never come upon the stage but a general satisfaction appears in every countenance of the whole people. When I dwell upon a note I behold all the men accompanying me with heads inclining and falling of their persons on one side, as dying away with me. The women too do justice to my merit, and no ill-natured

1 Mrs Tofts (see No. 22). On December 10, 1708, Lady Wentworth wrote a description of an opera rehearsal she had witnessed: ' The Dutchis of Molbery had gott the Etallian (Nicolini) to sing and he sent an excuse ; but the Dutchis of Shrosberry made him com, brought him in her coach ; but Mrs Taufs huft and would not sing becaus he had first put it ofe ; though she was thear yet she would not, but went away. I wish the house would al joyne to humble her and not receav her again' (*Wentworth Papers*, 1883, p. 66).

worthless creature cries 'The vain thing!' when I am
wrapped up in the performance of my part, and
sensibly touched with the effect my voice has upon all
who hear me.   I live here distinguished, as one whom
Nature has been liberal to in a graceful person, an
exalted mien, and heavenly voice.   These particularities in this strange country are arguments for respect
and generosity to her who is possessed of them.   The
Italians see a thousand beauties I am sensible I have
no pretence to, and abundantly make up to me the
injustice I received in my own country, of disallowing
me what I really had.   The humour of hissing, which
you have among you, I do not know anything of; and
their applauses are uttered in sighs, and bearing a part
at the cadences of voice with the persons who are
performing.   I am often put in mind of those complaisant lines of my own countryman[1], when he is
calling all his faculties together to hear Arabella :

> Let all be hushed, each softest motion cease,
> Be every loud tumultuous thought at peace ;
> And every ruder gasp of breath
> Be calm, as in the arms of death :
> And thou, most fickle, most uneasy part,
> Thou restless wanderer, my heart,
> Be still ; gently, ah ! gently leave,
> Thou busy, idle thing, to heave.
> Stir not a pulse ; and let my blood,
> That turbulent, unruly flood,
> Be softly staid :
> Let me be all but my attention dead.

The whole city of Venice is as still when I am
singing, as this polite hearer was to Mrs Hunt.   But
when they break that silence, did you know the
pleasure I am in, when every man utters his applause,
by calling me aloud the 'dear creature', the 'angel',
the 'Venus'.—'What attitude she moves with !——
Hush ! she sings again !'   We have no boisterous wits
who dare disturb an audience, and break the public
peace merely to show they dare.   Mr Spectator, I
write this to you thus in haste, to tell you I am very
much at ease here, that I know nothing but joy; and

[1] The verses are from Congreve's ode on 'Mrs Arabella Hunt
singing'.   Mrs Arabella Hunt was eminent both as a vocalist and
lutenist; and her beauty and wit brought her many friends.   She
died in 1705.

I will not return, but leave you in England to hiss all merit of your own growth off the stage.—I know, Sir, you were always my admirer, and therefore I am yours,                                           CAMILLA

*P.S.*—I am ten times better dressed than ever I was in England.

MR SPECTATOR,—The project in yours of the 11th instant [1], of furthering the correspondence and knowledge of that considerable part of mankind, the trading world, cannot but be highly commendable. Good lectures to young traders may have very good effects on their conduct : but beware you propagate no false notions of trade ; let none of your correspondents impose on the world, by putting forth base methods in a good light, and glazing them over with improper terms. I would have no means of profit set for copies to others, but such as are laudable in themselves. Let not noise be called industry, nor impudence courage. Let not good fortune be imposed on the world for good management, nor poverty be called folly ; impute not always bankruptcy to extravagance, nor an estate to foresight : niggardliness is not good husbandry, nor generosity profusion.

Honestus is a well-meaning and judicious trader, hath substantial goods, and trades with his own stock ; husbands his money to the best advantage, without taking all advantages of the necessities of his workmen, or grinding the face of the poor. Fortunatus is stocked with ignorance, and consequently with self-opinion ; the quality of his goods cannot but be suitable to that of his judgment. Honestus pleases discerning people, and keeps their custom by good usage ; makes modest profit by modest means, to the decent support of his family : whilst Fortunatus, blustering always, pushes on, promising much, and performing little, with obsequiousness offensive to people of sense ; strikes at all, catches much the greater part ; raises a considerable fortune by imposition on others, to the disencouragement and ruin of those who trade in the same way.

---

[1] No. 428.

I give here but loose hints, and beg you to be very circumspect in the province you have now undertaken : if you perform it successfully, it will be a very great good ; for nothing is more wanting, than that mechanic industry were set forth with the freedom and greatness of mind which ought always to accompany a man of a liberal education.

Your humble Servant,

R. C.

From my Shop under the
ROYAL EXCHANGE, *July* 14

*July* 24, 1712

MR SPECTATOR,—Notwithstanding the repeated censures that your spectatorial wisdom has passed upon people more remarkable for impudence than wit, there are yet some remaining, who pass with the giddy part of mankind for sufficient sharers of the latter, who have nothing but the former qualification to recommend them. Another timely animadversion is absolutely necessary ; be pleased therefore once for all to let these gentlemen know, that there is neither mirth nor good humour in hooting a young fellow out of countenance ; nor that it will ever constitute a wit, to conclude a tart piece of buffoonery with a ' What makes you blush ?' Pray please to inform them again, that to speak what they know is shocking, proceeds from ill-nature, and a sterility of brain ; especially when the subject will not admit of raillery, and their discourse has no pretension to satire but what is in their design to disoblige. I should be very glad too if you would take notice, that a daily repetition of the same overbearing insolence is yet more insupportable, and a confirmation of very extraordinary dulness. The sudden publication of this may have an effect upon a notorious offender of this kind, whose reformation would redound very much to the satisfaction and quiet of

Your most humble Servant,

T.                                           F. B.[1]

<hr>

Said to be Francis Beasniffe, whose nephew was recorder of Hull
he close of the eighteenth century.

*Wednesday, July 30, 1712*     [STEELE

*urient montes.* Hor., *Ars Poet.* 139 ]

much despair in the design of reform-
by my speculations, when I find there
rom one generation to another, succes-
id bubbles, as naturally as beasts of
o which are to be their food. There
an in the world, one would think, so
ot to know that the ordinary quack
publish their great abilities in little
distributed to all who pass by, are to
ors and murderers; yet such is the
o vulgar, and the impudence of these
it the affair still goes on, and new
but was never done before are made
'hat aggravates the jest is, that even
as been made as long as the memory
ice it, and yet nothing performed, and
ls. As I was passing along to-day, a
o my hand by a fellow without a nose
ows what good news is come to town,
re is now a certain cure for the French
entleman just come from his travels :

ourt, over against the Cannon-Ball, at
.rms in Drury Lane, is lately come from
rgeon who hath practised surgery and
sea and land these twenty-four years.
ssing) cures the yellow jaundice, green
y, dropsy, surfeits, long sea voyages,
women's miscarriages, lying-in, &c., as
it has been lame these thirty years can
rt, he cureth all diseases incident to
or children [2].

: fo'lo issue was Horace's

um tanto foret lie promissor hiatu.

as given in the follo issue, but was very properly
rint. The end was, 'He bleedeth for 3d, and
8 to 12, and from 2 till 6.

If a man could be so indolent as to look upon this havoc of the human species, which is made by vice and ignorance, it would be a good ridiculous work to comment upon the declaration of this accomplished traveller. There is something unaccountably taking among the vulgar in those who come from a great way off. Ignorant people of quality, as many there are of such, dote excessively this way; many instances of which every man will suggest to himself without my enumeration of them. The ignorants of lower order, who cannot, like the upper ones, be profuse of their money to those recommended by coming from a distance, are no less complaisant than the others, for they venture their lives from the same admiration.

'The doctor is lately come from his travels ', and has ' practised ' both by sea and land, and therefore cures the ' green sickness, long sea voyages, campaigns, and lying-in '. Both by sea and land!—— I will not answer for the distempers called ' sea voyages and campaigns '; but I dare say, those of green sickness and lying-in might be as well taken care of if the doctor stayed ashore. But the art of managing mankind is only to make them stare a little, to keep up their astonishment, to let nothing be familiar to them, but ever to have something in your sleeve, in which they must think you are deeper than they are. There is an ingenious fellow, a barber, of my acquaintance, who, besides his broken fiddle and a dried sea-monster, has a twine-cord, strained with two nails at each end, over his window, and the words ' rainy ', ' dry ', ' wet ', and so forth, written, to denote the weather according to the rising or falling of the cord. We very great scholars are not apt to wonder at this : but I observed a very honest fellow, a chance customer, who sat in the chair before me to be shaved, fix his eye upon this miraculous performance during the operation upon his chin and face. When those and his head also were cleared of all encumbrances and excrescences, he looked at the fish, then at the fiddle,

still grubbling [1] in his pockets, and casting his eye
again at the twine, and the words writ on each side;
then altered his mind as to farthings, and gave my
friend a silver sixpence. The business, as I said, is
to keep up the amazement, and if my friend had
had only the skeleton and kit [2], he must have been
contented with a less payment. But the doctor we
were talking of, adds to his long voyages the testimony of some people ' that has been thirty years
lame '. When I received my paper, a sagacious
fellow took one at the same time, and read till he
came to the thirty years' confinement of his friends,
and went off very well convinced of the doctor's
sufficiency. You have many of these prodigious
persons, who have had some extraordinary accident
at their birth, or a great disaster in some part of
their lives. Anything, however foreign from the
business the people want of you, will convince them
of your ability in that you profess. There is a
doctor [3] in Mouse Alley, near Wapping, who sets
up for curing cataracts, upon the credit of having,
as his bill sets forth, lost an eye in the emperor's
service. His patients come in upon this, and he
shows the muster-roll, which confirms that he was
in his imperial majesty's troops, and he puts out
their eyes with great success. Who would believe
that a man should be a doctor for the cure of
bursten children, by declaring that his father and
grandfather were born bursten? But Charles In-
goltson, next door to the Harp in Barbican, has
made a pretty penny by that asseveration. The

---

[1] Grubbing.                    [2] Fiddle.

[3] It is stated by Wadd (*Nugæ Chirurgicæ*, p. 72) that the quack here
satirised is Roger Grant (died 1724), whose skill is praised by a
correspondent in No. 472. Advertisements in the *British Apollo* for
1710 show, however, that at that time Grant was living in St
Christopher's Churchyard, near the Royal Exchange. He was the
chief rival of Sir William Read (see No. 472), and was appointed
oculist to Queen Anne and George I. He is said to have been a
Baptist preacher and a tinker or cobbler. Nichols thought that he
was more ingenious and reputable than most of his fellow oculists,
but, judging from his advertisements, not less vain or indelicate.

generality go upon their first conception, and think
no further; all the rest is granted. They take it,
that there is something uncommon in you, and give
you credit for the rest. You may be sure it is upon
that I go, when sometimes, let it be to the purpose
or not, I keep a Latin sentence in my front; and I
was not a little pleased when I observed one of my
readers say, casting his eye on my twentieth paper,
'More Latin still? What a prodigious scholar is
this man!' But as I have here taken much liberty
with this learned doctor, I must make up all I have
said by repeating what he seems to be in earnest in,
and honestly promise to those who will not receive
him as a great man: to wit, that from eight till
twelve, and from two till six, he attends for the good
of the public to bleed for threepence.        T.


No. 445.        *Thursday, July 31, 1712*        [ADDISON

*Tanti non es, ais. Sapis, Luperce.* MART., *Epig.* i, 118

THIS is the day on which many eminent authors
will probably publish their last words [1]. I am afraid

[1] In 1695 the Commons refused to renew the Licensing Act of
Charles II's reign; but under Queen Anne many journalists were
punished under the libel laws. In 1711 St John brought to the bar of
the House of Commons, under his warrant as Secretary of State,
fourteen printers and publishers. In the beginning of 1712, the
Queen's message had complained that by seditious papers and factious
rumours designing men had been able to sink credit, and the innocent
had suffered. On the 12th of February a committee of the whole
House was appointed to consider how to stop the abuse of the liberty
of the press. Some were for a renewal of the Licensing Act, some for
requiring writers' names after their articles. The Government carried
its own design of a halfpenny stamp by an Act (10 Anne, cap. 19)
passed on the 10th of June, which was to come in force on the first of
August 1712, and be in force for thirty-two years. 'Do you know',
wrote Swift to Stella five days after the date of this *Spectator* paper—
'do you know that all Grub Street is dead and gone last week? No
more ghosts or murders now for love or money. . . . Every single
half-sheet pays a halfpenny to the Queen. The *Observator* is fallen;
the *Medleys* are jumbled together with the *Flying Post;* the *Examiner*
is deadly sick; the *Spectator* keeps up and doubles its price; I know
not how long it will last.' It so happened that the mortality was
greatest among Government papers. The Act presently fell into

that few of our weekly historians, who are men that above all others delight in war, will be able to subsist under the weight of a stamp and an approaching peace. A sheet of blank paper that must have this new imprimatur clapped upon it, before it is qualified to communicate anything to the public, will make its way in the world but very heavily. In short, the necessity of carrying a stamp and the improbability of notifying a bloody battle, will, I am afraid, both concur to the sinking of those thin folios which have every other day retailed to us the history of Europe for several years last past. A facetious friend of mine, who loves a pun, calls this present mortality among authors ' The fall of the leaf.'

I remember, upon Mr Baxter's death[1], there was published a sheet of very good sayings, inscribed *The Last Words of Mr Baxter.* The title sold so great a number of these papers, that about a week after there came out a second sheet, inscribed *More Last Words of Mr Baxter.* In the same manner, I have reason to think, that several ingenious writers, who have taken their leave of the public in farewell papers, will not give over so, but intend to appear again, though perhaps under another form and with a different title. Be that as it will, it is my business in this place to give an account of my own intentions, and to acquaint my reader with the motives by which I act in this great crisis of the republic of letters.

I have been long debating in my own heart, whether I should throw up my pen as an author that is cashiered by the Act of Parliament, which is to operate within these four and twenty hours, or whether I should still persist in laying my speculations from day to day before the public. The

abeyance, was revived in 1725, and thenceforth maintained the taxation of newspapers until the abolition of the stamp in 1859. One of its immediate effects was a fall in the circulation of the *Spectator* (Morley). —Defoe argued against the Stamp Act in the *Review* for April 26, 1712, and the following numbers.

1 Richard Baxter died in 1691.

argument which prevails with me most on the first side of the question is, that I am informed by my bookseller he must raise the price of every single paper to twopence, or that he shall not be able to pay the duty of it. Now, as I am very desirous my readers should have their learning as cheap as possible, it is with great difficulty that I comply with him in this particular.

However, upon laying my reasons together in the balance, I find that those which plead for the continuance of this work have much the greater weight. For in the first place, in recompense for the expense to which this will put my readers, it is to be hoped they may receive from every paper so much instruction as will be a very good equivalent. And, in order to this, I would not advise any one to take it in who, after the perusal of it, does not find himself twopence the wiser or the better man for it; or who, upon examination, does not believe that he has had two pennyworth of mirth or instruction for his money.

But I must confess there is another motive which prevails with me more than the former. I consider that the tax on paper was given for the support of the Government; and as I have enemies who are apt to pervert everything I do or say, I fear they would ascribe the laying down my paper on such an occasion, to a spirit of malcontentedness, which I am resolved none shall ever justly upbraid me with. No, I shall glory in contributing my utmost to the weal public; and if my country receives five or six pounds a day by my labours, I shall be very well pleased to find myself so useful a member. It is a received maxim that no honest man should enrich himself by methods that are prejudicial 'to the community in which he lives, and by the same rule I think we may pronounce the person to deserve very well of his countrymen, whose labours bring more into the public coffers than into his own pocket.

Since I have mentioned the word enemies, I must explain myself so far as to acquaint my reader that I mean only the insignificant party zealots on both sides; men of such poor narrow souls, that they are not capable of thinking on anything but with an eye to Whig or Tory. During the course of this paper I have been accused by these despicable wretches of trimming, time-serving, personal reflection, secret satire, and the like. Now, though in these my compositions it is visible to any reader of common sense that I consider nothing but my subject, which is always of an indifferent nature, how is it possible for me to write so clear of party, as not to lie open to the censures of those who will be applying every sentence, and finding out persons and things in it which it has no regard to?

Several paltry scribblers and declaimers have done me the honour to be dull upon me in reflections of this nature; but notwithstanding my name has been sometimes traduced by this contemptible tribe of men, I have hitherto avoided all animadversions upon 'em. The truth of it is, I am afraid of making them appear considerable by taking notice of them, for they are like those imperceptible insects which are discovered by the microscope, and cannot be made the subject of observation without being magnified.

Having mentioned those few who have shown themselves the enemies of this paper, I should be very ungrateful to the public, did not I at the same time testify my gratitude to those who are its friends, in which number I may reckon many of the most distinguished persons of all conditions, parties, and professions in the isle of Great Britain. I am not so vain as to think this approbation is so much due to the performance as to the design. There is, and ever will be, justice enough in the world, to afford patronage and protection for those who endeavour to advance truth and virtue, without regard to the passions and prejudices of any particular cause or faction. If I have any other merit in me, it is that I have new-pointed all the batteries of ridicule. They have been generally planted against persons who have appeared serious rather than absurd; or at best, have aimed rather at what is unfashionable than what is vicious. For my own part, I have endeavoured to make nothing ridiculous that is not in some measure criminal. I have set up the immoral man as the object of derision. In short, if I have not formed a new weapon against vice and irreligion, I have at least shown how that weapon may be put to a right use, which has so often fought the battles of impiety and profaneness.                    C.

No. 446.     *Friday, August 1, 1712*     [ADDISON

*Quid deceat, quid non ; quo virtus, quo ferat error.*
HOR., *Ars Poet.* 308

SINCE two or three writers of comedy who are now living have taken their farewell of the stage, those who succeed them finding themselves incapable of rising up to their wit, humour, and good sense, have only imitated them in some of those loose unguarded strokes, in which they complied. with the corrupt taste of the more vicious part of their audience. When persons of a low genius attempt this kind of writing, they know no difference between being merry and being lewd. It is with an eye to some of these degenerate compositions that I have written the following discourse.

Were our English stage but half so virtuous as that of the Greeks or Romans, we should quickly see the influence of it in the behaviour of all the politer part of mankind. It would not be fashionable to ridicule religion, or its professors; the man of pleasure would not be the complete gentleman; vanity would be out of countenance, and every quality which is ornamental to human nature, would meet with that esteem which is due to it.

If the English stage were under the same regulations the Athenian was formerly, it would have the same effect that had, in recommending the religion, the government, and public worship of its country. Were our plays subject to proper inspections and limitations, we might not only pass away several of our vacant hours in the highest entertainments, but should always rise from them wiser and better than we sat down to them.

It is one of the most unaccountable things in our age, that the lewdness of our theatre should be so much complained of, so well exposed, and so little redressed. It is to be hoped, that some time or other we may be at leisure to restrain the licentiousness of the theatre, and make it contribute its assistance to the advancement of morality, and to the reformation of the age. As matters stand at present, multitudes are shut out from this noble diversion, by reason of those abuses and corruptions that accompany it. A father is often afraid that his daughter should be ruined by those entertainments, which were invented for the accomplishment and refining of human nature. The Athenian and Roman plays were written with such a regard to morality, that Socrates used to frequent the one, and Cicero the other.

It happened once indeed, that Cato dropped into the Roman theatre, when the Floralia were to be represented; and as in that performance, which was a kind of religious ceremony, there were several indecent parts to be acted, the people refused to see them whilst Cato was present. Martial on this hint made the following epigram [1], which we must suppose was applied to some grave friend of his, that had been accidentally present at some such entertainment :

Nosses jocosae dulce cum sacrum Florae,
Festosque lusus, et licentiam vulgi,
Cur in theatrum Cato severe venisti?
An ideo tantum veneras, ut exires?

1 *Epig.* 1, car, pr, 1.

Why dost thou come, great censor of thy age,
To see the loose diversions of the stage?
With awful conntenance and brow severe,
What in the name of goodness dost thou here?
See the mixed crowd! how giddy, lewd, and vain!
Didst thou come in but to go out again?

An accident of this nature might happen once in
an age among the Greeks or Romans; but they were
too wise and good to let the constant nightly entertainment be of such a nature that people of the most
sense and virtue could not be at it.    Whatever vices
are represented upon the stage, they ought to be so
marked and branded by the poet as not to appear
either laudable or amiable in the person who is
tainted with them.    But if we look in the English
comedies above mentioned, we would think they were
formed upon a quite contrary maxim, and that this
rule, though it held good upon the heathen stage,
was not to be regarded in Christian theatres.    There
is another rule likewise, which was observed by
authors of antiquity, and which these modern
geniuses have no regard to, and that was never to
choose an improper subject for ridicule.    Now a subject is improper for ridicule if it is apt to stir up
horror and commiseration rather than laughter.    For
this reason, we do not find any comedy in so polite
an author as Terence raised upon the violations of
the marriage-bed.    The falsehood of the wife or husband has given occasion to noble tragedies, but a
Scipio or a Lelius would have looked upon incest or
murder to have been as proper subjects for comedy.
On the contrary, cuckoldom is the basis of most of
our modern plays.    If an alderman appears upon the
stage, you may be sure it is in order to be cuckolded.
An husband that is a little grave or elderly generally
meets with the same fate.    Knights and baronets,
country squires and justices of the Quorum, come up
to town for no other purpose.    I have seen poor
Doggett [1] cuckolded in all these capacities.    In short,

---

[1] See No. 235.

English writers are as frequently severe upon
innocent unhappy creature, commonly known by
name of a cuckold, as the ancient comic writers
ɔ upon an eating parasite or a vainglorious soldier.
t the same time, the poet so contrives matters
tho two criminals are the favourites of the
.ence. We sit still and wish well to them
ugh the whole play, are pleased when they
t with proper opportunities, and out of humour
a they are disappointed. The truth of it is, the
mplished gentleman upon the English stage is
person that is familiar with other men's wives
indifferent to his own, as the fine woman is gener-
a composition of sprightliness and falsehood. I
ot know whether it proceeds from barrenness of
ation, depravation of manners, or ignorance of
ɔind; but I have often wondered that our ordi-
poets cannot frame to themselves the idea of a
man who is not a whoremaster, or of a fine
an that is not a jilt.

ave sometimes thought of compiling a system
hics out of the writings of these corrupt poets,
ɔ the title of ' Stage Morality '. But I have
diverted from this thought by a project which
con executed by an ingenious gentleman of my
cintance. He has composed, it seems, the his-
ɔf a young fellow who has taken all his notions
a world from the stage, and who has directed
lf in every circumstance of his life and con-
ɔion by the maxims and examples of the fine
men in English comedies. If I can prevail
him to give me a copy of this new-fashioned
I will bestow on it a place in my works, and
on not but it may have as good an effect upon
ama as ' Don Quixote ' had upon romance.

C.

No. 447.        *Saturday, August 2, 1712*        [ADDISON

Φημὶ πολυχρονίην μελέτην ἔμμεναι, φίλε· καὶ δὴ
Ταύτην ἀνθρώποισι τελευτῶσαν φύσιν εἶναι.

THERE is not a common saying which has a better
turn of sense in it than what we often hear in the
mouths of the vulgar, that custom is a second nature.
It is indeed able to form the man anew, and to give
him inclinations and capacities altogether different
from those he was born with.    Dr Plot, in his History
of Staffordshire [1], tells us of an idiot that chancing
to live within the sound of a clock, and always
amusing himself with counting the hour of the day
whenever the clock struck, the clock being spoiled by
some accident, the idiot continued to strike and count
the hour without the help of it in the same manner
as he had done when it was entire.    Though I dare
not vouch for the truth of this story, it is very certain that custom has a mechanical effect upon the
body, at the same time that it has a very extraordinary influence upon the mind.

I shall in this paper consider one very remarkable
effect which custom has upon human nature, and
which, if rightly observed, may lead us into very
useful rules of life.    What I shall here take notice
of in custom, is its wonderful efficacy in making
everything pleasant to us.    A person who is addicted
to play or gaming, though he took but little delight
in it at first, by degrees contracts so strong an inclination towards it, and gives himself up so entirely
to it, that it seems the only end of his being.    The
love of a retired or a busy life will grow upon a man
insensibly, as he is conversant in the one or the other,
until he is utterly unqualified for relishing that to

[1] *Natural History of Staffordshire*, by Robert Plot, D.C.L., 1686.
Dr Plot, who died in 1696, aged fifty-five, was one of the secretaries of
the Royal Society, first keeper of the Ashmolean Museum. Histori-
ographer-Royal, and Registrar at the Heralds' College.    Plot was
often misled by his informants, and his *Natural History of Staffordshire* contains numerous examples of his credulity.

which he has been for some time disused. Nay, a man may smoke, or drink, or take snuff, until he is unable to pass away his time without it; not to mention how our delight in any particular study, art, or science, rises and improves in proportion to the application which we bestow upon it. Thus what was at first an exercise, becomes at length an entertainment. Our employments are changed into our diversions. The mind grows fond of those actions she is accustomed to, and is drawn with reluctancy from those paths in which she has been used to walk.

Not only such actions as were at first indifferent to us, but even such as were painful, will by custom and practice become pleasant. Sir Francis Bacon observes in his *Natural Philosophy*, that our taste is never pleased better than with those things which at first created a disgust in it. He gives particular instances of claret, coffee, and other liquors, which the palate seldom approves upon the first taste; but when it has once got a relish of them, generally retains it for life. The mind is constituted after the same manner, and after having habituated herself to any particular exercise or employment, not only loses her first aversion towards it, but conceives a certain fondness and affection for it. I have heard one of the greatest geniuses this age has produced [1], who had been trained up in all the polite studies of antiquity, assure me, upon his being obliged to search into several rolls and records, that notwithstanding such an employment was at first very dry and irksome to him, he at last took an incredible pleasure in it, and preferred it even to the reading of Virgil or Cicero. The reader will observe, that I have not here considered custom as it makes things easy, but as it renders them delightful; and though others have often made the same reflections, it is possible they may not have drawn those uses from it, with which I intend to fill the remaining part of this paper.

If we consider attentively this property of human

[1] Atterbury.

nature, it may instruct us in very fine moralities. In the first place, I would have no man discouraged with that kind of life or series of action, in which the choice of others, or his own necessities, may have engaged him. It may perhaps be very disagreeable to him at first; but use and application will certainly render it not only less painful, but pleasing and satisfactory.

In the second place, I would recommend to every one that admirable precept which Pythagoras is said to have given to his disciples, and which that philosopher must have drawn from the observation I have enlarged upon : ' Optimum vitæ genus eligito, nam consuetudo faciet jucundissimum ' (Pitch upon that course of life which is the most excellent, and custom will render it the most delightful) [1]. Men, whose circumstances will permit them to choose their own way of life, are inexcusable if they do not pursue that which their judgment tells them is the most laudable. The voice of reason is more to be regarded than the bent of any present inclination, since, by the rule above mentioned, inclination will at length come over to reason, though we can never force reason to comply with inclination.

In the third place, this observation may teach the most sensual and irreligious man to overlook those hardships and difficulties which are apt to discourage him from the prosecution of a virtuous life. ' The gods ', said Hesiod [2], ' have placed labour before virtue; the way to her is at first rough and difficult, but grows more smooth and easy the further you advance in it '. The man who proceeds in it, with steadiness and resolution, will in a little time find that ' her ways are ways of pleasantness, and that all her paths are peace [3].'

To enforce this consideration, we may further observe, that the practice of religion will not only be attended with that pleasure which naturally accom-

---

[1] *Diogenes Laertius*, book viii.    [2] *Works and Days*, book i.
[3] *Proverbs* iii, 17.

panies those actions to which we are habituated, but with those supernumerary joys of heart that rise from the consciousness of such a pleasure, from the satisfaction of acting up to the dictates of reason, and from the prospect of an happy immortality.

In the fourth place, we may learn from this observation which we have made on the mind of man, to take particular care, when we are once settled in a regular course of life, how we too frequently indulge ourselves in any of the most innocent diversions and entertainments, since the mind may insensibly fall off from the relish of virtuous actions, and, by degrees, exchange that pleasure which it takes in the performance of its duty for delights of a much more inferior and unprofitable nature.

The last use which I shall make of this remarkable property in human nature, of being delighted with those actions to which it is accustomed, is to show how absolutely necessary it is for us to gain habits of virtue in this life, if we would enjoy the pleasures of the next. The state of bliss we call heaven will not be capable of affecting those minds which are not thus qualified for it; we must, in this world, gain a relish of truth and virtue, if we would be able to taste that knowledge and perfection which are to make us happy in the next. The seeds of those spiritual joys and raptures, which are to rise up and flourish in the soul to all eternity, must be planted in her, during this her present state of probation. In short, heaven is not to be looked upon only as the reward, but as the natural effect of a religious life.

On the other hand, those evil spirits, who by long custom have contracted in the body habits of lust and sensuality, malice and revenge, an aversion to everything that is good, just, or laudable, are naturally seasoned and prepared for pain and misery. Their torments have already taken root in them, they cannot be happy when divested of the body, unless we may suppose that Providence will, in a manner, create them anew, and work a miracle in the rectification of their faculties. They may, indeed, taste a kind of malignant pleasure in those actions to which they are accustomed whilst in this life, but when they are removed from all those objects which are here apt to gratify them, they will naturally become their own tormentors, and cherish in themselves those painful habits of mind which are called, in Scripture phrase, the worm which never dies. The notion of heaven and hell is so very comfortable to the light of nature, that it was discovered by several of the most exalted heathens. It has been finely improved by many eminent divines of the last age, as in particular by Archbishop Tillotson and Dr Sherlock, but there is none who has raised such noble speculations upon it as Dr Scott [1], in the first book of his *Christian Life*, which is one of the finest and most rational schemes of divinity that is written in our tongue, or in any other. That excellent author has shown how every particular custom and habit of virtue will, in its own nature, produce the heaven or a state of happiness in him who shall hereafter practise it. As, on the contrary, how every custom or habit of vice will be the natural hell of him in whom it subsists.

C.

No. 448.          *Monday, Aug. 4, 1712*          [STEELE

*Fœdius hoc aliquid quandoque audebis.* Juv., *Sat.* ii, 82

THE first steps towards ill are very carefully to be avoided, for men insensibly go on when they are once entered, and do not keep up a lively abhorrence of the least unworthiness. There is a certain frivolous falsehood that people indulge themselves in, which ought to be had in greater detestation than it commonly meets with. What I mean is a neglect of

[1] John Scott (1639–1695) began life as a tradesman, but was afterwards sent to Oxford, where he became D.D. in 1685. He was minister of St Thomas's, Southwark, Rector of St Giles-in-the-Fields, and Canon of St Paul's. His *Christian Life* was published in 1681, and was a very popular work. A ninth edition appeared in 1712.

promises made on small and indifferent occasions, such as parties of pleasure, entertainments, and sometimes meetings out of curiosity in men of like faculties to be in each other's company. There are many causes to which one may assign this light infidelity. Jack Sippet never keeps the hour he has appointed to come to a friend's to dinner, but he is an insignificant fellow who does it out of vanity. He could never, he knows, make any figure in company, but by giving a little disturbance at his entry, and therefore takes care to drop in when he thinks you are just seated. He takes his place after having discomposed everybody, and desires there may be no ceremony; then does he begin to call himself the saddest fellow, in disappointing so many places as he was invited to elsewhere. It is the fop's vanity to name houses of better cheer, and to acquaint you that he chose yours out of ten dinners which he was obliged to be at that day. The last time I had the fortune to eat with him, he was imagining how very fat he should have been had he eaten all he had ever been invited to. But it is impertinent to dwell upon the manners of such a wretch as obliges all whom he disappoints, though his circumstances constrain them to be civil to him. But there are those that every one would be glad to see, who fall into the same detestable habit. It is a merciless thing that any one can be at ease and suppose a set of people who have a kindness for him, at that moment waiting out of respect to him, and refusing to taste their food or conversation with the utmost impatience. One of these promisers sometimes shall make his excuses for not coming at all, so late that half the company have only to lament that they have neglected matters of moment to meet him whom they find a trifler. They immediately repent for the value they had for him; and such treatment repeated makes company never depend upon his promise any more, so that he often comes at the middle of a meal, where he is secretly slighted by the persons with whom he

eats, and cursed by the servants, whose dinner is
delayed by his prolonging their master's entertainment. It is wonderful that men guilty this way could
never have observed that the whiling time, and
gathering together, and waiting a little before dinner,
is the most awkwardly passed away of any part in
the four and twenty hours. If they did think at all,
they would reflect upon their guilt in lengthening
such a suspension of agreeable life. The constant
offending this way has, in a degree, an effect upon
the honesty of his mind who is guilty of it, as common swearing is a kind of habitual perjury. It makes
the soul inattentive to what an oath is, even while
it utters it at the lips. Phocion beholding a wordy
orator while he was making a magnificent speech to
the people full of vain promises, ' Methinks ', said
he, ' I am now fixing my eyes upon a cypress tree;
it has all the pomp and beauty imaginable in its
branches, leaves, and height, but alas it bears no
fruit.'

Though the expectation which is raised by impertinent promises is thus barren, their confidence, even
after failures, is so great that they subsist by still
promising on. I have heretofore discoursed of the
insignificant liar, the boaster, and the castle-builder [1],
and treated them as no ill-designing men (though
they are to be placed among the frivolously false
ones), but persons who fall into that way purely to
recommend themselves by their vivacities; but indeed
I cannot let heedless promisers, though in the most
minute circumstances, pass with so slight a censure.
If a man should take a resolution to pay only sums
above an hundred pounds, and yet contract with different people debts of five and ten, how long can we
suppose he will keep his credit? This man will as
long support his good name in business, as he will in
conversation who without difficulty makes assignations which he is indifferent whether he keeps or not.

I am the more severe upon this vice, because I

[1] Nos. 136, 167.

have been so unfortunate as to be a very great criminal myself. Sir Andrew Freeport, and all other my friends, who are scrupulous to promises of the meanest consideration imaginable from an habit of virtue that way, have often upbraided me with it. I take shame upon myself for this crime, and more particularly for the greatest I ever committed of the sort, that when as agreeable a company of gentlemen and ladies as ever were got together, and I forsooth, Mr Spectator, to be of the party with women of merit, like a booby as I was, mistook the time of meeting, and came the night following. I wish every fool who is negligent in this kind, may have as great a loss as I had in this; for the same company will never meet more, but are dispersed into various parts of the world, and I am left under the compunction that I deserve, in so many different places to be called a trifler.

This fault is sometimes to be accounted for, when desirable people are fearful of appearing precious and reserved by denials; but they will find the apprehension of that imputation will betray them into a childish impotence of mind, and make them promise all who are so kind to ask it of them. This leads such soft creatures into the misfortune of seeming to return overtures of goodwill with ingratitude. The first steps in the breach of a man's integrity are much more important than men are aware of. The man who scruples breaking his word in little things, would not suffer in his own conscience so great pain for failures of consequence, as he who thinks every little offence against truth and justice a disparagement. We should not make anything we ourselves disapprove habitual to us, if we would be sure of our integrity.

I remember a falsehood of the trivial sort, though not in relation to assignations, that exposed a man to a very uneasy adventure. Will Trap and Jack Stint were chamber-fellows in the Inner Temple about twenty-five years ago. They one night sat in the pit together at a comedy, where they both observed and liked the same young woman in the boxes. Their kindness for her entered both hearts deeper than they imagined. Stint had a good faculty at writing letters of love, and made his address privately that way; while Trap proceeded in the ordinary course, by money and her waiting-maid. The lady gave them both encouragement, receiving Trap into the utmost favour, and answering at the same time Stint's letters, and giving him appointments at third places. Trap began to suspect the epistolary correspondence of his friend, and discovered also that Stint opened all his letters which came to their common lodgings, in order to form his own assignations. After much anxiety and restlessness, Trap came to a resolution, which he thought would break off their commerce with one another without any hazardous explanation. He therefore writ a letter in a feigned hand to Mr Trap at his chambers in the Temple. Stint, according to custom, seized and opened it, and was not a little surprised to find the inside directed to himself, when, with great perturbation of spirit, he read as follows :

MR STINT,—You have gained a slight satisfaction at the expense of doing a very heinous crime. At the price of a faithful friend you have obtained an inconstant mistress. I rejoice in this expedient I have thought of to break my mind to you, and tell you, You are a base fellow, by a means which does not expose you to the affront except you deserve it. I know, sir, as criminal as you are, you have still shame enough to avenge yourself against the hardiness of any one that should publicly tell you of it. I therefore, who have received so many secret hurts from you, shall take satisfaction with safety to myself. I call you base, and you must bear it or acknowledge it; I triumph over you that you cannot come at me; nor do I think it dishonourable to come in armour to assault him, who was in ambuscade when he wounded me.

What need more be said to convince you of being

guilty of the basest practice imaginable, than that it
is such as has made you liable to be treated after this
manner, while you yourself cannot in your own conscience but allow the justice of the upbraidings of

Your injured friend,

T.                                RALPH TRAP

---

No. 449.      *Tuesday, August 5, 1712*      [STEELE

Tibi scriptus, matrona libellus.   MART., Epig. iii, 68

WHEN I reflect upon my labours for the public, I
cannot but observe, that part of the species, of which
I profess myself a friend and guardian, is sometimes
treated with severity; that is, there are in my
writings many descriptions given of ill persons, and
not yet any direct encomium made of those who are
good. When I was convinced of this error, I could
not but immediately call to mind several of the fair
sex of my acquaintance, whose characters deserve to
be transmitted to posterity in writings which will
long outlive mine. But I do not think that a reason
why I should not give them their place in my diurnal
as long as it will last. For the service therefore of
my female readers, I shall single out some characters
of maids, wives, and widows, which deserve the imitation of the sex. She who shall lead this small
illustrious number of heroines shall be the amiable
Fidelia.

Before I enter upon the particular parts of her
character, it is necessary to preface that she is the
only child of a decrepit father, whose life is bound
up in hers. This gentleman has used Fidelia from
her cradle with all the tenderness imaginable, and
has viewed her growing perfections with the partiality
of a parent that soon thought her accomplished above
the children of all other men, but never thought she
was come to the utmost improvement of which she
herself was capable. This fondness has had very
happy effects upon his own happiness, for she reads,

she dances, she sings, uses her spinet and lute to the
utmost perfection : and the lady's use of all these
excellences is to divert the old man in his easy-chair,
when he is out of the pangs of a chronical distemper.
Fidelia is now in the twenty-third year of her age;
but the application of many lovers, her vigorous time
of life, her quick sense of all that is truly gallant and
elegant in the enjoyment of a plentiful fortune, are
not able to draw her from the side of her good old
father. Certain it is, that there is no kind of affection so pure and angelic as that of a father to a
daughter. He beholds her both with and without
regard to her sex. In love to our wives there is
desire, to our sons there is ambition; but in that to
our daughters there is something which there are no
words to express. Her life is designed wholly domestic, and she is so ready a friend and companion, that
everything that passes about a man is accompanied
with the idea of her presence. Her sex also is naturally so much exposed to hazard, both as to fortune
and innocence, that there is perhaps a new cause of
fondness arising from that consideration also. None
but fathers can have a true sense of these sort of
pleasures and sensations; but my familiarity with the
father of Fidelia makes me let drop the words which
I have heard him speak and observe upon his tenderness towards her.

Fidelia on her part, as I was going to say, as accomplished as she is, with all her beauty, wit, air,
and mien, employs her whole time in care and attendance upon her father. How have I been charmed
to see one of the most beauteous women the age has
produced on her knees helping on an old man's slip-
per. Her filial regard to him is what she makes her
diversion, her business, and her glory. When she
was asked by a friend of her deceased mother to admit
of the courtship of her son, she answered, that she
had a great respect and gratitude to her for the overture in behalf of one so near to her, but that during
her father's life she would admit into her heart no

value for anything that should interfere with her
endeavour to make his remains of life as happy and
easy as could be expected in his circumstances. The
lady admonished her of the prime of life with a smile;
which Fidelia answered with a frankness that always
attends unfeigned virtue : ' It is true, madam, there
is to be sure very great satisfactions to be expected
in the commerce of a man of honour whom one tenderly loves : but I find so much satisfaction in the
reflection how much I mitigate a good man's pains,
whose welfare depends upon my assiduity about him,
that I willingly exclude the loose gratifications of
passion for the solid reflections of duty. I know not
whether any man's wife would be allowed, and (what
I still more fear) I know not whether I, a wife, should
be willing to be as officious as I am at present about
my parent.' The happy father has her declaration
that she will not marry during his life, and the pleasure of seeing that resolution not uneasy to her.
Were one to paint filial affection in its utmost beauty,
he could not have a more lively idea of it than in
beholding Fidelia serving her father at his hours of
rising, meals, and rest.

When the general crowd of female youth are consulting their glasses, preparing for balls, assemblies,
or plays; for a young lady, who could be regarded
among the foremost in those places, either for her
person, wit, fortune, or conversation, and yet contemn all these entertainments to sweeten the heavy
hours of a decrepit parent, is a resignation truly
heroic. Fidelia performs the duty of a nurse with
all the beauty of a bride; nor does she neglect her
person because of her attendance on him, when he is
too ill to receive company, to whom she may make an
appearance.

Fidelia, who gives him up her youth, does not
think it any great sacrifice to add to it the spoiling
of her dress. Her care and exactness in her habit
convince her father of the alacrity of her mind; and
she has of all women the best foundation for affecting

the praise of a seeming negligence. What adds to
the entertainment of the good old man is, that
Fidelia, where merit and fortune cannot be overlooked
by epistolary lovers, reads over the accounts of her
conquests, plays on her spinet the gayest airs (and
while she is doing so you would think her formed
only for gallantry), to intimate to him the pleasures
she despises for his sake.

Those who think themselves the patterns of good
breeding and gallantry would be astonished to hear,
that in those intervals when the old gentleman is at
ease and can bear company, there are at his house,
in the most regular order, assemblies of people of the
highest merit; where there is conversation without
mention of the faults of the absent, benevolence between men and women without passion, and the
highest subjects of morality treated of as natural and
accidental discourse; all which is owing to the genius
of Fidelia, who at once makes her father's way to
another world easy, and herself capable of being an
honour to his name in this.

MR SPECTATOR,—I was the other day at the bear-
garden [1], in hopes to have seen your short face; but
not being so fortunate, I must tell you by way of
letter, that there is a mystery among the gladiators
which has escaped your spectatorial penetration. For
being in a box, at an alehouse, near that renowned
seat of honour above mentioned, I overheard two
masters of the science agreeing to quarrel on the next
opportunity. This was to happen in the company of
a set of the fraternity of Basket-Hilts, who were to
meet that evening. When this was settled, one asked
the other, 'Will you give cuts, or receive?' The
other answered, 'Receive'. It was replied, 'Are you
a passionate man?'—'No, provided you cut no more
nor no deeper than we agree.' I thought it my duty
to acquaint you with this, that the people may not pay
their money for fighting and be cheated.

Your humble Servant,

SCABBARD RUSTY

1 See No. 436.

No. 450.        *Wednesday, August 6, 1712*        [STEELE

*Quærenda pecunia primum,*
*Virtus post nummos.*                    HOR., 1 *Ep.* i, 53

MR. SPECTATOR,—All men, through different paths,
make at the same common thing, Money [1]; and it is to
her we owe the politician, the merchant, and the
lawyer; nay, to be free with you, I believe to that
also we are beholden for our *Spectator*. I am apt to
think, that could we look into our own hearts, we
should see money engraved in them in more lively
and moving characters than self-preservation; for who
can reflect upon the merchant hoisting sail in a doubtful pursuit of her, and all mankind sacrificing their
quiet to her, but must perceive that the characters of
self-preservation (which were doubtless originally the
brightest) are sullied, if not wholly defaced; and that
those of money (which at first was only valuable as a
mean to security) are of late so brightened, that the
characters of self-preservation, like a less light set by
a greater, are become almost imperceptible? Thus
has money got the upper hand of what all mankind
formerly thought most dear, viz. security; and I wish
I could say she had here put a stop to her victories;
but, alas! common honesty fell a sacrifice to her. This
is the way scholastic men talk of the greatest good
in the world; but I, a tradesman, shall give you
another account of this matter in the plain narrative
of my own life. I think it proper, in the first place,
to acquaint my readers, that since my setting out in
the world, which was in the year 1660, I never wanted
money; having begun with an indifferent good stock
in the tobacco trade, to which I was bred; and by the
continual successes it has pleased Providence to bless
my endeavours with, am at last arrived at what they
call a plum [2]. To uphold my discourse in the manner
of your wits or philosophers, by speaking fine things,
or drawing inferences, as they pretend, from the nature
of the subject, I account it vain; having never found
anything in the writings of such men, that did not
favour more of the invention of the brain, or what is

[1] See No. 442 (end).                    [2] £100,000.

styled speculation, than of sound judgment, or profitable observation. I will readily grant indeed, that there is what the wits call natural in their talk; which is the utmost those curious authors can assume to themselves, and is indeed all they endeavour at, for they are but lamentable teachers. And what, I pray, is natural? That which is pleasing and easy. And what are pleasing and easy? Forsooth, a new thought or conceit dressed up in smooth quaint language, to make you smile and wag your head, as being what you never imagined before, and yet wonder why you had not; mere frothy amusements! fit only for boys or silly women to be caught with.

It is not my present intention to instruct my readers in the methods of acquiring riches—that may be the work of another essay—but to exhibit the real and solid advantages I have found by them in my long and manifold experience; nor yet all the advantages of so worthy and valuable a blessing (for who does not know or imagine the comforts of being warm or living at ease, and that power and pre-eminence are their inseparable attendants?), but only to instance the great supports they afford us under the severest calamities and misfortunes; to show that the love of them is a special antidote against immorality and vice, and that the same does likewise naturally dispose men to actions of piety and devotion: all which I can make out by my own experience, who think myself no ways particular from the rest of mankind, nor better nor worse by nature than generally other men are.

In the year 1665, when the Sickness was, I lost by it my wife and two children, which were all my stock. Probably I might have had more, considering I was married between four and five years; but finding her to be a teeming woman, I was careful, as having then little above a brace of thousand pounds to carry on my trade and maintain a family with. I loved them as usually men do their wives and children, and therefore could not resist the first impulses of nature on so wounding a loss; but I quickly roused myself, and found means to alleviate, and at last conquer my affliction, by reflecting how that she and her children having been no great expense to me, the best part of her fortune was still left; that my charge being reduced to myself, a journeyman, and a maid, I might live far cheaper than before; and that being now a childless widower, I might perhaps marry a no less deserving woman, and with a much better fortune than she brought, which was but £800. And to convince my readers that such considerations as these were proper and apt to produce such an effect, I remember it was the constant observation at that deplorable time, when so many hundreds were swept away daily, that the rich ever bore the loss of their families and relations far better than the poor; the latter having little or nothing beforehand, and living from hand to mouth, placed the whole comfort and satisfaction of their lives in their wives and children, and were therefore inconsolable.

The following year happened the Fire; at which time, by good Providence, it was my fortune to have converted the greatest part of my effects into ready money, on the prospect of an extraordinary advantage which I was preparing to lay hold on. This calamity was very terrible and astonishing, the fury of the flames being such that whole streets, at several distant places, were destroyed at one and the same time, so that (as it is well known) almost all our citizens were burnt out of what they had. But what did I then do? I did not stand gazing on the ruins of our noble metropolis; I did not shake my head, wring my hands, sigh and shed tears; I considered with myself what could this avail; I fell a plodding what advantages might be made of the ready cash I had, and immediately bethought myself that wonderful pennyworths might be bought of the goods that were saved out of the fire. In short, with about £2000 and a little credit, I bought as much tobacco as raised my estate to the value of £10,000. I then looked on the ashes of our city, and the misery of its late inhabitants, as an effect of the just wrath and indignation of Heaven towards a sinful and perverse people.

After this I married again, and that wife dying, I took another; but both proved to be idle baggages; the first gave me a great deal of plague and vexation by her extravagances, and I became one of the by-words of the city. I knew it would be to no manner of purpose to go about to curb the fancies and inclina-

tions of women, which fly out the more for being
restrained; but what I could I did. I watched her
narrowly, and by good luck found her in the embraces
(for which I had two witnesses with me) of a wealthy
spark of the court-end of the town; of whom I
recovered £15,000, which made me amends for what
she had idly squandered, and put a silence to all my
neighbours, taking off my reproach by the gain they
saw I had by it. The last died about two years after
I married her, in labour of three children. I conjec-
ture they were begotten by a country kinsman of hers,
whom, at her recommendation, I took into my family,
and gave wages to as a journeyman. What this creature expended in delicacies and high diet with her
kinsman (as well as I could compute by the poulterer's,
fishmonger's, and grocer's bills) amounted in the said
two years to one hundred eighty-six pounds, four
shillings, and fivepence halfpenny. The fine apparel,
bracelets, lockets, and treats, &c., of the other, according to the best calculation, came in three years and
about three quarters to seven hundred forty-four
pounds, seven shillings, and ninepence. After this I
resolved never to marry more, and found I had been
a gainer by my marriages, and the damages granted
me for the abuses of my bed (all charges deducted)
eight thousand three hundred pounds within a trifle.

I come now to show the good effects of the love of
money on the lives of men towards rendering them
honest, sober, and religious. When I was a young
man I had a mind to make the best of my wits, and
overreached a country chap in a parcel of unsound
goods; to whom upon his upbraiding, and threatening
to expose me for it, I returned the equivalent of his
loss; and upon his good advice, wherein he clearly
demonstrated the folly of such artifices, which can
never end but in shame, and the ruin of all correspondence, I never after transgressed. Can your courtiers, who take bribes, or your lawyers or physicians
in their practice, or even the divines who intermeddle
in worldly affairs, boast of making but one slip in their
lives, and of such a thorough and lasting reformation?
Since my coming into the world I do not remember I
was ever overtaken in drink, save nine times, one at
the christening of my first child, thrice at our city
feasts, and five times at driving of bargains. My refor-

mation I can attribute to nothing so much as the love and esteem of money, for I found myself to be extravagant in my drink, and apt to turn projector, and make rash bargains. As for women, I never knew any, except my wives : for my reader must know, and it is what he may confide in as an excellent recipe, that the love of business and money is the greatest mortifier of inordinate desires imaginable, as employing the mind continually in the careful oversight of what one has, in the eager quest after more, in looking after the negligences and deceits of servants, in the due entering and stating of accounts, in hunting after chaps¹, and in the exact knowledge of the state of markets; which things whoever thoroughly attends, will find enough and enough to employ his thoughts on every moment of the day; so that I cannot call to mind, that in all the time I was a husband, which, off and on, was about twelve years, I ever once thought of my wives but in bed. And, lastly, for religion, I have ever been a constant churchman, both forenoons and afternoons on Sundays, never forgetting to be thankful for any gain or advantage I had had that day; and on Saturday nights, upon casting up my accounts, I always was grateful for the sum of my week's profits, and at Christmas for that of the whole year. It is true, perhaps, that my devotion has not been the most fervent; which, I think, ought to be imputed to the evenness and sedateness of my temper, which never would admit of any impetuosities of any sort : and I can remember, that in my youth and prime of manhood, when my blood ran brisker, I took greater pleasure in religious exercises than at present, or many years past, and that my devotion sensibly declined as age, which is dull and unwieldy, came upon me.

I have, I hope, here proved that the love of money prevents all immorality and vice; which if you will not allow, you must, that the pursuit of it obliges men to the same kind of life as they would follow if they were really virtuous : which is all I have to say at present, only recommending to you, that you would think of it, and turn ready wit into ready money as fast as you can. I conclude,

Your Servant,

T.                                        EPHRAIM WEED

¹ Chapmen, purchasers.

No. 451.     *Thursday, August 7, 1712*     [ADDISON

*Jam sævus apertam
In rabiem cœpit verti jocus, et per honestas
Ire domos impune minax.*

HOR., 2 *Ep.* i, 148

THERE is nothing so scandalous to a government, and detestable in the eyes of all good men, as defamatory papers and pamphlets; but at the same time there is nothing so difficult to tame as a satirical author. An angry writer, who cannot appear in print, naturally vents his spleen in libels and lampoons. A gay old woman, says the fable, seeing all her wrinkles represented in a large looking-glass, threw it upon the ground in a passion, and broke it into a thousand pieces; but as she was afterwards surveying the fragments with a spiteful kind of pleasure, she could not forbear uttering herself in the following soliloquy: 'What have I got by this revengeful blow of mine! I have only multiplied my deformity, and see an hundred ugly faces, where before I saw but one.'

It has been proposed, to oblige every person that writes a book, or a paper, to swear himself the author of it, and enter down in a public register his name and place of abode.

This, indeed, would have effectually suppressed all printed scandal, which generally appears under borrowed names, or under none at all. But it is to be feared that such an expedient would not only destroy scandal, but learning. It would operate promiscuously, and root up the corn and tares together. Not to mention some of the most celebrated works of piety, which have proceeded from anonymous authors, who have made it their merit to convey to us so great a charity in secret, there are few works of genius that come out at first with the author's name. The writer generally makes a trial of them in the world before he owns them; and, I believe, very few who are capable of writing would set pen to paper, if they knew beforehand that they must not publish their productions on such such conditions. For my own part, I must declare the papers I present the public are like fairy favours, which shall last no longer than while the author is concealed.

That which makes it particularly difficult to restrain these sons of calumny and defamation is, that all sides are equally guilty of it, and that every dirty scribbler is countenanced by great names, whose interests he propagates by such vile and infamous methods. I have never yet heard of a ministry, who have inflicted an exemplary punishment on an author that has supported their cause with falsehood and scandal, and treated in a most cruel manner the names of those who have been looked upon as their rivals and antagonists. Would a government set an everlasting mark of their displeasure upon one of those infamous writers, who makes his court to them by tearing to pieces the reputation of a competitor, we should quickly see an end put to this race of vermin, that are a scandal to government, and a reproach to human nature. Such a proceeding would make a minister of state shine in history, and would fill all mankind with a just abhorrence of persons who should treat him unworthily, and employ against him those arms which he scorned to make use of against his enemies.

I cannot think that any one will be so unjust as to imagine what I have here said is spoken with a respect to any party or faction. Every one who has in him the sentiments either of a Christian or a gentleman cannot but be highly offended at this wicked and ungenerous practice, which is so much in use among us at present that it is become a kind of national crime, and distinguishes us from all the governments that lie about us. I cannot but look upon the finest strokes of satire which are aimed at particular persons, and which are supported even with the appearances of truth, to be the marks of an evil mind and highly criminal in themselves. Infamy, like other punishments, is under the direction and distribution of the magistrate, and not of any private person. Accordingly we learn from a fragment of Cicero [1], that though there were very few capital punishments in the twelve tables, a libel or lampoon which took away the good name of another was to be punished by death. But this is far from being our case. Our satire is nothing but ribaldry and Billingsgate. Scurrility passes for wit; and he who can call names in the greatest variety of phrases is looked upon to have the shrewdest pen. By this means the honour of families is ruined, the highest posts and greatest titles are rendered cheap and vile in the sight of the people; the noblest virtues and most exalted parts exposed to the contempt of the vicious and the ignorant. Should a foreigner, who knows nothing of our private factions, or one who is to act his part in the world, when our present heats and animosities are forgot—should, I say, such an one form to himself a notion of the greatest men of all sides in the British nation, who are now living, from the characters which are given them in some or other of those abominable writings which are daily published among us, what a nation of monsters must we appear!

As this cruel practice tends to the utter subversion of all truth and humanity among us, it deserves the utmost detestation and discouragement of all who have either the love of their country or the honour of their religion at heart. I would therefore earnestly recommend it to the consideration of those who deal in these pernicious arts of writing, and of those who take pleasure in the reading of them. As for the first, I have spoken of them in former papers, and have not stuck to rank them with the murderer and assassin. Every honest man sets as high a value upon a good name as upon life itself; and I cannot but think that those who privily assault the one would destroy the other, might they do it with the same secrecy and impunity.

As for persons who take pleasure in the reading

[1] *De Republica,* iv, 10.

and dispersing of such detestable libels, I am afraid they fall very far short of the guilt of the first composers.　By a law of the emperors Valentinian and Valens, it was made death for any person not only to write a libel, but if he met with one by chance, not to tear or burn it.　But because I would not be thought singular in my opinion of this matter, I shall conclude my paper with the words of Monsieur Bayle, who was a man of great freedom of thought, as well as of exquisite learning and judgment :

I cannot imagine that a man who disperses a libel is less desirous of doing mischief than the author himself.　But what shall we say of the pleasure which a man takes in the reading of a defamatory libel? Is it not an heinous sin in the sight of God? We must distinguish in this point.　This pleasure is either an agreeable sensation we are affected with, when we meet with a witty thought which is well expressed, or it is a joy which we conceive from the dishonour of the person who is defamed.　I will say nothing to the first of these cases ; for perhaps some would think that my morality is not severe enough if I should affirm that a man is not master of those agreeable sensations, any more than of those occasioned by sugar or honey when they touch his tongue ; but as to the second, every one will own that pleasure to be a heinous sin.　The pleasure in the first case is of no continuance ; it prevents [1] our reason and reflection, and may be immediately followed by a secret grief to see our neighbour's honour blasted.　If it does not cease immediately, it is a sign that we are not displeased with the ill-nature of the satirist, but are glad to see him defame his enemy by all kinds of stories ; and then we deserve the punishment to which the writer of the libel is subject.　I shall here add the words of a modern author : 'St Gregory, upon excommunicating those writers who had dishonoured Castorius, does not except those who read their works, because, says he, if calumnies have always been the delight of the hearers, and a gratification of those persons who have no other advantage over honest men, is not he who takes pleasure

---

[1] Anticipates.

in reading them as guilty as he who composed them?'
It is an incontested maxim, that they who approve an
action would certainly do it if they could; that is, if
some reason of self-love did not hinder them. There
is no difference, says Cicero, between advising a crime
and approving it when committed. The Roman law
confirmed this maxim, having subjected the approvers
and authors of this evil to the same penalty. We may
therefore conclude, that those who are pleased with
reading defamatory libels, so far as to approve the
authors and dispersers of them, are as guilty as if they
had composed them; for if they do not write such libels
themselves, it is because they have not the talent of
writing, or because they will run no hazard [1].

The author produces other authorities to confirm
his judgment in this particular.                C.


No. 452.     *Friday, August 8, 1712*     [ADDISON

*Est natura hominum novitatis avida.*
                    PLIN. *apud Lillium*

THERE is no humour in my countrymen which I
am more inclined to wonder at, than their general
thirst after news. There are about half-a-dozen ingenious men, who live very plentifully upon this
curiosity of their fellow-subjects. They all of them
receive the same advices from abroad, and very often
in the same words; but their way of cooking it is so
different, that there is no citizen, who has an eye to
the public good, that can leave the coffee-house with
peace of mind, before he has given every one of them
a reading. These several dishes of news are so very
agreeable to the palate of my countrymen, that they
are not only pleased with them when they are served
up hot, but when they are again set cold before them,
by those penetrating politicians who oblige the public
with their reflections and observations upon every
piece of intelligence that is sent us from abroad. The

_____
[1] *Dissertation upon Defamatory Libels*, sec. 17.

text is given us by one set of writers, and the comment by another.

But notwithstanding we have the same tale told us in so many different papers, and if occasion requires in so many articles of the same paper; notwithstanding in a scarcity of foreign posts we hear the same story repeated, by different advices from Paris, Brussels, the Hague, and from every great town in Europe; notwithstanding the multitude of annotations, explanations, reflections, and various readings which it passes through, our time lies heavy on our hands till the arrival of a fresh mail. We long to receive further particulars, to hear what will be the next step, or what will be the consequences of that which has been already taken. A westerly wind keeps the whole town in suspense, and puts a stop to conversation.

This general curiosity has been raised and inflamed by our late wars, and, if rightly directed, might be of good use to a person who has such a thirst awakened in him. Why should not a man, who takes delight in reading everything that is new, apply himself to history, travels, and other writings of the same kind, where he will find perpetual fuel for his curiosity, and meet with much more pleasure and improvement, than in these papers of the week? An honest tradesman, who languishes a whole summer in expectation of a battle, and perhaps is balked at last, may here meet with half-a-dozen in a day. He may read the news of a whole campaign, in less time than he now bestows upon the products of any single post. Fights, conquests, and revolutions lie thick together. The reader's curiosity is raised and satisfied every moment, and his passions disappointed or gratified, without being detained in a state of uncertainty from day to day, or lying at the mercy of sea and wind. In short, the mind is not here kept in a perpetual gape after knowledge, nor punished with that eternal thirst, which is the portion of all our modern newsmongers and coffee-house politicians.

All matters of fact, which a man did not know before, are news to him; and I do not see how any haberdasher in Cheapside is more concerned in the present quarrel of the Cantons, than he was in that of the League. At least, I believe every one will allow me, it is of more importance to an Englishman to know the history of his ancestors, than that of his contemporaries, who live upon the banks of the Danube or the Borysthenes. As for those who are of another mind, I shall recommend to them the following letter, from a projector, who is willing to turn a penny by this remarkable curiosity of his countrymen :

MR SPECTATOR,—You must have observed, that men who frequent coffee-houses, and delight in news, are pleased with everything that is matter of fact, so it be what they have not heard before. A victory or a defeat are equally agreeable to them. The shutting of a cardinal's mouth pleases them one post, and the opening of it another. They are glad to hear the French court is removed to Marli, and are afterwards as much delighted with its return to Versailles. They read the advertisements with the same curiosity as the articles of public news; and are as pleased to hear of a piebald horse that is strayed out of a field near Islington, as of a whole troop that has been engaged in any foreign adventure. In short, they have a relish for everything that is news, let the matter of it be what it will ; or to speak more properly, they are men of a voracious appetite, but no taste. Now, sir, since the great fountain of news, I mean the war, is very near being dried up ; and since these gentlemen have contracted such an inextinguishable thirst after it, I have taken their case and my own into consideration, and have thought of a project which may turn to the advantage of us both. I have thoughts of publishing a daily paper, which shall comprehend in it all the most remarkable occurrences in every little town, village, and hamlet that lie within ten miles of London, or in other words, within the verge of the penny post. I have pitched upon this scene of intelligence for two reasons ; first, because the carriage of letters will be very cheap ; and secondly, because I may receive them every day. By this means

my readers will have their news fresh and fresh, and
many worthy citizens, who cannot sleep with any satisfaction at present, for want of being informed how the
world goes, may go to bed contentedly, it being my
design to put out my paper every night at nine o'clock
precisely. I have already established correspondences
in these several places, and received very good intelligence.

By my last advices from Knightsbridge, I hear that
a horse was clapped into the pound on the third
instant, and that he was not released when the letters
came away.

We are informed from Pankridge[1], that a dozen
weddings were lately celebrated in the mother-church
of that place, but are referred to their next letters
for the names of the parties concerned.

Letters from Brompton advise, that the widow Blight
had received several visits from John Milldew, which
affords great matter of speculation in those parts.

By a fisherman which lately touched at Hammer-
smith, there is advice from Putney that a certain
person well known in that place, is like to lose his
election for churchwarden; but this being boat news,
we cannot give entire credit to it.

Letters from Paddington bring little more than that
William Squeak, the sow-gelder, passed through that
place the fifth instant.

They advise from Fulham, that things remained there
in the same state they were. They had intelligence,
just as the letters came away, of a tub of excellent
ale just set abroach at Parson's Green; but this wanted
confirmation.

I have here, sir, given you a specimen of the news
with which I intend to entertain the town, and which,
when drawn up regularly in the form of a newspaper,
will, I doubt not, be very acceptable to many of those
public-spirited readers, who take more delight in
acquainting themselves with other people's business
than their own. I hope a paper of this kind, which
lets us know what is done near home, may be more
useful to us than those which are filled with advices
from Zug and Bender, and make some amends for
that dearth of intelligence which we may justly apprehend from times of peace. If I find that you receive

[1] St. Pancras (*Pancratium*).

this project favourably, I will shortly trouble you with one or two more; and in the meantime am, most worthy sir, with all due respect,

Your most obedient,

C.                    And most humble Servant

No. 453.        *Saturday, August 9, 1712*        [ADDISON

*Non usitatâ nec tenui ferar*
*Pennâ.*                    HOR., 2 *Od.* xx, 1

THERE is not a more pleasing exercise of the mind than gratitude. It is accompanied with such an inward satisfaction, that the duty is sufficiently rewarded by the performance. It is not like the practice of many other virtues, difficult and painful, but attended with so much pleasure, that were there no positive command which enjoined it, nor any recompense laid up for it hereafter, a generous mind would indulge in it for the natural gratification that accompanies it.

If gratitude is due from man to man, how much more from man to his Maker? The Supreme Being does not only confer upon us those bounties which proceed more immediately from His hand, but even those benefits which are conveyed to us by others. Every blessing we enjoy, by what means soever it may be derived upon us, is the gift of Him who is the great Author of good and Father of mercies.

If gratitude, when exerted towards one another, naturally produces a very pleasing sensation in the mind of a grateful man, it exalts the soul into rapture when it is employed on this great object of gratitude, on this beneficent Being who has given us everything we already possess, and from whom we expect everything we yet hope for.

Most of the works of the pagan poets were either direct hymns to their deities, or tended indirectly to the celebration of their respective attributes and perfections. Those who are acquainted with the works of the Greek and Latin poets which are still extant,

will upon reflection find this observation so true, that
I shall not enlarge upon it.  One would wonder that
more of our Christian poets have not turned their
thoughts this way, especially if we consider that our
idea of the Supreme Being is not only infinitely more
great and noble than what could possibly enter into
the heart of an heathen, but filled with everything
that can raise the imagination, and give an opportunity for the sublimest thoughts and conceptions.

Plutarch tells us of a heathen who was singing an
hymn to Diana, in which he celebrated her for her
delight in human sacrifices, and other instances of
cruelty and revenge; upon which a poet who was
present at this piece of devotion, and seems to have
had a truer idea of the Divine Nature, told the
votary by way of reproof, that in recompense for his
hymn, he heartily wished he might have a daughter
of the same temper with the goddess he celebrated.
It was indeed impossible to write the praises of one
of those false deities, according to the pagan creed,
without a mixture of impertinence and absurdity.

The Jews, who before the times of Christianity
were the only people that had the knowledge of the
true God, have set the Christian world an example
how they ought to employ this divine talent of which
I am speaking.  As that nation produced men of
great genius, without considering them as inspired
writers, they have transmitted to us many hymns
and divine odes, which excel those that are delivered
down to us by the ancient Greeks and Romans in
the poetry, as much as in the subject to which it
was consecrated.  This I think might easily be shown,
if there were occasion for it.

I have already communicated to the public some
pieces of divine poetry, and as they have met with
a very favourable reception, I shall from time to
time publish any work of the same nature which has
not yet appeared in print, and may be acceptable to
my readers [1].

[1] This hymn is by Addison himself.  In 1776 Captain Thompson

### I

When all Thy mercies, oh my God,
　My rising soul surveys,
Transported with the view, I'm lost
　In wonder, love, and praise.

### II

Oh how shall words with equal warmth
　The gratitude declare
That glows within my ravished heart !
　But Thou canst read it there.

### III

Thy Providence my life sustained
　And all my wants redrest,
When in the silent womb I lay,
　And hung upon the breast.

### IV

To all my weak complaints and cries
　Thy mercy lent an ear,
Ere yet my feeble thoughts had learnt
　To form themselves in prayer.

### V

Unnumbered comforts to my soul
　Thy tender care bestowed,
Before my infant heart conceived
　From whom those comforts flowed.

### VI

When in the slippery paths of youth
　With heedless steps I ran,
Thine arm unseen conveyed me safe
　And led me up to man ;

### VII

Through hidden dangers, toils, and deaths,
　It gently cleared my way,
And through the pleasing snares of vice,
　More to be feared than they.

### VIII

When worn with sickness oft hast Thou
　With health renewed my face,
And when in sins and sorrows sunk
　Revived my soul with grace.

---

claimed it (together with the hymns in Nos. 461 and 465) for Marvell,
on the ground that he found the lines in a MS. commonplace book
which contained some verses in Marvell's handwriting. Evidently
these hymns had been added by a subsequent owner of the volume.

### IX

Thy bounteous hand with worldly bliss
    Has made my cup run o'er,
And in a kind and faithful Friend
    Has doubled all my store.

### X

Ten thousand thousand precious gifts
    My daily thanks employ :
Nor is the least a cheerful heart,
    That takes those gifts with joy.

### XI

Through every period of my life
    Thy goodness I'll pursue,
And after death in distant worlds
    The glorious theme renew.

### XII

When nature fails, and day and night
    Divide Thy works no more,
My ever-grateful heart, O Lord,
    Thy mercy shall adore.

### XIII

Through all eternity to Thee
    A joyful song I'll raise,
For oh ! eternity's too short
    To utter all Thy praise.

C.

No. 454.    *Monday, August 11, 1712*    [STEELE

*Sine me, vacivom tempus ne quod duim mihi
Laboris.*                    TER., *Heaut.*, Act i, sc. 1

IT is an inexpressible pleasure to know a little of
the world, and be of no character or significancy in
it.  To be ever unconcerned, and ever looking on
new objects with an endless curiosity, is a delight
known only to those who are turned for speculation :
nay, they who enjoy it must value things only as
they are the objects of speculation, without drawing
any worldly advantage to themselves from them, but
just as they are what contribute to their amusement,
or the improvement of the mind.  I lay one night
last week at Richmond ; and being restless, not out
of dissatisfaction, but a certain busy inclination one
sometimes has, I arose at four in the morning, and

took boat for London, with a resolution to rove by
boat and coach for the next four and twenty hours,
till the many different objects I must needs meet
with should tire my imagination, and give me an
inclination to a repose more profound than I was at
that time capable of. I beg people's pardon for an
odd humour I am guilty of, and was often that day,
which is saluting any person whom I like, whether
I know him or not. This is a particularity would be
tolerated in me, if they considered that the greatest
pleasure I know I receive at my eyes, and that I am
obliged to an agreeable person for coming abroad into
my view, as another is for the visit of conversation
at their own houses.

The hours of the day and night are taken up in
the cities of London and Westminster by people as
different from each other as those who are born in
different centuries. Men of six o'clock give way to
those of nine, they of nine to the generation of twelve,
and they of twelve disappear, and make room for the
fashionable world, who have made two o'clock the
noon of the day.

When we first put off from shore, we soon fell in
with a fleet of gardeners bound for the several market-
ports of London; and it was the most pleasing scene
imaginable to see the cheerfulness with which those
industrious people plied their way to a certain sale
of their goods. The banks on each side are as well
peopled, and beautified with as agreeable plantations,
as any spot on the earth; but the Thames itself,
loaded with the product of each shore, added very
much to the landscape. It was very easy to observe
by their sailing, and the countenances of the ruddy
virgins who were supercargoes, the parts of the town
to which they were bound. There was an air in the
purveyors for Covent Garden, who frequently converse
with morning rakes, very unlike the seemly sobriety
of those bound for Stocks Market [1].

[1] A market for fish and meat, on the site of the present Mansion
House. After the Great Fire, however, it was converted into a market

Nothing remarkable happened in our voyage; but I landed with ten sail of apricot boats at Strand Bridge, after having put in at Nine Elms, and taken in melons, consigned by Mr Cuffe of that place, to Sarah Sewell & Company, at their stall in Covent Garden. We arrived at Strand Bridge [1] at six of the clock, and were unloading; when the hackney-coachmen of the foregoing night took their leave of each other at the Dark House [2], to go to bed before the day was too far spent. Chimney-sweepers passed by us as we made up to the market, and some raillery happened between one of the fruit-wenches and those black men, about the devil and Eve, with allusion to their several professions. I could not believe any place more entertaining than Covent Garden, where I strolled from one fruit-shop to another, with crowds of agreeable young women around me, who were purchasing fruit for their respective families. It was almost eight of the clock before I could leave that variety of objects. I took coach and followed a young lady, who tripped into another just before me, attended by her maid. I saw immediately she was of the family of the Vainloves. There are a set of these, who of all things affect the play of Blind-man's Buff, and leading men into love for they know not whom, who are fled they know not where. This sort of woman is usually a jaunty slattern; she hangs on her clothes, plays her head, varies her posture, and changes place incessantly; and all with an appearance of striving at the same time to hide herself, and yet give you to understand she is in humour to laugh at you. You must have often seen the coachmen make signs with their fingers as they drive by each other, to intimate how much they have got that day. They can carry on that language to give intelligence where they are driving. In an instant my coachman took

for fruit and vegetables. A pair of stocks had been erected near this spot as early as the thirteenth century. See also No. 462.

[1] At the foot of Strand Lane.

[2] Another 'Dark House', at Billingsgate, is mentioned, as M Dobson points out, in Hogarth's *Five Days' Peregrination*.

the wink to pursue, and the lady's driver gave the hint that he was going through Long Acre towards St James's : while he whipped up St James Street [1], we drove for King Street, to save the pass at St Martin's Lane. The coachmen took care to meet, jostle, and threaten each other for way, and be entangled at the end of Newport Street and Long Acre. The fright, you must believe, brought down the lady's coach door, and obliged her, with her mask off, to inquire into the bustle, when she sees the man she would avoid. The tackle of the coach window is so bad she cannot draw it up again, and she drives on sometimes wholly discovered, and sometimes half escaped, according to the accident of carriages in her way. One of these ladies keeps her seat in an hackney coach as well as the best rider does on a managed horse. The laced shoe on her left foot, with a careless gesture, just appearing on the opposite cushion, held her both firm and in a proper attitude to receive the next jolt.

As she was an excellent coachwoman, many were the glances at each other which we had for an hour and a half in all parts of the town by the skill of our drivers; till at last my lady was conveniently lost with notice from her coachman to ours to make off, and he should hear where she went. This chase was now at an end, and the fellow who drove her came to us, and discovered that he was ordered to come again in an hour, for that she was a silkworm. I was surprised with this phrase, but found it was a cant among the hackney fraternity for their best customers, women who ramble twice or thrice a week from shop to shop, to turn over all the goods in town without buying anything. The silkworms are, it seems, indulged by the tradesmen; for though they never buy, they are ever talking of new silks, laces, and ribands, and serve the owners in getting them customers, as their common dunners do in making them pay.

[1] A turning out of the Great Piazza, Covent Garden.

The day of people of fashion began now to break, and carts and hacks were mingled with equipages of show and vanity; when I resolved to walk it out of cheapness; but my unhappy curiosity is such, that I find it always my interest to take coach, for some odd adventure among beggars, ballad-singers, or the like, detains and throws me into expense. It happened so immediately; for at the corner of Warwick Street, as I was listening to a new ballad, a ragged rascal, a beggar who knew me, came up to me, and began to turn the eyes of the good company upon me, by telling me he was extreme poor, and should die in the streets for want of drink, except I immediately would have the charity to give him sixpence to go into the next alehouse and save his life. He urged, with a melancholy face, that all his family had died of thirst. All the mob have humour, and two or three began to take the jest; by which Mr Sturdy carried his point, and let me sneak off to a coach. As I drove along, it was a pleasing reflection to see the world so prettily chequered since I left Richmond, and the scene still filling with children of a new hour. This satisfaction increased as I moved towards the city; and gay signs, well-disposed streets, magnificent public structures, and wealthy shops, adorned with contented faces, made the joy still rising till we came into the centre of the City, and centre of the world of trade, the Exchange of London. As other men in the crowds about me were pleased with their hopes and bargains, I found my account in observing them, in attention to their several interests. I, indeed, looked upon myself as the richest man that walked the Exchange that day; for my benevolence made me share the gains of every bargain that was made. It was not the least of the satisfactions in my survey, to go upstairs, and pass the shops of agreeable females [1]; to observe so many pretty hands busy

1 The Royal Exchange of Steele's day (see No. 69) had an upper storey, for the sale of fancy goods, ribbons, gloves, &c. Thomas Heywood described the similar arrangements in the earlier building, destroyed at the Fire of London, in his *Fair Maid of the Exchange*, 1607.

in the foldings of ribands, and the utmost eagerness
of agreeable faces in the sale of patches, pins, and
wires, on each side the counters, was an amusement
in which I should longer have indulged myself, had
not the dear creatures called to me to ask what I
wanted, when I could not answer only ' To look at
you '.  I went to one of the windows which opened
to the area below, where all the several voices lost
their distinction, and rose up in a confused humming;
which created in me a reflection that could not come
into the mind of any but of one a little too studious;
for I said to myself, with a kind of pun in thought,
' What nonsense is all the hurry of this world to those
who are above it?'  In these or not much wiser
thoughts I had like to have lost my place at the chop-
house; where every man, according to the natural
bashfulness or sullenness of our nation, eats in a
public room a mess of broth, or chop of meat, in dumb
silence, as if they had no pretence to speak to each
other on the foot of being men, except they were of
each other's acquaintance.

I went afterwards to Robin's [1], and saw people who
had dined with me at the fivepenny ordinary just
before, give bills for the value of large estates; and
could not but behold with great pleasure, property
lodged in, and transferred in a moment from such
as would never be masters of half as much as is
seemingly in them, and given from them every day
they live.  But before five in the afternoon I left the
City, came to my common scene of Covent Garden,
and passed the evening at Will's in attending the discourses of several sets of people, who relieved each
other within my hearing on the subjects of cards,
dice, love, learning, and politics.  The last subject
kept me till I heard the streets in the possession of
the bellman, who had now the world to himself, and
cried, ' Past two of clock '.  This roused me from
my seat, and I went to my lodging, led by a light,
whom I put into the discourse of his private economy,

[1] A coffee-house in Exchange Alley.

and made him give me an account of the charge, hazard, profit, and loss of a family that depended upon a link, with a design to end my trivial day with the generosity of sixpence, instead of a third part of that sum.   When I came to my chamber I writ down these minutes; but was at a loss what instruction I should propose to my reader from the enumeration of so many insignificant matters and occurrences; and I thought it of great use, if they could learn with me to keep their minds open to gratification, and ready to receive it from anything it meets with.   This one circumstance will make every face you see give you the satisfaction you now take in beholding that of a friend; will make every object a pleasing one; will make all the good which arrives to any man, an increase of happiness to yourself.                            T.


No. 455.    *Tuesday, August 12, 1712*        [STEELE

*Ego apis Matinæ
More modoque
Grata carpentis thyma per laborem
Plurimum.*                              Hor., 4 Od. ii, 27

THE following letters have in them reflections, which will seem of importance both to the learned world and to domestic life.   There is in the first an allegory so well carried on, that it cannot but be very pleasing to those who have a taste of good writing; and the other billets may have their use in common life :

MR SPECTATOR,—As I walked t'other day in a fine garden, and observed the great variety of improvements in plants and flowers beyond what they otherwise would have been, I was naturally led into a reflection upon the advantages of education, or modern culture; how many good qualities in the mind are lost for want of the like due care in nursing and skilfully managing them; how many virtues are choked by the multitude of weeds which are suffered to grow among them; how excellent parts are often starved and useless by being

planted in a wrong soil ; and how very seldom do these
moral seeds produce the noble fruits which might be
expected from them, by a neglect of proper manuring,
necessary pruning, and an artful management of our
tender inclinations and first spring of life.  These
obvious speculations made me at length conclude, that
there is a sort of vegetable principle in the mind of
every man when he comes into the world.  In infants
the seeds lie buried and undiscovered, until after a
while they sprout forth in a kind of rational leaves,
which are words ; and in a due season the flowers begin
to appear in variety of beautiful colours, and all the
gay pictures of youthful fancy and imagination; at
last the fruit knits and is formed, which is green perhaps first, and sour, unpleasant to the taste, and not
fit to be gathered; until ripened by due care and
application, it discovers itself in all the noble productions of philosophy, mathematics, close reasoning,
and handsome argumentation.  And these fruits, when
they arrive at a just maturity and are of a good kind
afford the most vigorous nourishment to the minds of
men.  I reflected further on the intellectual leaves
before mentioned, and found almost as great a variety
among them as in the vegetable world.  I could easily
observe the smooth shining Italian leaves ; the nimble
French aspen, always in motion; the Greek and Latin
evergreens, the Spanish myrtle, the English oak, the
Scotch thistle, the Irish shamrock, the prickly German and Dutch holly, the Polish and Russian nettle,
besides a vast number of exotics imported from Asia,
Africa, and America.  I saw several barren plants
which bore only leaves, without any hopes of flower
or fruit.  The leaves of some were fragrant and well
shaped, of others ill scented and irregular.  I wondered
at a set of old whimsical botanists, who spent their
whole lives in the contemplation of some withered
Egyptian, Coptic, Armenian, or Chinese leaves, while
others made it their business to collect in voluminous
herbals all the several leaves of some one tree.  The
flowers afforded a most diverting entertainment, in a
wonderful variety of figures, colours, and scents;
however, most of them withered soon, or at best are
but annuals.  Some professed florists make them their
constant study and employment, and despise all fruit;

and now and then a few fanciful people spend all their time in the cultivation of a single tulip or a carnation. But the most agreeable amusement seems to be the well choosing, mixing, and binding together these flowers in pleasing nosegays to present to ladies. The scent of Italian flowers is observed, like their other perfume, to be too strong and to hurt the brain; that of the French with glaring, gaudy colours, yet faint and languid; German and Northern flowers have little or no smell, or sometimes an unpleasant one. The ancients had a secret to give a lasting beauty, colour, and sweetness to some of their choice flowers, which flourish to this day, and which few of the moderns can effect. These are becoming enough and agreeable in their season, and do often handsomely adorn an entertainment; but an over-fondness of them seems to be a disease. It rarely happens to find a plant vigorous enough to have (like an orange tree) at once beautiful shining leaves, fragrant flowers, and delicious nourishing fruit.

Sir, Yours, &c.

August 6, 1712

DEAR SPEC.,—You have given us in your *Spectator* of Saturday last[1] a very excellent discourse upon the force of custom, and its wonderful efficacy in making everything pleasant to us. I cannot deny but that I received above two pennyworth of instruction from your paper, and in the general was very well pleased with it; but I am, without a compliment, sincerely troubled that I cannot exactly be of your opinion, that it makes everything pleasant to us. In short, I have the honour to be yoked to a young lady who is, in plain English, for her standing a very eminent scold. She began to break her mind very freely, both to me and to her servants, about two months after our nuptials; and though I have been accustomed to this humour of hers this three years, yet I do not know what's the matter with me, but I am no more delighted with it than I was at the very first. I have advised with her relations about her, and they all tell me that her mother, and her grandmother before her, were

[1] No. 447.

both taken much after the same manner; so that since it runs in the blood, I have but small hopes of her recovery. I should be glad to have a little of your advice in this matter. I would not willingly trouble you to contrive how it may be a pleasure to me; if you will but put me in a way that I may bear it with indifference, I shall rest satisfied.

Dear Spec.,<br>Your very humble Servant

*P.S.*—I must do the poor girl the justice to let you know that this match was none of her own choosing (or indeed of mine either), in consideration of which I avoid giving her the least provocation; and indeed we live better together than usually folks do, who hated one another when they were first joined. To evade the sin against parents, or at least to extenuate it, my dear rails at my father and mother, and I curse hers for making the match.

MR SPECTATOR,—I like the theme you lately gave out extremely [1], and should be as glad to handle it as any man living. But I find myself no better qualified to write about money than about my wife; for, to tell you a secret, which I desire may go no further, I am master of neither of those subjects.

Yours,

*Aug.* 8, 1712                    PILL GARLICK

MR SPECTATOR,—I desire you would print this in italic, so as it may be generally taken notice of. It is designed only to admonish all persons who speak either at the Bar, pulpit, or any public assembly whatsoever, how they discover their ignorance in the use of similes. There are in the pulpit itself, as well as other places, such gross abuses in this kind, that I give this warning to all I know. I shall bring them for the future before your Spectatorial authority. On Sunday last, one, who shall be nameless, reproving several of his congregation for standing at prayers, was pleased to say, ' One would think (like the elephant) you had no knees.' Now I

---

1 See Nos. 442, 450.

myself saw an elephant in Bartholomew Fair kneel down to take on his back the ingenious Mr William Pinkethman[1].

T.                    Your most humble Servant


No. 456.   *Wednesday, August 13, 1712*   [STEELE

*De quo libelli in celeberrimis locis proponuntur, huic ne perire quidem tacite conceditur.* TULL.

OTWAY, in his tragedy of *Venice Preserved*, has described the misery of a man whose effects are in the hands of the law with great spirit. The bitterness of being the scorn and laughter of base minds, the anguish of being insulted by men hardened beyond the sense of shame or pity, and the injury of a man's fortune being wasted, under pretence of justice, are excellently aggravated in the following speech of Pierre to Jaffier[2]:

> I passed this very moment by the doors,
> And found them guarded by a troop of villains,
> The sons of public rapine were destroying.
> They told me by the sentence of the law,
> They had commission to seize all thy fortune:
> Nay more, Priuli's cruel hand had signed it.
> Here stood a ruffian with a horrid face,
> Lording it o'er a pile of massy plate,
> Tumbled into a heap for public sale.
> There was another making villainous jests
> At thy undoing: he had ta'en possession
> Of all thy ancient most domestic ornaments;
> Rich hangings intermixed and wrought with gold;
> The very bed, which on thy wedding night
> Received thee to the arms of Belvidera,
> The scene of all thy joys, was violated
> By the coarse hands of filthy dungeon villains,
> And thrown amongst the common lumber.

Nothing indeed can be more unhappy than the condition of bankruptcy. The calamity which happens to us by ill fortune, or by the injury of others, has in it some consolation; but what arises from our own misbehaviour or error is the state of the most

---

[1] See No. 31.          [2] Act i, sc. 2.

exquisite sorrow.  When a man considers not only an
ample fortune, but even the very necessaries of life,
his pretence to food itself, at the mercy of his
creditors, he cannot but look upon himself in the
state of the dead, with his case thus much worse, that
the last office is performed by his adversaries instead
of his friends.  From this hour the cruel world does
not only take possession of his whole fortune, but
even of everything else which had no relation to it.
All his indifferent actions have new interpretations
put upon them; and those whom he has favoured in
his former life discharge themselves of their obligations to him by joining in the reproaches of his enemies.  It is almost incredible that it should be so;
but it is too often seen that there is a pride mixed
with the impatience of the creditor, and there are who
would rather recover their own by the downfall of a
prosperous man than be discharged to the common
satisfaction of themselves and their creditors.  The
wretched man, who was lately master of abundance,
is now under the direction of others; and the wisdom,
economy, good sense, and skill in human life before,
by reason of his present misfortune, are of no use to
him in the disposition of anything.  The incapacity
of an infant or a lunatic is designed for his provision
and accommodation; but that of a bankrupt, without
any mitigation in respect of the accidents by which it
arrived, is calculated for his utter ruin, except there
be a remainder ample enough after the discharge of
his creditors to bear also the expense of rewarding
those by whose means the effect of his labours was
transferred from him.  This man is to look on and
see others giving directions upon what terms and
conditions his goods are to be purchased, and all
this usually done not with an air of trustees to dispose of his effects, but destroyers to divide and tear
them to pieces.

There is something sacred in misery to great and
good minds; for this reason all wise lawgivers have
been extremely tender how they let loose even the

man who has right on his side to act with any mixture of resentment against the defendant. Virtuous and modest men, though they be used with some artifice, and have it in their power to avenge themselves, are slow in the application of that power, and are ever constrained to go into rigorous measures. They are careful to demonstrate themselves not only persons injured, but also that to bear it longer would be a means to make the offender injure others before they proceed. Such men clap their hands upon their hearts, and consider what it is to have at their mercy the life of a citizen. Such would have it to say to their own souls, if possible, that they were merciful when they could have destroyed, rather than when it was in their power to have spared a man, they destroyed. This is a due to the common calamity of human life, due in some measure to our very enemies. They who scruple doing the least injury are cautious of exacting the utmost justice.

Let any one who is conversant in the variety of human life reflect upon it, and he will find the man who wants mercy has a taste of no enjoyment of any kind. There is a natural disrelish of everything which is good in his very nature, and he is born an enemy to the world. He is ever extremely partial to himself in all his actions, and has no sense of iniquity but from the punishment which shall attend it. The law of the land is his gospel, and all his cases of conscience are determined by his attorney. Such men know not what it is to gladden the heart of a miserable man, that riches are the instruments of serving the purposes of heaven or hell, according to the disposition of the possessor. The wealthy can torment or gratify all who are in their power, and choose to do one or other as they are affected with love or hatred to mankind. As for such who are insensible of the concerns of others, but merely as they affect themselves, these men are to be valued only for their morality, and as we hope better things from their heirs. I could not but read with great delight a letter from an eminent citizen, who has failed, to one who was intimate with him in his better fortune, and able by his countenance to retrieve his lost condition :

SIR,—It is in vain to multiply words, and make apologies for what is never to be defended by the best advocate in the world, the guilt of being unfortunate. All that a man in my condition can do or say, will be received with prejudice by the generality of mankind, but I hope not with you : you have been a great instrument in helping me to get what I have lost, and I know (for that reason as well as kindness to me) you cannot but be in pain to see me undone. To show you I am not a man incapable of bearing calamity, I will, though a poor man, lay aside the distinction between us, and talk with the frankness we did when we were nearer to an equality : as all I do will be received with prejudice, all you do will be looked upon with partiality. What I desire of you is, that you, who are courted by all, would smile upon me who am shunned by all. Let that grace and favour which your fortune throws upon you, be turned to make up the coldness and indifference that is used towards me. All good and generous men will have an eye of kindness for me for my own sake, and the rest of the world will regard me for yours. There is an happy contagion in riches, as well as a destructive one in poverty ; the rich can make rich without parting with any of their store, and the conversation of the poor makes men poor, though they borrow nothing of them. How this is to be accounted for I know not ; but men's estimation follows us according to the company we keep. If you are what you were to me, you can go a great way towards my recovery ; if you are not, my good fortune, if ever it returns, will return by slower approaches.

I am, Sir,

Your affectionate Friend,

And humble Servant

This was answered with a condescension that did not, by long impertinent professions of kindness, insult his distress, but was as follows :

DEAR TOM,—I am very glad to hear that you have heart enough to begin the world a second time. I assure you, I do not think your numerous family at all diminished (in the gifts of Nature for which I have ever so much admired them) by what has so lately happened to you. I shall not only countenance your affairs with my appearance for you, but shall accommodate you with a considerable sum at common interest for three years. You know I could make more of it; but I have so great a love for you, that I can waive opportunities of gain to help you : for I do not care whether they say of me after I am dead, that I had an hundred or fifty thousand pounds more than I wanted when I was living.

T.　　　　　　　　Your obliged humble Servant

---

No. 457.　　*Thursday, August 14, 1712*　　[ADDISON

*Multa et præclara minantis.*　HOR., 2 Sat. iii, 9

I SHALL this day lay before my reader a letter, written by the same hand with that of last Friday [1], which contained proposals for a printed newspaper that should take in the whole circle of the penny post :

SIR,—The kind reception you gave my last Friday's letter, in which I broached my project of a newspaper, encourages me to lay before you two or three more; for, you must know, sir, that we look upon you to be the Lowndes [2] of the learned world, and cannot think any scheme practicable or rational before you have approved of it, though all the money we raise by it is on our own funds, and for our private use.

I have often thought that a 'News-Letter of Whispers', written every post, and sent about the kingdom,

---

1 No. 452.
2 William Lowndes was appointed Secretary to the Treasury in 1695, and held that post until his death in 1724. He was M.P. for Seaforth, St Mawes, and East Looe successively, and took a leading-part in questions of finance both in and out of the House of Commons. Walpole called him 'as able and honest a servant as ever the Crown had'.

after the same manner as that of Mr Dyer, Mr
Dawkes[1], or any other epistolary historian, might be
highly gratifying to the public, as well as beneficial to
the author.  By whispers I mean those pieces of news
which are communicated as secrets, and which bring a
double pleasure to the hearer ; first, as they are private
history, and in the next place, as they have always in
them a dash of scandal.  These are the two chief
qualifications in an article of news, which recommend
it, in a more than ordinary manner, to the ears of the
curious.  Sickness of persons in high posts, twilight
visits paid and received by ministers of state, clandestine courtships and marriages, secret amours, losses
at play, applications for places, with their respective
successes or repulses, are the materials in which I
chiefly intend to deal.  I have two persons, that are
each of them the representative of a species, who are
to furnish me with those whispers which I intend to
convey to my correspondents.  The first of these is
Peter Hush, descended from the ancient family of the
Hushes.  The other is the old Lady Blast, who has a
very numerous tribe of daughters in the two great
cities of London and Westminster.  Peter Hush has a
whispering-hole in most of the great coffee-houses about
town.  If you are alone with him in a wide room, he
carries you up into a corner of it, and speaks in your
ear.  I have seen Peter seat himself in a company of
seven or eight persons, whom he never saw before in
his life ; and after having looked about to see there was
no one that overheard him, has communicated to them
in a low voice, and under the seal of secrecy, the death
of a great man in the country, who was perhaps a fox-

---

[1] Some particulars of John Dyer will be found in a note to No. 43
(vol. i, p. 182).  'Honest Ichabod Dawks' (Tatler, No. 178) produced a
news-letter similar to Dyer's.  In his article on the distress of the
news-writers at the approach of peace (Tatler, No. 18), Addison wrote,
'I remember Mr Dyer, who is justly looked upon by all the fox-hunters
in the nation as the greatest statesman our country has produced,
was particularly famous for dealing in whales', three of which he
brought to the mouth of the Thames in five months.  'The judicious
and wary Mr Ichabod Dawks hath all along been the rival of this great
writer, and got himself a reputation from plagues and famines, by
which, in those days, he destroyed as great multitudes, as he has
lately done by the sword.'  In The Drummer (Act ii, sc. 1) Addison
makes Vellum believe his master is alive, 'because the news of his
death was first published in Dyer's Letter'.

hunting the very moment this account was giving of him. If upon your entering into a coffee-house you see a circle of heads bending over the table, and lying close by one another, it is ten to one but my friend Peter is among them. I have known Peter publishing the whisper of the day by eight o'clock in the morning at Garraway's, by twelve at Will's, and before two at the Smyrna. When Peter has thus effectually launched a secret, I have been very well pleased to hear people whispering it to one another at second hand, and spreading it about as their own; for you must know, sir, the great incentive to whispering is the ambition which every one has of being thought in the secret, and being looked upon as a man who has access to greater people than one would imagine. After having given you this account of Peter Hush, I proceed to that virtuous lady, the old Lady Blast, who is to communicate to me the private transactions of the crimp table, with all the arcana of the fair sex. The Lady Blast, you must understand, has such a particular malignity in her whisper, that it blights like an easterly wind, and withers every reputation that it breathes upon. She has a particular knack at making private weddings, and last winter married about five women of quality to their footmen. Her whisper can make an innocent young woman big with child, or fill an healthful young fellow with distempers that are not to be named. She can turn a visit into an intrigue, and a distant salute into an assignation. She can beggar the wealthy and degrade the noble. In short, she can whisper men base or foolish, jealous or ill-natured, or, if occasion requires, can tell you the slips of their great-grandmothers, and traduce the memory of honest coachmen that have been in their graves above these hundred years. By these, and the like helps, I question not but I shall furnish out a very handsome news-letter. If you approve my project, I shall begin to whisper by the very next post, and question not but every one of my customers will be very well pleased with me, when he considers that every piece of news I send him is a word in his ear, and lets him into a secret.

Having given you a sketch of this project, I shall, in the next place, suggest to you another for a monthly pamphlet, which I shall likewise submit to your Specta-

torial wisdom. I need not tell you, sir, that there are
several authors in France, Germany, and Holland, as
well as in our own country, who publish every month,
what they call 'An Account of the Works of the
Learned[1]', in which they give us an abstract of all
such books as are printed in any part of Europe. Now,
sir, it is my design to publish every month, 'An
Account of the Works of the Unlearned'. Several
late productions of my own countrymen, who many of
them make a very eminent figure in the illiterate world,
encourage me in this undertaking. I may, in this
work, possibly make a review of several pieces which
have appeared in the foreign accounts above mentioned,
though they ought not to have been taken notice of in
works which bear such a title. I may likewise take
into consideration such pieces as appear from time to
time under the names of those gentlemen who compliment one another, in public assemblies, by the title
of the 'Learned Gentlemen'. Our party authors will
also afford me a great variety of subjects, not to
mention editors, commentators, and others, who are
often men of no learning, or what is as bad, of no
knowledge. I shall not enlarge upon this ´hint; but
if you think anything can be made of it, I shall set
about it with all the pains and application that so useful a work deserves. I am ever,

C.                          Most worthy Sir, &c.

No. 458.        *Friday, August 15, 1712*        [ADDISON

Αἰδὼς δ' οὐκ ἀγαθή. HES., *Works and Days*, 315[2]
*Pudor malus.* HOR., 1 *Ep.* xvi, 24

I COULD not but smile at the account that was
yesterday given me of a modest young gentleman,
who being invited to an entertainment, though he
was not used to drink, had not the confidence to

---

1 'The History of the Works of the Learned, or an impartial Account
of Books, lately printed in all parts of Europe, with a particular
relation of the state of Learning in each Country: Done by several
hands', appeared in the form of quarto pamphlets from 1699 to 1712.
There had been an earlier 'Works of the Learned' in 1691-92, and the
title was revived in 1737.

2 This motto was added in the 1713 reprint.

refuse his glass in his turn, when on a sudden he grew so flustered that he took all the talk of the table into his own hands, abused every one of the company, and flung a bottle at the gentleman's head who treated him. This has given me occasion to reflect upon the ill effects of a vicious modesty, and to remember the saying of Brutus, as it is quoted by Plutarch, that 'the person has had but an ill education who has not been taught to deny anything.' This false kind of modesty has, perhaps, betrayed both sexes into as many vices as the most abandoned impudence, and is the more inexcusable to reason, because it acts to gratify others rather than itself, and is punished with a kind of remorse, not only like other vicious habits when the crime is over, but even at the very time that it is committed.

Nothing is more amiable than true modesty, and nothing is more contemptible than the false. The one guards virtue, the other betrays it. True modesty is ashamed to do anything that is repugnant to the rules of right reason : false modesty is ashamed to do anything that is opposite to the humour of the company. True modesty avoids everything that is criminal, false modesty everything that is unfashionable. The latter is only a general undetermined instinct; the former is that instinct, limited and circumscribed by the rules of prudence and religion.

We may conclude that modesty to be false and vicious which engages a man to do anything that is ill or indiscreet, or which restrains him from doing any that is of a contrary nature. How many men, in the common concerns of life, lend sums of money which they are not able to spare, are bound for persons whom they have but little friendship for, give recommendatory characters of men whom they are not acquainted with, bestow places on those whom they do not esteem, live in such a manner as they themselves do not approve, and all this merely because they have not the confidence to resist solicitation, importunity, or example?

Nor does this false modesty expose us only to such actions as are indiscreet, but very often to such as are highly criminal. When Xenophanes was called timorous because he would not venture his money in a game at dice, ' I confess ', said he, ' that I am exceeding timorous, for I dare not do an ill thing.' On the contrary, a man of vicious modesty complies with everything, and is only fearful of doing what may look singular in the company where he is engaged. He falls in with the torrent, and lets himself go to every action or discourse, however unjustifiable in itself, so it be in vogue among the present party. This, though one of the most common, is one of the most ridiculous dispositions in human nature, that men should not be ashamed of speaking or acting in a dissolute or irrational manner, but that one who is in their company should be ashamed of governing himself by the principles of reason and virtue.

In the second place, we are to consider false modesty as it restrains a man from doing what is good and laudable. My reader's own thoughts will suggest to him many instances and examples under this head. I shall only dwell upon one reflection, which I cannot make without a secret concern. We have in England a particular bashfulness in everything that regards religion. A well-bred man is obliged to conceal any serious sentiment of this nature, and very often to appear a greater libertine than he is, that he may keep himself in countenance among the men of mode. Our excess of modesty makes us shamefaced in all the exercises of piety and devotion. This humour prevails upon us daily; insomuch that at many well-bred tables the master of the house is so very modest a man that he has not the confidence to say grace at his own table : a custom which is not only practised by all the nations about us, but was never omitted by the heathens themselves. English gentlemen who travel into Roman Catholic countries are not a little surprised to meet with people of the best quality kneeling in their churches, and engaged in their private devotions, though it be not at the hours of public worship.  An officer of the army, or a man of wit and pleasure in those countries, would be afraid of passing not only for an irreligious, but an ill-bred man, should he be seen to go to bed, or sit down at table, without offering up his devotions on such occasions. The same show of religion appears in all the foreign reformed churches, and enters so much into their ordinary conversation that an Englishman is apt to term them hypocritical and precise.

This little appearance of a religious deportment in our nation may proceed in some measure from that modesty which is natural to us, but the great occasion of it is certainly this.  Those swarms of sectaries that overran the nation in the time of the great Rebellion, carried their hypocrisy so high that they had converted our whole language into a jargon of enthusiasm; insomuch that upon the Restoration men thought they could not recede too far from the behaviour and practice of those persons who had made religion a cloak to so many villainies.  This led them into the other extreme, every appearance of devotion was looked upon as puritanical, and falling into the hands of the ridiculers who flourished in that reign, and attacked everything that was serious, it has ever since been out of countenance among us.  By this means we are gradually fallen into that vicious modesty which has in some measure worn out from among us the appearance of Christianity in ordinary life and conversation, and which distinguishes us from all our neighbours [1].

Hypocrisy cannot indeed be too much detested, but at the same time is to be preferred to open impiety.  They are both equally destructive to the person who is possessed with them; but in regard to others, hypocrisy is not so pernicious as barefaced irreligion.  The due mean to be observed is to be

---

[1] 'All the nations that lie about us' (folio).

sincerely virtuous, and at the same time to let the world see we are so. I do not know a more dreadful menace in the Holy Writings, than that which is pronounced against those who have this perverted modesty, to be ashamed before men in a particular of such unspeakable importance.          C[1].

## No. 459.    *Saturday, August* 16, 1712    [ADDISON

*Quidquid dignum sapiente bonoque est.*  HOR., 1 *Ep.* iv, 5

RELIGION may be considered under two general heads. The first comprehends what we are to believe, the other what we are to practise. By those things which we are to believe, I mean whatever is revealed to us in the Holy Writings, and which we could not have obtained the knowledge of by the light of nature; by the things which we are to practise, I mean all those duties to which we are directed by reason or natural religion. The first of these I shall distinguish by the name of Faith, the second by that of Morality.

If we look into the more serious part of mankind, we find many who lay so great a stress upon faith, that they neglect morality; and many who build so much upon morality, that they do not pay a due regard to faith. The perfect man should be defective in neither of these particulars, as will be very evident to those who consider the benefits which arise from each of them, and which I shall make the subject of this day's paper.

Notwithstanding this general division of Christian duty into morality and faith, and that they have both their peculiar excellences, the first has the pre-eminence in several respects.

First, because the greatest part of morality (as I have stated the notion of it) is of a fixed eternal nature, and will endure when faith shall fail, and be lost in conviction.

Secondly, because a person may be qualified to do
_____
[1] No signature in the folio issue.

greater good to mankind, and become more beneficial to the world, by morality, without faith, than by faith without morality.

Thirdly, because morality gives a greater perfection to human nature, by quieting the mind, moderating the passions, and advancing the happiness of every man in his private capacity.

Fourthly, because the rule of morality is much more certain than that of faith, all the civilised nations of the world agreeing in the great points of morality, as much as they differ in those of faith.

Fifthly, because infidelity is not of so malignant a nature as immorality, or to put the same reason in another light, because it is generally owned, there may be salvation for a virtuous infidel (particularly in the case of invincible ignorance), but none for a vicious believer.

Sixthly, because faith seems to draw its principal, if not all its excellency, from the influence it has upon morality; as we shall see more at large, if we consider wherein consists the excellency of faith, or the belief of revealed religion; and this I think is:

First, in explaining, and carrying to greater heights, several points of morality.

Secondly, in furnishing new and stronger motives to enforce the practice of morality.

Thirdly, in giving us more amiable ideas of the Supreme Being, more endearing notions of one another, and a truer state of ourselves, both in regard to the grandeur and vileness of our natures.

Fourthly, by showing us the blackness and deformity of vice, which in the Christian system is so very great, that He who is possessed of all perfection and the Sovereign Judge of it, is represented by several of our divines as hating sin to the same degree that He loves the Sacred Person who was made the propitiation of it.

Fifthly, in being the ordinary and prescribed method of making morality effectual to salvation.

I have only touched on these several heads, which

every one who is conversant in discourses of this nature will easily enlarge upon in his own thoughts, and draw conclusions from them which may be useful to him in the conduct of his life. One I am sure is so obvious, that he cannot miss it, namely, that a man cannot be perfect in his scheme of morality, who does not strengthen and support it with that of the Christian faith.

Besides this, I shall lay down two or three other maxims which I think we may deduce from what has been said.

First, that we should be particularly cautious of making anything an article of faith, which does not contribute to the confirmation or improvement of morality.

Secondly, that no article of faith can be true and authentic, which weakens or subverts the practical part of religion, or what I have hitherto called morality.

Thirdly, that the greatest friend of morality, or natural religion, cannot possibly apprehend any danger from embracing Christianity as it is preserved pure and incorrupt in the doctrines of our national Church.

There is likewise another maxim which I think may be drawn from the foregoing considerations, which is this, that we should in all dubious points consider any ill consequences that may arise from them, supposing they should be erroneous, before we give up our assent to them.

For example, in that disputable point of persecuting men for conscience' sake, besides the imbittering their minds with hatred, indignation, and all the vehemence of resentment, and ensnaring them to profess what they do not believe, we cut them off from the pleasures and advantages of society, afflict their bodies, distress their fortunes, hurt their reputations, ruin their families, make their lives painful, or put an end to them. Sure when I see such dreadful consequences arising from a principle, I would be

as fully convinced of the truth of it as of a mathematical demonstration, before I would venture to
act upon it, or make it a part of my religion.

In this case the injury done our neighbour is plain
and evident, the principle that puts us upon doing
it, of a dubious and disputable nature. Morality
seems highly violated by the one, and whether or no
a zeal for what a man thinks the true system of faith
may justify it is very uncertain. I cannot but think,
if our religion produces charity as well as zeal, it
will not be for showing itself by such cruel instances.
But to conclude with the words of an excellent
author[1], 'We have just enough religion to make us
hate, but not enough to make us love one another.'

                                                    C.

No. 460.    *Monday, August* 18, 1712    [PARNELL[2]

*Decipimur specie recti.* HOR., *Ars Poet.* 25

OUR defects and follies are too often unknown to
us; nay, they are so far from being known to us,
that they pass for demonstrations of our worth. This
makes us easy in the midst of them, fond to show
them, fond to improve in them, and to be esteemed
for them. Then it is that a thousand unaccountable
conceits, gay inventions, and extravagant actions
must afford us pleasures, and display us to others
in the colours which we ourselves take a fancy to
glory in. And indeed there is something so amusing
for the time in this state of vanity and ill-grounded
satisfaction, that even the wiser world has chosen
an exalted word to describe its enchantments, and
called it ' The paradise of fools '.

Perhaps the latter part of this reflection may seem
a false thought to some, and bear another turn than
what I have given; but it is at present none of my

1 Probably Tillotson, in several of whose sermons a similar thought
occurs.
2 'A very ingenious gentleman . . . who was the author of the
Vision in the cccclx.th paper' (Addison, in No. 501).

business to look after it, who am going to confess that I have been lately amongst them in a vision.

Methought I was transported to a hill, green, flowery, and of an easy ascent. Upon the broad top of it resided squint-eyed Error and Popular Opinion with many heads; two that dealt in sorcery, and were famous for bewitching people with the love of themselves. To these repaired a multitude from every side, by two different paths which lead towards each of them. Some who had the most assuming air went directly of themselves to Error, without expecting a conductor; others of a softer nature went first to Popular Opinion, from whence, as she influenced and engaged them with their own praises, she delivered them over to his government.

When we had ascended to an open part of the summit where Opinion abode, we found her entertaining several who had arrived before us. Her voice was pleasing, she breathed odours as she spoke; she seemed to have a tongue for every one; every one thought he heard of something that was valuable in himself, and expected a paradise which she promised as the reward of his merit. Thus were we drawn to follow her, until she should bring us where it was to be bestowed; and it was observable, that all the way we went the company was either praising themselves for their qualifications, or one another for those qualifications which they took to be conspicuous in their own characters, or dispraising others for wanting theirs, or vying in the degrees of them.

At last we approached a bower, at the entrance of which Error was seated. The trees were thick woven, and the place where he sat artfully contrived to darken him a little. He was disguised in a whitish robe, which he put on that he might appear to us with a nearer resemblance to Truth; and as she has a light whereby she manifests the beauties of nature to the eyes of her adorers, so he had provided himself with a magical wand, that he might do something in imitation of it and please with delusions. This he lifted solemnly, and muttering to himself, bid the glories which he kept under enchantment to appear before us. Immediately we cast our eyes on that part of the sky to which he pointed, and observed a thin blue prospect, which cleared as mountains in a summer morning when the mists go off, and the palace of Vanity appeared to sight.

The foundation hardly seemed a foundation, but a set of curling clouds, which it stood upon by magical contrivance. The way by which we ascended was painted like a rainbow; and as we went, the breeze that played about us bewitched the senses. The walls were gilded all for show; the lowest set of pillars were of the slight fine Corinthian order, and the top of the building being rounded, bore so far the resemblance of a bubble.

At the gate the travellers neither met with a porter nor waited until one should appear; every one thought his merits a sufficient passport, and pressed forward. In the hall we met with several phantoms that roved amongst us, and ranged the company according to their sentiments. There was Decreasing Honour, that had nothing to show in but an old coat of his ancestors' achievements; there was Ostentation, that made himself his own constant subject, and Gallantry strutting upon his tiptoes. At the upper end of the hall stood a throne, whose canopy glittered with all the riches that gaiety could contrive to lavish on it; and between the gilded arms sat Vanity, decked in the peacock's feathers, and acknowledged for another Venus by her votaries. The boy who stood beside her for a Cupid, and who made the world to bow before her, was called Self-Conceit. His eyes had every now and then a cast inwards, to the neglect of all objects about him; and the arms which he made use of for conquest were borrowed from those against whom he had a design. The arrow which he shot at the soldier was fledged from his own plume of feathers; the dart he directed against the man of wit was winged from the quills he writ with; and that which he sent against those who presumed upon their riches was headed with gold out of their treasuries : he made nets for statesmen from their own contrivances; he took fire from the eyes of ladies, with which he melted their hearts; and lightning from the tongues of the eloquent, to inflame them with their own glories. At the foot of the throne sat three false Graces. Flattery with a shell of paint, Affectation with a mirror to practise at, and Fashion ever changing the posture of her clothes. These applied themselves to secure the conquests which Self-Conceit had gotten, and had each of them their particular politics. Flattery gave new colours and complexions to all things, Affectation new airs and appearances, which, as she said, were not vulgar, and Fashion both concealed some home defects, and added some foreign external beauties.

As I was reflecting upon what I saw, I heard a voice in the crowd bemoaning the condition of mankind, which is thus managed by the breath of Opinion, deluded by Error, fired by Self-Conceit, and given up to be trained in all the courses of Vanity, until Scorn or Poverty come upon us. These expressions were no sooner handed about, but I immediately saw a general disorder, until at last there was a parting in one place, and a grave old man, decent and resolute, was led forward to be punished for the words he had uttered. He appeared inclined to have spoken in his own defence, but I could not observe that any one was willing to hear him. Vanity cast a scornful smile at him, Self-Conceit was angry, Flattery, who knew him for Plain-dealing, put on a vizard and turned away, Affectation tossed her fan, made mouths, and called him Envy or Slander, and Fashion would have it, that at least he must be Ill-Manners. Thus slighted and despised by all, he was driven out for abusing people of merit and figure; and I heard it firmly resolved, that he should be used no better wherever they met with him hereafter.

I had already seen the meaning of most part of that warning which he had given, and was considering how the latter words should be fulfilled, when a mighty noise was heard without, and the door was blackened by a numerous train of harpies crowding in upon us. Folly and Broken Credit were seen in the house before they entered; Trouble, Shame, Infamy, Scorn, and Poverty brought up the rear. Vanity, with her Cupid and Graces, disappeared; her subjects ran into holes and corners; but many of them were found and carried off (as I was told by one who stood near me) either to prisons or cellars, solitude, or little company, the mean arts or the vilex crafts of life. 'But these', added he with a disdainful air, 'are such who would fondly live here when their merits neither matched the lustre of the place, nor their riches its expenses. We have seen such scenes as these before now; the glory you saw will all return when the hurry is over.' I thanked him for his information, and believing him so incorrigible as that he would stay until it was his turn to be taken, I made off to the door, and overtook some few who, though they would not hearken to Plaindealing, were now terrified to good purpose by the example of others : but when they had touched the threshold, it was a strange shock to them to find that the delusion of Error was gone, and they plainly discerned the building to hang a little up in the air without any real foundation. At first we saw nothing but a desperate leap remained for us, and I a thousand times blamed my unmeaning curiosity that had brought me into so much danger. But as they began to sink lower in their own minds, methought the palace sunk along with us, until they were arrived at the due point of Esteem which they ought to have for themselves; then the part of the building in which they stood touched the earth, and we departing out, it retired from our eyes. Now, whether they who stayed in the palace were sensible of this descent I cannot tell; it was then my opinion that they were not. However it be, my dream broke up at it, and has given me occasion all my life to reflect upon the fatal consequences of following the suggestions of Vanity.

MR SPECTATOR,—I write to you to desire that you would again [1] touch upon a certain enormity, which is chiefly in use among the politer and the better bred part of mankind : I mean the ceremonies, bows, curtsies, whisperings, smiles, winks, nods, with other familiar arts of salutation, which take up in our churches so much time that might be better employed, and which seem so utterly inconsistent with the duty and true intent of our entering into those religious assemblies. The resemblance which this bears to our indeed proper behaviour in theatres may be some instance of its incongruity in the above-mentioned places. In Roman Catholic churches and chapels abroad I myself have observed, more than once, persons of the first quality, of the nearest relation and intimatest acquaintance, passing by one another unknowing as it were and unknown, and with so little notices of each other that it looked like having their minds more suitably and more solemnly engaged; at least it was an acknowledgment that they ought to have been so. I have been told the same even of the Mahomedans, with relation to the propriety of their demeanour in the conventions of their erroneous worship; and I cannot but think either of them sufficient and laudable patterns for our imitation in this particular.

I cannot help upon this occasion remarking on the excellent memories of those devotionists, who upon returning from church shall give a particular account how two or three hundred people were dressed; a thing, by reason of its variety, so difficult to be digested and fixed in a head, that 'tis a miracle to me how two poor hours of divine service can be time sufficient for so elaborate an undertaking, the duty of the place too being jointly and, no doubt, oft pathetically performed along with it. Where it is said in Sacred Writ, that 'the woman ought to have a covering on her head, because of the angels [2]', that last word is by some

---

[1] See No. 259.        [2] 1 *Cor.* xi, 10.

thought to be metaphorically used, and to signify young men. Allowing this interpretation to be right, the text may not appear to be wholly foreign to our present purpose.

When you are in a disposition proper for writing on such a subject, I earnestly recommend this to you, and am,                         Sir,
    T.                    Your very humble Servant [1]


No. 461.     *Tuesday, August* 19, 1712     [STEELE

*Sed non ego credulus illis.* VIRG., *Eclog.* ix, 34

FOR want of time to substitute something else in the room of them, I am at present obliged to publish compliments above my desert in the following letters. It is no small satisfaction to have given occasion to ingenious men to employ their thoughts upon sacred subjects, from the approbation of such pieces of poetry as they have seen in my Saturday's papers. I shall never publish verse on that day but what is written by the same hand [2]; yet shall I not accompany those writings with eulogiums, but leave them to speak for themselves :


*For the* SPECTATOR [3]

MR SPECTATOR,—You very much promote the interests of virtue, while you reform the taste of a profane age, and persuade us to be entertained with

1 ' You will find a numerous concourse of people resort to afternoon's prayers, either to hear music or see the ladies. . . . There are gentlemen who walk about to make assignations, and make the house of God a public exchange. Some ladies you shall see at prayers, one part of the time with a fan before their face, at another time the fan is taken away, to be the better capable of beholding and being beheld ' (' *Original and genuine Letters sent to the* Tatler *and* Spectator ', 1725, i, 264–269).

2 Addison.

3 This letter and the version of the 114th Psalm are by Dr Isaac Watts, who was at this time thirty-eight years old, broken down by an attack of illness, and taking rest and change with his friend Sir Thomas Abney, at Theobalds. Isaac Watts, the son of a Nonconformist

divine poems. While we are distinguished by so many thousand humours, and split into so many different sects and parties, yet persons of every party, sect, and humour are fond of conforming their taste to yours. You can transfuse your own relish of a poem into all your readers, according to their capacity to receive; and when you recommend the pious passion that reigns in the verse, we seem to feel the devotion, and grow proud and pleased inwardly, that we have souls capable of relishing what the *Spectator* approves.

Upon reading the hymns that you have published in some late papers, I had a mind to try yesterday whether I could write one. The 114th Psalm appears to me an admirable ode, and I began to turn it into our language. As I was describing the journey of Israel from Egypt, and added the Divine Presence amongst them, I perceived a beauty in the psalm which was entirely new to me, and which I was going to lose; and that is, that the poet utterly conceals the presence of God in the beginning of it, and rather lets a possessive pronoun go without a substantive, than he will so much as mention anything of Divinity there. 'Judah was His sanctuary, and Israel His dominion or kingdom.' The reason now seems evident, and this conduct necessary. For if God had appeared before, there could be no wonder why the mountains should leap and the sea retire; therefore that this convulsion of Nature may be brought in with due surprise, His name is not mentioned till afterward, and then with a very

schoolmaster at Southampton, had injured his health by excessive study. After acting for a time as tutor to the son of Sir John Hartopp, he preached his first sermon in 1698, and three years later became pastor of the Nonconformist congregation in Mark Lane. By this office he abided, and with Sir Thomas Abney also he abided; his visit to Theobalds, in 1712, being, on all sides, so agreeable that he stayed there for the remaining thirty-six years of his life. There he wrote his *Divine and Moral Songs for Children*, his Hymns, and his metrical version of the Psalms. But his *Horæ Lyricæ*, published in 1709, had already attracted much attention when he contributed this psalm to the *Spectator*. In the Preface to that collection he had argued that Poesy, whose original is divine, had been desecrated to the vilest purpose, enticed unthinking youth to sin, and fallen into discredit among some weaker Christians. Watts bade them look into their Bibles and observe the boldness of its poetic imagery, and pointed to the way he had chosen for himself as a Biblical rhymer. He died in 1748, aged seventy-four (Morley).—Watts printed this version of the 114th Psalm as his own in his *Divine Psalms and Hymns*, 1719.

agreeable turn of thought God is introduced at once in all His majesty. This is what I have attempted to imitate in a translation without paraphrase, and to preserve what I could of the spirit of the sacred author.

If the following essay be not too incorrigible, bestow upon it a few brightenings from your genius, that I may learn how to write better, or to write no more.

Your daily admirer,<br>and humble Servant, &c.

## PSALM CXIV

### I

When Israel, freed from Pharaoh's hand,
Left the proud tyrant and his land,
The tribes with cheerful homage own
Their King, and Judah was His throne.

### II

Across the deep their journey lay,
The deep divides to make them way;
The streams of Jordan saw, and fled
With backward current to their head.

### III

The mountains shook like frighted sheep,
Like lambs the little hillocks leap;
Not Sinai on her base could stand,
Conscious of Sovereign Power at hand.

### IV

What power could make the deep divide?
Make Jordan backward roll his tide?
Why did ye leap, ye little hills?
And whence the fright that Sinai feels?

### V

Let every mountain, every flood
Retire, and know th' approaching God,
The King of Israel: see Him here;
Tremble, thou earth, adore and fear.

### VI

He thunders, and all nature mourns;
The rock to standing pools He turns;
Flints spring with fountains at His word,
And fires and seas confess their Lord.

Mr Spectator,—There are those who take the advantage of your putting an halfpenny value upon yourself above the rest of our daily writers[1], to defame you in public conversation, and strive to make you unpopular upon the account of the said halfpenny. But if I were you, I would insist upon that small acknowledgment for the superior merit of yours, as being a work of invention. Give me leave therefore to do you justice, and say in your behalf what you cannot yourself, which is, that your writings have made learning a more necessary part of good breeding than it was before you appeared : that modesty is become fashionable, and impudence stands in need of some wit, since you have put them both in their proper lights. Profaneness, lewdness, and debauchery are not now qualifications, and a man may be a very fine gentleman, though he is neither a keeper nor an infidel.

I would have you tell the town the story of the Sibyls, if they deny giving you twopence. Let them know, that those sacred papers were valued at the same rate after two-thirds of them were destroyed, as when there was the whole set. There are so many of us who will give you your own price, that you may acquaint your Nonconformist readers, that they shall not have it, except they come in within such a day, under threepence. I don't know but you might bring in the *Date obolum Bellisario*[2] with a good grace. The witlings come in clusters to two or three coffee-houses which have left you off, and I hope you will make us, who fine[3] to your wit, merry with their characters who stand out against it.

I am your most humble Servant

*P.S.*—I have lately got the ingenious authors of blacking for shoes, powder for colouring the hair, pomatum for the hands, cosmetic for the face, to be your constant customers[4] ; so that your advertisements will as much adorn the outward man, as your paper does the inward.    T.

---

[1] See No. 445.

[2] There is a story, discredited by Gibbon, that Belisarius, the great general, was neglected when blind and old by the Emperor Justinian, and was forced to beg for charity.    [3] *i. e.*, pay a fine.

[4] 'The famous Spanish blacking for gentlemen's shoes', and 'the famous Bavarian red liquor which gives such a delightful blushing colour to the cheeks', were often advertised in the *Spectator*.

No. 462.    *Wednesday, August* 20, 1712    [STEELE

*Nil ego prætulerim jucundo sanus amico.*    HOR., 1 *Sat.* v, 44

PEOPLE are not aware of the very great force which pleasantry in company has upon all those with whom a man of that talent converses. His faults are generally overlooked by all his acquaintance, and a certain carelessness that constantly attends all his actions, carries him on with greater success, than diligence and assiduity does others who have no share of this endowment. Dacinthus breaks his word upon all occasions both trivial and important; and when he is sufficiently railed at for that abominable quality, they who talk of him end with, ' After all he is a very pleasant fellow '. Dacinthus is an ill-natured husband, and yet the very women end their freedom of discourse upon his subject, ' But after all he is very pleasant company '. Dacinthus is neither in point of honour, civility, good breeding, or good nature unexceptionable, and yet all is answered, ' For he is a very pleasant fellow '. When this quality is conspicuous in a man who. has, to accompany it, manly and virtuous sentiments, there cannot certainly be anything which can give so pleasing gratification as the gaiety of such a person; but when it is alone, and serves only to gild a crowd of ill qualities, there is no man so much to be avoided as your pleasant fellow. A very pleasant fellow shall turn your good name to a jest, make your character contemptible, debauch your wife or daughter, and yet be received by the rest of the world with welcome wherever he appears. It is very ordinary with those of this character to be attentive only to their own satisfactions, and have very little bowels for the concerns or sorrows of other men; nay, they are capable of purchasing their own pleasures at the expense of giving pain to others. But they who do not consider this sort of man thus carefully, are

irresistibly exposed to his insinuations.   The author
of the following letter carries the matter so high, as
to intimate that the liberties of England have been
at the mercy of a prince merely as he was of this
pleasant character.

Mr. Spectator,—There is no one passion which all
mankind so naturally give in to as pride, nor any other
passion which appears in such different disguises; it
is to be found in all habits and all complexions.   Is
it not a question, whether it does more harm or good
in the world?   And if there be not such a thing as
what we may call a virtuous and laudable pride?
It is this passion alone, when misapplied, that lays
us so open to flatterers; and he who can agreeably
condescend to soothe our humour or temper, finds
always an open avenue to our soul, especially if the
flatterer happen to be our superior.
One might give many instances of this in a late
English monarch, under the title of ' The Gaieties of
King Charles II '.   This prince was by nature extremely
familiar, of very easy access, and much delighted to
see and be seen; and this happy temper, which in the
highest degree gratified his people's vanity, did him
more service with his loving subjects than all his other
virtues, though it must be confessed he had many.   He
delighted, though a mighty king, to give and take a
jest, as they say; and a prince of this fortunate disposition, who were inclined to make an ill use of his
power, may have anything of his people, be it never so
much to their prejudice.   But this good king made
generally a very innocent use, as to the public, of this
ensnaring temper; for it is well known he pursued
pleasure more than ambition.   He seemed to glory in
being the first man at cock-matches, horse-races, balls,
and plays; he appeared highly delighted on those
occasions, and never failed to warm and gladden the
heart of every spectator.   He more than once dined
with his good citizens of London on their Lord Mayor's
Day, and did so the year that Sir Robert Viner [1] was

---

[1] Sir Robert Viner, who is mentioned in several of Marvell's satires,
erected in Stocks Market, in 1672, a marble statue of Charles II, which
he had bought at Leghorn.   This statue was meant originally for John
Sobieski, trampling on a Turk.   The Turk was converted into Oliver

mayor. Sir Robert was a very loyal man, and if you
will allow the expression, very fond of his sovereign ;
but what with the joy he felt at heart for the honour
done him by his prince, and through the warmth he
was in with continual toasting healths to the royal
family, his lordship grew a little fond of his majesty,
and entered into a familiarity not altogether so graceful
in so public a place. The king understood very well
how to extricate himself on all kind of difficulties, and
with an hint to the company to avoid ceremony, stole
off and made towards his coach, which stood ready for
him in Guildhall Yard. But the mayor liked his company so well and was grown so intimate, that he pursued him hastily, and catching him fast by the hand,
cried out with a vehement oath and accent, ' Sir, you
shall stay and take t'other bottle.' The airy monarch
looked kindly at him over his shoulder, and with a
smile and graceful air (for I saw him at the time, and
do now) repeated this line of the old song :

He that's drunk is as great as a king,

and immediately turned back and complied with his
landlord.

I give you this story, Mr Spectator, because, as I
said, I saw the passage ; and I assure you it's very
true, and yet no common one ; and when I tell you the
sequel, you will say I have yet a better reason for't.
This very mayor afterwards erected the statue of his
merry monarch in Stocks Market [1], and did the Crown
many and great services ; and it was owing to this
humour of the king that his family had so great a
fortune shut up in the exchequer of their pleasant
sovereign. The many good-natured condescensions of
this prince are vulgarly known ; and it is excellently
said of him by a great hand [2] which writ his character,
that he was not a king a quarter of an hour together
in his whole reign. He would receive visits even from
fools and half madmen, and at times I have met with

Cromwell, but the turban remained on his head. The statue was
removed when the Mansion House was built in 1739, and in 1779 it
was given by the Corporation to one of Viner's descendants. Viner
was Lord Mayor in 1674-75, and by 1676 the king owed him £416,724,
and in order to repay the debt granted him £25,000 a year from the
excise duty.

[1] See No. 454.                    [2] John Sheffield, Duke of Buckingham.

people who have boxed, fought at backsword, and taken poison before King Charles II. In a word, he was so pleasant a man that no one could be sorrowful under his government. This made him capable of baffling, with the greatest ease imaginable, all suggestions of jealousy, and the people could not entertain notions of anything terrible in him whom they saw every way agreeable. This scrap of the familiar part of that prince's history I thought fit to send you, in compliance to the request you lately made to your correspondents.

I am, Sir,

T.          Your most humble Servant

No. 463.     *Thursday, August 21, 1712*     [ADDISON

*Omnia quæ sensu volvuntur vota diurno*
*Pectore sopito reddit amica quies.*
*Venator defessa toro cùm membra reponit,*
*Mens tamen ad sylvas et sua lustra redit.*
*Iudicibus lites, aurigis somnia currus,*
*Vanaque nocturnis meta cavetur equis.*
*Me quoque Musarum studium sub nocte silenti*
*Artibus assuetis sollicitare solet.*

CLAUD., In. vi, *Cons. Hon.*

I WAS lately entertaining myself with comparing Homer's balance, in which Jupiter is represented as weighing the fates of Hector and Achilles, with a passage of Virgil, wherein that deity is introduced as weighing the fates of Turnus and Æneas [1]. I then considered how the same way of thinking prevailed in the Eastern parts of the world, as in those noble passages of Scripture, wherein we are told that the great king of Babylon, the day before his death, had been weighed in the balance and been found wanting. In other places of the Holy Writings, the Almighty is described as weighing the mountains in scales, making the weight for the winds, knowing the balancings of the clouds, and in others as weighing the actions of men and laying their calamities together in a balance. Milton, as I have observed in a former paper [2], had an eye to several of these

[1] *Iliad*, viii, 69; *Æneid*, xii, 725.     [2] No. 326.

foregoing instances, in that beautiful description wherein he represents the Archangel and the Evil Spirit as addressing themselves for the combat, but parted by the balance which appeared in the heavens and weighed the consequences of such a battle :

The Eternal, to prevent such horrid fray,
Hung forth in heaven His golden scales, yet seen
Betwixt Astrea and the Scorpion sign,
Wherein all things created first He weighed,
The pendulous round earth with balanced air
In counterpoise ; now ponders all events,
Battles and realms ; in these He puts two weights,
The sequel each of parting and of fight ;
The latter quick up flew. and kicked the beam ;
Which Gabriel spying, thus bespake the fiend :
　'Satan, I know thy strength, and thou know'st mine ;
Neither our own, but given ; what folly then
To boast what arms can do ! since thine no more
Than heaven permits, nor mine, though doubled now
To trample thee as mire : for proof look up,
And read thy lot in yon celestial sign,
Where thou art weighed and shown how light, how weak
If thou resist.' The fiend looked up, and knew
His mounted scale aloft : nor more ; but fled
Murmuring, and with him fled the shades of night [1].

These several amusing thoughts having taken possession of my mind some time before I went to sleep, and mingling themselves with my ordinary ideas, raised in my imagination a very odd kind of vision. I was, methought, replaced in my study and seated in my elbow-chair, where I had indulged the foregoing speculations, with my lamp burning by me as usual. Whilst I was here meditating on several subjects of morality, and considering the nature of many virtues and vices, as materials for those discourses with which I daily entertain the public, I saw, methought, a pair of golden scales hanging by a chain of the same metal over the table that stood before me; when, on a sudden, there were great heaps of weights thrown down on each side of them. I found, upon examining these weights, they showed the value of everything that is in esteem among men. I made an essay of them

[1] *Paradise Lost*, iv, 996–1015.

by putting the weight of Wisdom in one scale and that of Riches in another, upon which the latter, to show its comparative lightness, immediately flew up and kicked the beam.

But before I proceed, I must inform my reader that these weights did not exert their natural gravity until they were laid in the golden balance, insomuch that I could not guess which was light or heavy whilst I held them in my hand. This I found by several instances, for upon my laying a weight in one of the scales, which was inscribed by the word Eternity; though I threw in that of Time, Prosperity, Affliction, Wealth, Poverty, Interest, Success, with many other weights, which in my hand seemed very ponderous, they were not able to stir the opposite balance, nor could they have prevailed though assisted with the weight of the sun, the stars, and the earth.

Upon emptying the scales, I laid several Titles and Honours, with Pomps, Triumphs, and many weights of the like nature, in one of them, and seeing a little glittering weight lie by me, I threw it accidentally into the other scale, when, to my great surprise, it proved so exact a counterpoise, that it kept the balance in an equilibrium. This little glittering weight was inscribed upon the edges of it with the word Vanity. I found there were several other weights which were equally heavy, and exact counterpoises to one another; a few of them I tried, as Avarice and Poverty, Riches and Content, with some others.

There were likewise several weights that were of the same figure, and seemed to correspond with each other, but were entirely different when thrown into the scales: as Religion and Hypocrisy, Pedantry and Learning, Wit and Vivacity, Superstition and Devotion, Gravity and Wisdom, with many others.

I observed one particular weight lettered on both sides, and upon applying myself to the reading of it, I found on one side written, ' In the Dialect of

Men ', and underneath it ' Calamities '; on the other side was written ' In the language of the gods ', and underneath ' Blessings '. I found the intrinsic value of this weight to be much greater than I imagined, for it overpowered Health, Wealth, Good Fortune, and many other weights, which were much more ponderous in my hand than the other.

There is a saying among the Scotch, that an ounce of mother is worth a pound of clergy; I was sensible of the truth of this saying when I saw the difference between the weight of Natural Parts and that of Learning. The observation which I made upon these two weights opened to me a new field of discoveries, for notwithstanding the weight of Natural Parts was much heavier than that of Learning, I observed that it weighed an hundred times heavier than it did before, when I put Learning into the same scale with it. I made the same observation upon Faith and Morality [1]; for notwithstanding the latter outweighed the former separately, it received a thousand times more additional weight from its conjunction with the former than what it had by itself. This odd phenomenon showed itself in other particulars, as in Wit and Judgment, Philosophy and Religion, Justice and Humanity, Zeal and Charity, Depth of Sense and Perspicuity of Style, with innumerable other particulars, too long to be mentioned in this paper.

As a dream seldom fails of dashing seriousness with impertinence, mirth with gravity, methought I made several other experiments of a more ludicrous nature, by one of which I found that an English octavo was very often heavier than a French folio; and by another, that an old Greek or Latin author weighed down a whole library of moderns. Seeing one of my *Spectators* lying by me, I laid it into one of the scales, and flung a twopenny piece into the other. The reader will not inquire into the event if he remembers the first trial which I have recorded in this paper [2]. I afterwards threw both the sexes into the

[1] No. 459.    [2] See No. 445.

balance; but as it is not for my interest to disoblige either of them, I shall desire to be excused from telling the result of this experiment. Having an opportunity of this nature in my hands, I could not forbear throwing into one scale the principles of a Tory, and in the other those of a Whig; but as I have all along declared this to be a neutral paper, I shall likewise desire to be silent under this head also, though upon examining one of the weights, I saw the word TEKEL engraven on it in capital letters [1].

I made many other experiments, and though I have not room for them all in this day's speculation, I may perhaps reserve them for another. I shall only add, that upon my awaking I was sorry to find my golden scales vanished, but resolved for the future to learn this lesson from them, not to despise or value any things for their appearances, but to regulate my esteem and passions towards them according to their real and intrinsic value.          C.


No. 464.     *Friday, August 22, 1712*     [ADDISON

*Auream quisquis mediocritatem
Diligit, tutus caret obsoleti
Sordibus tecti, caret invidenda.
Sobrius aula.*          HOR., 2 Od. x, 5

I AM wonderfully pleased when I meet with any passage in an old Greek or Latin author that is not blown upon, and which I have never met with in a quotation. Of this kind is a beautiful saying in Theognis : ' Vice is covered by wealth, and virtue by poverty '; or to give it in the verbal translation, ' Among men there are some who have their vices concealed by wealth, and others who have their virtues concealed by poverty.' Every man's observation will supply him with instances of rich men, who have several faults and defects that are overlooked, if not entirely hidden, by means of their

[1] *Daniel v, 27.*

riches; and, I think, we cannot find a more natural description of a poor man, whose merits are lost in his poverty, than that in the words of the wise man : ' There was a little city, and few men within it; and there came a great king against it, and besieged it, and built great bulwarks against it : now there was found in it a poor wise man, and he by his wisdom delivered the city: yet no man remembered that same poor man. Then said I, Wisdom is better than strength : nevertheless, the poor man's wisdom is despised, and his words are not heard [1].'

The middle condition seems to be the most advantageously situated for the gaining of wisdom. Poverty turns our thoughts too much upon the supplying of our wants, and riches upon enjoying our superfluities; and as Cowley has said in another case, ' It is hard for a man to keep a steady eye upon truth, who is always in a battle or a triumph.'

If we regard poverty and wealth, as they are apt to produce virtues or vices in the mind of man, one may observe that there is a set of each of those growing out of poverty, quite different from that which rises out of wealth. Humility and patience, industry and temperance, are very often the good qualities of a poor man. Humanity and good-nature, magnanimity, and a sense of honour, are as often the qualifications of the rich. On the contrary, poverty is apt to betray a man into envy, riches into arrogance; poverty is too often attended with fraud, vicious compliance, repining, murmur, and discontent. Riches expose a man to pride and luxury, a foolish elation of heart, and too great a fondness for the present world. In short, the middle condition is most eligible to the man who would improve himself in virtue; as I have before shown, it is the most advantageous for the gaining of knowledge. It was upon this consideration that Agar founded his prayer, which for the wisdom of it is recorded in Holy Writ : ' Two things have I required of Thee; deny me them not before I die : remove far from me vanity and lies : give me neither poverty nor riches; feed me with food convenient for me : lest I be full, and deny Thee, and say, Who is the Lord? or lest I be poor, and steal, and take the name of my God in vain [1].'

I shall fill the remaining part of my paper with a very pretty allegory, which is wrought into a play [2] by Aristophanes the Greek comedian. It seems originally designed as a satire upon the rich, though in some parts of it 'tis, like the foregoing discourse, a kind of comparison between wealth and poverty.

Chremylus, who was an old and a good man, and withal exceeding poor, being desirous to leave some riches to his son, consults the oracle of Apollo upon the subject. The oracle bids him follow the first man he should see upon his going out of the temple. The person he chanced to see was to appearance an old sordid blind man, but upon his following him from place to place, he at last found by his own confession that he was Plutus, the god of riches, and that he was just come out of the house of a miser. Plutus further told him, that when he was a boy he used to declare that as soon as he came to age he would distribute wealth to none but virtuous and just men; upon which Jupiter, considering the pernicious consequences of such a resolution, took his sight away from him, and left him to stroll about the world in the blind condition wherein Chremylus beheld him. With much ado Chremylus prevailed upon him to go to his house, where he met an old woman in a tattered raiment, who had been his guest for many years, and whose name was Poverty. The old woman refusing to turn out so easily as he would have her, he threatened to banish her not only from his own house, but out of all Greece, if she made any more words upon the matter. Poverty on this occasion pleads her cause very notably, and represents to her old landlord, that should she be driven out of the country, all their trades, arts,

[1] *Proverbs* xxx, 7-9.  [2] *Plutus.*

and sciences would be driven out with her; and that if every one was rich, they would never be supplied with those pomps, ornaments, and conveniences of life which made riches desirable. She likewise represented to him the several advantages which she bestowed upon her votaries, in regard to their shape, their health, and their activity, by preserving them from gouts, dropsies, unwieldiness, and intemperance. But whatever she had to say for herself, she was at last forced to troop off. Chremylus immediately considered how he might restore Plutus to his sight; and in order to it conveyed him to the temple of Æsculapius, who was famous for cures and miracles of this nature. By this means the deity recovered his eyes, and begun to make a right use of them, by enriching every one that was distinguished by piety towards the gods, and justice towards men [1]; and at the same time by taking away his gifts from the impious and undeserving. This produces several merry incidents, until in the last act Mercury descends with great complaints from the gods, that since the good men were grown rich they had received no sacrifices, which is confirmed by a priest of Jupiter, who enters with a remonstrance, that since this late innovation he was reduced to a starving condition, and could not live upon his office. Chremylus, who in the beginning of the play was religious in his poverty, concludes it with a proposal which was relished by all the good men who were now grown rich as well as himself, that they should carry Plutus in a solemn procession to the temple, and instal him in the place of Jupiter. This allegory instructed the Athenians in two points; first, as it vindicated the conduct of Providence in its ordinary distributions of wealth; and in the next place, as it showed the great tendency of riches to corrupt the morals of those who possessed them.

C.

---

[1] 'Man' (folio).

No. 465.     *Saturday, August 23, 1712*     [ADDISON

*Quâ ratione queas traducere leniter ævum.*
*Nè te semper inops agitet vexetque cupido ;*
*Num pavor et rerum mediocriter utilium spes.*
                              HOR., 1 *Ep.* xviii, 97

HAVING endeavoured in my last Saturday's paper [1]
to show the great excellency of faith, I shall here
consider what are the proper means of strengthening
and confirming it in the mind of man. Those who
delight in reading books of controversy, which are
written on both sides of the question in points of
faith, do very seldom arrive at a fixed and settled
habit of it. They are one day entirely convinced of
its important truths, and the next meet with something that shakes and disturbs them. The doubt
which was laid revives again, and shows itself in
new difficulties, and that generally for this reason,
because the mind which is perpetually tossed in con-
troversies and disputes, is apt to forget the reasons
which had once set it at rest, and to be disquieted
with any former perplexity, when it appears in a
new shape, or is started by a different hand. As
nothing is more laudable than an inquiry after truth,
so nothing is more irrational than to pass away our
whole lives, without determining ourselves one way
or other in those points which are of the last importance to us. There are indeed many things from
which we may withhold our assent; but in cases by
which we are to regulate our lives, it is the greatest
absurdity to be wavering and unsettled, without
closing with that side which appears the most safe
and the most probable. The first rule therefore
which I shall lay down is this, that when by reading
or discourse we find ourselves thoroughly convinced
of the truth of any article, and of the reasonableness
of our belief in it, we should never after suffer ourselves to call it into question. We may perhaps

                    [1] No. 459.

forget the arguments which occasioned our conviction, but we ought to remember the strength they
had with us, and therefore still to retain the conviction which they once produced. This is no more
than what we do in every common art or science,
nor is it possible to act otherwise, considering the
weakness and limitation of our intellectual faculties.
It was thus that Latimer, one of the glorious army
of martyrs who introduced the Reformation in England, behaved himself in that great conference which
was managed between the most learned among the
Protestants and Papists in the reign of Queen Mary.
This venerable old man, knowing how his abilities
were impaired by age, and that it was impossible for
him to recollect all those reasons which had directed
him in the choice of his religion, left his companions,
who were in the full possession of their parts and
learning, to baffle and confound their antagonists by
the force of reason. As for himself, he only repeated
to his adversaries the articles in which he firmly
believed, and in the profession of which he was determined to die. It is in this manner that the mathe-
matician proceeds upon propositions which he has
once demonstrated, and though the demonstration
may have slipped out of his memory, he builds upon
the truth, because he knows it was demonstrated.
This rule is absolutely necessary for weaker minds,
and in some measure for men of the greatest abilities;
but to these last I would propose, in the second place,
that they should lay up in their memories, and
always keep by them in a readiness, those arguments
which appear to them of the greatest strength, and
which cannot be got over by all the doubts and cavils
of infidelity.

But, in the third place, there is nothing which
strengthens faith more than morality. Faith and
morality naturally produce each other. A man is
quickly convinced of the truth of religion, who finds
it is not against his interest that it should be true.
The pleasure he receives at present, and the happi-

ness which he promises himself from it hereafter, will both dispose him very powerfully to give credit to it, according to the ordinary observation that we are easy to believe what we wish. It is very certain, that a man of sound reason cannot forbear closing with religion upon an impartial examination of it; but at the same time it is as certain, that faith is kept alive in us, and gathers strength from practice more than from speculation.

There is still another method which is more persuasive than any of the former, and that is an habitual adoration of the Supreme Being, as well in constant acts of mental worship, as in outward forms. The devout man does not only believe but feels there is a Deity. He has actual sensations of Him; his experience concurs with his reason; he sees Him more and more in all his intercourses with Him, and even in this life almost loses his faith in conviction.

The last method which I shall mention for the giving life to a man's faith, is frequent retirement from the world, accompanied with religious meditation. When a man thinks of anything in the darkness of the night, whatever deep impressions it may make in his mind, they are apt to vanish as soon as the day breaks about him. The light and noise of the day, which are perpetually soliciting his senses, and calling off his attention, wear out of his mind the thoughts that imprinted themselves in it, with so much strength, during the silence and darkness of the night. A man finds the same difference as to himself in a crowd and in a solitude; the mind is stunned and dazzled amidst that variety of objects which press upon her in a great city: she cannot apply herself to the consideration of those things which are of the utmost concern to her. The cares or pleasures of the world strike in with every thought, and a multitude of vicious examples give [1] a kind of justification to [2] our folly. In our retire-

1 'Give us' (folio).                    2 'In' (folio).

ments everything disposes us to be serious.  In courts and cities we are entertained with the works of men, in the country with those of God.  One is the province of art, the other of nature.  Faith and devotion naturally grow in the mind of every reasonable man, who sees the impressions of Divine power and wisdom in every object on which he casts his eye.  The Supreme Being has made the best arguments for His own existence, in the formation of the heavens and the earth, and these are arguments which a man of sense cannot forbear attending to, who is out of the noise and hurry of human affairs.  Aristotle says, that should a man live underground, and there converse with works of art and mechanism, and should afterwards be brought up into the open day, and see the several glories of the heaven and earth, he would immediately pronounce them the works of such a Being as we define God to be.  The Psalmist has very beautiful strokes of poetry to this purpose, in that exalted strain : ' The heavens declare the glory of God : and the firmament showeth His handywork.  One day telleth another : and one night certifieth another.  There is neither speech nor language : but their voices are heard among them.  Their sound is gone out into all lands : and their words into the ends of the world [1].'  As such a bold and sublime manner of thinking furnishes very noble matter for an ode, the reader may see it wrought into the following one [2]:

I

The spacious firmament on high,
With all the blue ethereal sky,
And spangled heav'ns, a shining frame
Their great Original proclaim :
Th' unwearied sun, from day to day,
Does his Creator's power display.

### II

Soon as the evening shades prevail,
The moon takes up the wond'rous tale,
And nightly to the list'ning earth
Repeats the story of her birth:
Whilst all the stars that round her burn,
And all the planets, in their turn,
Confirm the tidings as they roll,
And spread the truth from pole to pole.

### III

What though, in solemn silence, all
Move round the dark terrestrial ball?
What though no real voice nor sound
Amid their radiant orbs be found?
In reason's ear they all rejoice,
And utter forth a glorious voice,
For ever singing, as they shine,
'The hand that made us is Divine.'

C.

No. 466.        *Monday, August 25, 1712*        [STEELE

*Vera incessu patuit dea.* VIRG., *Æn.* i, 405

WHEN Æneas, the hero of Virgil, is lost in the
wood, and a perfect stranger in the place on which
he is landed, he is accosted by a lady in an habit
for the chase. She inquires of him whether he has
seen pass by that way any young woman dressed as
she was? whether she were following the sport in
the wood, or any other way employed, according to
the custom of huntresses? The hero answers with
the respect due to the beautiful appearance she
made, tells her he saw no such person as she inquired
for; but intimates that he knows her to be of the
deities, and desires she would conduct a stranger.
Her form from her first appearance manifested she
was more than mortal; but though she was certainly
a goddess, the poet does not make her known to be
the goddess of beauty till she moved : all the charms
of an agreeable person are then in their highest
exertion, every limb and feature appears with its
respective grace. It is from this observation that I
cannot help being so passionate an admirer as I am

of good dancing[1]. As all art is an imitation of
Nature, this is an imitation of Nature in its highest
excellence, and at a time when she is most agreeable.
The business of dancing is to display beauty, and for
that reason all distortions and mimicries, as such, are
what raise aversion instead of pleasure : but things
that are in themselves excellent, are ever attended
with imposture and false imitation.    Thus, as in
poetry there are laborious fools who write anagrams
and acrostics, there are pretenders in dancing, who
think merely to do what others cannot is to excel.
Such creatures should be rewarded like him who had
acquired the knack of throwing a grain of corn
through the eye of a needle, with a bushel to keep
his hand in use.    The dancers[2] on our stages are very
faulty in this kind ; and what they mean by writhing
themselves into such postures, as it would be a pain
for any of the spectators to stand in, and yet hope
to please those spectators, is unintelligible.    Mr
Prince has a genius, if he were encouraged, would
prompt them to better things.    In all the dances he
invents, you see he keeps close to the characters he
represents.    He does not hope to please by making
his performers move in a manner in which no one
else ever did, but by motions proper to the characters
he represents.    He gives to clowns and lubbers
clumsy graces ; that is, he makes them practise what
they would think graces ; and I have seen dances of
his, which might give hints that would be useful to
a comic writer.    These performances have pleased
the taste of such as have not reflection enough to
know their excellence, because they are in Nature ;
and the distorted motions of others, have offended
those who could not form reasons to themselves for
their displeasure from their being a contradiction to
Nature.
      When one considers the inexpressible advantage
there is in arriving at some excellence in this art, it

---

[1] See Nos. 66, 67, 334, 370, 376.
[2] 'Dancing', in original edition.

is monstrous to behold it so much neglected. The following letter has in it something very natural on the subject :

MR SPECTATOR,—I am a widower with but one daughter ; she was by nature much inclined to be a romp, and I had no way of educating her, but commanding a young woman, whom I entertained to take care of her, to be very watchful in her care and attendance about her. I am a man of business, and obliged to be much abroad. The neighbours have told me that in my absence our maid has let in the spruce servants in the neighbourhood to junketings, while my girl played and romped even in the street. To tell you the plain truth, I catched her once, at eleven years old, at chuck-farthing among the boys. This put me upon new thoughts about my child, and I determined to place her at a boarding-school, and at the same time gave a very discreet young gentlewoman her maintenance at the same place and rate to be her companion. I took little notice of my girl from time to time, but saw her now and then in good health, out of harm's way, and was satisfied. But by much importunity, I was lately prevailed with to go to one of their balls. I cannot express to you the anxiety my silly heart was in, when I saw my romp, now fifteen, taken out : I never felt the pangs of a father upon me so strongly in my whole life before ; and I could not have suffered more had my whole fortune been at stake. My girl came on with the most becoming modesty I had ever seen, and casting a respectful eye, as if she feared me more than all the audience, I gave a nod, which, I think, gave her all the spirit she assumed upon it, but she rose properly to that dignity of aspect. My romp, now the most graceful person of her sex, assumed a majesty which commanded the highest respect ; and when she returned to me and saw my face in rapture, she fell into the prettiest smile, and I saw in all her motion that she exulted in her father's satisfaction. You, Mr Spectator, will, better than I can tell you, imagine to yourself all the different beauties and changes of aspect in an accomplished young woman, setting forth all her beauties with a design to please no one so much as her father. My girl's lover can never know half the satisfaction that I did in her that day. I could not possibly have imagined that so great improvement could have been wrought by an art that I always held in itself ridiculous and contemptible. There is, I am convinced, no method like this to give young women a sense of their own value and dignity; and I am sure there can be none so expeditious to communicate that value to others. As for the flippant insipidly gay, and wantonly forward, whom you behold among dancers, that carriage is more to be attributed to the perverse genius of the performers than imputed to the art itself. For my part, my child has danced herself into my esteem, and I have as great an honour for her as ever I had for her mother, from whom she derived those latent good qualities which appeared in her countenance when she was dancing; for my girl, though I say it myself, showed in one quarter of an hour the innate principles of a modest virgin, a tender wife, a generous friend, a kind mother, and an indulgent mistress. I'll strain hard, but I will purchase for her an husband suitable to her merit. I am your convert in the admiration of what I thought you jested when you recommended; and if you please to be at my house on Thursday next, I make a ball for my daughter, and you shall see her dance, or, if you will do her that honour, dance with her.

I am, Sir,<br>Your most humble Servant,<br>PHILIPATER

I have some time ago spoken of a treatise written by Mr Weaver [1] on this subject, which is now, I understand, ready to be published. This work sets this matter in a very plain and advantageous light; and I am convinced from it, that if the art was under proper regulations it would be a mechanic way of implanting insensibly in minds, not capable of receiving it so well by any other rules, a sense of good breeding and virtue.

Were any one to see Mariamne dance, let him be

---

[1] See No. 334. 'This day is published, An Essay towards a History of Dancing, in which the whole art, and its various excellences, are in some measure explained' (*Spectator*, folio, No. 481).

never so sensual a brute, I defy him to entertain any thoughts but of the highest respect and esteem towards her. I was showed last week a picture in a lady's closet, for which she had an hundred different dresses that she could clap on round the face, on purpose to demonstrate the force of habits in the diversity of the same countenance. Motion, and change of posture and aspect, has an effect no less surprising on the person of Mariamne when she dances.

Chloe is extremely pretty, and as silly as she is pretty. This idiot has a very good ear and a most agreeable shape; but the folly of the thing is such, that it smiles so impertinently and affects to please so sillily, that while she dances you see the simpleton from head to foot. For you must know (as trivial as this art is thought to be) no one ever was a good dancer that had not a good understanding. If this be a truth, I shall leave the reader to judge from that maxim what esteem they ought to have for such impertinents as fly, hop, caper, tumble, twirl, turn round, and jump over their heads, and, in a word, play a thousand pranks which many animals can do better than a man, instead of performing to perfection what the human figure only is capable of performing.

It may perhaps appear odd that I, who set up for a mighty lover, at least, of virtue, should take so much pains to recommend what the soberer part of mankind look upon to be a trifle; but, under favour of the soberer part of mankind, I think they have not enough considered this matter, and for that reason only disesteem it. I must also, in my own justification, say that I attempt to bring into the service of honour and virtue everything in Nature that can pretend to give elegant delight. It may possibly be proved that vice is in itself destructive of pleasure, and virtue in itself conducive to it. If the delights of a free fortune were under proper regulations this truth would not want much argument to support it;

but it would be obvious to every man, that there is a strict affinity between all things that are truly laudable and beautiful, from the highest sentiment of the soul to the most indifferent gesture of the body.    T.

---

No. 467.    *Tuesday, August 26, 1712*    [HUGHES [1]

*Quodcunque meæ poterunt audere Camœnæ*
*Seu tibi par poterunt, seu, quod spes abnuit, ultra;*
*Sive minus; certeque canent minus; omne vovemus*
*Hoc tibi; ne tanto careat mihi nomine charta.*
TIBULL., *ad Messalam*, 1 *Eleg.* iv, 24

THE love of praise is a passion deeply fixed in the mind of every extraordinary person, and those who are most affected with it seem most to partake of that particle of the divinity which distinguishes mankind from the inferior creation.  The Supreme Being itself is most pleased with praise and thanksgiving; the other part of our duty is but an acknowledgment of our faults, whilst this is the immediate adoration of His perfections.  'Twas an excellent observation, ' That we then only despise commendation when we cease to deserve it '; and we have still extant two orations of Tully and Pliny, spoken to the greatest and best princes of all the Roman emperors [2], who, no doubt, heard with the greatest satisfaction what even the most disinterested persons, and at so large a distance of time, cannot read without admiration. Cæsar thought his life consisted in the breath of praise when he professed he had lived long enough for himself when he had for his glory; others have sacrificed themselves for a name which was not to begin till they were dead, giving away themselves to purchase a sound which was not to commence till they were out of hearing; but by merit and superior excellences not only to gain, but, whilst living, to enjoy a great and universal reputation, is the last degree of happiness which we can hope for here.  Bad characters

---

[1] This paper is attributed to Hughes ; but see No. 404.
[2] Julius Cæsar and Trajan. Cicero flattered Cæsar in his speech *Pro Marcello*, and Pliny the younger wrote a panegyric upon Trajan.

are dispersed abroad with profusion, I hope for example sake, and (as punishments are designed by the civil power) more for the deterring the innocent than the chastising the guilty. The good are less frequent, whether it be that there are indeed fewer originals of this kind to copy after, or that, through the malignity of our nature, we rather delight in the ridicule than the virtues we find in others. However, it is but just, as well as pleasing, even for variety, sometimes to give the world a representation of the bright side of human nature, as well as the dark and gloomy. The desire of imitation may, perhaps, be a greater incentive to the practice of what is good than the aversion we may conceive at what is blamable; the one immediately directs you what you should do, whilst the other only shows you what you should avoid; and I cannot at present do this with more satisfaction than by endeavouring to do some justice to the character of Manilius [1].

It would far exceed my present design, to give a particular description of Manilius through all the parts of his excellent life : I shall now only draw him in his retirement, and pass over in silence the various arts, the courtly manners, and the undesigning honesty by which he attained the honours he has enjoyed, and which now give a dignity and veneration to the ease he does enjoy. 'Tis here that he looks back with pleasure on the waves and billows through which he has steered to so fair an haven; he is now intent upon the practice of every virtue, which a great knowledge and use of mankind has discovered to be the most useful to them. Thus in his private domestic employments he is no less glorious than in his public; for 'tis in reality a more difficult task to be conspicuous in a sedentary inactive life, than in one that is spent in hurry and business; persons engaged in the latter, like bodies violently agitated, from the

---

[1] Probably Earl Cowper, the Lord Chancellor. See No. 38. At the time this paper was written Lord Cowper was in opposition, having resigned office in September 1710, after the fall of the Whig government.

swiftness of their motion have a brightness added to
them, which often vanishes when they are at rest;
but if it then still remain, it must be the seeds of
intrinsic worth that thus shine out without any
foreign aid or assistance.

His liberality in another might almost bear the
name of profusion; he seems to think it laudable
even in the excess, like that river which most enriches
when it overflows : but Manilius has too perfect a
taste of the pleasure of doing good, ever to let it be
out of his power; and for that reason he will have
a just economy, and a splendid frugality at home, the
fountain from whence those streams should flow
which he disperses abroad. He looks with disdain
on those who propose their death as the time when
they are to begin their munificence; he will both
see and enjoy (which he then does in the highest
degree) what he bestows himself; he will be the living
executor of his own bounty, whilst they who have
the happiness to be within his care and patronage,
at once pray for the continuation of his life, and their
own good fortune. No one is out of the reach of his
obligations; he knows how, by proper and becoming
methods, to raise himself to a level with those of the
highest rank; and his good nature is a sufficient warrant against the want of those who are so unhappy as
to be in the very lowest. One may say of him, as
Pindar bids his muse say of Theron [1] :

> Swear, that Theron sure has sworn,
> No one near him should be poor.
> Swear that none e'er had such a graceful art
> Fortune's free-gifts as freely to impart,
> With an unenvious hand, and an unbounded heart.

Never did Atticus succeed better in gaining the
universal love and esteem of all men, nor steer with
more success betwixt the extremes of two contending
parties. 'Tis his peculiar happiness, that while he
espouses neither with an intemperate zeal, he is not
only admired, but, what is a more rare and unusual

[1] Second Olympic Ode.

felicity, he is beloved and caressed by both; and I never yet saw any person, of whatsoever age or sex, but was immediately struck with the merit of Manilius.   There are many who are acceptable to some particular persons, whilst the rest of mankind look upon them with coldness and indifference; but he is the first whose entire good fortune it is ever to please and to be pleased, wherever he comes to be admired, and wherever he is absent to be lamented.   His merit fares like the pictures of Raphael, which are either seen with admiration by all, or at least no one dare own he has no taste for a composition which has received so universal an applause.   Envy and malice find it against their interest to indulge slander and obloquy.   'Tis as hard for an enemy to detract from, as for a friend to add to his praise.   An attempt upon his reputation is a sure lessening of one's own; and there is but one way to injure him, which is to refuse him his just commendations, and be obstinately silent.

It is below him to catch the sight with any care of dress; his outward garb is but the emblem of his mind, it is genteel, plain, and unaffected; he knows that gold and embroidery can add nothing to the opinion which all have of his merit, and that he gives a lustre to the plainest dress, whilst 'tis impossible the richest should communicate any to him.   He is still the principal figure in the room : he first engages your eye, as if there were some point of light which shone stronger upon him than on any other person.

He puts me in mind of a story of the famous Bussy d'Amboise [1], who at an assembly at court, where every one appeared with the utmost magnificence, relying upon his own superior behaviour, instead of adorning himself like the rest, put on that day a plain suit of clothes, and dressed all his servants in the

---

[1] Bussy d'Amboise killed a relation at the massacre of St Bartholomew, in order to obtain a title, and was killed by the Comte de Montsorean.  His story was made familiar in English through George Chapman's tragedy, of which there was an adaptation by D'Urfey in 1691.

most costly gay habits he could procure.  The event
was, that the eyes of the whole court were fixed upon
him; all the rest looked like his attendants, whilst
he alone had the air of a person of quality and
distinction.

Like Aristippus, whatever shape or condition he
appears in, it still sits free and easy upon him; but
in some part of his character, 'tis true, he differs
from him; for as he is altogether equal to the largeness of his present circumstances, the rectitude of
his judgment has so far corrected the inclinations of
his ambition, that he will not trouble himself with
either the desires or pursuits of anything beyond his
present enjoyments.

A thousand obliging things flow from him upon
every occasion, and they are always so just and
natural, that it is impossible to think he was at the
least pains to look for them.  One would think it
were the demon of good thoughts that discovered
to him those treasures, which he must have blinded
others from seeing, they lay so directly in their way.
Nothing can equal the pleasure is taken in hearing
him speak, but the satisfaction one receives in the
civility and attention he pays to the discourse of
others.  His looks are a silent commendation of
what is good and praiseworthy, and a secret reproof
to what is licentious and extravagant.  He knows
how to appear free and open without danger of in-
trusion, and to be cautious without seeming reserved.
The gravity of his conversation is always enlivened
with his wit and humour, and the gaiety of it is tempered with something that is instructive, as well as
barely agreeable.  Thus with him you are sure not
to be merry at the expense of your reason, nor serious
with the loss of your good humour; but by a happy
mixture in his temper, they either go together, or
perpetually succeed each other.  In fine, his whole
behaviour is equally distant from constraint and negligence, and he commands your respect, whilst he
gains your heart.

There is in his whole carriage such an engaging softness, that one cannot persuade one's self he is ever actuated by those rougher passions, which, wherever they find place, seldom fail of showing themselves in the outward demeanour of the persons they belong to : but his constitution is a just temperature between indolence on one hand and violence on the other. He is mild and gentle, wherever his affairs will give him leave to follow his own inclinations; but yet never failing to exert himself with vigour and resolution in the service of his prince, his country, or his friend.                    Z.


No. 468.    *Wednesday, August 27, 1712*    [STEELE

*Erat homo ingeniosus, acutus, acer, et qui plurimum et salis haberet et fellis, nec candoris minus.* PLIN., *Epist.*

MY paper is in a kind a letter of news, but it regards rather what passes in the world of conversation than that of business. I am very sorry that I have at present a circumstance before me which is of very great importance to all who have a relish for gaiety, wit, mirth, or humour. I mean the death of poor Dick Estcourt [1]. I have been obliged to him for so many hours of jollity, that it is but a small recompense, though all I can give him, to pass a moment or two in sadness for the loss of so agreeable a man. Poor Estcourt! the last time I saw him, we were plotting to show the town his great capacity for acting in its full light, by introducing him as dictating to a set of young players, in what manner to speak this sentence, and utter t'other passion—he had so exquisite a discerning of what was defective in any object before him, that in an instant he could show you the ridiculous side of what would pass for beautiful and just, even to men of no ill judgment, before

[1] Estcourt was buried at St Paul's, Covent Garden, on August 27, 1712, the date of this paper. See Nos. 264, 358, 370. Soon afterwards there appeared a foolish ' Letter from Dick Estcourt, the Comedian, to the *Spectator* '.

he had pointed at the failure.  He was no less skilful in the knowledge of beauty; and, I dare say, there is no one who knew him well but can repeat more well-turned compliments, as well as smart repartees, of Mr Estcourt's than of any other man in England. This was easily to be observed in his inimitable faculty of telling a story, in which he would throw in natural and unexpected incidents, to make his court to one part, and rally the other part of the company.  Then he would vary the usage he gave them, according as he saw them bear kind or sharp language.  He had the knack to raise up a pensive temper, and mortify an impertinently gay one, with the most agreeable skill imaginable.  There are a thousand things which crowd into my memory, which make me too much concerned to tell on about him. Hamlet, holding up the skull which the gravedigger threw to him with an account that it was the head of the king's jester, falls into very pleasing reflections, and cries out to his companion :

Alas, poor Yorick!  I knew him, Horatio : a fellow of infinite jest, of most excellent fancy : he hath borne me on his back a thousand times; and now, how abhorred in my imagination it is!  my gorge rises at it.  Here hung those lips, that I have kissed I know not how oft. Where be your gibes now?  your gambols?  your songs? your flashes of merriment, that were wont to set the table on a roar?  Not one now, to mock your own grinning?  quite chap-fallen?  Now get you to my lady's chamber, and tell her, let her paint an inch thick, to this favour she must come; make her laugh at that [1].

It is an insolence natural to the wealthy to affix, as much as in them lies, the character of a man to his circumstances.  Thus it is ordinary with them to praise faintly the good qualities of those below them, and say it is very extraordinary in such a man as he is, or the like, when they are forced to acknowledge

[1] *Hamlet*, Act v, sc. 1.

the value of him whose lowness upbraids their exaltation. It is to this humour only that it is to be ascribed that a quick wit in conversation, a nice judgment upon any emergency that could arise, and a most blameless inoffensive behaviour, could not raise this man above being received only upon the foot of contributing to mirth and diversion. But he was as easy under that condition as a man of so excellent talents was capable; and since they would have it that to divert was his business, he did it with all the seeming alacrity imaginable, though it stung him to the heart that it was his business. Men of sense, who could taste his excellences, were well satisfied to let him lead the way in conversation, and play after his own manner; but fools, who provoked him to mimicry, found he had the indignation to let it be at their expense who called for it, and he would show the form of conceited heavy fellows as jests to the company at their own request, in revenge for interrupting him from being a companion to put on the character of a jester.

What was peculiarly excellent in this memorable companion was, that in the accounts he gave of persons and sentiments, he did not only hit the figure of their faces and manner of their gestures, but he would in his narration fall into their very way of thinking, and this when he recounted passages wherein men of the best wit were concerned, as well as such wherein were represented men of the lowest rank of understanding [1]. It is certainly as great an instance of self-love to a weakness, to be impatient of being mimicked, as any can be imagined. There

[1] Cibber says (*Apology*, 1740, p. 69): 'This man was so amazing and extraordinary a mimic that no man or woman, from the coquette to the privy-councillor, ever moved or spoke before him, but he could carry their voice, look, mien, and motion, instantly into another company. I have heard him make long harangues, and form various arguments even in the manner of thinking, of an eminent pleader at the Bar, with every the least article and singularity of his utterance so perfectly imitated, that he was the very *alter ipse*, scarce to be distinguished from his original.' But Cibber says that these gifts deserted Estcourt on the stage, where he was a 'languid, unaffecting actor'.

were none but the vain, the formal, the proud, or those who were incapable of amending their faults, that dreaded him; to others he was in the highest degree pleasing; and I do not know any satisfaction of any indifferent kind I ever tasted so much, as having got over an impatience of seeing myself in the air he could put me when I have displeased him. It is indeed to his exquisite talent this way, more than any philosophy I could read on the subject, that my person is very little of my care; and it is indifferent to me what is said of my shape, my air, my manner, my speech, or my address. It is to poor Estcourt I chiefly owe that I am arrived at the happiness of thinking nothing a diminution to me, but what argues a depravity of my will.

It has as much surprised me as anything in Nature to have it frequently said that he was not a good player : but that must be owing to a partiality for former actors in the parts in which he succeeded them, and judging by comparison of what was liked before, rather than by the nature of the thing. When a man of his wit and smartness could put on an utter absence of common sense in his face, as he did in the character of Bullfinch in the *Northern Lass* [1], and an air of insipid cunning and vivacity in the character of Pounce in the *Tender Husband* [2], it is folly to dispute his capacity and success, as he was an actor.

Poor Estcourt! let the vain and proud be at rest; they will no more disturb their admiration of their dear selves, and thou art no longer to drudge in raising the mirth of stupids, who know nothing of thy merit, for thy maintenance.

It is natural for the generality of mankind to run into reflections upon our mortality when disturbers of the world are laid at rest, but to take no notice when they who can please and divert are pulled from us : but for my part, I cannot but think the loss of such talents as the man of whom I am speaking was

1 By Richard Brome, 1632.        2 By Steele, 1705.

master of, a more melancholy instance of mortality than the dissolution of persons of never so high characters in the world, whose pretensions were that they were noisy and mischievous.

But I must grow more succinct, and, as a Spectator, give an account of this extraordinary man who, in his way, never had an equal in any age before him, or in that wherein he lived. I speak of him as a companion, and a man qualified for conversation. His fortune exposed him to an obsequiousness towards the worst sort of company, but his excellent qualities rendered him capable of making the best figure in the most refined. I have been present with him among men of the most delicate taste a whole night, and have known him (for he saw it was desired) keep the discourse to himself the most part of it, and maintain his good humour with a countenance, in a language so delightful, without offence to any person or thing upon earth, still preserving the distance his circumstances obliged him to; I say, I have seen him do all this in such a charming manner that I am sure none of those I hint at will read this without giving him some sorrow for their abundant mirth, and one gush of tears for so many bursts of laughter. I wish it were any honour to the pleasant creature's memory that my eyes are too much suffused to let me go on [1]. 　　　　T.

[1] The following sentences, which appeared in the folio issue, were not reprinted in the collected edition :

‘ It is a felicity his friends may rejoice in, that he had his senses, and used them as he ought to do, in his last moments. It is remarkable that his judgment was in its calm perfection to the utmost article, for when his wife out of her fondness, desired she might send for a certain illiterate humorist (whom he had accompanied in a thousand mirthful moments, and whose insolence makes fools think he assumes from conscious merit) he answered, " *Do what you please, but he won't come near me.*" Let poor Estcourt's negligence about this message convince the unwary of a triumphant empiric's ignorance and inhumanity.’

This passage refers to the neglect of Estcourt in his last illness by Dr John Radcliffe, the physician, who made numerous enemies, and was often called an empiric by other doctors.

No. 469.    *Thursday, August 28, 1712*    [ADDISON

*Detrahere aliquid alteri, et hominem hominis incommodo suum augere commodum, magis est contra naturam, quam mors, quam paupertas, quam dolor, quam cætera quæ possunt aut corpori accidere, aut rebus externis.* TULL.

I AM persuaded there are few men, of generous principles, who would seek after great places, were it not rather to have an opportunity in their hands of obliging their particular friends, or those whom they look upon as men of worth, than to procure wealth and honour for themselves. To an honest mind the best perquisites of a place are the advantages it gives a man of doing good.

Those who are under the great officers of state, and are the instruments by which they act, have more frequent opportunities for the exercise of compassion, and benevolence, than their superiors themselves. These men know every little case that is to come before the great man, and if they are possessed with honest minds, will consider poverty as a recommendation in the person who applies himself to them, and makes the justice of his cause the most powerful solicitor in his behalf. A man of this temper, when he is in a post of business, becomes a blessing to the public: he patronises the orphan and the widow, assists the friendless, and guides the ignorant: he does not reject the person's pretensions, who does not know how to explain them, or refuse doing a good office for a man because he cannot pay the fee of it. In short, though he regulates himself in all his proceedings by justice and equity, he finds a thousand occasions for all the good-natured offices of generosity and compassion.

A man is unfit for such a place of trust, who is of a sour intractable nature, or has any other passion that makes him uneasy to those who approach him. Roughness of temper is apt to discountenance the timorous or modest. The proud man discourages those from approaching him, who are of a mean condition, and who most want his assistance. The impatient man will not give himself time to be informed of the matter that lies before him. An officer with one or more of these unbecoming qualities, is sometimes looked upon as a proper person to keep off impertinence and solicitation from his superior; but this is a kind of merit that can never atone for the injustice which may very often arise from it.

There are two other vicious qualities which render a man very unfit for such a place of trust. The first of these is a dilatory temper, which commits innumerable cruelties without design. The maxim which several have laid down for a man's conduct in ordinary life, should be inviolable with a man in office, never to think of doing that to-morrow which may be done to-day. A man who defers doing what ought to be done, is guilty of injustice so long as he defers it. The despatch of a good office is very often as beneficial to the solicitor as the good office itself. In short, if a man compared the inconveniences which another suffers by his delays, with the trifling motives and advantages which he himself may reap by such a delay, he would never be guilty of a fault which very often does an irreparable prejudice to the person who depends upon him, and which might be remedied with little trouble to himself.

But in the last place, there is no man so improper to be employed in business, as he who is in any degree capable of corruption; and such an one is the man, who upon any pretence whatsoever receives more than what is the stated and unquestioned fee of his office. Gratifications, tokens of thankfulness, despatch money, and the like specious terms, are the pretences under which corruption very frequently shelters itself. An honest man will, however, look on all these methods as unjustifiable, and will enjoy himself better in a moderate fortune that is gained with honour and reputation, than in an overgrown estate that is cankered with the acquisitions of rapine and exaction. Were all our offices discharged with such an inflexible integrity, we should not see men in all ages, who grow up to exorbitant wealth with the abilities which are to be met with in an ordinary mechanic. I cannot but think that such a corruption proceeds chiefly from men's employing the first that offer themselves, or those who have the character of shrewd worldly men, instead of searching out such as have had a liberal education, and have been trained up in the studies of knowledge and virtue.

It has been observed, that men of learning who take to business, discharge it generally with greater honesty than men of the world. The chief reason for it I take to be as follows : A man that has spent his youth in reading, has been used to find virtue extolled, and vice stigmatised. A man that has passed his time in the world, has often seen vice triumphant, and virtue discountenanced. Extortion, rapine, and injustice, which are branded with infamy in books, often give a man a figure in the world; while several qualities which are celebrated in authors, as generosity, ingenuity, and good-nature, impoverish and ruin him. This cannot but have a proportionable effect on men, whose tempers and principles are equally good and vicious.

There would be at least this advantage in employing men of learning and parts in business, that their prosperity would sit more gracefully on them, and that we should not see many worthless persons shot up into the greatest figures of life.      C.

No. 470.      *Friday, August* 29, 1712      [ADDISON

*Turpe est difficiles habere nugas,*
*Et stultus est labor ineptiarum.*
MART., 2 *Epig.* lxxxvi, 9

I HAVE been very often disappointed of late years, when upon examining the new edition of a classic author, I have found about half the volume taken up with various readings. When I have expected to meet with a learned note upon a doubtful passage in

a Latin poet, I have only been informed that such or
such ancient manuscripts for an *et* write an *ac*, or of
some other notable discovery of the like importance.
Indeed, when a different reading gives us a different
sense, or a new elegance in an author, the editor
does very well in taking notice of it; but when he
only entertains us with the several ways of spelling
the same word, and gathers together the various
blunders and mistakes of twenty or thirty different
transcribers, they only take up the time of the learned
reader and puzzle the minds of the ignorant.  I have
often fancied with myself how enraged an old Latin
author would be, should he see the several absurdities in sense and grammar which are imputed to
him by some or other of these various readings.  In
one he speaks nonsense; in another makes use of a
word that was never heard of; and, indeed, there is
scarce a solecism in writing which the best author
is not guilty of, if we may be at liberty to read him
in the words of some manuscript, which the laborious
editor has thought fit to examine in the prosecution
of his work.

I question not but the ladies and pretty fellows
will be very curious to understand what it is that
I have been hitherto talking of, I shall therefore
give them a notion of this practice, by endeavouring
to write after the manner of several persons who
make an eminent figure in the republic of letters.
To this end we will suppose that the following song
is an old ode [1] which I present to the public in a
new edition, with the several various readings which
I find of it in former editions and in ancient manuscripts [2].  Those who cannot relish the various read-

---

[1] 'Following song, which by the way is a beautiful descant upon a
single thought, like the compositions of the best ancient lyric poets.
I say, we will suppose this song is an old ode' (folio).

[2] 'This satire on the pedantry of editors appears to have special
reference to the edition of the *Perrigilium Veneris*, which was published
at the Hague in 1712.  This work was satirised also in 1714 in *Le Chef
d'Œuvre d'un Inconnu*, which contained a witty commentary celebrated
in some lines by Bolingbroke' (Nichols's *Select Collection of Poems*,
vii, 68).

ings, will perhaps find their account in the song, which never before appeared in print :

My love was fickle once and changing,
  Nor e'er would settle in my heart ;
From beauty still to beauty ranging,
  In every face I found a dart.

'Twas first a charming shape enslaved me ;
  An eye then gave the fatal stroke :
'Till by her wit Corinna saved me,
  And all my former fetters broke.

But now a long and lasting anguish
  For Belvidera I endure ;
Hourly I sigh and hourly languish,
  Nor hope to find the wonted cure.

For here the false inconstant lover,
  After a thousand beauties shown,
Does new surprising charms discover,
  And finds variety in one.

## Various Readings

Stanza the first, verse the first : *And changing.* The *and* in some manuscripts is written thus &, but that in the Cotton Library writes it in three distinct letters.

Verse the second : *Nor e'er would.* Aldus reads it *ever would;* but as this would hurt the metre we have restored it to its genuine reading, by observing that syrænesis which had been neglected by ignorant transcribers.

Ibid : *In my heart.* Scaliger and others, *on my heart.*

Verse the fourth : *I found a dart.* The Vatican manuscript for *I* reads *it*, but this must have been the hallucination of the transcriber, who probably mistook the dash of the *I* for a *T*.

Stanza the second, verse the second : *The fatal stroke.* Scioppius, Salmasius, and many others for *the* read *a*, but I have stuck to the usual reading.

Verse the third : *'Till by her wit.* Some manuscripts have it *his wit*, others *your*, others *their wit*.

But as I find Corinna to be the name of a woman in other authors, I cannot doubt but it should be *her.*

Stanza the third, verse the first : *A long and lasting anguish.* The German manuscript reads *a lasting passion,* but the rhyme will not admit it.

Verse the second : *For Belvidera I endure.* Did not all the manuscripts reclaim, I should change *Belvidera* into *Pelvidera;* pelvis being used by several of the ancient comic writers for a looking-glass, by which means the etymology of the word is very visible, and Pelvidera will signify a lady who often looks in her glass, as indeed she had very good reason, if she had all those beauties which our poet here ascribes to her.

Verse the third : *Hourly I sigh and hourly languish.* Some for the word *hourly* read *daily,* and others *nightly;* the last has great authorities of its side.

Verse the fourth : *The wonted cure.* The elder Stevens reads *wanted cure.*

Stanza the fourth, verse the second : *After a thousand beauties.* In several copies we meet with a *hundred beauties,* by the usual error of the transcribers, who probably omitted a cipher, and had not taste enough to know that the word *thousand* was ten times a greater compliment to the poet's mistress than a *hundred.*

Verse the fourth : *And finds variety in one.* Most of the ancient manuscripts have it *in two.* Indeed so many of them concur in this last reading, that I am very much in doubt whether it ought not to take place. There are but two reasons which incline me to the reading, as I have published it; first, because the rhyme, and, secondly, because the sense is preserved by it. It might likewise proceed from the oscitancy of transcribers, who, to despatch their work the sooner, used to write all numbers in cipher, and seeing the figure 1 followed by a little dash of the pen, as is customary in old manuscripts, they perhaps mistook the dash for a second figure, and by casting-up both together, composed out of them the figure 2. But this I shall leave to the learned, without determining anything in a matter of so great uncertainty.                                             C.

No. 471.     *Saturday, August 30, 1712*     [ADDISON

'Εν ελπίσιν χρη τους σοφους έχειν βίον. EURIPID.

THE time present seldom affords sufficient employment to the mind of man. Objects of pain or pleasure, love or admiration, do not lie thick enough together in life to keep the soul in constant action, and supply an immediate exercise to its faculties. In order, therefore, to remedy this defect, that the mind may not want business, but always have materials for thinking, she is endowed with certain powers, that can recall what is passed, and anticipate what is to come.

That wonderful faculty, which we call the memory, is perpetually looking back, when we have nothing present to entertain us. It is like those repositories in several animals, that are filled with stores of their former food, on which they may ruminate when their present pasture fails.

As the memory relieves the mind in her vacant moments, and prevents any chasms of thought by ideas of what is past, we have other faculties that agitate and employ her upon what is to come. These are the passions of hope and fear.

By these two passions we reach forward into futurity, and bring up to our present thoughts objects that lie hid in the remotest depths of time. We suffer misery, and enjoy happiness before they are in being; we can set the sun and stars forward, or lose sight of them by wandering into those retired parts of eternity, when the heavens and earth shall be no more.

By the way, who can imagine that the existence

of a creature is to be circumscribed by time, whose thoughts are not? But I shall, in this paper, confine myself to that particular passion which goes by the name of Hope.

Our actual enjoyments are so few and transient, that man would be a very miserable being, were he not endowed with this passion, which gives him a taste of those good things that may possibly come into his possession. ' We should hope for every-thing that is good ', says the old poet Linus[1], ' be-cause there is nothing which may not be hoped for, and nothing but what the gods are able to give us.' Hope quickens all the still parts of life, and keeps the mind awake in her most remiss and indolent hours. It gives habitual serenity and good humour. It is a kind of vital heat in the soul, that cheers and gladdens her, when she does not attend to it. It makes pain easy, and labour pleasant.

Beside these several advantages which rise from hope, there is another which is none of the least, and that is, its great efficacy in preserving us from setting too high a value on present enjoyments. The saying of Cæsar is very well known. When he had given away all his estate in gratuities among his friends, one of them asked what he had left for him-self; to which that great man replied, ' Hope '. His natural magnanimity hindered him from prizing what he was certainly possessed of, and turned all his thoughts upon something more valuable that he had in view. I question not but every reader will draw a moral from this story, and apply it to himself with-out my direction.

The old story of Pandora's box (which many of the learned believe was formed among the heathens upon the tradition of the fall of man) shows us how deplorable a state they thought the present life with-out hope. To set forth the utmost condition of misery, they tell us that our forefather, according to the pagan theology, had a great vessel presented

[1] Fragment on Hope.

him by Pandora. 'Upon his lifting up the lid of it', says the fable, 'there flew out all the calamities and distempers incident to men, from which, until that time, they had been altogether exempt. Hope, who had been enclosed in the cup with so much bad company, instead of flying off with the rest, stuck so close to the lid of it, that it was shut down upon her.'

I shall make but two reflections upon what I have hitherto said. First, that no kind of life is so happy as that which is full of hope, especially when the hope is well grounded, and when the object of it is of an exalted kind, and in its nature proper to make the person happy who enjoys it. This proposition must be very evident to those who consider how few are the present enjoyments of the most happy man, and how insufficient to give him an entire satisfaction and acquiescence in them.

My next observation is this, that a religious life is that which most abounds in a well-grounded hope, and such an one as is fixed on objects that are capable of making us entirely happy. This hope in a religious man, is much more sure and certain than the hope of any temporal blessing, as it is strengthened not only by reason, but by faith. It has at the same time its eye perpetually fixed on that state, which implies in the very notion of it the most full and the most complete happiness.

I have before shown how the influence of hope in general sweetens life, and makes our present condition supportable, if not pleasing; but a religious hope has still greater advantages. It does not only bear up the mind under her sufferings, but makes her rejoice in them, as they may be the instruments of procuring her the great and ultimate end of all her hope.

Religious hope has likewise this advantage above any other kind of hope, that it is able to revive the dying man, and to fill his mind not only with secret comfort and refreshment, but sometimes with rapture and transport. He triumphs in his agonies, whilst the soul springs forward with delight to the great object which she has always had in view, and leaves the body with an expectation of being reunited to her in a glorious and joyful resurrection.

I shall conclude this essay with those emphatical expressions of a lively hope, which the Psalmist made use of in the midst of those dangers and adversities which surrounded him, for the following passage had its present and personal, as well as its future and prophetic sense : ' I have set the Lord always before me : because He is at my right hand, I shall not be moved. Therefore my heart is glad, and my glory rejoiceth : my flesh also shall rest in hope. For Thou wilt not leave my soul in hell; neither wilt Thou suffer Thine Holy One to see corruption. Thou wilt shew me the path of life : in Thy presence is fulness of joy; at Thy right hand there are pleasures for evermore [1].'                                C.

No. 472.        *Monday, Sept. 1, 1712*        [STEELE

*Voluptas*
*Solamenque mali.*        VIRG., *Æn.* iii, 660

I RECEIVED some time ago a proposal, which had a preface to it, wherein the author discoursed at large of the innumerable objects of charity in a nation, and admonished the rich, who were afflicted with any distemper of body, particularly to regard the poor in the same species of affliction, and confine their tenderness to them, since it is impossible to assist all who are presented to them. The proposer had been relieved from a malady in his eyes by an operation performed by Sir William Read [2]; and being a man of condition,

[1] *Psalm* xvi, 8–11.
[2] Sir William Read, who died on May 24, 1715, was a well-known oculist who was often regarded as a quack, and was certainly uneducated, though his abilities are recognised in Sir Hans Sloane's correspondence. On his death he left a considerable portion of his property to Marischal College, Aberdeen. In the *Tatler* (No. 219) he advertised that he had been thirty-five years in the practice of couching cataracts, taking off wens, curing wry-necks and hare-lips,

had taken a resolution to maintain three poor blind men during their lives, in gratitude for that great blessing. This misfortune is so very great and un-frequent, that one would think an establishment for all the poor under it might be easily accomplished, with the addition of a very few others to those wealthy who are in the same calamity. However, the thought of the proposer arose from a very good motive, and the parcelling of ourselves out, as called to particular acts of beneficence, would be a pretty cement of society and virtue. It is the ordinary foun-dation of men's holding a commerce with each other, and becoming familiar, that they agree in the same sort of pleasure; and sure it may also be some reason for amity, that they are under one common distress. If all the rich who are lame in the gout, from a life of ease, pleasure, and luxury, would help those few who have it without a previous life of pleasure, and add a few of such laborious men, who are become lame from unhappy blows, falls, or other accidents of age or sickness; I say, would such gouty persons administer to the necessities of men disabled like themselves, the consciousness of such a behaviour would be the best julep, cordial, and anodyne in the feverish, faint, and tormenting vicissitudes of that miserable distemper. The same may be said of all other, both bodily and intellectual evils. These classes of charity would certainly bring down bless-ings upon an age and people; and if men were not petrified with the love of this world, against all sense of the commerce which ought to be among them, it would not be an unreasonable bill for a poor man in the agony of pain, aggravated by want and poverty, to draw upon a sick alderman after this form:

vending styptic water, &c. In 1711 Swift wrote of Read: ' He has been a mountebank, and is the queen's oculist. He makes admirable punch, and treats you in golden vessels.' He had been knighted in 1705. After Read's death his widow, ' the Lady Read in Durham Yard in the Strand,' announced that she was continuing her husband's business, in which she had had fifteen years' experience, and great success ' in curing multitudes of blind and defective in their sight particularly several who were born blind '.

MR. BASIL PLENTY

SIR,—You have the gout and stone, with sixty thousand pounds sterling; I have the gout and stone, not worth one farthing : I shall pray for you, and desire you would pay the bearer twenty shillings for value received from,

Sir,
Your humble Servant,
CRIPPLEGATE,                        LAZARUS HOPEFUL
*Aug.* 29, 1712

The reader's own imagination will suggest to him the reasonableness of such correspondences, and diversify them into a thousand forms; but I shall close this as I began upon the subject of blindness. The following letter seems to be written by a man of learning, who is returned to his study after a suspense of an ability to do so. The benefit he reports himself to have received may well claim the handsomest encomium he can give the operator.

MR. SPECTATOR,—Ruminating lately on your admirable discourses on the 'Pleasures of the Imagination[1]', I began to consider to which of our senses we are obliged for the greatest and most important share of those pleasures; and I soon concluded that it was to the sight : that is the sovereign of the senses and mother of all the arts and sciences, that have refined the rudeness of the uncultivated mind to a politeness that distinguishes the fine spirits from the barbarous *goût* of the great vulgar and the small. The sight is the obliging benefactress that bestows on us the most transporting sensations that we have from the various and wonderful products of Nature. To the sight we owe the amazing discoveries of the height, magnitude, and motion of the planets; their several revolutions about their common centre of light, heat, and motion, the sun. The sight travels yet farther to the fixed stars, and furnishes the understanding with solid reasons to prove that each of them is a sun moving on its own axis, in the centre of its own vortex or tur-

[1] No. 411 *seq.*

billion, and performing the same offices to its dependent planets that our glorious sun does to this. But the inquiries of the sight will not be stopped here, but make their progress through the immense expanse to the Milky Way, and there divide the blended fires of the Galaxy into infinite and different worlds, made up of distinct suns and their peculiar equipages of planets; till unable to pursue this track any further, it deputes the imagination to go on to new discoveries till it fill the unbounded space with endless worlds.

The sight informs the statuary's chisel with power to give breath to lifeless brass and marble, and the painter's pencil to swell the flat canvas with moving figures actuated by imaginary souls. Music indeed may plead another original, since Jubal, by the different falls of his hammer on the anvil, discovered by the ear the first rude music that pleased the antediluvian fathers; but then the sight has not only reduced those wilder sounds into artful order and harmony, but conveys that harmony to the most distant parts of the world without the help of sound. To the sight we owe not only all the discoveries of philosophy, but all the divine imagery of poetry that transport the intelligent reader of Homer, Milton, and Virgil.

As the sight has polished the world so does it supply us with the most grateful and lasting pleasure. Let love, let friendship, paternal affection, filial piety, and conjugal duty declare the joys the sight bestows on a meeting after absence. But it would be endless to enumerate all the pleasures and advantages of sight; every one that has it, every hour he makes use of it, finds them, feels them, enjoys them.

Thus as our greatest pleasures and knowledge are derived from the sight, so has Providence been more curious in the formation of its seat, the eye, than of the organs of the other senses. That stupendous machine is composed in a wonderful manner of muscles, membranes, and humours. Its motions are admirably directed by the muscles; the perspicuity of the humours transmit the rays of light; the rays are regularly refracted by their figure; the black lining of the sclerotics effectually prevents their being confounded by reflection. It is wonderful indeed to consider how many objects the eye is fitted to take in at once, and successively in an instant, and at the same time to make a judgment of their position, figure, and colour. It watches against our dangers, guides our steps, and lets in all the visible objects, whose beauty and variety instruct and delight.

The pleasures and advantages of sight being so great, the loss must be very grievous; of which Milton, from experience, gives the most sensible idea, both in the third book of his *Paradise Lost* and in his *Samson Agonistes*:

To Light, in the former :

> Thee I revisit safe,
> And feel thy sovereign vital lamp ; but thou
> Revisit'st not these eyes, that roll in vain
> To find thy piercing ray, but [1] find no dawn [2].

And a little after :

> Seasons return ; but not to me returns
> Day, or the sweet approach of even or morn,
> Or sight of vernal bloom, or summer's rose,
> Or flocks, or herds, or human face divine ;
> But cloud instead, and everduring dark
> Surrounds me, from the cheerful ways of men
> Cut off, and for the book of knowledge fair
> Presented with a universal blank
> Of nature's works, to me expunged and razed,
> And wisdom at one entrance quite shut out [3].

Again, in *Samson Agonistes* :

> But chief of all,
> O loss of sight? of thee I most complain,
> Blind among enemies, O worse than chains,
> Dungeon, or beggary, or decrepit age !
> Light, the prime work of God, to me's extinct,
> And all her various objects of delight
> Annulled [4].

> Still as a fool,
> In power of others, never in my own.
> Scarce half I seem to live, dead more than half :
> O dark ! dark ! dark ! amid the blaze of noon !
> Irrecoverably dark, total eclipse,
> Without all hope of day [5] !

The enjoyment of sight then being so great a blessing, and the loss of it so terrible an evil, how excellent and valuable is the skill of that artist which can
restore the former, and redress the latter? My frequent perusal of the advertisements in the public newspapers (generally the most agreeable entertainment they
afford) has presented me with many and various benefits
of this kind done to my countrymen by that skilful
artist Dr Grant [1], her Majesty's oculist extraordinary,
whose happy hand has brought and restored to sight
several hundreds in less than four years. Many have
received sight by his means who came blind from their
mother's womb, as in the famous instance of Jones of
Newington [2]. I myself have been cured by him of a
weakness in my eyes next to blindness, and am ready
to believe anything that is reported of his ability this
way; and know that many, who could not purchase his
assistance with money, have enjoyed it from his charity.
But a list of particulars would swell my letter beyond
its bounds, what I have said being sufficient to comfort
those who are in the like distress, since they may conceive hopes of being no longer miserable in this kind,
while there is yet alive so able an oculist as Dr Grant.

I am,

The Spectator's humble Servant,

PHILANTHROPUS

No. 473.        Tuesday, Sept. 2, 1712        [STEELE

Quid, si quis vultu torvo ferus et pede nudo
Exiguæque togæ simulet textore Catonem ;
Virtutemne repræsentet moresque Catonis?

HOR., 1 Ep. xix, 12

To the SPECTATOR

SIR,—I am now in the country, and employ most of
my time in reading, or thinking upon what I have read.

[1] See No. 444.
[2] *A full and true Account of a Miraculous Cure of a Young Man in
Newington* was published in 1707, and the story is told in the *Tatler*,
No. 55. Jones seems not to have been born blind, but only with an
imperfection in his sight. Testimonies to the genuineness of the cure
will, however, be found in the *British Apollo*, vol. ii, Nos. 39, 91, a
paper in which Grant frequently advertised.

Your paper comes constantly down to me, and it affects me so much that I find my thoughts run into your way; and I recommend to you a subject upon which you have not yet touched, and that is the satisfaction some men seem to take in their imperfections, I think one may call it glorying in their insufficiency; a certain great author is of opinion it is the contrary to envy, though perhaps it may proceed from it. Nothing is so common as to hear men of this sort speaking of themselves, add to their own merit (as they think) by impairing it, in praising themselves for their defects, freely allowing they commit some few frivolous errors, in order to be esteemed persons of uncommon talents and great qualifications. They are generally professing an injudicious neglect of dancing, fencing, and riding, as also an unjust contempt for travelling and the modern languages; as for their part (say they) they never valued or troubled their head about them. This panegyrical satire on themselves certainly is worthy of your animadversion. I have known one of these gentlemen think himself obliged to forget the day of an appointment, and sometimes even that you spoke to him; and when you see 'em, they hope you'll pardon 'em, for they have the worst memory in the world. One of 'em started up t'other day in some confusion, and said, 'Now I think on't, I'm to meet Mr Mortmain the attorney about some business, but whether it is to-day or to-morrow, faith, I can't tell.' Now to my certain knowledge he knew his time to a moment, and was there accordingly. These forgetful persons have, to heighten their crime, generally the best memories of any people, as I have found out by their remembering sometimes through inadvertency. Two or three of them that I know can say most of our modern tragedies by heart. I asked a gentleman the other day that is famous for a good carver (at which acquisition he is out of countenance, imagining it may detract from some of his more essential qualifications) to help me to something that was near him; but he excused himself, and blushing told me, of all things he could never carve in his life; though it can be proved upon him, that he cuts up, disjoints, and uncases with incomparable dexterity. I would not be understood as if I thought it laudable for a man of quality and fortune to rival the acquisitions of artificers, and endeavour to excel in little handy qualities; no, I argue only against being ashamed at what is really praiseworthy. As these pretences to ingenuity show themselves several ways, you'll often see a man of this temper ashamed to be clean, and setting up for wit only from negligence in his habit. Now I am upon this head, I can't help observing also upon a very different folly proceeding from the same cause. As these above mentioned arise from affecting an equality with men of greater talents from having the same faults, there are others who would come at a parallel with those above them, by possessing little advantages which they want. I heard a young man not long ago, who has sense, comfort himself in his ignorance of Greek, Hebrew, and the Orientals. At the same time that he published his aversion to these languages, he said that the knowledge of 'em was rather a diminution than an advancement of a man's character, though at the same time I know he languishes and repines he is not master of them himself. Whenever I take any of these fine persons, thus detracting from what they don't understand, I tell them I will complain to you, and say I am sure you will not allow it an exception against a thing, that he who contemns it is an ignorant in it.

I am, Sir,

Your most humble Servant,

S. P.

MR SPECTATOR,—I am a man of a very good estate, and am honourably in love. I hope you will allow, when the ultimate purpose is honest, there may be, without trespass against innocence, some toying by the way. People of condition are perhaps too distant and formal on those occasions; but, however that is, I am to confess to you, that I have writ some verses to atone for my offence. You professed authors are a little severe upon us, who write like gentlemen. But if you are a friend to love, you will insert my poem. You cannot imagine how much service it will do me with my fair one, as well as reputation with all my friends, to have something of mine in the *Spectator*. My crime was, that I snatched a kiss, and my poetical excuse as follows :

### I

Belinda, see from yonder flowers
  The bee flies loaded to its cell;
Can you perceive what it devours?
  Are they impaired in show or smell?

### II

So, though I robbed you of a kiss,
  Sweeter than their ambrosial dew,
Why are you angry at my bliss?
  Has it at all impoverished you?

### III

'Tis by this cunning I contrive,
  In spite of your unkind reserve,
To keep my fam'shed love alive,
  Which you inhumanly would starve.

I am, Sir,
Your humble Servant,
TIMOTHY STANZA

*Aug.* 23, 1712

SIR,—Having a little time upon my hands, I could not think of bestowing it better, than in writing an epistle to the *Spectator*, which I now do, and am,
Sir,
Your humble Servant,
BOB SHORT

*P.S.*—If you approve of my style, I am likely enough to become your correspondent. I desire your opinion of it. I design it for that way of writing called by the judicious the ' familiar[1] '.          T.

No. 474.          *Wednesday, Sept. 3, 1712*          [STEELE

*Asperitas agrestis et inconcinna.*   Hor., 1 *Ep.* xviii, 6

MR SPECTATOR,—Being of the number of those that have lately retired from the centre of business and pleasure, my uneasiness in the country where I am, arises rather from the society than the solitude of it.

[1] See No. 485.

To be obliged to receive and return visits from and to a circle of neighbours, who through diversity of age or inclinations can neither be entertaining nor serviceable to us, is a vile loss of time, and a slavery from which a man should deliver himself, if possible : for why must I lose the remaining part of my life, because they have thrown away the former part of theirs? It is to me an insupportable affliction, to be tormented with the narrations of a set of people, who are warm in their expressions, of the quick relish of that pleasure which their dogs and horses have a more delicate taste of. I do also in my heart detest and abhor that damnable doctrine and position of the necessity of a bumper, though to one's own toast; for though 'tis pretended that these deep politicians[1] are used only to inspire gaiety, they certainly drown that cheerfulness which would survive a moderate circulation. If at these meetings it were left to every stranger either to fill his glass according to his own inclination, or to make his retreat when he finds he has been sufficiently obedient to that of others, these entertainments would be governed with more good sense, and consequently with more good breeding, than at present they are. Indeed where any of the guests are known to measure their fame or pleasure by their glass, proper exhortations might be used to these to push their fortunes in this sort of reputation; but where 'tis unseasonably insisted on to a modest stranger, this drench may be said to be swallowed with the same necessity, as if it had been tendered in the horn[2] for that purpose, with this aggravating circumstance, that it distresses the entertainer's guest in the same degree as it relieves his horses.

To attend without impatience an account of five-barred gates, double ditches and precipices, and to survey the orator with desiring eyes, is to me extremely difficult, but absolutely necessary, to be upon tolerable terms with him : but then the occasional burstings out into laughter, is of all other accomplishments the most requisite. I confess at present I have not the command of these convulsions, as is necessary to be good com-

---

1 'Politicians,' the reading of the original and subsequent editions seems to be a misprint for 'potations.'
2 A horn used to administer potions to horses.

pany; therefore I beg you would publish this letter, and let me be known all at once for a queer fellow, and avoided. It is monstrous to me, that we, who are given to reading and calm conversation, should ever be visited by these roarers : but they think they themselves, as neighbours, may come into our rooms with the same right that they and their dogs hunt in our grounds.

Your institution of clubs I have always admired, in which you constantly endeavoured the union of the metaphorically defunct, that is, such as are neither serviceable to the busy and enterprising part of mankind, nor entertaining to the retired and speculative. There should certainly therefore in each county be established a club of the persons whose conversations I have described, who for their own private, as also the public emolument, should exclude, and be excluded all other society. Their attire should be the same with their huntsmen's, and none should be admitted into this green conversation-piece, except he had broke his collarbone thrice. A broken rib or two might also admit a man without the least opposition. The president must necessarily have broken his neck, and have been taken up dead once or twice. For the more maims this brotherhood shall have met with, the easier will their conversation flow and keep up; and when any one of these vigorous invalids had finished his narration of the collar-bone, this naturally would introduce the history of the ribs. Besides, the different circumstances of their falls and fractures would help to prolong and diversify their relations. There should also be another club of such men, who have not succeeded so well in maiming themselves, but are however in the constant pursuit of these accomplishments. I would by no means be suspected by what I have said to traduce in general the body of fox-hunters; for whilst I look upon a reasonable creature full speed after a pack of dogs, by way of pleasure, and not of business, I shall always make honourable mention of it.

But the most irksome conversation of all others I have met with in the neighbourhood, has been among two or three of your travellers, who have overlooked men and manners, and have passed through France and Italy with the same observation that the carriers and stage-coachmen do through Great Britain; that is, their stops and stages have been regulated according to the liquor they have met with in their passage. They indeed remember the names of abundance of places, with the particular fineries of certain churches : but their distinguishing mark is certain prettinesses of foreign languages, the meaning of which they could have better expressed in their own. The entertainment of these fine observers Shakespeare [1] has described to consist

> In talking of the Alps and Apennines,
> The Pyrenæan, and the river Po.

And then concludes with a sigh :

> Now this is worshipful society.

I would not be thought in all this to hate such honest creatures as dogs; I am only unhappy that I cannot partake in their diversions. But I love them so well, as dogs, that I often go with my pockets stuffed with bread to dispense my favours or make my way through them at neighbours' houses. There is in particular a young hound of great expectation, vivacity, and enterprise, that attends my flights wherever he spies me. This creature observes my countenance, and behaves himself accordingly. His mirth, his frolic, and joy upon the sight of me has been observed, and I have been gravely desired not to encourage him so much, for it spoils his parts; but I think he shows them sufficiently in the several boundings, friskings, and scourings, when he makes his court to me; but I foresee in a little time he and I must keep company with one another only, for we are fit for no other in these parts. Having informed you how I do pass my time in the country where I am, I must proceed to tell you how I would pass it had I such a fortune as would put me above the observance of ceremony and custom.

My scheme of a country life then should be as follows. As I am happy in three or four very agreeable friends, these I would constantly have with me; and the freedom we took with one another at school and the university we would maintain and exert upon all occasions with great courage. There should be

---

[1] *King John*, Act i, sc. 1.

certain hours of the day to be employed in reading,
during which time it should be impossible for any one
of us to enter the other's chamber, unless by storm.
After this we would communicate the trash or treasure
we had met with, with our own reflections upon the
matter; the justness of which we would controvert
with good-humoured warmth, and never spare one
another out of that complaisant spirit of conversation
which makes others affirm and deny the same matter
in a quarter of an hour.  If any of the neighbouring
gentlemen, not of our turn, should take it in their
heads to visit me, I should look upon these persons
in the same degree enemies to my particular state of
happiness as ever the French were to that of the
public, and I would be at an annual expense in spies
to observe their motions.  Whenever I should be surprised with a visit, as I hate drinking, I would be
brisk in swilling bumpers, upon this maxim, that it is
better to trouble others with my impertinence than to
be troubled myself with theirs.  The necessity of an
infirmary makes me resolve to fall into that project;
and as we should be but five, the terrors of an involun-
tary separation, which our number cannot so well admit
of, would make us exert ourselves in opposition to all
the particulars mentioned in your institution of that
equitable confinement.  This my way of life I know
would subject me to the imputation of a morose,
covetous, and singular fellow.  These and all other hard
words, with all manner of insipid jests, and all other
reproach, would be matter of mirth to me and my
friends : besides, I would destroy the application of
the epithets morose and covetous by a yearly relief of
my undeservedly necessitous neighbours, and by treating my friends and domestics with an humanity that
should express the obligation to lie rather on my side ;
and as for the word singular, I was always of opinion
every man must be so to be what one would desire
him.

Your very humble Servant,

J. R. [1]

---

[1] The author of this letter appears to have been Richard Parker,
a college friend of Steele's who became Fellow of Merton and Vicar
of Embleton, Northumberland.  At Parker's suggestion Steele
destroyed a comedy which he had written at Oxford.

Mr Spectator,—About two years ago I was called upon by the younger part of a country family, by my mother's side related to me, to visit Mr Campbell, the dumb man [1]; for they told me that that was chiefly what brought them to town, having heard wonders of him in Essex. I, who always wanted faith in matters of that kind, was not easily prevailed on to go; but lest they should take it ill, I went with them, when, to my surprise, Mr Campbell related all their past life (in short, had he not been prevented, such a discovery would have come out as would have ruined the next design of their coming to town, viz., buying wedding clothes). Our names, though he never heard of us before—and we endeavoured to conceal—were as familiar to him as to ourselves. To be sure, Mr Spectator, he is a very learned and wise man. Being impatient to know my fortune, having paid my respects in a family Jacobus, he told me (after his manner) among several other things, that in a year and nine months I should fall ill of a new fever, be given over by my physicians, but should with much difficulty recover: that the first time I took the air afterwards I should be addressed to by a young gentleman of a plentiful fortune, good sense, and a generous spirit. Mr Spectator, he is the purest man in the world, for all he said has come to pass, and I am the happiest she in Kent. I have been in quest of Mr Campbell these three months, and cannot find him out. Now hearing you are a dumb man too, I thought you might correspond, and be able to tell me something, for I think myself highly obliged to make his fortune as he has mine. 'Tis very possible your worship, who has spies all over this town, can inform me how to send to him: if you can, I beseech you be as speedy as possible, and you will highly oblige

Your constant Reader and Admirer,
Dulcibella Thankley

Ordered, that the inspector I employ about Wonders, inquire at the Golden Lion, opposite to the Half-Moon Tavern in Drury Lane, into the merit of this silent sage, and report accordingly.     T.

1 See No. 323.

No. 475.     *Thursday, Sept. 4, 1712*     [ADDISON

*Quæ res in se neque consilium neque modum*
*Habet ullum, eam consilio regere non potes.*
                              TER., *Eun.*, Act 1, sc. 1

IT is an old observation, which has been made of
politicians who would rather ingratiate themselves
with their sovereign than promote his real service,
that they accommodate their counsels to his inclinations, and advise him to such actions only as his
heart is naturally set upon.  The privy-councillor of
one in love must observe the same conduct, unless
he would forfeit the friendship of the person who
desires his advice.  I have known several odd cases
of this nature.  Hipparchus was going to marry a
common woman, but being resolved to do nothing
without the advice of his friend Philander, he consulted him upon the occasion.  Philander told him
his mind freely, and represented his mistress to him
in such strong colours, that the next morning he received a challenge for his pains, and before twelve
o'clock was run through the body by the man who
had asked his advice.  Celia was more prudent on the
like occasion; she desired Leonilla to give her opinion
freely upon a young fellow who made his addresses
to her.  Leonilla, to oblige her, told her with great
frankness that she looked upon him as one of the
most worthless—— Celia, foreseeing what a character she was to expect, begged her not to go on, for
that she had been privately married to him above a
fortnight.  The truth of it is, a woman seldom asks
advice before she has bought her wedding clothes.
When she has made her own choice, for form sake
she sends a *congé d'élire* to her friends.

If we look into the secret springs and motives that
set people at work in these occasions, and put them
upon asking advice which they never intend to take,
I look upon it to be none of the least, that they are
incapable of keeping a secret which is so very pleasing
to them.  A girl longs to tell her confidante that she

hopes to be married in a little time, and in order to talk of the pretty fellow that dwells so much in her thoughts, asks her very gravely what she would advise her to in a case of so much difficulty. Why else should Melissa, who had not a thousand pound in the world, go into every quarter of the town to ask her acquaintance whether they would advise her to take Tom Townly, that made his addresses to her, with an estate of five thousand a year? 'Tis very pleasant, on this occasion, to hear the lady propose her doubts, and to see the pains she is at to get over them.

I must not here omit a practice that is in use among the vainer part of our own sex, who will often ask a friend's advice in relation to a fortune whom they are never likely to come at. Will Honeycomb, who is now on the verge of threescore, took me aside not long since, and asked me in his most serious look, whether I would advise him to marry my Lady Betty Single, who, by the way, is one of the greatest fortunes about town. I stared him full in the face upon so strange a question; upon which he immediately gave me an inventory of her jewels and estate, adding that he was resolved to do nothing in a matter of such consequence without my approbation. Finding he would have an answer, I told him if he could get the lady's consent he had mine. This is about the tenth match which, to my knowledge, Will has consulted his friends upon, without ever opening his mind to the party herself.

I have been engaged in this subject by the following letter, which comes to me from some notable young female scribe, who, by the contents of it, seems to have carried matters so far that she is ripe for asking advice; but as I would not lose her goodwill, nor forfeit the reputation which I have with her for wisdom, I shall only communicate the letter to the public, without returning any answer to it.

Mr. Spectator,—Now, sir, the thing is this: Mr Shapely is the prettiest gentleman about town. He is very tall, but not too tall neither. He dances like

an angel. His mouth is made I don't know how, but
'tis the prettiest that I ever saw in my life. He is
always laughing, for he has an infinite deal of wit.
If you did but see how he rolls his stockings! He
has a thousand pretty fancies, and I am sure if you
saw him you would like him. He is a very good
scholar, and can talk Latin as fast as English. I wish
you could but see him dance. Now you must understand poor Mr Shapely has no estate; but how can he
help that, you know? And yet my friends are so
unreasonable as to be always teasing me about him,
because he has no estate. But, I am sure, he has that
that is better than an estate; for he is a good-natured,
ingenuous, modest, civil, tall, well-bred, handsome man,
and I am obliged to him for his civilities ever since I
saw him. I forgot to tell you that he has black eyes,
and looks upon me now and then as if he had tears in
them. And yet my friends are so unreasonable, that
they would have me be uncivil to him. I have a good
portion which they cannot hinder me of, and I shall
be fourteen on the 29th day of August next, and am
therefore willing to settle in the world as soon as I can,
and so is Mr Shapely. But everybody I advise with
here is poor Mr Shapely's enemy. I desire therefore
you will give me your advice, for I know you are a wise
man, and if you advise me well I am resolved to follow
it. I heartily wish you could see him dance, and am,

Sir,

Your most humble Servant,

B. D.

He loves your *Spectators* mightily.                    C.


No. 476.          *Friday, Sept. 5*, 1712          [ADDISON

*Lucidus ordo.* HOR., *Ars Poet.* 41

AMONG my daily papers which I bestow on the public, there are some which are written with regularity
and method, and others that run out into the wildness of those compositions which go by the name of
essays. As for the first, I have the whole scheme of
the discourse in my mind before I set pen to paper.

In the other kind of writing it is sufficient that I have several thoughts on a subject, without troubling myself to range them in such order that they may seem to grow out of one another, and be disposed under the proper heads.  Seneca and Montaigne are patterns for writing in this last kind, as Tully and Aristotle excel in the other.  When I read an author of genius who writes without method, I fancy myself in a wood that abounds with a great many noble objects, rising among one another in the greatest confusion and disorder.  When I read a methodical discourse, I am in a regular plantation, and can place myself in its several centres, so as to take a view of all the lines and walks that are struck from them. You may ramble in the one a whole day together, and every moment discover something or other that is new to you; but when you have done you will have but a confused imperfect notion of the place : in the other, your eye commands the whole prospect, and gives you such an idea of it as is not easily worn out of the memory.

Irregularity and want of method are only supportable in men of great learning or genius, who are often too full to be exact, and therefore choose to throw down their pearls in heaps before the reader rather than be at the pains of stringing them.

Method is of advantage to a work both in respect to the writer and the reader.  In regard to the first, it is a great help to his invention.  When a man has planned his discourse he finds a great many thoughts rising out of every head that do not offer themselves upon the general survey of a subject.  His thoughts are at the same time more intelligible, and better discover their drift and meaning when they are placed in their proper lights, and follow one another in a regular series, than when they are thrown together without order and connection.  There is always an obscurity in confusion, and the same sentence that would have enlightened the reader in one part of a discourse perplexes him in another.  For the same reason, likewise, every thought in a methodical discourse shows itself in its greatest beauty, as the several figures in a piece of painting receive new grace from their disposition in the picture. The advantages of a reader from a methodical discourse are correspondent with those of the writer. He comprehends everything easily, takes it in with pleasure, and retains it long.

Method is not less requisite in ordinary conversation than in writing, provided a man would talk to make himself understood. I, who hear a thousand coffee-house debates every day, am very sensible of this want of method in the thoughts of my honest countrymen. There is not one dispute in ten which is managed in those schools of politics where, after the three first sentences, the question is not entirely lost. Our disputants put me in mind of the cuttlefish, that when he is unable to extricate himself, blackens all the water about him till he becomes invisible. The man who does not know how to methodise his thoughts has always, to borrow a phrase from the ' Dispensary [1] ', ' a barren superfluity of words '; the fruit is lost amidst the exuberance of leaves.

Tom Puzzle is one of the most eminent immethodical disputants of any that has fallen under my observation. Tom has read enough to make him very impertinent; his knowledge is sufficient to raise doubts, but not to clear them. It is pity that he has so much learning, or that he has not a great deal more. With these qualifications Tom sets up for a Freethinker, finds a great many things to blame in the constitution of his country, and gives shrewd intimations that he does not believe another world. In short, Puzzle is an atheist as much as his parts will give him leave. He has got about half-a-dozen commonplace topics, into which he never fails to turn the conversation, whatever was the occasion of it:

---

[1] In Garth's *Dispensary* (ii, 95), it is said of Colon :

Hourly his learned impertinence affords
A barren superfluity of words.

though the matter in debate be about Douay or Denain [1], it is ten to one but half his discourse runs upon the unreasonableness of bigotry and priestcraft. This makes Mr Puzzle the admiration of all those who have less sense than himself, and the contempt of all those who have more. There is none in town whom Tom dreads so much as my friend Will Dry. Will, who is acquainted with Tom's logic, when he finds him running off the question, cuts him short with a ' What then? We allow all this to be true, but what is it to our present purpose?' I have known Tom eloquent half-an-hour together, and triumphing as he thought in the superiority of the argument, when he has been nonplussed on a sudden by Mr Dry's desiring him to tell the company what it was that he endeavoured to prove. In short, Dry is a man of a clear methodical head but few words, and gains the same advantage over Puzzle that a small body of regular troops would gain over a numberless undisciplined militia.     C.

No. 477.     *Saturday, Sept. 6, 1712*     [ADDISON

*An me ludit amabilis
Insania? audire et videor pios
Errare per lucos, amœnæ
Quos et aquæ subeunt et auræ.*

HOR., 3 Od. iv, 5

SIR,—Having lately read your essay on the ' Pleasures of the Imagination [2] ', I was so taken with your thoughts upon some of our English gardens [3], that I cannot forbear troubling you with a letter upon that subject. I am one, you must know, who am looked upon as a humorist in gardening. I have several acres about my house, which I call my garden, and which a skilful gardener would not know what to call. It is a

---

[1] Douay was besieged by Marlborough and Prince Eugene in 1710, and capitulated on June 26, after two months' resistance. Prince Eugene's forces were defeated at Denain on July 24, 1712; and soon afterwards Douay was retaken by the French. Addison's paper was published on September 5, 1712.

[2] Nos. 411–421.     [3] See No. 414.

confusion of kitchen and parterre, orchard and flower-
garden, which lie so mixed and interwoven with one
another, that if a foreigner who had seen nothing of
our country should be conveyed into my garden at his
first landing, he would look upon it as a natural wilderness, and one of the uncultivated parts of our country.
My flowers grow up in several parts of the garden in
the greatest luxuriancy and profusion. I am so far
from being fond of any particular one, by reason of its
rarity, that if I meet with any one in a field which
pleases me, I give it a place in my garden. By this
means, when a stranger walks with me, he is surprised
to see several large spots of ground covered with ten
thousand different colours, and has often singled out
flowers that he might have met with under a common
hedge, in a field, or in a meadow, as some of the
greatest beauties of the place. The only method I
observe in this particular, is to range in the same
quarter the products of the same season, that they
may make their appearance together, and compose a
picture of the greatest variety. There is the same
irregularity in my plantations, which run into as great
a wildness as their natures will permit. I take in none
that do not naturally rejoice in the soil, and am pleased
when I am walking in a labyrinth of my own raising,
not to know whether the next tree I shall meet with
is an apple or an oak, an elm or a pear-tree. My
kitchen has likewise its particular quarters assigned it ;
for besides the wholesome luxury which that place
abounds with, I have always thought a kitchen-garden
a more pleasant sight than the finest orangery, or
artificial greenhouse. I love to see everything in its
perfection, and am more pleased to survey my rows of
colworts and cabbages, with a thousand nameless pot-
herbs, springing up in their full fragrancy and verdure,
than to see the tender plants of foreign countries kept
alive by artificial heats, or withering in an air and
soil that are not adapted to them. I must not omit,
that there is a fountain rising in the upper part of my
garden, which forms a little wandering rill, and
administers to the pleasure as well as the plenty of the
place : I have so conducted it, that it visits most of my
plantations, and have taken particular care to let it
run in the same manner as it would do in an open field,

so that it generally passes through banks of violets and
primroses, plats of willow, or other plants, that seem
to be of its own producing. There is another circumstance in which I am very particular, or, as my neighbours call me, very whimsical : as my garden invites
into it all the birds of the country, by offering them
the conveniency of springs and shades, solitude and
shelter, I do not suffer any one to destroy their nests
in the spring, or drive them from their usual haunts
in fruit-time. I value my garden more for being full
of blackbirds than cherries, and very frankly give them
fruit for their songs. By this means I have always the
music of the season in its perfection, and am highly
delighted to see the jay or the thrush hopping about
my walks, and shooting before my eye across the several
little glades and alleys that I pass through. I think
there are as many kinds of gardening as of poetry :
your makers of parterres and flower-gardens are epi-
grammists and sonneteers in this art, contrivers of
bowers and grottoes, treillages and cascades, are
romance writers. Wise and London[1] are our heroic
poets ; and if, as a critic, I may single out any passage
of their works to commend, I shall take notice of that
part in the upper garden at Kensington, which was at
first nothing but a gravel-pit. It must have been a fine
genius for gardening, that could have thought of forming such an unsightly hollow into so beautiful an area,
and to have hit the eye with so uncommon and agreeable a scene as that which it is now wrought into. To
give this particular spot of ground the greater effect,
they have made a very pleasing contrast ; for as on

---

[1] See No. 5. London and Wise, who set the fashion for stiff Dutch
gardening, had a nursery at Brompton. Evelyn said we had some
advantages in gardening which no other country could attain to,
advantages which were 'much due to the industry of Mr London and
Mr Wise, and to such as shall imitate their laudable undertakings'.
Many years after the *Spectator*, Pope, in his fourth Moral Essay (*On
False Taste*), satirised the success of the formal style of gardening :

> Grove nods on grove, each alley has a brother,
> And half the platform just reflects the other.
> The suffering eye inverted Nature sees,
> Trees cut to statues, statues thick as trees ;
> With here a fountain, never to be played,
> And there a summer-house, that knows no shade :
> Here Amphitrite sails through myrtle bowers ;
> There gladiators fight, or die, in flowers.

one side of the walk you see this hollow basin, with
its several little plantations lying so conveniently under
the eye of the beholder; on the other side of it there
appears a seeming mount, made up of trees rising one
higher than another in proportion as they approach the
centre. A spectator, who has not heard this account
of it, would think this circular mount was not only a
real one, but that it had been actually scooped out of
that hollow space which I have before mentioned. I
never yet met with any one who had walked in this
garden, who was not struck with that part of it which
I have here mentioned. As for myself, you will find,
by the account which I have already given you, that
my compositions in gardening are altogether after the
Pindaric manner, and run into the beautiful wildness
of nature, without affecting the nicer elegances of art.
What I am now going to mention will, perhaps, deserve
your attention more than anything I have yet said. I
find that in the discourse which I spoke of at the
beginning of my letter, you are against filling an
English garden with evergreens; and indeed I am so
far of your opinion, that I can by no means think the
verdure of an evergreen comparable to that which
shoots out annually, and clothes our trees in the
summer season. But I have often wondered that those
who are like myself, and love to live in gardens, have
never thought of contriving a winter garden, which
should consist of such trees only as never cast their
leaves. We have very often little snatches of sunshine and fair weather in the most uncomfortable parts
of the year, and have frequently several days in
November and January that are as agreeable as any
in the finest months. At such times, therefore, I think
there could not be a greater pleasure than to walk in
such a winter garden as I have proposed. In the
summer season the whole country blooms, and is a kind
of garden, for which reason we are not so sensible of
those beauties that at this time may be everywhere
met with; but when Nature is in her desolation, and
presents us with nothing but bleak and barren prospects, there is something unspeakably cheerful in a
spot of ground which is covered with trees that smile
amidst all the rigours of winter, and give us a view
of the most gay season in the midst of that which is

the most dead and melancholy. I have so far indulged myself in this thought, that I have set apart a whole acre of ground for the executing of it. The walls are covered with ivy instead of vines. The laurel, the hornbeam, and the holly, with many other trees and plants of the same nature, grow so thick in it, that you cannot imagine a more lively scene. The glowing redness of the berries, with which they are hung at this time, vies with the verdure of their leaves, and are apt to inspire the heart of the beholder with that vernal delight which you have somewhere taken notice of in your former papers [1]. It is very pleasant, at the same time, to see the several kinds of birds retiring into this little green spot, and enjoying themselves among the branches and foliage, when my great garden, which I have before mentioned to you, does not afford a single leaf for their shelter.

You must know, sir, that I look upon the pleasure which we take in a garden, as one of the most innocent delights in human life. A garden was the habitation of our first parents before the fall. It is naturally apt to fill the mind with calmness and tranquillity, and to lay all its turbulent passions at rest. It gives us a great insight into the contrivance and wisdom of Providence, and suggests innumerable subjects for meditation. I cannot but think the very complacency and satisfaction which a man takes in these works of Nature, to be a laudable, if not a virtuous habit of mind. For all which reasons I hope you will pardon the length of my present letter.

C.                                    I am, Sir, &c.

---

No. 478.          *Monday, Sept. 8, 1712*          [STEELE

*Usus*
*Quem penes arbitrium est, et jus et norma.*
HOR., *Ars Poet.* 72

MR SPECTATOR,—It happened lately, that a friend of mine, who had many things to buy for his family, would oblige me to walk with him to the shops. He was very nice in his way, and fond of having everything shown, which at first made me very uneasy; but

1 See No. 393.

as his humour still continued, the things which I had been staring at along with him began to fill my head, and led me into a set of amusing thoughts concerning them.

I fancied it must be very surprising to any one who enters into a detail of fashions, to consider how far the vanity of mankind has laid itself out in dress, what a prodigious number of people it maintains, and what a circulation of money it occasions. Providence in this case makes use of the folly which we will not give up, and it becomes instrumental to the support of those who are willing to labour. Hence it is that fringe-makers, lace-men, tire-women, and a number of other trades, which would be useless in a simple state of nature, draw their subsistence; though it is seldom seen that such as these are extremely rich, because their original fault of being founded upon vanity, keeps them poor by the light inconstancy of its nature. The variableness of fashion turns the stream of business, which flows from it now into one channel, and anon into another; so that different sets of people sink or flourish in their turns by it.

From the shops we retired to the tavern, where I found my friend express so much satisfaction for the bargains he had made, that my moral reflections (if I had told them) might have passed for a reproof; so I chose rather to fall in with him, and let the discourse run upon the use of fashions.

Here we remembered how much man is governed by his senses, how lively he is struck by the objects which appear to him in an agreeable manner, how much clothes contribute to make us agreeable objects, and how much we owe it to ourselves that we should appear so.

We considered man as belonging to societies: societies as formed of different ranks, and different ranks distinguished by habits, that all proper duty or respect might attend their appearance.

We took notice of several advantages which are met with in the occurrences of conversation. How the bashful man has been sometimes so raised, as to express himself with an air of freedom, when he imagines that his habit introduces him to company with a becoming manner. And again, how a fool in fine clothes shall be suddenly heard with attention, until he has betrayed himself; whereas a man of sense appearing with a dress of negligence, shall be but coldly received, until he be proved by time, and established in a character. Such things as these we could recollect to have happened to our own knowledge so very often, that we concluded the author [1] had his reasons, who advises his son to go in dress rather above his fortune than under it.

At last the subject seemed so considerable, that it was proposed to have a repository builded for fashions, as there are chambers for medals and other rarities. The building may be shaped as that which stands among the Pyramids, in the form of a woman's head [2]. This may be raised upon pillars, whose ornaments shall bear a just relation to the design. Thus there may be an imitation of fringe carved in the base, a sort of appearance of lace in the frieze, and a representation of curling locks with bows of ribbon sloping over them, may fill up the work of the cornice. The inside may be divided into two apartments, appropriated to each sex. The apartments may be filled with shelves, on which boxes are to stand as regularly as books in a library. These are to have folding doors, which being opened you are to behold a baby [3] dressed out in some fashion which has flourished, and standing upon a pedestal, where the time of its reign is marked down. For its further regulation let it be ordered that every one who invents a fashion shall bring in his box, whose front he may at pleasure have either worked or painted with some amorous or gay device, that, like books with gilded leaves and covers, it may the sooner draw the eyes of the beholders. And to the end that these may be preserved with all due care, let there be a keeper appointed, who shall be a gentleman qualified with a competent knowledge in clothes; so that by this means the place will be a comfortable support for some beau who has spent his estate in dressing.

The reasons offered, by which we expected to gain the approbation of the public, were as follows:

First, that every one who is considerable enough to be a mode, and has any imperfection of nature or chance, which it is possible to hide by the advantage of clothes, may, by coming to this repository, be

---

[1] Osborne, *Advice to his Son.*     [2] The Sphinx.     [3] Doll.

furnished herself, and furnish all who are under the same misfortunes, with the most agreeable manner of concealing it; and that on the other side, every one who has any beauty in face or shape, may also be furnished with the most agreeable manner of showing it.

Secondly, that whereas some of our young gentlemen who travel, give us great reason to suspect that they only go abroad to make or improve a fancy for dress, a project of this nature may be a means to keep them at home, which is in effect the keeping of so much money in the kingdom. And perhaps the balance of fashion in Europe, which now leans upon the side of France, may be so altered for the future, that it may become as common with Frenchmen to come to England for their finishing stroke of breeding, as it has been for Englishmen to go to France for it.

Thirdly, whereas several great scholars, who might have been otherwise useful to the world, have spent their time in studying to describe the dresses of the ancients from dark hints, which they are fain to interpret and support with much learning, it will from henceforth happen that they shall be freed from the trouble, and the world from useless volumes. This project will be a registry to which posterity may have recourse for the clearing such obscure passages as tend that way in authors, and therefore we shall not for the future submit ourselves to the learning of etymology, which might persuade the age to come that the farthingal was worn for cheapness, or the furbelow for warmth.

Fourthly, whereas they who are old themselves have often a way of railing at the extravagance of youth, and the whole age in which their children live, it is hoped that this ill humour will be much suppressed when we can have recourse to the fashions of their times, produce them in our vindication, and be able to show that it might have been as expensive in Queen Elizabeth's time only to wash and quill a ruff, as it is now to buy cravats or neck-handkerchiefs.

We desire also to have it taken notice of, that because we would show a particular respect to foreigners, which may induce them to perfect their breeding here in a knowledge which is very proper for pretty gentlemen, we have conceived the motto for the house in the learned language. There is to be a picture over the door, with a looking-glass and a dressing-chair in the middle of it. Then on one side are to be seen, above one another, patch-boxes, pin-cushions, and little bottles; on the other, powder-bags, puffs, combs, and brushes; beyond these, swords with fine knots, whose points are hidden, and fans almost closed, with the handles downward, are to stand out interchangeably from the sides, till they meet at the top and form a semicircle over the rest of the figures. Beneath all the writing is to run in this pretty sounding manner :

> Adeste, O quotquot sunt, Veneres, Gratiæ, Cupidines,
> En vobis adsunt in promptu
> Faces, Vincula, Spicula,
> Hinc eligite, sumite, regite.

I am, Sir,
Your most humble Servant,
A. B.

The proposal of my correspondent I cannot but look upon as an ingenious method of placing persons (whose parts make them ambitious to exert themselves in frivolous things) in a rank by themselves. In order to this, I would propose, that there be a board of directors of the fashionable society; and because it is a matter of too much weight for a private man to determine alone, I should be highly obliged to my correspondents if they would give in lists of persons qualified for this trust. If the chief coffee-houses, the conversations of which places are carried on by persons each of whom has his little number of followers and admirers, would name from among themselves two or three to be inserted, they should be put up with great faithfulness. Old beaux are to be presented in the first place; but as that sect, with relation to dress, is almost extinct, it will, I fear, be absolutely necessary to take in all time-servers, properly so deemed; that is, such as, without any conviction of conscience, or view of interest, change with the world, and that merely from a terror of being out of fashion. Such also, who from facility of temper, and too much obsequiousness, are vicious against their will, and follow leaders whom they do not approve, for want of courage to go their own way, are capable persons for this superintendency. Those who are loth to grow old, or would do anything contrary to the course and order of things, out of fondness to be in fashion, are proper candidates. To conclude, those who are in fashion without apparent merit, must be supposed to have latent qualities, which would appear in a post of direction, and therefore are to be regarded in forming these lists. Any who shall be pleased, according to these, or what further qualifications may occur to himself, to send a list, is desired to do it within fourteen days after this date.

N.B.—The place of the physician to this society, according to the last-mentioned qualification, is already engaged.                                        T.

No. 479.     *Tuesday, Sept. 9, 1712*     [STEELE

*Dare jura maritis.*  HOR., *Ars Poet.* 398

MANY are the epistles I every day receive from husbands, who complain of vanity, pride, but above all ill-nature, in their wives. I cannot tell how it is, but I think I see in all their letters that the cause of their uneasiness is in themselves; and indeed I have hardly ever observed the married condition unhappy, but from want of judgment or temper in the man. The truth is, we generally make love in a style, and with sentiments very unfit for ordinary life : they are half theatrical, half romantic. By this means we raise our imaginations to what is not to be expected in human life; and because we did not beforehand think of the creature we were enamoured of as subject to dishumour, age, sickness, impatience, or sullenness, but altogether considered her as the object of joy, human nature itself is often imputed to her as her particular imperfection or defect.

I take it to be a rule proper to be observed in all occurrences of life, but more especially in the domestic or matrimonial part of it, to preserve always a disposition to be pleased. This cannot be supported but by considering things in their right light, and as Nature has formed them, and not as our own fancies or appetites would have them. He then who took a young lady to his bed, with no other consideration than the expectation of scenes of dalliance, and thought of her (as I said before) only as she was to administer to the gratification of desire; as that desire flags, will, without her fault, think her charms and her merit abated : from hence must follow indifference, dislike, peevishness, and rage. But the man who brings his reason to support his passion, and beholds what he loves as liable to all the calamities of human life both in body and mind, and even at the best, what must bring upon him new cares and new relations; such a lover, I say, will form himself accordingly, and adapt his mind to the nature of his circumstances. This latter person will be prepared to be a father, a friend, an advocate, a steward for people yet unborn, and has proper affections ready for every incident in the marriage state. Such a man can hear the cries of children with pity instead of anger; and when they run over his head, he is not disturbed at their noise, but is glad of their mirth and health. Tom Trusty has told me, that he thinks it doubles his attention to the most intricate affair he is about, to hear his children, for whom all his cares are applied, make a noise in the next room : on the other side, Will Sparkish cannot put on his periwig, or adjust his cravat at the glass, for the noise of those damned nurses and squalling brats; and then ends with a gallant reflection upon the comforts of matrimony, runs out of the hearing, and drives to the chocolate-house.

According as the husband is disposed in himself, every circumstance of his life is to give him torment or pleasure. When the affection is well placed, and supported by the considerations of duty, honour, and friendship, which are in the highest degree engaged in this alliance, there can nothing rise in the common course of life, or from the blows or favours of fortune, in which a man will not find matters of some delight unknown to a single condition.

He that sincerely loves his wife and family, and studies to improve that affection in himself, conceives pleasure from the most indifferent things; while the married man, who has not bid adieu to the fashions and false gallantries of the town, is perplexed with everything around him. In both these cases man cannot, indeed, make a sillier figure, than in repeating such pleasures and pains to the rest of the world; but I speak of them only as they sit upon those who are involved in them. As I visit all sorts of people, I cannot indeed but smile, when the good lady tells her husband what extraordinary things the child spoke since he went out. No longer than yesterday I was prevailed with to go home with a fond husband; and his wife told him, that his son, of his own head, when the clock in the parlour struck two, said papa would come to dinner presently. While the father has him in a rapture in his arms, and is drowning him with kisses, the wife tells me he is but just four years old. Then they both struggle for him, and bring him up to me, and repeat his observation of two o'clock. I was called upon, by looks upon the child and then at me, to say something; and I told the father that this remark of the infant of his coming home, and joining the time with it, was a certain indication that he would be a great historian and chronologer. They are neither of them fools, yet received my compliment with great acknowledgment of my prescience. I fared very well at dinner, and heard many other notable sayings of their heir, which would have given very little entertainment to one less turned to reflection than I was; but it was a pleasing speculation to remark on the happiness of a life in which things of no moment give occasion of hope, self-satisfaction, and triumph.   On the other hand, I have known an ill-natured coxcomb, who was hardly improved in anything but bulk, for want of this disposition silence the whole family as a set of silly women and children for recounting things which were really above his own capacity.

When I say all this, I cannot deny but there are perverse jades that fall to men's lots, with whom it requires more than common proficiency in philosophy to be able to live.   When these are joined to men of warm spirits, without temper or learning, they are frequently corrected with stripes; but one of our famous lawyers is of opinion that this ought to be used sparingly [1].   As I remember those are his very words; but as it is proper to draw some spiritual use out of all afflictions, I should rather recommend to those who are visited with women of spirit, to form themselves for the world by patience at home. Socrates, who is by all accounts the undoubted head of the sect of the henpecked, owned and acknowledged that he owed great part of his virtue to the exercise which his useful wife constantly gave it.   There are several good instructions may be drawn from his wise answers to people of less fortitude than himself on the subject.   A friend, with indignation, asked how so good a man could live with so violent a creature? He observed to him, that they who learn to keep a good seat on horseback, mount the least manageable they can get, and when they have mastered them, they are sure never to be discomposed on the backs of steeds less restive [2].   At several times, to different persons on the same subject, he has said, ' My dear friend, you are beholden to Xantippe, that I bear so well your flying-out in a dispute.'   To another, ' My hen clacks very much, but she brings me chickens.   They that live in a trading street are not disturbed at the passage of carts.'   I would have, if

---

1 See Henry de Bracton's *De Legibus et Consuetudinibus Angliæ*, Book i, chap. x.
2 Xenophon's *Symposium*, Book ii.

possible, a wise man be contented with his lot, even
with a shrew; for though he cannot make her better,
he may, you see, make himself better by her means.

But, instead of pursuing my design of displaying
conjugal love in its natural beauties and attractions,
I am got into tales to the disadvantage of that state
of life. I must say, therefore, that I am verily persuaded that whatever is delightful in human life
is to be enjoyed in greater perfection in the married
than in the single condition. He that has this passion in perfection, in occasions of joy can say to
himself, besides his own satisfaction, ' How happy
will this make my wife and children!' Upon occurrences of distress or danger can comfort himself,
' But all this while my wife and children are safe.'
There is something in it that doubles satisfactions,
because others participate them; and dispels afflictions, because others are exempt from them. All
who are married without this relish of their circumstance are in either a tasteless indolence and negligence, which is hardly to be attained, or else live
in the hourly repetition of sharp answers, eager upbraidings, and distracting reproaches. In a word,
the married state, with and without the affection
suitable to it, is the completest image of heaven
and hell we are capable of receiving in this life [1].

T.

No. 480.        *Wednesday, Sept. 10, 1712*        [STEELE

*Responsare cupidinibus, contemnere honores*
*Fortis, et in se ipso totus, teres atque rotundus.*
HOR., 2 *Sat.* vii, 85

THE other day, looking over those old manuscripts,
of which I have formerly given some account, and
which relate to the character of the mighty Pharamond of France, and the close friendship between
him and his friend Eucrate [2], I found, among the

[1] See Nos. 482, 486.        [2] See Nos. 76, 84, 97.

letters which had been in the custody of the latter, an epistle from a country gentleman to Pharamond, wherein he excuses himself from coming to court. The gentleman, it seems, was contented with his condition, had formerly been in the king's service, but at the writing the following letter had, from leisure and reflection, quite another sense of things than that which he had in the more active part of his life.

### Monsieur Chezluy *to* Pharamond

Dread Sir,—I have from your own hand (enclosed under the cover of Mr Eucrate of your majesty's bed-chamber) a letter which invites me to court. I understand this great honour to be done me out of respect and inclination to me, rather than regard to your own service : for which reasons I beg leave to lay before your majesty my reasons for declining to depart from home ; and will not doubt but, as your motive in desiring my attendance was to make me an happier man, when you think that will not be effected by my remove, you will permit me to stay where I am. Those who have an ambition to appear in courts, have ever an opinion that their persons or their talents are particularly formed for the service or ornament of that place ; or else are hurried by downright desire of gain, or what they call honour, or take upon themselves whatever the generosity of their master can give them opportunities to grasp at. But your goodness shall not be thus imposed upon by me : I will therefore confess to you that frequent solitude, and long conversation with such who know no arts which polish life, have made me the plainest creature in your dominions. Those less capacities of moving with a good grace, bearing a ready affability to all around me, and acting with ease before many, have quite left me. I am come to that, with regard to my person, that I consider it only as a machine I am obliged to take care of, in order to enjoy my soul in its faculties with alacrity ; well remembering that this habitation of clay will in a few years be a meaner piece of earth than any utensil about my house. When this is, as it really is, the most frequent reflection I have, you will easily imagine how well I should become a drawing-room : add to this, what shall a man without desires do about the generous Pharamond? Monsieur Eucrate has hinted to me, that you have thoughts of distinguishing me with titles. As for myself, in the temper of my present mind, appellations of honour would but embarrass discourse, and new behaviour towards me perplex me in every habitude of life. I am also to acknowledge to you, that my children, of whom your majesty condescended to inquire, are all of them mean both in their persons and genius. The estate my eldest son is heir to is more than he can enjoy with a good grace. My self-love will not carry me so far as to impose upon mankind the advancement of persons (merely for their being related to me) into high distinctions, who ought for their own sakes, as well as that of the public, to affect obscurity. I wish, my generous prince, as it is in your power to give honours and offices, it were also to give talents suitable to them : were it so, the noble Pharamond would reward the zeal of my youth with abilities to do him service in my age.

Those who accept of favour without merit, support themselves in it at the expense of your majesty. Give me leave to tell you, sir, this is the reason that we in the country hear so often repeated the word *prerogative*. That part of your law which is reserved in yourself for the readier service and good of the public, slight men are eternally buzzing in our ears to cover their own follies and miscarriages. It would be an addition to the high favour you have done me if you would let Eucrate send me word how often, and in what cases you allow a constable to insist upon the prerogative. From the highest to the lowest officer in your dominions, something of their own carriage they would exempt from examination under the shelter of the word *prerogative*. I would fain, most noble Pharamond, see one of your officers assert your prerogative by good and gracious actions. When is it used to help the afflicted, to rescue the innocent, to comfort the stranger? Uncommon methods, apparently undertaken to attain worthy ends, would never make power invidious. You see, sir, I talk to you with the freedom your noble nature approves in all whom you admit to your conversation.

But, to return to your majesty's letter, I humbly conceive that all distinctions are useful to men only as they are to act in public; and it would be a romantic madness for a man to be a lord in his closet. Nothing can be honourable to a man apart from the world but the reflection upon worthy actions; and he that places honour in a consciousness of well-doing will have but little relish for any outward homage that is paid him, since what gives him distinction to himself cannot come within the observation of his beholders. Thus all the words of *Lordship*, *Honour*, and *Grace*, are only repetitions to a man that the king has ordered him to be called so; but no evidences that there is anything in himself that would give the man who applies to him those ideas, without the creation of his master.

I have, most noble Pharamond, all honours and all titles in your own approbation; I triumph in them as they are your gift, I refuse them as they are to give me the observation of others. Indulge me, my noble master, in this chastity of renown; let me know myself in the favour of Pharamond, and look down upon the applause of the people. I am, in all duty and loyalty,

Your Majesty's most obedient
Subject and Servant,
JEAN CHEZLUY

SIR,—I need not tell you with what disadvantages men of low fortunes and great modesty come into the world, what wrong measures their diffidence of themselves and fear of offending often obliges them to take, and what a pity it is that their greatest virtues and qualities, that should soonest recommend them, are the main obstacle in the way of their preferment.

This, sir, is my case: I was bred at a country school, where I learned Latin and Greek. The misfortunes of my family forced me up to town, where a profession of the politer sort has protected me against infamy and want. I am now clerk to a lawyer, and, in times of vacancy and recess from business, have made myself master of Italian and French; and though the progress I have made in my business has gained me reputation enough for one of my standing, yet my mind suggests to me every day that it is not upon that foundation I am to build my fortune.

The person I have my present dependence upon, has it in his nature, as well as in his power, to advance me, by recommending me to a gentleman that is going beyond sea in a public employment. I know the printing this letter would point me out to those I want confidence to speak to, and I hope it is not in your power to refuse making anybody happy.

Yours, &c.,<br>M. D.[1]

*September* 9, 1712

No. 481.　　　*Thursday, Sept.* 11, 1712　　　[ADDISON

*Uti non*<br>
*Compositum melius cum Bitho Bacchius; in jus*<br>
*Acres procurrunt.*

HOR., 1 *Sat.* vii, 19

IT is something [2] pleasant enough to consider the different notions, which different persons have of the same thing. If men of low condition very often set a value on things, which are not prized by those who are in an higher station of life, there are many things these esteem, which are in no value among persons of an inferior rank. Common people are, in particular, very much astonished, when they hear of those solemn contests and debates, which are made among the great upon the punctilios of a public ceremony, and wonder to hear that any business of consequence should be retarded by those little circumstances, which they represent to themselves as trifling and insignificant. I am mightily pleased with a porter's decision, in one of Mr Southerne's plays [3], which is founded upon that fine distress of a virtuous

---

1 This letter was by Mr Robert Harper, a conveyancer of Lincoln's Inn ; but the original draft in Harper's letter-book—which was seen by Nichols—shows that Steele made alterations and omissions. The letter was sent to the *Spectator* on August 9, 1712. Dr Grosart kindly informs me that Harper's letter-book is now in his possession. The original of this letter has this postscript : 'I know the printing this letter would point me out to those I want confidence to speak to, and I hope it is not in your power to refuse making anybody happy.'

2 'Sometimes' (folio).

3 *The Fatal Marriage ; or, the Innocent Adultery*, v, 1.

woman's marrying a second husband, while her first
was yet living. The first husband, who was supposed
to have been dead, returning to his house after a long
absence, raises a noble perplexity for the tragic part
of the play. In the meanwhile the nurse and the
porter conferring upon the difficulties that would
ensue in such a case, honest Sampson thinks the
matter may be easily decided, and solves it very
judiciously, by the old proverb, that if his master
be still living, 'The man must have his mare again.'
There is nothing in my time which has so much
surprised and confounded the greatest part of my
honest countrymen, as the present controversy between Count Rechteren and Monsieur Mesnager,
which employs the wise heads of so many nations,
and holds all the affairs of Europe in suspense [1].

[1] The negotiations for peace which were going on at Utrecht had
been checked by the complaint of Count Rechteren, deputy for the
Province of Overyssel. On the 24th of July the French, under
Marshal Villars, had obtained a great victory at Denain. Count
Rechteren complained that, a few days after this battle, when he
was riding in his carriage by the gate of M. Ménager, the French
Plenipotentiary, that gentleman's lackeys insulted his lackeys with
grimaces and indecent gestures. He sent his secretary to complain
to M. Ménager, demand satisfaction, and say that if it were not
given, he should take it. Ménager replied, in writing, that although
this was but an affair between lackeys, he was far from approving ill
behaviour in his servants towards other servants, particularly towards
servants of Count Rechteren, and he was ready to send to the count
those lackeys whom he had seen misbehaving, or even those whom
his other servants should point out as guilty of the offensive conduct.
Rechteren admitted that he had not himself seen the grimaces and
insulting gestures, but he ought, he said, to be at liberty to send his
servants into Ménager's house for the detection of the offenders. A
few days afterwards Ménager and Rechteren were on the chief
promenade of Utrecht, with others who were Plenipotentiaries of the
United Provinces, and Rechteren said that he was still awaiting satisfaction. Ménager replied that his lackeys all denied the charge
against them, and he refused to allow the accusers of his servants to
come into his house and be their judges. Rechteren said he would
have justice yet upon master and men; he was not a man to take
insults. He then spoke some words in Dutch to his attendants, and
presently Ménager's lackeys came with complaint that the lackeys o
Rechteren tripped them up behind, threw them upon their faces, and
threatened them with knives. Rechteren told the French Plenipotentiary that he would pay them for doing that, and discharge them
if they did not do it. Rechteren's colleagues did what they could to
cover or excuse his folly, and begged that the matter might be left
to the arbitration of English Plenipotentiaries. This the French

Upon my going into a coffee-house yesterday, and lending an ear to the next table, which was encompassed with a circle of inferior politicians, one of them, after having read over the news very attentively, broke out into the following remarks : ' I am afraid ', says he, ' this unhappy rupture between the footmen at Utrecht will retard the peace of Christendom.' I wish the Pope may not be at the bottom of it. His holiness has a very good hand at fomenting a division, as the poor Swiss cantons have lately experienced to their cost. If Monsieur What-d'ye-call-him's domestics will not come to an accommodation, I do not know how the quarrel can be ended, but by a religious war.'

' Why truly ', says a wiseacre that sate by him, ' were I as the King of France, I would scorn to take part with the footmen of either side. Here's all the business of Europe stands still, because Monsieur Mesnager's man has had his head broke. If Count Rectrum had given them a pot of ale after it, all would have been well, without any of this bustle; but they say he's a warm man, and does not care to be made mouths at.'

Upon this, one that had held his tongue hitherto began to exert himself; declaring that he was very well pleased the plenipotentiaries of our Christian princes took this matter into their serious consideration; for that lackeys were never so saucy and pragmatical as they are nowadays, and that he should be glad to see them taken down in the treaty of peace, if it might be done without prejudice to the public affairs.

assented to, but they now demanded satisfaction against Rechteren, and refused to accept the excuse made for him, that he was drunk. 'Louis XIV might, under other circumstances', says M. Torcy, the French minister of the time, in his account of the peace negotiations, 'have dismissed the petty quarrel of servants by accepting such an excuse; but', says M. de Torcy, 'it was desirable to retard the conferences, and this dispute gave a plausible reason' (*Mémoires de Torcy*, iii, 411–413). This was the high policy of the affair of the lackeys, which, as Addison says, held all the affairs of Europe in suspense, a policy avowed by the high politician who was puller of the strings Morley).

One, who sate at the other end of the table, and seemed to be in the interests of the French king, told them, that they did not take the matter right, for that his most Christian majesty did not resent this matter because it was an injury done to Monsieur Mesnager's footmen; ' for ', says he, ' what are Monsieur Mesnager's footmen to him?' but because it was done to his subjects. ' Now ', says he, ' let me tell you, it would look very odd for a subject of France to have a bloody nose, and his sovereign not to take notice of it. He is obliged in honour to defend his people against hostilities; and if the Dutch will be so insolent to a crowned head, as in any wise to cuff or kick those who are under his protection, I think he is in the right to call them to an account for it.'

This distinction set the controversy upon a new foot, and seemed to be very well approved by most that heard it, until a little warm fellow, who declared himself a friend to the House of Austria, fell most unmercifully upon his Gallic majesty, as encouraging his subjects to make mouths at their betters, and afterwards screening them from the punishment that was due to their insolence. To which he added, that the French nation was so addicted to grimace, that if there was not a stop put to it at the General Congress, there would be no walking the streets for them in a time of peace, especially if they continued masters of the West Indies. The little man proceeded with a great deal of warmth, declaring that if the allies were of his mind, he would oblige the French king to burn his galleys and tolerate the Protestant religion in his dominions, before he would sheath his sword. He concluded with calling Monsieur Mesnager an insignificant prig.

The dispute was now growing very warm, and one does not know where it would have ended, had not a young man of about one and twenty, who seems to have been brought up with an eye to the law, taken the debate into his hand, and given it as his opinion that neither Count Rechteren nor

Monsieur Mesnager had behaved themselves right in this affair. ' Count Rechteren ', says he, ' should have made affidavit that his servants had been affronted, and then Monsieur Mesnager would have done him justice by taking away their liveries from them, or some other way that he might have thought the most proper; for let me tell you, if a man makes a mouth at me, I am not to knock the teeth out of it for his pains. Then again, as for Monsieur Mesnager, upon his servants being beaten, why, he might have had his action of assault and battery. But as the case now stands, if you will have my opinion, I think they ought to bring it to referees.'

I heard a great deal more of this conference, but I must confess, with little edification; for all I could learn at last from these honest gentlemen, was that the matter in debate was of too high a nature for such heads as theirs or mine to comprehend.

O.

No. 482.      *Friday, Sept. 12, 1712*      [ADDISON

*Floriferis ut apes in saltibus omnia libant.* LUCR., iii, 11

WHEN I have published any single paper that falls in with the popular taste and pleases more than ordinary, it always brings me in a great return of letters. My Tuesday's discourse [1], wherein I gave several admonitions to the fraternity of the Henpecked, has already produced me very many correspondents; the reason I cannot guess at, unless it be that such a discourse is of general use, and every married man's money. An honest tradesman, who dates his letter from Cheapside, sends me thanks in the name of a club, who, he tells me, meet as often as their wives will give them leave, and stay together until they are sent for home. He informs me that my paper has administered great consolation to their whole club, and desires me to give some further

1 No. 479.

account of Socrates, and to acquaint them in whose reign he lived, whether he was a citizen or a courtier, whether he buried Xantippe, with many other particulars; for that by his sayings he appears to have been a very wise man, and a good Christian. Another, who writes himself Benjamin Bamboo, tells me that, being coupled with a shrew, he had endeavoured to tame her by such lawful means as those which I mentioned in my last Tuesday's paper, and that in his wrath he had often gone further than Bracton allows in those cases; but that for the future he was resolved to bear it like a man of temper and learning, and consider her only as one who lives in his house to teach him philosophy. Tom Dapperwit says that he agrees with me in that whole discourse, excepting only the last sentence, where I affirm the married state to be either an heaven or an hell. Tom has been at the charge of a penny upon this occasion, to tell me that by his experience it is neither one nor the other, but rather that middle kind of state commonly known by the name of Purgatory.

The fair sex have likewise obliged me with their reflections upon the same discourse. A lady, who calls herself Euterpe, and seems a woman of letters, asks me whether I am for establishing the Salic law in every family, and why it is not fit that a woman who has discretion and learning should sit at the helm, when the husband is weak and illiterate? Another, of a quite contrary character, subscribes herself Xantippe, and tells me that she follows the example of her namesake; for being married to a bookish man who has no knowledge of the world, she is forced to take their affairs into her own hands, and to spirit him up now and then, that he may not grow musty and unfit for conversation.

After this abridgment of some letters which are come to my hands upon this occasion, I shall publish one of them at large :

Mr. Spectator,—You have given us a lively picture of
that kind of husband who comes under the denomination of the Henpecked; but I do not remember that you
have ever touched upon one that is of the quite different character, and who, in several places of England,
goes by the name of a Cotquean. I have the misfortune
to be joined for life with one of this character, who in
reality is more a woman than I am[1]. He was bred up
under the tuition of a tender mother, until she had
made him as good an housewife as herself. He could
preserve apricots and make jellies before he had been
two years out of the nursery. He was never suffered to
go abroad for fear of catching cold; when he should
have been hunting down a buck, he was by his mother's
side learning how to season it, or put it in crust; and
was making paper boats with his sisters, at an age when
other young gentlemen are crossing the seas, or travelling into foreign countries. He has the whitest hand
that you ever saw in your life, and raises paste better
than any woman in England. These qualifications make
him a sad husband : he is perpetually in the kitchen,
and has a thousand squabbles with the cook-maid. He
is better acquainted with the milk-score than his
steward's accounts. I fret to death when I hear him
find fault with a dish that is not dressed to his liking,
and instructing his friends that dine with him in the
best pickle for a walnut, or sauce for an haunch of
venison. With all this, he is a very good-natured
husband, and never fell out with me in his life but
once, upon the over-roasting of a dish of wild-fowl : at
the same time I must own I would rather he was a man
of a rough temper, that would treat me harshly sometimes, than of such an effeminate busy nature in a
province that does not belong to him. Since you have
given us the character of a wife who wears the breeches,
pray say something of a husband that wears the petticoat. Why should not a female character be as ridiculous in a man, as a male character in one of our sex?

O.                                    I am, &c.

---

[1] 'Than myself' (folio).

No. 483.       *Saturday, Sept. 13, 1712*       [ADDISON

*Nec Deus intersit, nisi dignus vindice nodus*
*Inciderit.*                                    HOR., *Ars Poet.* 191

WE cannot be guilty of a greater act of un-
charitableness, than to interpret the afflictions which
befall our neighbours, as punishments and judgments.
It aggravates the evil to him who suffers, when he
looks upon himself as the mark of Divine vengeance,
and abates the compassion of those towards him, who
regard him in so dreadful a light. This humour of
turning every misfortune into a judgment, proceeds
from wrong notions of religion, which, in its own
nature, produces goodwill towards men, and puts
the mildest construction upon every accident that
befalls them. In this case, therefore, it is not
religion that sours a man's temper, but it is his
temper that sours his religion : people of gloomy un-
cheerful imaginations, or of envious malignant tempers, whatever kind of life they are engaged in, will
discover their natural tincture of mind in all their
thoughts, words, and actions. As the finest wines
have often the taste of the soil, so even the most
religious thoughts often draw something that is particular from the constitution of the mind in which
they arise. When folly or superstition strike in with
this natural depravity of temper, it is not in the power
even of religion itself to preserve the character of the
person who is possessed with it, from appearing highly
absurd and ridiculous.

An old maiden gentlewoman, whom I shall conceal
under the name of Nemesis, is the greatest discoverer
of judgments that I have met with. She can tell
you what sin it was that set such a man's house on
fire, or blew down his barns. Talk to her of an
unfortunate young lady that lost her beauty by the
small-pox, she fetches a deep sigh, and tells you,
that when she had a fine face she was always looking
on it in her glass. Tell her of a piece of good fortune

that has befallen one of her acquaintance, and she wishes it may prosper with her; but her mother used one of her nieces very barbarously. Her usual remarks turn upon people who had great estates, but never enjoyed them, by reason of some flaw in their own or their fathers' behaviour. She can give you the reason why such an one died childless; why such an one was cut off in the flower of his youth; why such an one was unhappy in her marriage; why one broke his leg on such a particular spot of ground, and why another was killed with a back-sword [1], rather than with any other kind of weapon. She has a crime for every misfortune that can befall any of her acquaintance, and when she hears of a robbery that has been made, or a murder that has been committed, enlarges more on the guilt of the suffering person, than on that of the thief or the assassin. In short, she is so good a Christian, that whatever happens to herself is a trial, and whatever happens to her neighbour is a judgment.

The very description of this folly, in ordinary life, is sufficient to expose it; but when it appears in a pomp and dignity of style, it is very apt to amuse and terrify the mind of the reader. Herodotus and Plutarch very often apply their judgments as impertinently as the old woman I have before mentioned, though their manner of relating them makes the folly itself appear venerable. Indeed, most historians, as well Christian as Pagan, have fallen into this idle superstition, and spoken of ill success, unforeseen disasters, and terrible events, as if they had been let into the secrets of Providence, and made acquainted with that private conduct by which the world is governed. One would think several of our own historians in particular had many revelations of this kind made to them. Our old English monks seldom let any of their kings depart in peace, who had endeavoured to diminish the power or wealth of which the ecclesiastics were in those times pos-

[1] A sword with one sharp edge.

sessed. William the Conqueror's race generally found
their judgments in the New Forest, where their
father had pulled down churches and monasteries.
In short, read one of the chronicles written by an
author of this frame of mind, and you would think
you were reading an history of the kings of Israel
or Judah, where the historians were actually inspired,
and where, by a particular scheme of Providence,
the kings were distinguished by judgments or blessings, according as they promoted idolatry or the
worship of the true God.

I cannot but look upon this manner of judging
upon misfortunes not only to be very uncharitable in
regard to the person whom they befall, but very pre-
sumptuous in regard to him who is supposed to inflict
them.   It is a strong argument for a state of retribu-
tion hereafter, that in this world virtuous persons
are very often unfortunate, and vicious persons prosperous, which is wholly repugnant to the nature of a
Being who appears infinitely wise and good in all His
works, unless we may suppose that such a promis-
cuous and undistinguishing distribution of good and
evil, which was necessary for carrying on the designs
of Providence in this life, will be rectified and made
amends for in another.   We are not, therefore, to
expect that fire should fall from heaven in the
ordinary course of Providence; nor when we see triumphant guilt or depressed virtue in particular persons, that Omnipotence will make bare its holy arm
in the defence of the one or punishment of the other.
It is sufficient that there is a day set apart for the
hearing and requiting of both according to their respective merits.

The folly of ascribing temporal judgments to any
particular crimes may appear from several considerations.   I shall only mention two: first, that generally speaking, there is no calamity or affliction which
is supposed to have happened as a judgment to a
vicious man, which does not sometimes happen to
men of approved religion and virtue.   When Diagoras

the atheist was on board one of the Athenian ships, there arose a very violent tempest; upon which the mariners told him that it was a just judgment upon them for having taken so impious a man on board. Diagoras begged them to look upon the rest of the ships that were in the same distress, and asked them whether or no Diagoras was on board every vessel in the fleet [1]. We are all involved in the same calamities, and subject to the same accidents; and when we see any one of the species under any particular oppression, we should look upon it as arising from the common lot of human nature, rather than from the guilt of the person who suffers.

Another consideration that may check our presumption in putting such a construction upon a misfortune is this, that it is impossible for us to know what are calamities and what are blessings. How many accidents have passed for misfortunes which have turned to the welfare and prosperity of the persons in whose lot they have fallen? How many disappointments have, in their consequences, saved a man from ruin? If we could look into the effects of everything, we might be allowed to pronounce boldly upon blessings and judgments; but for a man to give his opinion of what he sees but in part, and in its beginnings, is an unjustifiable piece of rashness and folly. The story of Biton and Clitobus [2], which was in great reputation among the heathens, for we see it quoted by all the ancient authors, both Greek and Latin, who have written upon the immortality of the soul, may teach us a caution in this matter. These two brothers, being the sons of a lady who was priestess to Juno, drew their mother's chariot to the temple at the time of a great solemnity, the persons being absent who by their office were to have drawn her chariot on that occasion. The mother was so

---

[1] Cicero, *De Natura Deorum*. iii, 37. Diagoras the Melian attacked the Eleusinian mysteries, and a price having been set on his head, left Athens 411 B.C.

[2] A mistake for Cleobis (Herodotus, i, 31).

transported with this instance of filial duty that she petitioned her goddess to bestow upon them the greatest gift that could be given to men; upon which they were both cast into a deep sleep, and the next morning found dead in the temple.  This was such an event as would have been construed into a judgment had it happened to the two brothers after an act of disobedience, and would doubtless have been represented as such by any ancient historian who had given us an account of it.                    O.

No. 484.    *Monday, Sept. 15, 1712*    [STEELE

*Neque cuiquam tam statim clarum ingenium est, ut possit emergere; nisi illi materia, occasio, fautor etiam, commendatorque contingat.*
                                    PLIN., Epist.

MR. SPECTATOR,—Of all the young fellows who are in their progress through any profession, none seem to have so good a title to the protection of the men of eminence in it as the modest man; not so much because his modesty is a certain indication of his merit, as because 'tis a certain obstacle to the producing of it. Now, as of all professions this virtue is thought to be more particularly unnecessary in that of the law than in any other, I shall only apply myself to the relief of such who follow this profession with this disadvantage.  What aggravates the matter is that those persons who, the better to prepare themselves for this study, have made some progress in others, have, by addicting themselves to letters, increased their natural modesty, and consequently heightened the obstruction to this sort of preferment; so that every one of these may emphatically be said to be such a one as 'laboureth and taketh pains, and is still the more behind'. It may be a matter worth discussing, then, Why that which made a youth so amiable to the ancients should make him appear so ridiculous to the moderns? and why in our days there should be neglect, and even oppression of young beginners, instead of that protection which was the pride of theirs?  In the profession spoken of, 'tis obvious to every one whose attendance is required at Westminster Hall, with what difficulty a youth of any modesty has

been permitted to make an observation that could in
no wise detract from the merit of his elders, and is
absolutely necessary for the advancing his own.  I have
often seen one of these not only molested in his utter-
ance of something very pertinent, but even plundered
of his question, and by a strong serjeant shouldered out
of his rank, which he has recovered with much difficulty and confusion.  Now as great part of the business
of this profession might be despatched by one that
perhaps

> Abest virtute diserti
> Messalæ, nec scit quantum Cascellius Aulus.  Hor.[1]

So I can't conceive the injustice done to the public
if the men of reputation in this calling would introduce such of the young ones into business whose application to this study will let them into the secrets of it,
as much as their modesty will hinder them from the
practice : I say, it would be laying an everlasting
obligation upon a young man to be introduced at first
only as a mute, until by this countenance, and a resolution to support the good opinion conceived of him in his
betters, his complexion shall be so well settled that the
litigious of this island may be secure of his obstreperous
aid.  If I might be indulged to speak in the style of a
lawyer I would say, that any one about thirty years
of age might make a common motion to the Court with
as much elegance and propriety as the most aged advo-
cates in the hall.

I can't advance the merit of modesty by any argument of my own so powerfully as by inquiring into the
sentiments the greatest among the ancients of different
ages entertained upon this virtue.  If we go back to
the days of Solomon, we shall find favour a necessary
consequence to a shamefaced man.  Pliny, the greatest
lawyer and most elegant writer of the age he lived in,
in several of his epistles is very solicitous in recommending to the public some young men of his own
profession, and very often undertakes to become an
advocate, upon condition that some one of these his
favourites might be joined with him in order to produce
the merit of such whose modesty otherwise would have
suppressed it.  It may seem very marvellous to a

----

1 *Ars Poet.* 370.

saucy modern, that *Multum sanguinis, multum vere-cundiæ, multum solicitudinis in ore*[1] (to have the face first full of blood, then the countenance dashed with modesty, and then the whole aspect as of one dying with fear, when a man begins to speak) should be esteemed by Pliny the necessary qualifications of a fine speaker. Shakespeare also has expressed himself in the same favourable strain of modesty when he says :

> In the modesty of fearful duty
> I read as much as from the rattling tongue
> Of fancy and audacious eloquence[2].

Now since these authors have professed themselves for the modest man, even in the utmost confusions of speech and countenance, why should an intrepid utter-ance and a resolute vociferation thunder so success-fully in our courts of justice? and why should that con-fidence of speech and behaviour which seems to acknow-ledge no superior and to defy all contradiction, prevail over that deference and resignation with which the modest man implores that favourable opinion which the other seems to command.

As the case at present stands, the best consolation that I can administer to those who cannot get into that stroke of business (as the phrase is) which they deserve, is to reckon every particular acquisition of knowledge in this study as a real increase of their fortune; and fully to believe that one day this imagin-ary gain will certainly be made out by one more sub-stantial. I wish you would talk to us a little on this head; you would oblige,

Sir,

Your most humble Servant

The author of this letter is certainly a man of good sense; but I am perhaps particular in my opinion on this occasion, for I have observed that, under the notion of modesty, men have indulged themselves in a spiritless sheepishness, and been for ever lost to themselves, their families, their friends, and their country. When a man has taken care to pretend to

---

1 Pliny's *Epistles*, Book v, Epist. 17.
2 *Midsummer Night's Dream*, v, i.

nothing but what he may justly aim at, and can
execute as well as any other without injustice to
any other, it is ever want of breeding or courage to
be browbeaten or elbowed out of his honest ambition.
I have said often, modesty must be an act of the
will, and yet it always implies self-denial: for if a
man has an ardent desire to do what is laudable for
him to perform, and, from an unmanly bashfulness,
shrinks away, and lets his merits languish in silence,
he ought not to be angry at the world that a more
unskilful actor succeeds in his part, because he has
not confidence to come upon the stage himself. The
generosity my correspondent mentions of Pliny cannot be enough applauded. To cherish the dawn
of merit and hasten its maturity was a work worthy
a noble Roman and a liberal scholar. That concern
which is described in the letter is to all the world
the greatest charm imaginable; but then the modest
man must proceed, and show a latent revolution in
himself; for the admiration of his modesty arises
from the manifestation of his merit. I must confess,
we live in an age wherein a few empty blusterers
carry away the praise of speaking, while a crowd of
fellows overstocked with knowledge are run down by
them—I say overstocked, because they certainly are
so as to their service of mankind, if from their very
store they raise to themselves ideas of respect and
greatness of the occasion, and I know not what, to
disable themselves from explaining their thoughts.
I must confess, when I have seen Charles Frankair
rise up with a commanding mien and torrent of
handsome words, talk a mile off the purpose, and
drive down twenty bashful boobies of ten times his
sense, who at the same time were envying his impudence and despising his understanding, it has been
matter of great mirth to me; but it soon ended in a
secret lamentation, that the foundations of everything praiseworthy in these realms, the universities,
should be so muddied with a false sense of this virtue
as to produce men capable of being so abused. I

will be bold to say, that it is a ridiculous education which does not qualify a man to make his best appearance before the greatest man and the finest woman to whom he can address himself. Were this judiciously corrected in the nurseries of learning, pert coxcombs would know their distance; but we must bear with this false modesty in our young nobility and gentry until they cease at Oxford and Cambridge to grow dumb in the study of eloquence.

T.

No. 485.     *Tuesday, Sept. 16, 1712*     [STEELE

*Nihil tam firmum est, cui periculum non sit, etiam ab invalido.*
QUINT. CURT., Lib. vii, c. 8

MR SPECTATOR,—My Lord Clarendon has observed, 'That few men have done more harm than those who have been thought to be able to do least; and there cannot be a greater error than to believe a man whom we see qualified with too mean parts to do good, to be therefore incapable of doing hurt. There is a supply of malice, of pride, of industry, and even of folly in the weakest when he sets his heart upon it, that makes a strange progress in mischief.' What may seem to the reader the greatest paradox in the reflection of the historian is, I suppose, that folly, which is generally thought incapable of contriving or executing any design, should be so formidable to those whom it exerts itself to molest. But this will appear very plain, if we remember that Solomon says, 'It is as sport to a fool to do mischief[1]'; and that he might the more emphatically express the calamitous circumstances of him that falls under the displeasure of this wanton person, the same author adds further, 'That a stone is heavy and the sand weighty, but a fool's wrath is heavier than them both[2].' It is impossible to suppress my own illustration upon this matter, which is, that as the man of sagacity bestirs himself to distress his enemy by methods probable and reducible to reason, so the same reason will fortify his enemy to elude these his regular efforts; but your fool projects, acts, and con-

[1] *Proverbs* x, 23.      [2] *Proverbs* xxvii, 3.

cludes with such notable inconsistence, that no regular course of thought can evade or counterplot his prodigious machinations. My frontispiece, I believe, may be extended to imply that several of our misfortunes arise from things, as well as persons, that seem of very little consequence. Into what tragical extravagance does Shakespeare hurry Othello upon the loss of an handkerchief only? And what barbarities does Desdemona suffer from a slight inadvertency in regard to this fatal trifle?[1] If the schemes of all the enterprising spirits were to be carefully examined, some intervening accident, not considerable enough to occasion any debate upon, or give 'em any apprehension of ill consequence from it, will be found to be the occasion of their ill success, rather than any error in points of moment and difficulty, which naturally engaged their maturest deliberations. If you go to the levee of any great man, you will observe him exceeding gracious to several very insignificant fellows; and this upon this maxim, that the neglect of any person must arise from the mean opinion you have of his capacity to do you any service or prejudice; and that this calling his sufficiency in question must give him inclination, and where this is there never wants strength or opportunity to annoy you. There is nobody so weak of invention, that can't aggravate or make some little stories to vilify his enemy; and there are very few but have good inclinations to hear 'em, and 'tis infinite pleasure to the majority of mankind to level a person superior to his neighbours. Besides, in all matter of controversy, that party which has the greatest abilities labours under this prejudice, that he will certainly be supposed, upon account of his abilities, to have done an injury when perhaps he has received one. It would be tedious to enumerate the strokes that nations and particular friends have suffered from persons very contemptible.

'I think Henry IV of France, so formidable to his neighbours, could no more be secured against the resolute villainy of Ravillac, than Villiers, Duke of Buckingham, could be against that of Felton. And there is no incensed person so destitute but can provide himself with a knife or a pistol, if he finds stomach to apply 'em. That things and persons of no moment should

[1] *Othello*, Act iii, sc. 3, *seq.*

give such powerful revolutions to the progress of those
of the greatest, seems a providential disposition to baffle
and abate the pride of human sufficiency; as also to
engage the humanity and benevolence of superiors to
all below 'em, by letting them into this secret, that the
stronger depends upon the weaker.

I am, Sir,<br>
Your very humble Servant

TEMPLE, PAPER BUILDINGS

DEAR SIR,—I received a letter from you some time
ago, which I should have answered sooner, had you
informed me in yours to what part of this island I
might have directed my impertinence; but having been
let into the knowledge of that matter, this handsome
excuse is no longer serviceable. My neighbour Pretty-
man shall be the subject of this letter; who falling in
with the *Spectator's* doctrine concerning the month of
May [1], began from that season to dedicate himself to
the service of the fair in the following manner. I
observed at the beginning of the month he bought him
a new night-gown, either side to be worn outwards, both
equally gorgeous and attractive; but until the end of
the month I did not enter so fully into the knowledge
of his contrivance, as the use of that garment has since
suggested to me. Now you must know that all new
clothes raise and warm the bearer's imagination into
a conceit of his being a much finer gentleman than he
was before, banishing all sobriety and reflection, and
giving him up to gallantry and amour. Inflamed therefore with this way of thinking, and full of the spirit
of the month of May, did this merciless youth resolve
upon the business of captivating. At first he confined
himself to his room only, now and then appearing at
his window in his night-gown, and practising that easy
posture which expresses the very top and dignity of
languishment. It was pleasant to see him diversify his
loveliness, sometimes obliging the passengers only with
a side-face, with a book in his hand; sometimes being
so generous as to expose the whole in the fulness of its
beauty; at the other times, by a judicious throwing
back of his periwig, he would throw in his ears. You

[1] See Nos. 365, 395, 425.

know he is that sort of person which the mob call a handsome jolly man; which appearance can't miss of captives in this part of the town. Being emboldened by daily success, he leaves his room with a resolution to extend his conquests; and I have apprehended him in his night-gown smiting in all parts of this neighbourhood.

This I, being of an amorous complexion, saw with indignation, and had thoughts of purchasing a wig in these parts; into which, being at a greater distance from the earth, I might have thrown a very liberal mixture of white horse-hair, which would make a fairer, and consequently a handsomer appearance, while my situation would secure me against any discoveries. But the passion to the handsome gentleman seems to be so fixed to that part of the building, that it will be extremely difficult to divert it to mine; so that I am resolved to stand boldly to the complexion of my own eyebrow, and prepare me an immense black wig of the same sort of structure with that of my rival. Now, though by this I shall not, perhaps, lessen the number of the admirers of his complexion, I shall have a fair chance to divide the passengers by the irresistible force of mine.

I expect sudden despatches from you, with advice of the family you are in now, how to deport myself upon this so delicate a conjunction; with some comfortable resolutions in favour of the handsome black man against the handsome fair one.

I am, Sir,

Your most humble Servant,

C.

*N.B.*—He who writ this is a black man two pair of stairs; the gentleman of whom he writes is fair, and one pair of stairs.


MR SPECTATOR,—I only say, that it is impossible for me to say how much I am

Yours,

ROBIN SHORTER

*P.S.*—I shall think it a little hard, if you do not take as much notice of this epistle as you have of the ingenious Mr Short's[1]. I am not afraid to let the world see which is the deeper man of the two.

## ADVERTISEMENT

LONDON, *September* 15

Whereas a young woman on horseback, in an equestrian habit, on the 13th instant in the evening, met the Spectator, within a mile and an half of this town, and flying in the face of justice, pulled off her hat, in which there was a feather, with the mien and air of a young officer[2], saying at the same time, 'Your servant, Mr Spec.', or words to that purpose; this is to give notice, that if any person can discover the name, and place, and abode of the said offender, so as she can be brought to justice, the informant shall have all fitting encouragement.    T.

No. 486.    *Wednesday*, Sept. 17, 1712    [STEELE

*Audire est operæ pretium, procedere recte
Qui mœchos non vultis.*    HOR., 1 *Sat.* ii, 38

MR SPECTATOR,—There are very many of my acquaintance followers of Socrates, with more particular regard to that part of his philosophy which we, among ourselves, call his 'Domestics', under which denomination, or title, we include all the conjugal joys and sufferings. We have indeed, with very great pleasure, observed the honour you do the whole fraternity of the Henpecked, in placing that illustrious man at our head[3]; and it does in a very great measure baffle the raillery of pert rogues, who have no advantage above us, but in that they are single. But when you look about into the crowd of mankind, you will find the fair sex reigns with greater tyranny over lovers than husbands. You shall hardly meet one in a thousand who is wholly exempt from their dominion, and those that are so are

1 See No. 473.
2 In No. 435, Addison spoke of women who dressed 'in a hat and feather, a riding-coat and a periwig', in imitation of men.
3 Nos. 479, 482.

capable of no taste of life, and breathe and walk about
the earth as insignificants. But I am going to desire
your further favour in behalf of our harmless brotherhood, and hope you will show in a true light the
unmarried henpecked, as well as you have done justice
to us, who submit to the conduct of our wives. I am
very particularly acquainted with one who is under
entire submission to a kind girl, as he calls her; and
though he knows I have been witness both to the ill-
usage he has received from her, and his inability to
resist her tyranny, he still pretends to make a jest of
me for a little more than ordinary obsequiousness to
my spouse. No longer than Tuesday last he took me
with him to visit his mistress; and he having, it seems,
been a little in disgrace before, thought by bringing
me with him she would constrain herself, and insensibly
fall into general discourse with him; and so he might
break the ice, and save himself all the ordinary com-
punctions and mortifications she used to make him
suffer before she would be reconciled after any act of
rebellion on his part. When we came into the room,
we were received with the utmost coldness; and when
he presented me as Mr Such-a-one, his very good friend,
she just had patience to suffer my salutation; but when
he himself, with a very gay air, offered to follow me,
she gave him a thundering box on the ear, called him
pitiful poor-spirited wretch, how durst he see her face?
His wig and hat fell on different parts of the floor.
She seized the wig too soon for him to recover it, and
kicking it downstairs, threw herself into an opposite
room, pulling the door after her with a force, that you
would have thought the hinges would have given way.
We went down, you must think, with no very good
countenances; and as we sneaked off, and were driving
home together, he confessed to me that her anger was
thus highly raised, because he did not think fit to fight
a gentleman who had said she was what she was;
'but', says he, 'a kind letter or two, or fifty pieces,
will put her in humour again'. I asked him why he
did not part with her; he answered, he loved her with
all the tenderness imaginable, and she had too many
charms to be abandoned for a little quickness of spirit.
Thus does this illegitimate henpecked overlook the
hussy's having no regard to his very life and fame, in

putting him upon an infamous dispute about her reputation; yet has he the confidence to laugh at me, because I obey my poor dear in keeping out of harm's way, and not staying too late from my own family, to pass through the hazards of a town full of ranters and debauchees. You that are a philosopher should urge in our behalf, that when we bear with a froward woman, our patience is preserved, in consideration that a breach with her might be a dishonour to children who are descended from us, and whose concern make us tolerate a thousand frailties, for fear they should redound dishonour upon the innocent. This and the like circumstances, which carry with them the most valuable regards of human life, may be mentioned for our long-suffering; but in the case of gallants, they swallow ill-usage from one to whom they have no obligation, but from a base passion which it is mean to indulge, and which it would be glorious to overcome.

These sort of fellows are very numerous, and some have been conspicuously such without shame; nay, they have carried on the jest in the very article of death, and, to the diminution of the wealth and happiness of their families, in bar of those honourably near to them, have left immense wealth to their paramours. What is this but being a cully in the grave! Sure this is being henpecked with a vengeance! But without dwelling upon these less frequent instances of eminent cullyism, what is there so common as to hear a fellow curse his fate that he cannot get rid of a passion to a jilt, and quote an half line out of a miscellany poem to prove his weakness is natural. If they will go on thus, I have nothing to say to it; but then let them not pretend to be free all this while, and laugh at us poor married patients.

I have known one wench in this town carry an haughty dominion over her lovers so well, that she has at the same time been kept by a sea captain in the Straits, a merchant in the city, a country gentleman in Hampshire, and had all her correspondences managed by one she kept for her own uses. This happy man (as the phrase is) used to write very punctually every post letters for the mistress to transcribe. He would sit in his night-gown and slippers, and be as grave giving an account, only changing names, that there was nothing in these idle reports they had heard of such a scoundrel as one of the other lovers was; and how could he think she could condescend so low, after such a fine gentleman as each of them? For the same epistle said the same thing to and of every one of them. And so Mr Secretary and his lady went to bed with great order.

To be short, Mr Spectator, we husbands shall never make the figure we ought in the imaginations of young men growing up in the world, except you can bring it about that a man of the town shall be as infamous a character as a woman of the town. But of all that I have met in my time, commend me to Betty Duall. She is the wife of a sailor, and the kept mistress of a man of quality; she dwells with the latter during the seafaring of the former. The husband asks no questions, sees his apartments furnished with riches not his, when he comes into port, and the lover is as joyful as a man arrived at his haven when the other puts to sea. Betty is the most eminently victorious of any of her sex, and ought to stand recorded the only woman of the age in which she lives, who has possessed at the same time two abused and two contented——[1]

                                                T.


No. 487.          *Thursday, Sept. 18, 1712*          [ADDISON

*Cum prostrata sopore*
*Urget membra quies, et mens sine pondere ludit.* PETR.

THOUGH there are many authors who have written on dreams, they have generally considered them only as revelations of what has already happened in distant parts of the world, or as presages of what is to happen in future periods of time.

I shall consider this subject in another light, as dreams may give us some idea of the great excellency of an human soul, and some intimation of its independency on matter.

In the first place, our dreams are great instances of that activity which is natural to the human soul, and which it is not in the power of sleep to deaden

[1] See No. 500.

or abate. When the man appears tired and worn
out with the labours of the day, this active part in
his composition is still busy and unwearied. When
the organs of sense want their due repose and necessary reparations, and the body is no longer able to
keep pace with that spiritual substance to which it
is united, the soul exerts herself in her several faculties, and continues in action until her partner is
again qualified to bear her company. In this case
dreams look like the relaxations and amusements of
the soul when she is disencumbered of her machine,
her sports and recreations when she has laid her
charge asleep.

In the second place, dreams are an instance of
that agility and perfection which is natural to the
faculties of the mind, when they are disengaged
from the body. The soul is clogged and retarded
in her operations, when she acts in conjunction with
a companion that is so heavy and unwieldy in its
motions. But in dreams it is wonderful to observe
with what a sprightliness and alacrity she exerts
herself. The slow of speech make unpremeditated
harangues, or converse readily in languages that they
are but little acquainted with. The grave abound
in pleasantries, the dull in repartees and points of
wit. There is not a more painful action of the mind
than invention; yet in dreams it works with that
ease and activity, that we are not sensible when the
faculty is employed. For instance, I believe every
one some time or other dreams that he is reading
papers, books, or letters, in which case the invention
prompts so readily that the mind is imposed upon,
and mistakes its own suggestions for the compositions
of another.

I shall, under this head, quote a passage out of
the *Religio Medici* [1], in which the ingenious author

1 Part II, sec. 11. This passage is preceded by the following words
of Sir Thomas Browne: 'Surely it is not a melancholy conceit to
think we are all asleep in this world, and that the conceits of this
life are as mere dreams to those of the next, as the phantasms of the
night to the conceit of the day.'

gives an account of himself in his dreaming and his waking thoughts : ' We are somewhat more than ourselves in our sleeps, and the slumber of the body seems to be but the waking of the soul. It is the ligation of sense, but the liberty of reason, and our waking conceptions do not match the fancies of our sleeps. At my nativity my ascendant was the watery sign of Scorpius : I was born in the planetary hour of Saturn, and I think I have a piece of that leaden planet in me. I am no way facetious nor disposed for the mirth and galliardise of company; yet in one dream I can compose a whole comedy, behold the action, apprehend the jests, and laugh myself awake at the conceits thereof. Were my memory as faithful as my reason is then fruitful, I would never study but in my dreams; and this time also would I choose for my devotions; but our grosser memories have then so little hold of our abstracted understandings, that they forget the story, and can only relate to our awaked souls a confused and broken tale of that that has passed. . . . . Thus it is observed that men sometimes, upon the hour of their departure, do speak and reason above themselves, for then the soul beginning to be freed from the ligaments of the body, begins to reason like herself, and to discourse in a strain above mortality.'

We may likewise observe in the third place, that the passions affect the mind with greater strength when we are asleep than when we are awake. Joy and sorrow give us more vigorous sensations of pain or pleasure at this time than at any other. Devotion likewise, as the excellent author above mentioned has hinted, is in a very particular manner heightened and inflamed when it rises in the soul at a time that the body is thus laid at rest. Every man's experience will inform him in this matter, though it is very probable that this may happen differently in different constitutions. I shall conclude this head with the two following problems, which I shall leave to the solution of my reader.

Supposing a man always happy in his dreams and
miserable in his waking thoughts, and that his life
was equally divided between them, whether would
he be more happy or miserable?   Were a man a
king in his dreams and a beggar awake, and dreamt
as consequentially and in as continued unbroken
schemes as he thinks when awake, whether he would
be in reality a king or beggar, or rather whether he
would not be both?

There is another circumstance which methinks
gives us a very high idea of the nature of the soul
in regard to what passes in dreams, I mean that
innumerable multitude and variety of ideas which
then arise in her.   Were that active watchful being
only conscious of her own existence at such a time,
what a painful solitude would her hours of sleep
be?   Were the soul sensible of her being alone in
her sleeping moments, after the same manner that
she is sensible of it while awake, the time would
hang very heavy on her, as it often actually does
when she dreams that she is in such a solitude :

> Semperque relinqui
> Sola sibi, semper longam incomitata videtur
> Ire viam.   VIRG.[1]

But this observation I only make by the way.
What I would here remark is that wonderful power
in the soul of producing her own company on these
occasions.   She converses with numberless beings of
her own creation, and is transported into ten thousand scenes of her own raising.   She is herself the
theatre, the actors, and the beholder.   This puts me
in mind of a saying which I am infinitely pleased
with, and which Plutarch[2] ascribes to Heraclitus,
' That all men whilst they are awake are in one
common world; but that each of them, when he is
asleep, is in a world of his own.'   The waking man
is conversant in the world of Nature, when he sleeps
he retires to a private world that is particular to

---

[1] _Æneid_, iv, 466.        [2] _On Superstition_, chap. iii.

himself. There seems something in this consideration that intimates to us a natural grandeur and perfection in the soul, which is rather to be admired
than explained.

I must not omit that argument for the excellency
of the soul, which I have seen quoted out of Ter-
tullian [1], namely, its power of divining in dreams.
That several such divinations have been made, none
can question who believes the Holy Writings, or who
has but the least degree of a common historical
faith, there being innumerable instances of this nature
in several authors, both ancient and modern, sacred
and profane. Whether such dark presages, such
visions of the night proceed from any latent power
in the soul during this her state of abstraction, or
from any communication with the Supreme Being,
or from any operation of subordinate spirits, has
been a great dispute among the learned; the matter
of fact is, I think, incontestable, and has been looked
upon as such by the greatest writers, who have been
never suspected either of superstition or enthusiasm.

I do not suppose that the soul in these instances
is entirely loose and unfettered from the body : it is
sufficient, if she is not so far sunk and immersed in
matter, nor entangled and perplexed in her operations, with such motions of blood and spirits as when
she actuates the machine in its waking hours. The
corporeal union is slackened enough to give the mind
more play. The soul seems gathered within herself,
and recovers that spring which is broke and weakened
when she operates more in concert with the body.

The speculations I have here made, if they are
not arguments, they are at least strong intimations,
not only of the excellency of an human soul, but
of its independence on the body; and if they do not
prove, do at least confirm these two great points,
which are established by many other reasons that are
altogether unanswerable.                                O.

[1] *On the Soul.* Chapters xliii to xlix relate to Sleep and Dreams.

## No. 488.      *Friday*, Sept. 19, 1712      [ADDISON

*Quanti emptæ ? Parvo.   Quanti ergo ? Octussibus.   Eheu !*
HOR., 2 Sat. iii, 156

I FIND, by several letters which I receive daily, that many of my readers would be better pleased to pay three-halfpence for my paper than twopence[1]. The ingenious T. W.[2] tells me that I have deprived him of the best part of his breakfast, for that, since the rise of my paper, he is forced every morning to drink his dish of coffee by itself, without the addition of the *Spectator*, that used to be better than lace[3] to it. Eugenius informs me very obligingly, that he never thought he should have disliked any passage in my paper, but that of late there have been two words in every one of them, which he could heartily wish left out, viz., ' Price twopence '. I have a letter from a soap-boiler, who condoles with me very affectionately upon the necessity we both lie under of setting an higher price on our commodities, since the late tax has been laid upon them, and desiring me, when I write next on that subject, to speak a word or two upon the present duties on Castle soap[4]. But there is none of these my correspondents who writes with a greater turn of good sense and elegance of expression than the generous Philomedes[5], who advises me to value every *Spectator* at sixpence, and promises that he himself will engage for above an hundred of his acquaintance, who shall take it at that price.

Letters from the female world are likewise come to me in great quantities upon the same occasion,

1 See No. 445.
2 Probably Dr Thomas Walker (died 1728, aged eighty), who was head-master of the Charterhouse when Addison and Steele were at that school.
3 Spirits added to tea or coffee. Prior (*The Chameleon*) says, ' He drinks his coffee without lace.'
4 Castile soap—called ' Castle ' by the soap-boiler—was introduced in the reign of James I.
5 ' Philomeides ', laughter-loving.

and as I naturally bear a great deference to this part of our species, I am very glad to find that those who approve my conduct in this particular are much more numerous than those who condemn it. A large family of daughters have drawn me up a very handsome remonstrance, in which they set forth that their father having refused to take in the *Spectator* since the additional price was set upon it, they offered him unanimously to bate him the article of bread and butter in the tea-table account, provided the *Spectator* might be served up to them every morning as usual. Upon this the old gentleman, being pleased, it seems, with their desire of improving themselves, has granted them the continuance both of the *Spectator* and their bread and butter; having given particular orders that the tea-table shall be set forth every morning with its customary bill of fare, and without any manner of defalcation. I thought myself obliged to mention this particular, as it does honour to this worthy gentleman; and if the young lady Lætitia, who sent me this account, will acquaint me with his name, I will insert it at length in one of my papers if he desires it.

I should be very glad to find out any expedient that might alleviate the expense which this my paper brings to any of my readers, and, in order to it, must propose two points to their consideration. First, that if they retrench any the smallest particular in their ordinary expense, it will easily make up the halfpenny a day which we have now under consideration. Let a lady sacrifice but a single riband to her morning studies, and it will be sufficient: let a family burn but a candle a night less than the usual number, and they may take in the *Spectator* without detriment to their private affairs.

In the next place, if my readers will not go to the price of buying my papers by retail, let them have patience, and they may buy them in the lump without the burthen of a tax upon them. My speculations, when they are sold single, like cherries upon the stick, are delights for the rich and wealthy; after some time they come to market in greater quantities, and are every ordinary man's money. The truth of it is, they have a certain flavour at their first appearance from several accidental circumstances of time, place, and person, which they may lose if they are not taken early; but in this case every reader is to consider whether it is not better for him to be half a year behindhand with the fashionable and polite part of the world, than to strain himself beyond his circumstances. My bookseller has now about ten thousand of the third and fourth volumes, which he is ready to publish, having already disposed of as large an edition both of the first and second volume. As he is a person whose head is very well turned to his business, he thinks they would be a very proper present to be made to persons at christenings, marriages, visiting days, and the like joyful solemnities, as several other books are frequently given at funerals. He has printed them in such a little portable volume [1] that many of them may be ranged together upon a single plate, and is of opinion that a salver of *Spectators* would be as acceptable an entertainment to the ladies as a salver of sweetmeats.

I shall conclude this paper with an epigram lately sent to the writer of the *Spectator*, after having returned my thanks to the ingenious author of it :

SIR,—Having heard the following epigram very much commended, I wonder that it has not yet had a place in any of your papers; I think the suffrage of our poet-laureate [2] should not be overlooked, which shows the opinion he entertains of your paper, whether the

---

[1] There was a reprint in 12mo in 1712-13, besides the 8vo edition.

[2] Nahum Tate (1652-1715) succeeded Thomas Shadwell as poet-laureate in 1692. Tate wrote the greater portion of the second part of Dryden's *Absalom and Achitophel*, and published a new version of Shakespeare's *King Lear*, besides producing a version of the *Psalms* in concert with Dr Nicholas Brady. He died in poverty in the Mint. The epigram here printed appeared on p. 28 of *The Tunbridge Miscellany: consisting of poems, &c., written at Tunbridge Wells this summer*, published by Curll in 1712.

notion he proceed upon be true or false. I make bold
to convey it to you, not knowing if it has yet come to
your hands :

### ON THE *SPECTATOR*

#### BY MR TATE

*Aliusque et idem*
*Nasceris.* HOR.[1]

When first the *Tatler* to a mute was turned,
Great Britain for her censor's silence mourned.
Robbed of his sprightly beams she wept the night,
'Till the *Spectator* rose, and blazed as bright.
So the first man the sun's first setting viewed,
And sighed, 'till circling day his joys renewed ;
Yet doubtful how that second sun to name,
Whether a bright successor, or the same.
So we : but now from this suspense are freed,
Since all agree, who doth with judgment read,
'Tis the same sun, and does himself succeed.

O.

---

**No. 489.** *Saturday, Sept. 20, 1712* [ADDISON

Βαθυρρείταο μέγα σθένος Ὠκεανοῖο. HOM., *Iliad*, xxi, 175

SIR,—Upon reading your essay concerning the Pleasures of the Imagination, I find, among the three
sources of those pleasures which you have discovered,
that Greatness is one. This has suggested to me the
reason why, of all objects that I have ever seen, there
is none which affects my imagination so much as the
sea or ocean. I cannot see the heavings of this prodigious bulk of waters, even in a calm, without a very
pleasing astonishment, but when it is worked up in a
tempest, so that the horizon on every side is nothing
but foaming billows and floating mountains, it is impossible to describe the agreeable horror that arises
from such a prospect. A troubled ocean, to a man who
sails upon it, is I think the biggest object that he can
see in motion, and consequently gives his imagination
one of the highest kinds of pleasure that can arise from
greatness. I must confess, it is impossible for me to

[1] *Carm.*, Sec. 10.

survey this world of fluid matter without thinking on the hand that first poured it out, and made a proper channel for its reception. Such an object naturally raises in my thoughts the idea of an Almighty Being, and convinces me of His existence as much as a metaphysical demonstration. The imagination prompts the understanding, and by the greatness of the sensible object, produces in it the idea of a Being who is neither circumscribed by time nor space.

As I have made several voyages upon the sea, I have often been tossed in storms, and on that occasion have frequently reflected on the descriptions of them in ancient poets. I remember Longinus [1] highly recommends one in Homer, because the poet has not amused himself with little fancies upon the occasion, as authors of an inferior genius, whom he mentions, had done, but because he has gathered together those circumstances which are the most apt to terrify the imagination, and which really happen in the raging of a tempest. It is for the same reason that I prefer the following description of a ship in a storm, which the Psalmist has made, before any other I have ever met with : ' They that go down to the sea in ships, that do business in great waters ; these see the works of the Lord, and His wonders in the deep. For He commandeth, and raiseth the stormy wind, which lifteth up the waters thereof. They mount up to the heaven, they go down again to the depths : their soul is melted because of trouble. They reel to and fro, and stagger like a drunken man, and are at their wit's end. Then they cry unto the Lord in their trouble, and He bringeth them out of their distresses. He maketh the storm a calm, so that the waves thereof are still. Then they are glad because they be quiet ; so He bringeth them unto their desired haven [2].'

By the way, how much more comfortable, as well as rational, is this system of the Psalmist, than the Pagan scheme in Virgil and other poets, where one deity is represented as raising a storm, and another as laying it. Were we only to consider the sublime in

[1] *On the Sublime*, sec. 10, where Longinus compares a description by Aristaeus the Proconnesian with an account of a storm in Book xv of the *Iliad*.
[2] *Psalm* cvii, 23–30.

this piece of poetry, what can be nobler than the idea it gives us, or the Supreme Being thus raising a tumult among the elements, and recovering them out of their confusion, thus troubling and becalming nature?

Great painters do not only give us landscapes of gardens, groves, and meadows, but very often employ their pencils upon sea-pieces : I could wish you would follow their example. If this small sketch may deserve a place among your works, I shall accompany it with a divine ode, made by a gentleman[1] upon the conclusion of his travels :

I

How are Thy servants blest, O Lord !
How sure is their defence !
Eternal wisdom is their guide,
Their help Omnipotence.

II

In foreign realms, and lands remote,
Supported by Thy care,
Through burning climes I passed unhurt,
And breathed in tainted air.

III

Thy mercy sweetened every soil,
Made every region please ;
The hoary Alpine hills it warmed,
And smoked the Tyrrhene seas :

IV

Think, oh my soul, devoutly think,
How with affrighted eyes
Thou saw'st the wide extended deep
In all its horrors rise !

V

Confusion dwelt in every face,
And fear in every heart ;
When waves on waves, and gulfs in gulfs,
O'ercame the pilot's art.

VI

Yet then from all my griefs, O Lord,
Thy mercy set me free,
Whilst in the confidence of prayer
My soul took hold on Thee.

### VII

For though in dreadful whirls we hung
  High on the broken wave,
I knew Thou wert not slow to hear,
  Nor impotent to save.

### VIII

The storm was laid, the winds retired,
  Obedient to Thy will ;
The sea, that roared at Thy command,
  At Thy command was still.  ●

### IX

In midst of dangers, fears, and death,
  Thy goodness I'll adore,
And praise Thee for Thy mercies past,
  And humbly hope for more.

### X

My life, if Thou preserv'st my life,
  Thy sacrifice shall be ;
And death, if death must be my doom,
  Shall join my soul to Thee.

C.

No. 490.    *Monday, Sept. 22, 1712*    [STEELE

*Domus et placens Uxor.* HOR., 2 *Od.* xiv, 21-2

I HAVE very long entertained an ambition to make
the word *wife* the most agreeable and delightful name
in nature. If it be not so in itself, all the wiser
part of mankind, from the beginning of the world to
this day, has consented in an error : but our unhappi-
ness in England has been, that a few loose men of
genius, for pleasure, have turned it all to the gratification of ungoverned desires, in despite of good sense,
form, and order; when, in truth, any satisfaction
beyond the boundaries of reason, is but a step towards
madness and folly. But is the sense of joy and accomplishment of desire no way to be indulged or
attained? and have we appetites given us to be at all
gratified? Yes, certainly. Marriage is an institution
calculated for a constant scene of as much delight

as our being is capable of. Two persons who have chosen each other out of all the species, with design to be each other's mutual comfort and entertainment, have in that action bound themselves to be good-humoured, affable, discreet, forgiving, patient, and joyful, with respect to each other's frailties and perfections, to the end of their lives. The wiser of the two (and it always happens one of them is such) will, for her or his own sake, keep things from outrage with the utmost sanctity. When this union is thus preserved (as I have often said) the most indifferent circumstance administers delight. Their condition is an endless source of new gratifications. The married man can say, ' If I am unacceptable to all the world beside, there is one, whom I entirely love, that will receive me with joy and transport, and think herself obliged to double her kindness and caresses of me from the gloom with which she sees me overcast. I need not dissemble the sorrow of my heart to be agreeable there, that very sorrow quickens her affection.'

This passion towards each other, when once well fixed, enters into the very constitution, and the kindness flows as easily and silently as the blood in the veins. When this affection is enjoyed in the most sublime degree, unskilful eyes see nothing of it; but when it is subject to be changed, and has an alloy in it that may make it end in distaste, it is apt to break into rage, or overflow into fondness, before the rest of the world.

Uxander and Viramira are amorous and young, and have been married these two years; yet do they so much distinguish each other in company, that in your conversation with the dear things you are still put to a sort of cross-purposes. Whenever you address yourself in ordinary discourse to Viramira, she turns her head another way, and the answer is made to the dear Uxander. If you tell a merry tale, the application is still directed to her dear; and when she should ommend you, she says to him, as if he had spoke it,

' That is, my dear, so pretty——' This puts me in mind of what I have somewhere read in the admired memoirs of the famous Cervantes, where, while honest Sancho Panza is putting some necessary humble question concerning Rozinante, his supper, or his lodgings, the knight of the sorrowful countenance is ever improving the harmless lowly hints of his squire to the poetical conceit, rapture, and flight, in contemplation of the dear Dulcinea of his affections.

On the other side, Dictamnus and Moria are ever squabbling, and you may observe them all the time they are in company in a state of impatience. As Uxander and Viramira wish you all gone, that they may be at freedom for dalliance, Dictamnus and Moria wait your absence, that they may speak their harsh interpretations on each other's words and actions during the time you were with them.

It is certain that the greater part of the evils attending this condition of life arises from fashion. Prejudice in this case is turned the wrong way, and instead of expecting more happiness than we shall meet with in it, we are laughed into a prepossession, that we shall be disappointed if we hope for lasting satisfactions.

With all persons who have made good sense the rule of action, marriage is described as the state capable of the highest human felicity. Tully has epistles full of affectionate pleasure, when he writes to his wife or speaks of his children. But above all the hints of this kind I have met with in writers of ancient date, I am pleased with an epigram of Martial [1], in honour of the beauty of his wife Cleopatra. Commentators say it was written in the day after his wedding-night. When his spouse was retired to the bathing-room in the heat of the day, he, it seems, came in upon her when she was just going into the water. To her beauty and carriage on this occasion we owe the following epigram, which I

[1] *Epig.* iv, 22.

showed my friend Will Honeycomb in French, who
has translated it as follows, without understanding
the original. I expect it will please the English
better than the Latin reader.

> When my bright consort, now nor wife nor maid,
> Ashamed and wanton, of embrace afraid,
> Fled to the streams, the streams my fair betrayed.
> To my fond eyes she all transparent stood,
> She blushed, I smiled at the slight covering flood.
> Thus through the glass the lovely lily glows,
> Thus through the ambient gem shines forth the rose.
> I saw new charms, and plunged to seize my store:
> Kisses I snatched, the waves prevented more.

My friend would not allow that this luscious account could be given of a wife, and therefore used
the word consort, which, he learnedly said, would
serve for a mistress as well, and give a more gentle-
manly turn to the epigram. But, under favour of
him and all other such fine gentlemen, I cannot be
persuaded but that the passion a bridegroom has for
a virtuous young woman, will, by little and little,
grow into friendship, and then it is ascended to
an higher pleasure than it was in its first fervour.
Without this happens, he is a very unfortunate man
who has entered into this state, and left the habitudes
of life he might have enjoyed with a faithful friend.
But when the wife proves capable of filling serious
as well as joyous hours, she brings happiness unknown to friendship itself. Spenser speaks of each
kind of love with great justice, and attributes the
highest praise to friendship; and indeed there is no
disputing that point, but by making that friendship
take place [1] between two married persons.

> Hard is the doubt, and difficult to deem,
> When all three kinds of love together meet,
> And do dispart the heart with power extreme,
> Whether shall weigh the balance down ; to wit,
> The dear affection unto kindred sweet,
> Or raging fire of love to womenkind,
> Or zeal of friends, combined by virtues meet.
> But, of them all, the band of virtuous mind,
> Methinks [2] the gentle heart should most assured bind.

For natural affection soon doth cease,
And quenchèd is with Cupid's greater flame ;
But faithful friendship doth them both suppress,
And then with mastering discipline does tame,
Through thoughts aspiring to eternal fame.
For as the soul doth rule the earthly mass,
And all the service of the body frame ;
So love of soul doth love of body pass,
No less than perfect gold surmounts the meanest brass [1].

T.

No. 491.     *Tuesday, Sept. 23, 1712*     [STEELE

*Digna satis fortuna revisit.* VIRG., *Æn.* iii, 318

IT is common with me to run from book to book
to exercise my mind with many objects, and qualify
myself for my daily labours. After an hour spent
in this loitering way of reading, something will remain to be food to the imagination. The writings
that please me most on such occasions are stories
for the truth of which there is good authority. The
mind of a man is naturally a lover of justice, and
when we read a story wherein a criminal is overtaken, in whom there is no quality which is the object
of pity, the soul enjoys a certain revenge for the
offence done to its nature in the wicked actions committed in the preceding part of the history. This
will be better understood by the reader from the following narration [2] itself, than from anything which
I can say to introduce it :

When Charles Duke of Burgundy, surnamed the
Bold, reigned over spacious dominions now swallowed
up by the power of France, he heaped many favours
and honours upon Claudius Rhynsault, a German who
had served him in his wars against the insults of his
neighbours. A great part of Zealand was at that
time in subjection to that dukedom. The prince

[1] *Faerie Queene,* Book iv, canto ix, 1, 2.
[2] Based upon Note N to the memoir of Charles of Burgundy in
Bayle's *Dictionary.*

himself was a person of singular humanity and justice. Rhynsault, with no other real quality than courage, had dissimulation enough to pass upon his generous and unsuspicious master for a person of blunt honesty and fidelity, without any vice that could bias him from the execution of justice. His highness, prepossessed to his advantage, upon the decease of the governor of his chief town of Zealand gave Rhynsault that command. He was not long seated in that government, before he cast his eyes upon Sapphira, a woman of exquisite beauty, the wife of Paul Danvelt, a wealthy merchant of the city under his protection and government. Rhynsault was a man of a warm constitution, and violent inclination to women, and not unskilled in the soft arts which win their favour. He knew what it was to enjoy the satisfactions which are reaped from the possession of beauty, but was an utter stranger to the decencies, honours, and delicacies that attend the passion towards them in elegant minds. However, he had so much of the world, that he had a great share of the language which usually prevails upon the weaker part of that sex, and he could with his tongue utter a passion with which his heart was wholly untouched. He was one of those brutal minds which can be gratified with the violation of innocence and beauty, without the least pity, passion, or love to that with which they are so much delighted. Ingratitude is a vice inseparable to a lustful man; and the possession of a woman by him who has no thought but allaying a passion painful to himself, is necessarily followed by distaste and aversion. Rhynsault was resolved to accomplish his will on the wife of Danvelt, left no arts untried to get into a familiarity at her house; but she knew his character and disposition too well, not to shun all occasions that might ensnare her into his conversation. The governor, despairing of success by ordinary means, apprehended and imprisoned her husband, under pretence of an information that he was guilty of a correspondence with the enemies of the duke, to betray the town into their possession. This design had its desired effect; and the wife of the unfortunate Danvelt, the day before that which was appointed for his execution, presented herself in the hall of the governor's house, and as he passed through the apartment, threw herself at his feet, and holding his knees, beseeched his mercy. Rhynsault beheld her with a dissembled satisfaction, and assuming an air of thought and authority, he bid her arise, and told her she must follow him to his closet; and asking her whether she knew the hand of the letter he pulled out of his pocket, went from her, leaving this admonition aloud, ' If you would serve your husband, you must give me an account of all you know without prevarication; for everybody is satisfied he was too fond of you to be able to hide from you the names of the rest of the conspirators, or any other particulars whatsoever.' He went to his closet, and soon after the lady was sent for to an audience. The servant knew his distance when matters of state were to be debated; and the governor, laying aside the air with which he had appeared in public, began to be the supplicant, to rally an affliction, which it was in her power easily to remove. She easily perceived his intention, and bathed in tears, began to deprecate so wicked a design, and relieve an innocent man from his imprisonment. Lust, like ambition, takes in all the faculties of the mind and body into its service and subjection. Her becoming tears, her honest anguish, the wringing of her hands, and the many changes of her posture and figure in the vehemence of speaking, were but so many attitudes in which he beheld her beauty, and further incentives of his desire. All humanity was lost in that one appetite, and he signified to her in so many plain terms, that he was unhappy, until he had possessed her, and nothing less should be the price of her husband's life; and she must, before the following noon, pronounce the death or enlargement of Danvelt. After this notification, when he saw Sapphira enough again distracted to make the subject of their discourse to common eyes appear different from what it was, he called servants to conduct her to the gate. Loaded with insupportable affliction, she immediately repairs to her husband, and having signified to his gaolers that she had a proposal to make to her husband from the governor, she was left alone with him, revealed to him all that had passed, and represented the endless conflict she was in between love to his person, and fidelity to his bed. It is easy to imagine the sharp affliction this honest pair was in upon such an incident, in lives not used to any but ordinary occurrences. The man was bridled by shame from speaking what his fear prompted upon so near an approach of death; but let fall words that signified to her, he should not think her polluted, though she had not yet confessed to him that the governor had violated her person, since he knew her will had no part in the action. She parted from him with this oblique permission to save a life he had not resolution enough to resign for the safety of his honour.

The next morning the unhappy Sapphira attended the governor, and being led into a remote apartment, submitted to his desires. Rhynsault commended her charms, claimed a familiarity after what passed between them, and with an air of gaiety, in the language of a gallant, bid her return, and take her husband out of prison : ' but ', continued he, ' my fair one must not be offended that I have taken care he should not be an interruption to our future assignations '. These last words foreboded what she found when she came to the gaol, her husband executed by the order of Rhynsault.

It was remarkable that the woman, who was full of tears and lamentations during the whole course of her affliction, uttered neither sigh nor complaint, but stood fixed with grief at this consummation of her misfortunes. She betook herself to her abode, and, after having in solitude paid her devotions to

Him who is the avenger of innocence, she repaired privately to court. Her person, and a certain grandeur of sorrow negligent of forms, gained her passage into the presence of the duke her sovereign. As soon as she came into the presence, she broke forth into the following words : ' Behold, O mighty Charles, a wretch weary of life, though it has always been spent with innocence and virtue. It is not in your power to redress my injuries, but it is to avenge them. And if the protection of the distressed, the punishment of oppressors, is a task worthy a prince, I bring the Duke of Burgundy ample matter for doing honour to his own great name, and wiping infamy off of mine.'

When she had spoke this, she delivered the duke a paper reciting her story. He read it with all the emotions that indignation and pity could raise in a prince jealous of his honour in the behaviour of his officers, and prosperity of his subjects.

Upon an appointed day Rhynsault was sent for to court, and in the presence of a few of the council, confronted by Sapphira, the prince asking, ' Do you know that lady?' Rhynsault, as soon as he could recover his surprise, told the duke he would marry her, if his highness would please to think that a reparation. The duke seemed contented with his answer, and stood by during the immediate solemnisation of the ceremony. At the conclusion of it he told Rhynsault, ' Thus far you have done as constrained by my authority : I shall not be satisfied of your kind usage of her, without you sign a gift of your whole estate to her after your decease.' To the performance of this also the duke was a witness. When these two acts were executed, the duke turned to the lady, and told her, ' It now remains for me to put you in quiet possession of what your husband has so bountifully bestowed on you '; and ordered the immediate execution of Rhynsault.     T.

No. 492.    *Wednesday, Sept. 24, 1712*    [STEELE

*Quicquid est boni moris levitate extinguitur.*    SEN.

TUNBRIDGE, *Sept.* 18

DEAR MR SPECTATOR,— I am a young woman of eighteen years of age, and, I do assure you, a maid of unspotted reputation, founded upon a very careful carriage in all my looks, words, and actions. At the same time I must own to you, that it is with much constraint to flesh and blood that my behaviour is so strictly irreproachable; for I am naturally addicted to mirth, to gaiety, to a free air, to motion and gadding. Now what gives me a great deal of anxiety, and is some discouragement in the pursuit of virtue, is, that the young women who run into greater freedoms with the men are more taken notice of than I am. The men are such unthinking sots, that they do not prefer her who restrains all her passions and affections, and keeps much within the bounds of what is lawful, to her who goes to the utmost verge of innocence, and parleys at the very brink of vice, whether she shall be a wife or a mistress. But I must appeal to your Spectatorial wisdom, who, I find, have passed very much of your time in the study of women, whether this is not a most unreasonable proceeding. I have read somewhere, that Hobbes of Malmesbury asserts that continent persons have more of what they contain, than those who give a loose to their desires. According to this rule, let there be equal age, equal wit, and equal good humour, in the woman of prudence, and her of liberty, what stores has he to expect who takes the former? what refuse must he be contented with who chooses the latter? Well, but I sate down to write to you to vent my indignation against several pert creatures who are addressed to and courted in this place, while poor I, and two or three like me, are wholly unregarded.

Every one of these affect gaining the hearts of your sex. This is generally attempted by a particular manner of carrying themselves with familiarity. Glycera has a dancing walk, and keeps time in her ordinary gait. Chloe, her sister, who is unwilling to interrupt her conquests, comes into the room before her with a familiar run. Dulcissa takes advantage of the approach of the winter, and has introduced a very pretty shiver, closing up her shoulders, and shrinking as she moves. All that are in this mode carry their fans between both hands before them. Dulcissa herself, who is author of this air, adds the pretty run to it; and has also, when she is in very good humour, a taking familiarity in throwing herself into the lowest seat in the room, and letting her hooped petticoats fall with a lucky decency about her. I know she practises this way of sitting down in her chamber; and indeed she does it as well as you may have seen an actress fall down dead in a tragedy. Not the least indecency in her posture. If you have observed what pretty carcasses are carried off at the end of a verse at the theatre, it will give you a notion how Dulcissa plumps into her chair. Here's a little country girl that's very cunning, that makes her use of being young and unbred, and outdoes the ensnarers, who are almost twice her age. The air that she takes is to come into company after a walk, and is very successfully out of breath upon occasion. Her mother is in the secret, and calls her 'romp', and then looks round to see what young men stare at her.

It would take up more than can come into one of your papers, to enumerate all the particular airs of the younger company in this place. But I cannot omit Dulceorella, whose manner is the most indolent imaginable, but still as watchful of conquest as the busiest virgin among us. She has a peculiar art of staring at a young fellow, until she sees she has got him, and inflamed him by so much observation. When she sees she has him, and he begins to toss his head upon it, she is immediately short-sighted, and labours to observe what he is at a distance with her eyes half shut. Thus the captive that thought her first struck, is to make very near approaches, or be wholly disregarded. This artifice has done more execution than all the ogling of the rest of the women here, with the utmost variety of half glances, attentive heedlessnesses, childish inadvertences, haughty contempts, or artificial oversights. After I have said thus much of ladies among us who fight thus regularly, I am to complain to you of a set of familiar romps, who have broken through all common rules, and have thought of a very effectual way of showing more charms than all of us. These, Mr Spectator, are the swingers. You are to know these careless pretty creatures are very innocents again; and it is to be no matter what they do, for 'tis all harmless freedom. They get on ropes, as you must have seen the children, and are swung by their men visitants. The jest is, that Mr Such-a-one can name the colour of Mrs Such-a-one's stockings; and she tells him, he is a lying thief, so he is, and full of roguery; and she'll lay a wager, and her sister shall tell the truth if he says right, and he can't tell what colour her garters are of. In this diversion there are very many pretty shrieks, not so much for fear of falling, as that their petticoats should untie. For there is a great care had to avoid improprieties; and the lover who swings the lady, is to tie her clothes very close with his hatband before she admits him to throw up her heels.

Now, Mr Spectator, except you can note these wantonnesses in their beginnings, and bring us sober girls into observation, there is no help for it, we must swim with the tide, the coquettes are too powerful a party for us. To look into the merit of a regular and well-behaved woman, is a slow thing. A loose trivial song gains the affections, when a wise homily is not attended to. There is no other way but to make war upon them, or we must go over to them. As for my part, I will show all the world it is not for want of charms that I stand so long unasked; and if you do not take measures for the immediate redress of us rigids, as the fellows call us, I can move with a speaking mien, can look significantly, can lisp, can trip, can loll, can start, can blush, can rage, can weep, if I must do it, and can be frighted, as agreeably as any she in England. All which is humbly submitted to your Spectatorial consideration with all humility, by
Your most humble Servant,
T.                                 MATILDA MOHAIR [1]

---

[1] This letter, with that in No. 496, are printed in Curll's *Tunbridge Miscellany*, 1712, under the title, 'The Swingers described, in the following letters to the *Spectator*'.

No. 493.     *Thursday, Sept. 25, 1712*     [STEELE

*Qualem commendes, etiam atque etiam adspice, ne mox*
*Incutiant aliena tibi peccata pudorem.*

HOR., 1 *Ep.* xviii, 76

IT is no unpleasant matter of speculation to consider the recommendatory epistles that pass round this town from hand to hand, and the abuse people put upon one another in that kind. It is indeed come to that pass, that instead of being the testimony of merit in the person recommended, the true reading of a letter of this sort is : ' The bearer hereof is so uneasy to me, that it will be an act of charity in you to take him off my hands; whether you prefer him or not it is all one, for I have no manner of kindness for him, or obligation to him or his; and do what you please as to that.' As negligent as men are in this respect, a point of honour is concerned in it, and there is nothing a man should be more ashamed of than passing a worthless creature into the service or interests of a man who has never injured you. The women indeed are a little too keen in their resentments to trespass often this way; but you shall sometimes know that the mistress and the maid shall quarrel, and give each other very free language, and at last the lady shall be pacified to turn her out of doors, and give her a very good word to anybody else. Hence it is that you see, in a year and a half's time, the same face a domestic in all parts of the town. Good breeding and good nature lead people in a great measure to this injustice : when suitors of no consideration will have confidence enough to press upon their superiors, those in power are tender of speaking the exceptions they have against them, and are mortgaged into promises out of their impatience of importunity. In this latter case it would be a very useful inquiry to know the history of recommendations : there are, you must know, certain abettors of this way of torment who make it a profession to manage the affairs of candidates : these gentlemen

let out their impudence to their clients, and supply
any defective recommendation, by informing how
such and such a man is to be attacked. They will
tell you, get the least scrap from Mr Such-a-one,
and leave the rest to them. When one of these
undertakers have your business in hand, you may
be sick, absent, in town or country, and the patron
shall be worried, or you prevail. I remember to
have been shown a gentleman, some years ago, who
punished a whole people for their facility in giving
their credentials [1]. This person had belonged to a
regiment which did duty in the West Indies, and
by the mortality of the place happened to be commanding officer in the colony. He oppressed his
subjects with great frankness till he became sensible
that he was heartily hated by every man under his
command. When he had carried his point, to be
thus detestable, in a pretended fit of dishumour,
and feigned uneasiness of living where he found he
was so universally unacceptable, he communicated
to the chief inhabitants a design he had to return
for England, provided they would give him ample
testimonials of their approbation. The planters came
into it to a man, and in proportion to his deserving
the quite contrary, the words justice, generosity, and
courage were inserted in his commission, not omit-
ting the general good-liking of people of all conditions in the colony. The gentleman returns for
England, and within few months after came back
to them their governor on the strength of their own
testimonials.

Such a rebuke as this cannot indeed happen to

[1] Mr. Darnell Davis (*The Spectator's Essays relating to the West
Indies*, pp. 14, 15) suggests that Steele may here have had in mind
Sir Richard Dutton, an unpopular governor of Barbados. In 1683,
when Dutton was leaving Barbados, the grand jury drew up an
address to be presented to the king by ' their noble and high deserving governor', who, as they said, ' had stifled and discountenanced
faction and fanaticism in the very embryo'. Oldmixon observes that
the grand jury little thought how soon they would have reason to
turn their addresses to remonstrances; for Dutton returned to
Barbados in the following year.

easy recommenders, in the ordinary case of things
from one hand to another; but how would a man
bear to have it said to him, ' The person I took into
confidence on the credit you gave him has proved
false, unjust, and has not answered any way the
character you gave me of him '?

I cannot but conceive very good hopes of that rake
Jack Toper of the Temple, for an honest scrupulous-
ness in this point. A friend of his meeting with a
servant that had formerly lived with Jack, and having
a mind to take him, sent to him to know what
faults the fellow had, since he could not please such
a careless fellow as he was. His answer was as
follows :

Sir,—Thomas that lived with me was turned away
because he was too good for me. You know I live in
taverns ; he is an orderly sober rascal, and thinks much
to sleep in an entry until two in a morning. He told
me one day when he was dressing me, that he wondered
I was not dead before now, since I went to dinner in
the evening, and went to supper at two in the morning.
We were coming down Essex Street one night a little
flustered, and I was giving him the word to alarm the
watch ; he had the impudence to tell me it was against
the law. You that are married, and live one day after
another the same way, and so on the whole week, I
daresay will like him, and he will be glad to have his
meat in due season : the fellow is certainly very
honest. My service to your lady. Yours,
J. T.

Now this was very fair dealing. Jack knew very
well, that though the love of order made a man very
awkward in his equipage, it was a valuable quality
among the queer people who live by rule; and had
too much good sense and good nature to let the
fellow starve, because he was not fit to attend his
vivacities.

I shall end this discourse with a letter of recommendation from Horace to Claudius Nero [1]. You

[1] 1 Epist., ix.

will see, in that letter, a slowness to ask a favour, a strong reason for being unable to deny his good word any longer, and that it is a service to the person to whom he recommends, to comply with what is asked : all which are necessary circumstances, both in justice and good breeding, if a man would ask so as to have reason to complain of a denial; and indeed a man should not in strictness ask otherwise. In hopes the authority of Horace, who perfectly understood how to live with great men, may have a good effect towards amending this facility in people of condition, and the confidence of those who apply to them without merit, I have translated the epistle :

### *To* CLAUDIUS NERO

SIR,—Septimius, who waits upon you with this, is very well acquainted with the place you are pleased to allow me in your friendship. For when he beseeches me to recommend him to your notice in such a manner as to be received by you, who are delicate in the choice of your friends and domestics, he knows our intimacy and understands my ability to serve him better than I do myself. I have defended myself against his ambition to be yours as long as I possibly could; but fearing the imputation of hiding my power in you out of mean and selfish considerations, I am at last prevailed upon to give you this trouble. Thus, to avoid the appearance of a greater fault, I have put on this confidence. If you can forgive this transgression of modesty in behalf of a friend, receive this gentleman into your interests and friendship, and take it from me that he is an honest and a brave man.    T.

No. 494.    *Friday, Sept. 26, 1712*    [ADDISON

*Ægritudinem laudare, unam rem maxime detestabilem, quorum est tandem philosophorum ?*  CIC.

ABOUT an age ago it was the fashion in England, for every one that would be thought religious, to

throw as much sanctity as possible into his face,
and in particular to abstain from all appearances of
mirth and pleasantry, which were looked upon as
the marks of a carnal mind. The saint was of a
sorrowful countenance, and generally eaten up with
spleen and melancholy. A gentleman, who was
lately a great ornament to the learned world[1], has
diverted me more than once with an account of the
reception which he met with from a very famous
Independent minister, who was head of a college in
those times[2]. This gentleman was then a young
adventurer in the republic of letters, and just fitted
out for the university with a good cargo of Latin and
Greek. His friends were resolved that he should
try his fortune at an election which was drawing
near in the college of which the Independent minister, whom I have before mentioned, was governor.
The youth, according to custom, waited on him in
order to be examined. He was received at the door
by a servant, who was one of that gloomy generation
that were then in fashion. He conducted him, with
great silence and seriousness, to a long gallery which
was darkened at noonday, and had only a single
candle burning in it. After a short stay in this
melancholy apartment, he was led into a chamber
hung with black, where he entertained himself for
some time by the glimmering of a taper, until at
length the head of the college came out to him from
an inner room, with half-a-dozen nightcaps upon his
head, and a religious horror in his countenance. The

[1] Supposed to be Anthony Henley, a friend of Swift and Steele
who contributed to the *Tatler*, and died in 1711.
[2] Dr Thomas Goodwin (1600–1679) was one of those who went to
Holland to escape from persecution, and was pastor of the English
church at Arnheim, till in the Civil Wars he came to London, and sat
at Westminster as one of the Assembly of Divines. In 1649 Cromwell
made him president of Magdalen College. As Oliver Cromwell's
chaplain, he prayed with and for him in his last illness. At the
Restoration Dr Goodwin was deprived of his post at Oxford, and he
then preached in London to an assembly of Independents till his
death (Morley). Anthony à Wood mentions that the undergraduates
used to call Goodwin 'Nine-caps', from the care that he took to
protect his head from cold (Arnold).

young man trembled; but his fears increased when, instead of being asked what progress he had made in learning, he was examined how he abounded in grace. His Latin and Greek stood him in little stead. He was to give an account only of the state of his soul, whether he was of the number of the elect; what was the occasion of his conversion; upon what day of the month and hour of the day it happened; how it was carried on, and when completed? The whole examination was summed up with one short question, namely, whether he was prepared for death? The boy, who had been bred up by honest parents, was frighted out of his wits at the solemnity of the proceeding, and by the last dreadful interrogatory; so that upon making his escape out of this house of mourning, he could never be brought a second time to the examination, as not being able to go through the terrors of it.

Notwithstanding this general form and outside of religion is pretty well worn out among us, there are many persons who, by a natural uncheerfulness of heart, mistaken notions of piety, or weakness of understanding, love to indulge this uncomfortable way of life, and give up themselves a prey to grief and melancholy. Superstitious fears and groundless scruples cut them off from the pleasures of conversation, and all those social entertainments which are not only innocent but laudable; as if mirth was made for reprobates, and cheerfulness of heart denied those who are the only persons that have a proper title to it.

Sombrius is one of these sons of sorrow. He thinks himself obliged in duty to be sad and disconsolate. He looks on a sudden fit of laughter as a breach of his baptismal vow. An innocent jest startles him like blasphemy. Tell him of one who is advanced to a title of honour, he lifts up his hands and eyes; describe a public ceremony, he shakes his head; show him a gay equipage, he blesses himself. All the little ornaments of life are pomps and vanities. Mirth is wanton and wit profane. He is scandalised at youth for being lively, and at childhood for being playful. He sits at a christening or a marriage feast as at a funeral; sighs at the conclusion of a merry story; and grows devout when the rest of the company grow pleasant. After all, Sombrius is a religious man, and would have behaved himself very properly had he lived when Christianity was under a general persecution.

I would by no means presume to tax such characters with hypocrisy, as is done too frequently, that being a vice which I think none but He who knows the secrets of men's hearts should pretend to discover in another, where the proofs of it do not amount to a demonstration. On the contrary, as there are many excellent persons who are weighed down by this habitual sorrow of heart, they rather deserve our compassion than our reproaches. I think, however, they would do well to consider, whether such a behaviour does not deter men from a religious life, by representing it as an unsociable state, that extinguishes all joy and gladness, darkens the face of nature, and destroys the relish of being itself.

I have, in former papers, shown how great a tendency there is to cheerfulness in religion, and how such a frame of mind is not only the most lovely, but the most commendable in a virtuous person. In short, those who represent religion in so unamiable a light, are like the spies sent by Moses to make a discovery of the Land of Promise, when by their reports they discouraged the people from entering upon it. Those who show us the joy, the cheerfulness, the good humour, that naturally spring up in this happy state, are like the spies bringing along with them the clusters of grapes, and delicious fruits, that might invite their companions into the pleasant country which produced them [1].

An eminent Pagan writer has made a discourse [2], to show that the atheist, who denies a God, does

---

[1] *Numbers*, chap. xiii.　　[2] Plutarch, *On Superstition*, chap. x.

Him less dishonour than the man who owns His being, but at the same time believes Him to be cruel, hard to please, and terrible to human nature. ' For my own part ', says he, ' I would rather it should be said of me, that there was never any such man as Plutarch, than that Plutarch was ill-natured, capricious, or inhuman.'

If we may believe our logicians, man is distinguished from all other creatures by the faculty of laughter. He has an heart capable of mirth, and naturally disposed to it. It is not the business of virtue to extirpate the affections of the mind, but to regulate them. It may moderate and restrain, but was not designed to banish gladness from the heart of man. Religion contracts the circle of our pleasures, but leaves it wide enough for her votaries to expatiate in. The contemplation of the Divine Being, and the exercise of virtue, are in their own nature so far from excluding all gladness of heart, that they are perpetual sources of it. In a word, the true spirit of religion cheers, as well as composes the soul : it banishes indeed all levity of behaviour, all vicious and dissolute mirth, but in exchange fills the mind with a perpetual serenity, uninterrupted cheerfulness, and an habitual inclination to please others, as well as to be pleased in itself.       O.

No. 495.    *Saturday, Sept. 27, 1712*    [ADDISON

*Duris ut ilex tonsa bipennibus*
*Nigrœ feraci frondis in Algido,*
*Per damna, per cœdes ab ipso*
*Ducit opes animumque ferro.*  HOR., 4 Od. iv, 57

As I am one who, by my profession, am obliged to look into all kinds of men, there are none whom I consider with so much pleasure, as those who have anything new or extraordinary in their characters, or ways of living. For this reason I have often amused myself with speculations on the race of people called

Jews, many of whom I have met with in most of the considerable towns which I have passed through in the course of my travels. They are, indeed, so disseminated through all the trading parts of the world, that they are become the instruments by which the most distant nations converse with one another, and by which mankind are knit together in a general correspondence. They are like the pegs and nails in a great building, which, though they are but little valued in themselves, are absolutely necessary to keep the whole frame together.

That I may not fall into any common beaten tracks of observation, I shall consider this people in three views : first, with regard to their number; secondly, their dispersion; and thirdly, their adherence to their religion; and afterwards endeavour to show, first, what natural reasons, and secondly, what providential reasons may be assigned for these three remarkable particulars.

The Jews are looked upon by many to be as numerous at present as they were formerly in the land of Canaan.

This is wonderful, considering the dreadful slaughter made of them under some of the Roman emperors, which historians describe by the death of many hundred thousands in a war, and the innumerable massacres and persecutions they have undergone in Turkey, as well as in all Christian nations of the world. Their Rabbins, to express the great havoc which has been sometimes made of them, tell us, after their usual manner of hyperbole, that there were such torrents of holy blood shed, as carried rocks of an hundred yards in circumference above three miles into the sea.

Their dispersion is the second remarkable particular in this people. They swarm over all the East, and are settled in the remotest parts of China : they are spread through most of the nations of Europe and Africa, and many families of them are established in the West Indies. Not to mention whole nations bordering on Prester John's country [1], and discovered in the inner parts of America, if we may give any credit to their own writers.

Their firm adherence to their religion is no less remarkable than their numbers and dispersion, especially considering it as persecuted or contemned over the face of the whole earth. This is likewise the more remarkable if we consider the frequent apostasies of this people when they lived under their kings in the Land of Promise, and within sight of their temple.

If in the next place we examine what may be the natural reasons for these three particulars which we find in the Jews, and which are not to be found in any other religion or people, I can in the first place attribute their numbers to nothing but their constant employment, their abstinence, their exemption from wars, and, above all, their frequent marriages; for they look on celibacy as an accursed state, and generally are married before twenty, as hoping the Messiah may descend from them.

The dispersion of the Jews into all the nations of the earth is the second remarkable particular of that people, though not so hard to be accounted for. They were always in rebellions and tumults while they had the temple and holy city in view, for which reason they have often been driven out of their old habitations in the Land of Promise: they have as often been banished out of most other places where they have settled, which must very much disperse and scatter a people, and oblige them to seek a livelihood where they can find it. Besides, the whole people is now a race of such merchants as are wanderers by profession, and, at the same time, are in most if not all places incapable of either lands or offices that might engage them to make any part of the world their home.

[1] In the thirteenth and fourteenth centuries it was believed that a powerful king, who was both a Christian and a priest, ruled in Central Asia about A.D. 1200.

This dispersion would probably have lost their religion had it not been secured by the strength of its constitution : for they are to live all in a body and generally within the same enclosure, to marry among themselves, and to eat no meats that are not killed or prepared their own way. This shuts them out from all table conversation, and the most agreeable intercourses of life; and, by consequence, excludes them from the most probable means of conversion.

If, in the last place, we consider what providential reason may be assigned for these three particulars, we shall find that their numbers, dispersion, and adherence to their religion have furnished every age, and every nation of the world, with the strongest arguments for the Christian faith, not only as these very particulars are foretold of them, but as they themselves are the depositaries of these, and all the other prophecies which tend to their own confusion. Their number furnishes us with a sufficient cloud of witnesses that attest the truth of the old Bible. Their dispersion spreads these witnesses through all parts of the world. The adherence to their religion makes their testimony unquestionable. Had the whole body of Jews been converted to Christianity, we should certainly have thought all the prophecies of the Old Testament that relate to the coming and history of our Blessed Saviour, forged by Christians, and have looked upon them, with the prophecies of the sibyls, as made many years after the events they pretended to foretell.                O.

No. 496.        *Monday, Sept. 29, 1712*        [STEELE

*Gnatum pariter uti his decuit aut etiam amplius,*
*Quod illa ætas magis ad hæc utenda idonea est.*
                        TER., *Heaut.*, Act i, sc. 1

MR. SPECTATOR,—Those ancients who were the most accurate in their remarks on the genius and temper of mankind, by considering the various bent and scope of

our actions throughout the progress of life, have with
great exactness allotted inclinations and objects of
desire particular to every stage, according to the different
circumstances of our conversation and fortune, through
the several periods of it.  Hence they were disposed
easily to excuse those excesses which might possibly
arise from a too eager pursuit of the affections more
immediately proper to each state : they indulged the
levity of childhood with tenderness, overlooked the
gaiety of youth with good nature, tempered the forward ambition and impatience of ripened manhood
with discretion, and kindly imputed the tenacious
avarice of old men to their want of relish for any
other enjoyment.  Such allowances as these were no
less advantageous to common society than obliging to
particular persons; for by maintaining a decency and
regularity in the course of life, they supported the
dignity of human nature, which then suffers the
greatest violence when the order of things is inverted;
and in nothing is it more remarkably vilified and
ridiculous than when feebleness preposterously attempts
to adorn itself with that outward pomp and lustre,
which serve only to set off the bloom of youth with
better advantage.  I was insensibly carried into reflections of this nature by just now meeting Paulino (who
is in his climacteric) bedecked with the utmost splendour of dress and equipage, and giving an unbounded
loose to all manner of pleasure, whilst his only son is
debarred all innocent diversion, and may be seen
frequently solacing himself in the Mall, with no other
attendance than one antiquated servant of his father's,
for a companion and director.

It is a monstrous want of reflection, that a man
cannot consider that when he cannot resign the
pleasures of life in his decay of appetite and inclination to them, his son must have a much uneasier task
to resist the impetuosity of growing desires.  The skill,
therefore, should methinks be to let a son want no
lawful diversion, in proportion to his future fortune,
and the figure he is to make in the world.  The first
step towards virtue that I have observed in young men
of condition that have run into excesses, has been that
they had a regard to their quality and reputation in
the management of their vices.  Narrowness in their

circumstances has made many youths, to supply themselves as debauchees, commence cheats and rascals.
The father who allows his son to his utmost ability,
avoids this latter evil, which as to the world is much
greater than the former.   But the contrary practice
has prevailed so much among some men, that I have
known them deny them what was merely necessary for
education suitable to their quality.   Poor young Antonio
is a lamentable instance of ill conduct in this kind.
The young man did not want natural talents; but the
father of him was a coxcomb, who affected being a
fine gentleman so unmercifully, that he could not
endure in his sight, or the frequent mention of one,
who was his son growing into manhood, and thrust-
ing him out of the gay world.   I have often thought
the father took a secret pleasure in reflecting, that
when that fine house and seat came into the next
hands, it would revive his memory, as a person who
knew how to enjoy them, from observation of the
rusticity and ignorance of his successor.   Certain it
is that a man may, if he will, let his heart close to
the having no regard to anything but his dear self,
even with exclusion of his very children.   I recommend this subject to your consideration, and am,
Sir,
Your most humble Servant,
T. B.

LONDON, Sept. 26, 1712

MR SPECTATOR,—I am just come from Tunbridge,
and have since my return read Mrs Matilda Mohair's
letter to you[1].   She pretends to make a mighty story
about the diversion of swinging in that place.   What
was done, was only among relations; and no man
swung any woman who was not second cousin at
farthest.   She is pleased to say, 'Care was taken that
the gallants tied the ladies' legs before they were
wafted into the air.'   Since she is so spiteful, I'll tell
you the plain truth.   There was no such nicety
observed, since we were all, as I just now told you,
near relations; but Mrs Mohair herself has been swung

1 See No. 492.

there, and she invents all this malice because it was observed she has crooked legs, of which I was an eye-witness.　　Your humble Servant,

RACHEL SHOESTRING

TUNBRIDGE, *Sept.* 26, 1712

MR SPECTATOR,—We have just now read your paper containing Mrs Mohair's letter. It is an invention of her own from one end to the other; and I desire you would print the enclosed letter by itself, and shorten it so as to come within the compass of your half-sheet. She is the most malicious minx in the world, for all she looks so innocent. Don't leave out that part about her being in love with her father's butler, which makes her shun men; for that is the truest of it all.

Your humble Servant,

SARAH TRICE

*P.S.*—She has crooked legs.

TUNBRIDGE, *Sept.* 26, 1712

MR SPECTATOR,—All that Mrs Mohair is so vexed at against the good company of this place is, that we all know she has crooked legs. This is certainly true. I don't care for putting my name, because one would not be in the power of the creature.

Your humble Servant unknown

TUNBRIDGE, *Sept.* 26, 1712

MR SPECTATOR,—That insufferable prude Mrs Mohair, who has told such stories of the company here, is with child, for all her nice airs and her crooked legs. Pray be sure to put her in for both those two things, and you'll oblige everybody here, especially

Your humble Servant,

ALICE BLUEGARTER

No. 497.     *Tuesday, Sept.* 30, 1712     [STEELE

'Οὗτός ἐστι γαλεώτης γέρων.   MENANDER

A FAVOUR well bestowed, is almost as great an honour to him who confers it as to him who receives it. What indeed makes for the superior reputation of the patron in this case, is, that he is always surrounded with specious pretences of unworthy candidates, and is often alone in the kind inclination he has towards the well-deserving. Justice is the first quality in the man who is in a post of direction; and I remember to have heard an old gentleman talk of the Civil Wars, and in his relation gave an account of a general officer, who with this one quality, without any shining endowments, became so peculiarly beloved and honoured, that all decisions between man and man were laid before him by the parties concerned in a private way, and they would lay by their animosities implicitly if he bid them be friends, or submit themselves in the wrong without reluctance, if he said it, without waiting the judgment of court-martials. His manner was to keep the dates of all commissions in his closet, and wholly dismiss from the service such who were deficient in their duty, and after that took care to prefer according to the order of battle. His familiars were his entire friends, and could have no interested views in courting his acquaintance; for his affection was no step to their preferment, though it was to their reputation. By this means a kind aspect, a salutation, a smile, and giving out his hand, had the weight of what is esteemed by vulgar minds more substantial. His business was very short, and he who had nothing to do but justice, was never affronted with a request of a familiar daily visitant for what was due to a brave man at a distance. Extraordinary merit he used to recommend to the king for some distinction at home, until the order of battle made way for his rising in the troops. Add to this, that he had an excellent manner of getting rid of such whom he observed were good at ' an Halt ', as his phrase was. Under this description he comprehended all those who were contented to live without reproach, and had no promptitude in their minds towards glory. These fellows were also recommended to the king, and taken off the general's hands into posts wherein diligence and common honesty were all that were necessary. This general had no weak part in his line; but every man had as much care upon him, and as much honour to lose as himself. Every officer could answer for what passed where he was, and the general's presence was never necessary anywhere but where he had placed himself at the first disposition, except that accident happened from extraordinary efforts of the enemy which he could not foresee; but it was remarkable that it never fell out from failure in his own troops. It must be confessed, the world is just so much out of order, as an unworthy person possesses what should be in the direction of him who has better pretensions to it.

Instead of such conduct as this old fellow used to describe in his general, all the evils which have ever happened among mankind have arose from the wanton disposition of the favours of the powerful. It is generally all that men of modesty and virtue can do to fall in with some whimsical turn in a great man, to make way for things of real and absolute service. In the time of Don Sebastian of Portugal, or some time since, the first minister would let nothing come near him but what bore the most profound face of wisdom and gravity. They carried it so far, that, for the greater show of their profound knowledge, a pair of spectacles, tied on their noses with a black riband round their heads, was what completed the dress of those who made their court at his levee, and none with naked noses were admitted to his presence. A blunt honest fellow, who had a command in the train of artillery, had attempted to make an impression upon the porter, day after day, in vain, until at length he made his appearance in a very thoughtful dark suit of clothes, and two pair of spectacles on at once.  He was conducted from room to room, with great deference, to the minister, and carrying on the farce of the place, he told his excellence that he had pretended in this manner to be wiser than he really was, but with no ill intention; but he was honest Such-a-one of the train, and he came to tell him that they wanted wheelbarrows and pickaxes.  The thing happened not to displease, the great man was seen to smile, and the successful officer was reconducted with the same profound ceremony out of the house.

When Leo the Tenth reigned Pope of Rome, his holiness, though a man of sense, and of an excellent taste of letters, of all things affected fools, buffoons, humorists, and coxcombs.  Whether it were from vanity, and that he enjoyed no talents in other men but what were inferior to him, or whatever it was, he carried it so far, that his whole delight was in finding out new fools, and, as our phrase is, playing them off, and making them show themselves to advantage.  A priest of his former acquaintance[1] suffered a great many disappointments in attempting to find access to him in a regular character, until at last in despair he retired from Rome, and returned in an equipage so very fantastical, both as to the dress of himself and servants, that the whole court were in an emulation who should first introduce him to his holiness.  What added to the expectation his holiness had of the pleasure he should have in his follies, was, that this fellow, in a dress the most exquisitely ridiculous, desired he might speak to him alone, for he had matters of the highest importance, upon which he wanted a conference.  Nothing could be denied to a coxcomb of so great hope; but when they were apart, the impostor revealed himself, and spoke as follows :

[1] This story is taken from Bayle's *Dictionary*, ' Leo X ', Note F.

'Do not be surprised, most holy father, at seeing, instead of a coxcomb to laugh at, your old friend, who has taken this way of access to admonish you of your own folly. Can anything show your holiness how unworthily you treat mankind, more than my being put upon this difficulty to speak with you? It is a degree of folly to delight to see it in others, and it is the greatest insolence imaginable to rejoice in the disgrace of human nature. It is a criminal humility in a person of your holiness's understanding, to believe you cannot excel but in the conversation of half-wits, humorists, coxcombs, and buffoons. If your holiness has a mind to be diverted like a rational man, you have a great opportunity for it, in disrobing all the impertinents you have favoured of all their riches and trappings at once, and bestowing them on the humble, the virtuous, and the meek. If your holiness is not concerned for the sake of virtue and religion, be pleased to reflect, that for the sake of your own safety it is not proper to be so very much in jest. When the Pope is thus merry, the people will in time begin to think many things, which they have hitherto beheld with great veneration, are in themselves objects of scorn and derision. If they once get a trick of knowing how to laugh, your holiness's saying this sentence in one nightcap and t'other with the other, the change of your slippers, bringing you your staff in the midst of a prayer, then stripping you of one vest and clapping on a second, during divine service, will be found out to have nothing in it. Consider, sir, that at this rate a head will be reckoned never the wiser for being bald; and the ignorant will be apt to say, that going barefoot does not at all help on in the way to heaven. The red cap and the cowl will fall under the same contempt; and the vulgar will tell us to our faces, that we shall have no authority over them but from the force of our arguments and the sanctity of our lives.'　　T.

No. 498.     *Wednesday, Oct. 1, 1712*     [STEELE

*Frustra retinacula tendens
Fertur equis auriga, neque audit currus habenas.*
VIRG., *Georg.* i, 513

*To the* SPECTATOR-GENERAL OF GREAT BRITAIN

*From the farther end of the Widow's Coffee-House in* DEVEREUX COURT[1],
*Monday evening, 28 Minutes and a half past Six*

DEAR DUMB,—In short, to use no further preface, if I should tell you that I have seen a hackney-coachman, when he has come to set down his fare, which has consisted of two or three very fine ladies, hand them out, and salute every one of them with an air of familiarity, without giving the least offence, you would perhaps think me guilty of a gasconade. But to clear myself from that imputation, and to explain this matter to you, I assure you that there are many illustrious youths within this city, who frequently recreate themselves by driving of a hackney-coach : but those whom, above all others, I would recommend to you, are the young gentlemen belonging to our Inns of Court. We have, I think, about a dozen coachmen, who have chambers here in the Temple ; and as it is reasonable to believe others will follow their example, we may perhaps in time (if it shall be thought convenient) be drove to Westminster by our own fraternity, allowing every fifth person to apply his meditations this way, which is but a modest computation as the humour is now likely to take. It is to be hoped, likewise, that there are in the other nurseries of the law to be found a proportionable number of these hopeful plants, springing up to the everlasting renown of their native country. Of how long standing this humour has been, I know not ; the first time I had any particular reason to take notice of it was about this time twelvemonth, when, being upon Hampstead Heath with some of these studious young men, who went thither purely for the sake of contemplation, nothing would serve them but

[1] The Grecian Coffee-House and Tom's Coffee-House were both in Devereux Court, Strand, near St Clement's Danes Church.

I must go through a course of this philosophy too; and being ever willing to embellish myself with any commendable qualifications, it was not long ere they persuaded me into the coach-box; nor indeed much longer before I underwent the fate of my brother Phaeton, for having drove about fifty paces with pretty good success, through my own natural sagacity, together with the good instructions of my tutors, who, to give them their due, were on all hands encouraging and assisting me in this laudable undertaking; I say, sir, having drove about fifty paces with pretty good success, I must needs be exercising the lash, which the horses resented so ill from my hands, that they gave a sudden start, and thereby pitched me directly upon my head, as I very well remembered about half-an-hour afterwards, which not only deprived me of all the knowledge I had gained for fifty yards before, but had like to have broken my neck into the bargain. After such a severe reprimand, you may imagine I was not very easily prevailed with to make a second attempt; and indeed, upon mature deliberation, the whole science seemed, at least to me, to be surrounded with so many difficulties, that notwithstanding the unknown advantages which might have accrued to me thereby, I gave over all hopes of attaining it, and I believe had never thought of it more, but that my memory has been lately refreshed by seeing some of these ingenious gentlemen ply in the open streets, one of which I saw receive so suitable a reward to his labours, that though I know you are no friend to story-telling, yet I must beg leave to trouble you with this at large.

About a fortnight since, as I was diverting myself with a pennyworth of walnuts at the Temple Gate, a lively young fellow in a fustian jacket shot by me, beckoned a coach, and told the coachman he wanted to go as far as Chelsea: they agreed upon the price, and this young gentleman mounts the coach-box; the fellow staring at him, desired to know if he should not drive until they were out of town. 'No, no', replied he: he was then going to climb up to him, but received another check, and was then ordered to get into the coach, or behind it, for that he wanted no instructors; 'but be sure, you dog you', says he, 'don't you bilk me'. The fellow thereupon surrendered his whip, scratched his head, and crept into the coach. Having myself occasion to go into the Strand, about the same time, we started both together; but the street being very full of coaches, and he not so able a coachman as perhaps he imagined himself, I had soon got a little way before him; often, however, having the curiosity to cast my eye back upon him to observe how he behaved himself in this high station, which he did with great composure until he came to the 'pass', which is a military term the brothers of the whip had given the strait at St Clement's Church; when he was arrived near this place, where are always coaches in waiting, the coachmen began to suck up the muscles of their cheeks, and to tip the wink upon each other, as if they had some roguery in their heads, which I was immediately convinced of; for he no sooner came within reach, but the first of them with his whip took the exact dimension of his shoulders, which he very ingeniously called endorsing; and, indeed, I must say that every one of them took due care to endorse him as he came through their hands. He seemed at first a little uneasy under the operation, and was going in all haste to take the numbers of their coaches; but at length, by the mediation of the worthy gentleman in the coach, his wrath was assuaged, and he prevailed upon to pursue his journey; though, indeed, I thought they had clapped such a spoke in his wheel as had disabled him from being a coachman for that day at least: for I am only mistaken, Mr Spec., if some of these endorsements were not wrote in so strong a hand that they are still legible. Upon my inquiring the reason of this unusual salutation, they told me that it was a custom among them, whenever they saw a brother tottering or unstable in his post, to lend him a hand in order to settle him again therein: for my part, I thought their allegations but reasonable, and so marched off. Besides our coachmen, we do abound in divers other sorts of ingenious robust youth who, I hope, will not take it ill if I refer giving you an account of their several recreations to another opportunity. In the meantime, if you would but bestow a little of your wholesome advice upon our coachmen, it might perhaps be a reprieve to some of their necks. As I understand you have several inspectors under you, if you would but send one amongst us here in the Temple, I am persuaded he would not want employment. But I leave this to your own consideration, and am,

Sir,

Your very humble Servant,

MOSES GREENBAG [1]

*P.S.*—I have heard our critics in the coffee-houses hereabout talk mightily of the unity of time and place : according to my notion of the matter, I have endeavoured at something like it in the beginning of my epistle. I desire to be informed a little as to that particular. In my next I design to give you some account of excellent watermen who are bred to the law, and far outdo the land-students above mentioned.

T.

No. 499.    *Thursday, Oct. 2, 1712*    [ADDISON

*Nimis uncis*
*Naribus indulges.*    PERS., *Sat.* i, 40

MY friend Will Honeycomb has told me, for above this half year, that he had a great mind to try his hand at a *Spectator*, and that he would fain have one of his writing in my works. This morning I received from him the following letter, which, after having rectified some little orthographical mistakes, I shall make a present of to the public :

DEAR SPEC.,—I was, about two nights ago, in company with very agreeable young people of both sexes, where, talking of some of your papers which are written on conjugal love, there arose a dispute among us whether there were not more bad husbands in the world than bad wives. A gentleman, who was advocate for the ladies, took this occasion to tell us the story of a famous siege in Germany, which I have since found related in my Historical Dictionary after the following manner : ' When the Emperor Conrad the Third had besieged Guelphus, Duke of Bavaria, in the city of Hensberg, the women finding that the town could not possibly hold out long, petitioned the Emperor that

[1] See No. 526.

they might depart out of it with so much as each of
them could carry. The Emperor, knowing they could
not convey away many of their effects, granted them
their petition : when the women, to his great surprise,
came out of the place with every one her husband upon
her back. The Emperor was so moved at the sight
that he burst into tears, and after having very much
extolled the women for their conjugal affection, gave
the men to their wives, and received the duke into his
favour.'

The ladies did not a little triumph at this story,
asking us, at the same time, whether in our consciences
we believed that the men of any town in Great Britain
would, upon the same offer, and at the same conjunc-
ture, have loaden themselves with their wives; or
rather, whether they would not have been glad of such
an opportunity to get rid of them? To this my very
good friend Tom Dapperwit, who took upon him to
be the mouth of our sex, replied that they would be
very much to blame if they would not do the same
good office for the women, considering that their
strength would be greater, and their burdens lighter.
As we were amusing ourselves with discourses of this
nature, in order to pass away the evening, which now
begins to grow tedious, we fell into that laudable and
primitive diversion of 'Questions and commands'. I
was no sooner vested with the regal authority but I
enjoined all the ladies, under pain of my displeasure,
to tell the company ingenuously, in case they had been
in the siege above mentioned, and had the same offers
made them as the good women of that place, what
every one of them would have brought off with her,
and have thought most worth the saving? There were
several merry answers made to my question, which
entertained us until bedtime. This filled my mind with
such an huddle of ideas, that upon my going to sleep
I fell into the following dream :

I saw a town of this island, which shall be nameless,
invested on every side, and the inhabitants of it so
straitened as to cry for quarter. The general refused
any other terms than those granted to the above-mentioned town of Hensberg, namely, that the married
women might come out with what they could bring

along with them. Immediately the city gates flew
open, and a female procession appeared, multitudes of
the sex following one another in a row, and staggering
under their respective burdens. I took my stand upon
an eminence in the enemy's camp, which was appointed
for the general rendezvous of these female carriers,
being very desirous to look into their several ladings.
The first of them had an huge sack upon her shoulders,
which she set down with great care : upon the opening
of it, when I expected to have seen her husband shot
out of it, I found it was filled with chinaware. The
next appeared in a more decent figure, carrying an
handsome young fellow upon her back : I could not
forbear commending the young woman for her conjugal
affection, when, to my great surprise, I found that she
had left the good man at home, and brought away her
gallant. I saw the third at some distance, with a little
withered face peeping over her shoulder, whom I could
not suspect for any but her spouse, until upon her
setting him down I heard her call him dear Pugg, and
found him to be her favourite monkey. A fourth
brought a huge bale of cards along with her ; and the
fifth a Bolonia lapdog, for her husband it seems being
a very burly man, she thought it would be less trouble
for her to bring away little Cupid. The next was the
wife of a rich usurer, loaden with a bag of gold ; she
told us that her spouse was very old, and by the course
of nature could not expect to live long, and that to
show her tender regards for him she had saved that
which the poor man loved better than his life. The
next came towards us with her son upon her back, who,
we were told, was the greatest rake in the place, but
so much the mother's darling that she left her husband
behind, with a large family of hopeful sons and
daughters, for the sake of this graceless youth.

It would be endless to mention the several persons,
with their several loads, that appeared to me in this
strange vision. All the place about me was covered
with packs of ribands, brocades, embroidery, and ten
thousand other materials, sufficient to have furnished
a whole street of toyshops. One of the women, having
an husband who was none of the heaviest, was bringing him off upon her shoulders at the same time that
she carried a great bundle of Flanders lace under her

arm; but finding herself so overloaden that she could not save both of them, she dropped the good man, and brought away the bundle. In short, I found but one husband among this great mountain of baggage, who was a lively cobbler, that kicked and spurred all the while his wife was carrying him on, and, as it was said, had scarce passed a day in his life without giving her the discipline of the strap.

I cannot conclude my letter, dear SPEC., without telling thee one very odd whim in this my dream. I saw, methoughts, a dozen women employed in bringing off one man; I could not guess who it should be, until upon his nearer approach I discovered thy short phiz. The women all declared that it was for the sake of thy works, and not thy person, that they brought thee off, and that it was on condition that thou shouldst continue the *Spectator*. If thou thinkest this dream will make a tolerable one it is at thy service, from,

Dear SPEC.,<br>Thine sleeping and waking,<br>WILL. HONEYCOMB

The ladies will see, by this letter, what I have often told them, that Will is one of those old-fashioned men of wit and pleasure of the town, that shows his parts by raillery on marriage, and one who has often tried his fortune that way without success. I cannot however dismiss his letter without observing, that the true story on which it is built does honour to the sex, and that in order to abuse them the writer is obliged to have recourse to dream and fiction [1].                               O.

[1] In October 1712 Tonson joined Buckley in the publishing of the *Spectator*, and the colophon in this and following numbers reads thus: 'London: Printed for S. Buckley and J. Tonson: and sold by A Baldwin in Warwick Lane.'

No. 500.          *Friday, Oct. 3, 1712*          [ADDISON

*Huc natas adjice septem*
*Et totidem juvenes, et mox generosque nurusque:*
*Quærite nunc, habeat quam nostra superbia causam.*
OVID, *Met.* vi, 182

SIR,—You, who are so well acquainted with the story of Socrates, must have read how, upon his making a discourse concerning love, he pressed his point with so much success that all the bachelors in his audience took a resolution to marry by the first opportunity, and that all the married men immediately took horse and galloped home to their wives. I am apt to think your discourses, in which you have drawn so many agreeable pictures of marriage, have had a very good effect this way in England. We are obliged to you at least for having taken off that senseless ridicule which for many years the witlings of the town have turned upon their fathers and mothers. For my own part, I was born in wedlock, and I don't care who knows it : for which reason, among many others, I should look upon myself as a most insufferable coxcomb did I endeavour to maintain that cuckoldom was inseparable from marriage, or to make use of 'husband' and 'wife' as terms of reproach. Nay, sir, I will go one step further, and declare to you before the whole world, that I am a married man, and at the same time I have so much assurance as not to be ashamed of what I have done.

Among the several pleasures that accompany this state of life, and which you have described in your former papers, there are two you have not taken notice of, and which are seldom cast into the account by those who write on this subject. You must have observed, in your speculations on human nature, that nothing is more gratifying to the mind of man than power or dominion, and this I think myself amply possessed of, as I am the father of a family. I am perpetually taken up in giving out orders, in prescribing duties, in hearing parties, in administering justice, and in distributing rewards and punishments. To speak in the language of the centurion, 'I say unto one, Go, and he goeth; and to another, Come, and he cometh; and to

my servant, Do this, and he doeth it [1]'. In short, sir,
I look upon my family as a patriarchal sovereignty, in
which I am myself both king and priest. All great
governments are nothing else but clusters of these little
private royalties, and therefore I consider the masters
of families as small deputy-governors presiding over
the several little parcels and divisions of their fellow-
subjects. As I take great pleasure in the administra-
tion of my government in particular, so I look upon
myself not only as a more useful, but as a much greater
and happier man than any bachelor in England of
my [2] rank and condition.

There is another accidental advantage in marriage,
which has likewise fallen to my share, I mean the
having a multitude of children. These I cannot but
regard as very great blessings. When I see my little
troop before me, I rejoice in the additions which I
have made to my species, to my country, and to my
religion, in having produced such a number of reasonable creatures, citizens, and Christians. I am pleased
to see myself thus perpetuated, and as there is no production comparable to that of a human creature, I am
more proud of having been the occasion of ten such
glorious productions, than if I had built an hundred
pyramids at my own expense, or published as many
volumes of the finest wit and learning. In what a
beautiful light has the Holy Scripture represented
Abdon, one of the judges of Israel, who had forty sons
and thirty grandsons that rode on threescore and ten
ass colts, according to the magnificence of the Eastern
countries [3]? How must the heart of the old man
rejoice, when he saw such a beautiful procession of
his own descendants, such a numerous cavalcade of his
own raising? For my own part, I can sit in my parlour
with great content, when I take a review of half-a-
dozen of my little boys mounting upon hobby-horses,
and of as many little girls tutoring their babies [4], each
of them endeavouring to excel the rest, and to do something that may gain my favour and approbation. I
cannot question but He who has blessed me with so
many children, will assist my endeavours in providing
for them. There is one thing I am able to give each

1 *Matthew* viii, 9.    2 'My own' (folio).
3 *Judges* xii, 14.    4 Dolls.

of them, which is a virtuous education. I think it is Sir Francis Bacon's observation, that in a numerous family of children the eldest is often spoiled by the prospect of an estate, and the youngest by being the darling of the parent; but that some one or other in the middle, who has not perhaps been regarded, has made his way in the world and overtopped the rest. It is my business to implant in every one of my children the same seeds of industry and the same honest principles. By this means I think I have a fair chance that one or other of them may grow considerable in some or other way of life, whether it be in the army, or in the fleet, in trade, or any of the three learned professions; for you must know, sir, that from long experience and observation, I am persuaded of what seems a paradox to most of those with whom I converse, namely, that a man who has many children and gives them a good education, is more likely to raise a family than he who has but one, notwithstanding he leaves him his whole estate. For this reason I cannot forbear amusing myself with finding out a general, an admiral, or an alderman of London, a divine, a physician, or a lawyer among my little people who are now perhaps in petticoats; and when I see the motherly airs of my little daughters when they are playing with their puppets, I cannot but flatter myself that their husbands and children will be happy in the possession of such wives and mothers.

If you are a father you will not, perhaps, think this letter impertinent, but if you are a single man you will not know the meaning of it, and probably throw it into the fire : whatever you determine of it, you may assure yourself that it comes from one who is,

Your most humble Servant<br>and Well-wisher,

O.                                          PHILOGAMUS

No. 501.     *Saturday*, *Oct.* 4, 1712     [PARNELL [1]

*Durum : sed levius fit patientia*
*Quicquid corrigere est nefas.*

HOR., 1 *Od.* xxiv, 19

As some of the finest compositions among the ancients are in allegory, I have endeavoured in several of my papers to revive that way of writing, and hope I have not been altogether unsuccessful in it. For I find there is always a great demand for those particular papers, and cannot but observe that several authors have endeavoured of late to excel in works of this nature. Among these I do not know any one who has succeeded better than a very ingenious gentleman, to whom I am obliged for the following piece, and who was the author of the vision in the cccclxth paper :          O.

How are we tortured with the absence of what we covet to possess, when it appears to be lost to us! What excursions does the soul make in imagination after it! And how does it turn into itself again, more foolishly fond and dejected, at the disappointment! Our grief, instead of having recourse to reason, which might restrain it, searches to find a further nourishment. It calls upon memory to relate the several passages and circumstances of satisfactions which we formerly enjoyed; the pleasures we purchased by those riches that are taken from us; or the power and splendour of our departed honours; or the voice, the words, the looks, the temper, and affections of our friends that are deceased. It needs must happen from hence, that the passion should often swell to such a size as to burst the heart which contains it, if time did not make these circumstances less strong and lively, so that reason should become a more equal match for the passion, or if another desire which becomes more present did not overpower them with a livelier representation. These are thoughts which I had when I fell into a kind of vision upon this subject, and may therefore stand for a proper introduction to a relation of it.

[1] The introductory paragraph is Addison's.

I found myself upon a naked shore, with company whose afflicted countenances witnessed their conditions. Before us flowed a water deep, silent, and called the River of Tears, which, issuing from two fountains on an upper ground, encompassed an island that lay before us. The boat which plied in it was old and shattered, having been sometimes overset by the impatience and haste of single passengers to arrive at the other side. This immediately was brought to us by Misfortune, who steers it, and we were all preparing to take our places, when there appeared a woman of a mild and composed behaviour, who began to deter us from it, by representing the dangers which would attend our voyage. Hereupon some who knew her for Patience, and some of those too who until then cried the loudest, were persuaded by her, and returned back. The rest of us went in, and she (whose good-nature would not suffer her to forsake persons in trouble) desired leave to accompany us, that she might at least administer some small comfort or advice while we sailed. We were no sooner embarked but the boat was pushed off, the sheet was spread, and being filled with sighs, which are the winds of that country, we made a passage to the farther bank, through several difficulties of which the most of us seemed utterly regardless.

When we landed, we perceived the island to be strangely overcast with fogs, which no brightness could pierce, so that a kind of gloomy horror sat always brooding over it. This had something in it very shocking to easy tempers, insomuch that some others, whom Patience had by this time gained over, left us here, and privily conveyed themselves round the verge of the island to find a ford by which she told them they might escape.

For my part, I still went along with those who were for piercing into the centre of the place; and joining ourselves to others whom we found upon the same journey, we marched solemnly as at a funeral, through bordering hedges of rosemary, and through a grove of yew-trees, which love to overshadow tombs and flourish in churchyards. Here we heard on every side the wailings and complaints of several of the inhabitants, who had cast themselves disconsolately at the feet of trees; and as we chanced to approach any of these, we might perceive them wringing their hands, beating their breasts, tearing their hair, or after some other manner visibly agitated with vexation. Our sorrows were heightened by the influence of what we heard and saw, and one of our number was wrought up to such a pitch of wildness, as to talk of hanging himself upon a bough which shot temptingly across the path we travelled in, but he was restrained from it by the kind endeavours of our above-mentioned companion.

We had now gotten into the most dusky, silent part of the island, and by the redoubled sounds of sighs, which made a doleful whistling in the branches, the thickness of air which occasioned faintish respiration, and the violent throbbings of heart which more and more affected us, we found that we approached the Grotto of Grief. It was a wide, hollow, and melancholy cave, sunk deep in a dale, and watered by rivulets that had a colour between red and black. These crept slow and half congealed amongst its windings, and mixed their heavy murmur with the echo of groans that rolled through all the passages. In the most retired part of it sat the Doleful Being herself, the path to her was strewed with goads, stings, and thorns, and her throne on which she sat was broken into a rock, with ragged pieces pointing upwards for her to lean upon. A heavy mist hung above her; her head, oppressed with it, reclined upon her arm : thus did she reign over her disconsolate subjects, full of herself to stupidity, in eternal pensiveness, and the profoundest silence. On one side of her stood Dejection just dropping into a swoon, and Paleness wasting to a skeleton; on the other side were Care inwardly tormented with imaginations, and Anguish suffering outward troubles to suck the blood from her heart in the shape of vultures. The whole vault had a genuine dismalness in it, which a few scattered lamps, whose bluish flames arose and sunk in their urns, discovered to our eyes with increase. Some of us fell down, overcome and spent with what they suffered in the way, and were given over to those tormentors that stood on either hand of the presence; others, galled and mortified with pain, recovered the entrance, where Patience, whom we had left behind, was still waiting to receive us.

With her (whose company was now become more grateful to us by the want we had found of her) we winded round the grotto, and ascended at the back of it, out of the mournful dale in whose bottom it lay. On this eminence we halted, by her advice, to pant for breath, and lifting our eyes, which until then were fixed downwards, felt a sullen sort of satisfaction in observing through the shades what numbers had entered the island. This satisfaction, which appears to have ill-nature in it, was excusable, because it happened at a time when we were too much taken up with our own concern to have respect to that of others, and therefore we did not consider them as suffering, but ourselves as not suffering in the most forlorn estate. It had also the groundwork of humanity and compassion in it, though the mind was then too dark and too deeply engaged to perceive it; but as we proceeded onwards it began to discover itself, and from observing that others were unhappy, we came to question one another, when it was that we met, and what were the sad occasions that brought us together. Then we heard our stories, we compared them, we mutually gave and received pity, and so by degrees became tolerable company.

A considerable part of the troublesome road was thus deceived[1], at length the openings among the trees grew larger, the air seemed thinner, it lay with less oppression upon us, and we could now and then discern tracks in it of a lighter greyness, like the breakings of day, short in duration, much enlivening, and called in that country Gleams of Amusement. Within a short while these gleams began to appear more frequent, and then brighter and of a longer continuance; the sighs, that hitherto filled the air with so much dolefulness, altered to the sound of common breezes, and in general the horrors of the island were abated.

When we had arrived at last at the ford by which we were to pass out, we met with those fashionable mourners who had been ferried over along with us,

---

[1] Wiled away.  *Cf.* Dryden (Virgil, *Eclog.* x),

This while I sung, my sorrows I deceived;

and who being unwilling to go as far as we, had coasted by the shore to find the place, where they waited our coming, that by showing themselves to the world only at the time when we did, they might seem also to have been among the troubles of the grotto. Here the waters, that rolled on the other side so deep and silent, were much dried up, and it was an easier matter for us to wade over.

The river being crossed, we were received upon the further bank by our friends and acquaintance, whom Comfort had brought out to congratulate our appearance in the world again. Some of these blamed us for staying so long away from them, others advised us against all temptations of going back again; every one was cautious not to renew our trouble, by asking any particulars of the journey; and all concluded, that in a case of so much melancholy and affliction, we could not have made choice of a fitter companion than Patience. Here Patience, appearing serene at her praises, delivered us over to Comfort. Comfort smiled at his receiving the charge, immediately the sky purpled on that side to which we turned, and double day at once broke in upon me.

## No. 502.        *Monday, Oct. 6, 1712*        [STEELE

*Melius, pejus, prosit, obsit, nil vident nisi quod lubent.*
TER., *Heaut.*, Act iv, sc. 1

WHEN men read, they taste the matter with which they are entertained according as their own respective studies and inclinations have prepared them, and make their reflections accordingly. Some perusing a Roman writer, would find in them, whatever the subject of the discourses were, parts which implied the grandeur of that people in their warfare or their politics. As for my part, who am a mere spectator, I drew this morning conclusions of their eminence in what I think great, to wit, in having worthy sentiments, from the reading a comedy of Terence. The play was *The Self-Tormentor*. It is from the beginning to the end a perfect picture of human life,

but I did not observe in the whole one passage that
could raise a laugh. How well disposed must that
people be, who could be entertained with satisfaction
by so sober and polite mirth! In the first scene of
the comedy, when one of the old men accuses the
other of impertinence for interposing in his affairs,
he answers, ' I am a man, and cannot help feeling
any sorrow that can arrive at man [1].' It is said
this sentence was received with an universal applause. There cannot be a greater argument of the
general good understanding of a people, than a sudden
consent to give their approbation of a sentiment
which has no emotion in it. If it were spoken with
never so great skill in the actor, the manner of
uttering that sentence could have nothing in it which
could strike any but people of the greatest humanity,
nay, people elegant and skilful in observations upon
it. It is possible he might have laid his hand on
his breast, and with a winning insinuation in his
countenance, expressed to his neighbour that he was
a man who made his case his own; yet I'll engage
a player in Covent Garden might hit such an attitude a thousand times before he would have been
regarded. I have heard that the minister of state
in the reign of Queen Elizabeth had all manner of
books and ballads brought to him, of what kind
soever, and took great notice how much they took
with the people [2]; upon which he would, and certainly might, very well judge of their present dispositions, and the most proper way of applying them
according to his own purposes. What passes on the
stage, and the reception it meets from the audience,
is a very useful instruction of this kind. According
to what you may observe there on our stage, you
see them often moved so directly against all common
sense and humanity, that you would be apt to pro-

---

[1] 'Homo sum: humani nihil a me alienum puto' (*Heaut.*, Act i,
sc. 1).

[2] *Cf.* the saying of Andrew Fletcher of Saltoun: 'I knew a very
wise man that believed, that if a man were permitted to make all
the ballads, he need not care who should make the laws, of a nation.'

nounce us a nation of savages. It cannot be called a mistake of what is pleasant, but the very contrary to it is what most assuredly takes with them. The other night an old woman carried off with a pain in her side, with all the distortions and anguish of countenance which is natural to one in that condition, was laughed and clapped off the stage. Terence's comedy, which I am speaking of, is indeed written as if he hoped to please none but such as had as good a taste as himself. I could not but reflect upon the natural description of the innocent young woman made by the servant to his master [1]. ' When I came to the house ', said he, ' an old woman opened the door, and I followed her in, because I could by entering upon them unawares better observe what was your mistress's ordinary manner of spending her time, the only way of judging any one's inclinations and genius. I found her at her needle in a sort of second mourning, which she wore for an aunt she had lately lost. She had nothing on but what showed she dressed only for herself. Her hair hung negligently about her shoulders. She had none of the arts with which others use to set themselves off, but had that negligence of person which is remarkable in those who are careful of their minds. . . . Then she had a maid who was at work near her, that was a slattern, because her mistress was careless; which I take to be another argument of your security in her; for the go-betweens of women of intrigue are rewarded too well to be dirty. When you were named, and I told her you desired to see her, she threw down her work for joy, covered her face, and decently hid her tears. . . .' He must be a very good actor, and draw attention rather from his own character than the words of the author, that could gain it among us for this speech, though so full of nature and good sense.

The intolerable folly and confidence of players putting in words of their own, does in a great measure

[1] *Heaut.*, Act ii, sc. 3.

feed the absurd taste of the audience. But, however that is, it is ordinary for a cluster of coxcombs to take up the house to themselves, and equally insult both the actors and the company. These savages, who want all manner of regard and deference to the rest of mankind, come only to show themselves to us, without any other purpose than to let us know they despise us.

The gross of an audience is composed of two sorts of people, those who know no pleasure but of the body, and those who improve or command corporeal pleasures by the addition of fine sentiments of the mind. At present the intelligent part of the company are wholly subdued by the insurrections of those who know no satisfactions but what they have in common with all other animals.

This is the reason that when a scene tending to procreation is acted, you see the whole pit in such a chuckle, and old lechers, with mouths open, stare at the loose gesticulations on the stage with shameful earnestness, when the justest pictures of human life in its calm dignity, and the properest sentiments for the conduct of it, pass by like mere narration, as conducing only to somewhat much better which is to come after. I have seen the whole house at some times in so proper a disposition, that indeed I have trembled for the boxes, and feared the entertainment would end in the representation of the *Rape of the Sabines.*

I would not be understood in this talk to argue, that nothing is tolerable on the stage but what has an immediate tendency to the promotion of virtue. On the contrary, I can allow, provided there is nothing against the interests of virtue, and is not offensive to good manners, that things of an indifferent nature may be represented. For this reason I ave no exception to the well-drawn rusticities in *The Country Wake;* and there is something so miraculously pleasant in Doggett's acting the awkward triumph and comic sorrow of Hob in different circumstances, that I shall not be able to stay away whenever it is acted [1]. All that vexes me is, that the gallantry of taking the cudgels for Gloucestershire, with the pride of heart in tucking himself up, and taking aim at his adversary, as well as the other's protestation in the humanity of low romance, that he could not promise the squire to break Hob's head, but he would, if he could, do it in love; then flourish and begin: I say, what vexes me is, that such excellent touches as these, as well as the squire's being out of all patience at Hob's success, and venturing himself into the crowd, are circumstances hardly taken notice of, and the height of the jest is only in the very point that heads are broken. I am confident, were there a scene written wherein Penkethman [2] should break his leg by wrestling with Bullock [3], and Dicky [4] come in to set it, without one word said but what should be according to the exact rules of surgery in making this extension, and binding up the leg, the whole house should be in a roar of applause at the dissembled anguish of the patient, the help given by him who threw him down, and the handy address and arch looks of the surgeon. To enumerate the entrance of ghosts, the embattling of armies, the noise of heroes in love, with a thousand other enormities, would be to transgress the bounds of this paper, for which reasons it is possible they may have hereafter distinct discourses; not forgetting any of the audience who shall set up for actors, and interrupt the play on the stage; and players who shall prefer the applause of fools to that of the reasonable part of the company [5].      T.

---

1 Doggett had recently acted as Hob in *The Country Wake* at Drury Lane. He was himself the author of this farce, which was first printed in 1715.

2 See Nos. 31, 370.      3 See No. 36.      4 Richard Norris; see No. 44.

5 See No. 521, postscript.  In No. 50 of the *Guardian*, the writer of a letter in praise of Addison's *Cato* says, 'Such virtuous and moral sentiments were never before put into the mouth of a British actor; and I congratulate my countrymen on the virtue they have shown in giving them (as you tell me) such loud and repeated applauses. They have now cleared themselves of the imputation which a late writer had thrown upon them in his 502nd Speculation.'

No. 503.        *Tuesday, Oct. 7, 1712*        [STEELE

*Deleo omnes dehinc ex animo mulieres.*

TER., *Eun.*, Act ii, sc. 3

MR SPECTATOR,—You have often mentioned with great vehemence and indignation the misbehaviour of people at church [1]; but I am at present to talk to you on that subject, and complain to you of one, whom at the same time I know not what to accuse of, except it be looking too well there, and diverting the eyes of the congregation to that one object. However, I have this to say, that she might have stayed at her own parish, and not come to perplex those who are otherwise intent upon their duty.

Last Sunday was sevennight I went into a church not far from London Bridge; but I wish I had been contented to go to my own parish, I am sure it had been better for me : I say I went to church thither, and got into a pew very near the pulpit. I had hardly been accommodated with a seat, before there entered into the aisle a young lady in the very bloom of youth and beauty, and dressed in the most elegant manner imaginable. Her form was such, that it engaged the eyes of the whole congregation in an instant, and mine among the rest. Though we were all thus fixed upon her, she was not in the least out of countenance, or under the least disorder, though unattended by any one, and not seeming to know particularly where to place herself. However, she had not in the least a confident aspect, but moved on with the most graceful modesty, every one making way, until she came to a seat just over against that in which I was placed. The deputy of the ward sat in that pew, and she stood opposite to him ; and at a glance into the seat, though she did not appear the least acquainted with the gentleman, was let in, with a confusion that spoke much

---

[1] See Nos. 53. 242. 259, 460. Writing to her daughter, Lady Bute, in 1755, Lady M. W. Montague says: 'I am of opinion the world improves every day. I confess I remember to have dressed for St James's Chapel with the same thoughts your daughters will have at the opera ; but am not of the *Rambler's* mind, that the church is the proper place to make love in; and the peepers behind a fan, who divided their glances between their lovers and their prayer-book, were not at all modester than those that now laugh aloud in public walks.'

admiration at the novelty of the thing.  The service
immediately began, and she composed herself for it
with an air of so much goodness and sweetness, that
the confession, which she uttered so as to be heard
where I sate, appeared an act of humiliation more than
she had occasion for.  The truth is, her beauty had
something so innocent, and yet so sublime, that we all
gazed upon her like a phantom.  None of the pictures
which we behold of the best Italian painters, have anything like the spirit which appeared in her countenance,
at the different sentiments expressed in the several
parts of divine service : that gratitude and joy at a
thanksgiving, that lowliness and sorrow at the prayers
for the sick and distressed, that triumph at the passages which gave instances of the Divine mercy, which
appeared respectively in her aspect, will `be in my
memory to my last hour.  I protest to you, sir, she
suspended the devotion of every one around her ; and
the ease she did everything with, soon dispersed the
churlish dislike and hesitation in approving what is
excellent, too frequent amongst us, to a general attention and entertainment in observing her behaviour.  All
the while that we were gazing at her, she took notice
of no object about her, but had an art of seeming
awkwardly attentive, whatever else her eyes were accidentally thrown upon.  One thing indeed was particular,
she stood the whole service, and never kneeled or sat.
I do not question but that was to show herself with
the greater advantage, and set forth to better grace
her hands and arms, lifted up with the most ardent
devotion, and her bosom, the fairest that ever was seen,
bare to observation ; while she, you must think, knew
nothing of the concern she gave others any other than
as an example of devotion, that threw herself out,
without regard to dress or garment, all contrition, and
loose of all worldly regards, in ecstasy of devotion.
Well, now the organ was to play a voluntary, and she
was so skilful in music, and so touched with it, that she
kept time, not only with some motion of her head, but
also with a different air in her countenance.  When the
music was strong and bold, she looked exalted, but
serious ; when lively and airy, she was smiling and
gracious ; when the notes were more soft and languish-
ing, she was kind and full of pity.  When she had now

made it visible to the whole congregation, by her motion and ear, that she could dance, and she wanted now only to inform us that she could sing too, when the psalm was given out, her voice was distinguished above all the rest, or rather people did not exert their own in order to hear her. Never was any heard so sweet and so strong. The organist observed it, and he thought fit to play to her only, and she swelled every note; when she found she had thrown us all out, and had the last verse to herself in such a manner, as the whole congregation was intent upon her, in the same manner as you see in cathedrals, they are on the person who sings alone the anthem. Well, it came at last to the sermon, and our young lady would not lose her part in that neither; for she fixed her eye upon the preacher, and as he said anything she approved, with one of Charles Mather's[1] fine tablets she set down the sentence, at once showing her fine hand, the golden pen, her readiness in writing, and her judgment in choosing what to write. To sum up what I intend by this long and particular account, I mean to appeal to you, whether it is reasonable that such a creature as this shall come from a jaunty part of the town, and give herself such violent airs, to the disturbance of an innocent and inoffensive congregation, with her sublimities. The fact, I assure you, was as I have related; but I had like to have forgot another very considerable particular. As soon as church was done, she immediately stepped out of her pew, and fell into the finest pitty-pat air forsooth, wonderfully out of countenance, tossing her head up and down as she swam along the body of the church. I, with several others of the inhabitants, followed her out, and saw her hold up her fan to an hackney coach at a distance, who immediately came up to her, and she whipped into it with great nimbleness, pulled the door with a bowing mien, as if she had been used to a better glass. She said aloud, 'You know where to go', and drove off. By this time the best of the congregation was at the church door, and I could hear some say, 'A very fine lady'; others, 'I'll warrant ye, she's no better than she should be'; and one very wise old lady said, 'She ought to have been taken up.' Mr Spectator, I think this matter

1 See No. 328.

lies wholly before you; for the offence does not come under any law, though it is apparent this creature came among us only to give herself airs, and enjoy her full swing in being admired. I desire you would print this that she may be confined to her own parish; for I can assure you there is no attending anything else in a place where she is a novelty. She has been talked of among us ever since under the name of the Phantom: but I would advise her to come no more; for there is so strong a party made by the women against her that she must expect they will not be excelled a second time in so outrageous a manner without doing her some insult. Young women who assume after this rate, and affect exposing themselves to view in congregations at t'other end of the town, are not so mischievous, because they are rivalled by more of the same ambition, who will not let the rest of the company be particular: but, in the name of the whole congregation where I was, I desire you to keep these agreeable disturbances out of the city, where sobriety of manners is still preserved, and all glaring and ostentatious behaviour, even in things laudable, discountenanced. I wish you may never see the Phantom, and am,

Sir,

Your most humble Servant,

T.   RALPH WONDER [1]

---

No. 504.   *Wednesday, Oct. 8, 1712*   [STEELE

*Lepus tute es, et pulpamentum quæris.* TER., *Eun.*, Act iii, sc. 1

IT is a great convenience to those who want wit to furnish out a conversation that there is something or other in all companies where it is wanted substituted in its stead, which, according to their taste, does the business as well. Of this nature is the agreeable pastime in the country halls of Cross Purposes, Questions and Commands, and the like [2]. A little superior to these are those who can play at Crambo [3], or cap verses. Then above them are such as can

[1] For a further letter see No. 515.
[2] See No. 245.   [3] See No. 63.

make verses, that is rhyme; and among those who
have the Latin tongue, such as used to make what
they call golden verses.  Commend me also to those
who have not brains enough for any of these exercises, and yet do not give up their pretensions to
mirth.  These can slap you on the back unawares,
laugh loud, ask you how you do with a twang on
your shoulders, say you are dull to-day, and laugh a
voluntary to put you in humour; the laborious way
among the minor poets of making things come into
such and such a shape [1], as that of an egg, a hand,
an axe, or anything that nobody had ever thought on
before for that purpose, or which would have cost
a great deal of pains to accomplish it if they did.
But all these methods, though they are mechanical,
and may be arrived at with the smallest capacity,
do not serve an honest gentleman who wants wit
for his ordinary occasions; therefore it is absolutely
necessary that the poor in imagination should have
something which may be serviceable to them at all
hours upon all common occurrences.  That which
we call punning is, therefore, greatly affected by
men of small intellects.  These men need not be
concerned with you for the whole sentence, but if
they can say a quaint thing, or bring in a word
which sounds like any one word you have spoken to
them, they can turn the discourse, or distract you
so that you cannot go on, and by consequence if
they cannot be as witty as you are, they can hinder
your being any wittier than they are.  Thus if you
talk of a candle, he *can deal* with you; and if you
ask to help you to some bread, a punster should
think himself very ill *bred* if he did not; and if he
is not as well *bred* as yourself, he hopes for *grains* of
allowance.  If you do not understand that last fancy,
you must recollect that bread is made of grain; and
so they go on for ever, without possibility of being
exhausted.

There are another kind of people of small faculties,

[1] See No. 58.

who supply want of wit with want of breeding; and because women are both by nature and education more offended at anything which is immodest than we men are, these are ever harping upon things they ought not to allude to, and deal mightily in double meanings. Every one's own observation will suggest instances enough of this kind, without my mentioning any; for your double meaners are dispersed up and down through all parts of town or city where there are any to offend, in order to set off themselves. These men are mighty loud laughers, and held very pretty gentlemen with the sillier and unbred part of womankind. But above all already mentioned, or any who ever were, or ever can be in the world, the happiest and surest to be pleasant are a sort of people whom we have not indeed lately heard much of, and those are your Biters.

A biter [1] is one who tells you a thing you have no reason to disbelieve in itself, and perhaps has given you, before he bit you, no reason to disbelieve it for his saying it; and if you give him credit, laughs in your face, and triumphs that he has deceived you. In a word, a biter is one who thinks you a fool, because you do not think him a knave. This description of him one may insist upon to be a just one, for what else but a degree of knavery is it to depend upon deceit for what you gain of another, be it in point of wit or interest, or anything else?

This way of wit is called biting by a metaphor taken from beasts of prey, which devour harmless and unarmed animals, and look upon them as their food wherever they meet them. The sharpers about town very ingeniously understood themselves to be to the undesigning part of mankind what foxes are

---

[1] See No. 47. 'Gamesters, banterers, biters, swearers, and twenty new-born insects more are, in their several species, the modern men of wit' (*Tatler*, No. 12). A comedy by Rowe, called *The Biter*, was published in 1705. In Lillie's *Letters sent to the Tatler and Spectator* (ii, 232), is a letter from a tradesman, complaining of a set of female 'biters and hunters', who amused themselves by driving about in bad weather, and calling out shopmen on fool's errands in order that they might get wet through.

to lambs, and therefore used the word *biting* to express any exploit wherein they had overreached any innocent and inadvertent man of his purse. These rascals of late years have been the gallants of the town, and carried it with a fashionable haughty air, to the discouragement of modesty and all honest arts. Shallow fops, who are governed by the eye, and admire everything that struts in vogue, took up from the sharpers the phrase of *biting*, and used it upon all occasions, either to disown any nonsensical stuff they should talk themselves, or evade the force of what was reasonably said by others. Thus when one of these cunning creatures was entered into a debate with you, whether it was practicable in the present state of affairs to accomplish such a proposition, and you thought he had let fall what destroyed his side of the question, as soon as you looked with an earnestness ready to lay hold of it, he immediately cried, ' Bite ', and you were immediately to acknowledge all that part was in jest. To carry this to all the extravagance imaginable, and if one of these witlings knows any particulars which may give authority to what he says, he is still the more ingenious if he imposes upon your credulity. I remember a remarkable instance of this kind. There came up a shrewd young fellow to a plain young man, his countryman, and taking him aside with a grave concerned countenance, goes on at this rate : ' I see you here, and have you heard nothing out of Yorkshire? You look so surprised you could not have heard of it—and yet the particulars are such, that it cannot be false. I am sorry I am got into it so far, that I now must tell you; but I know not but it may be for your service to know——On Tuesday last, just after dinner—you know his manner is to smoke, opening his box—your father fell down dead in an apoplexy.' The youth showed the filial sorrow which he ought—upon which the witty man cried, ' Bite, there was nothing in all this——'

To put an end to this silly, pernicious, frivolous

way at once, I will give the reader one late instance
of a bite, which no biter for the future will ever be
able to equal, though I heartily wish him the same
occasion. It is a superstition with some surgeons,
who beg the bodies of condemned malefactors, to go
to the gaol, and bargain for the carcass with the
criminal himself. A good honest fellow did so last
sessions, and was admitted to the condemned men
on the morning wherein they died. The surgeon
communicated his business, and fell into discourse
with a little fellow, who refused twelve shillings,
and insisted upon fifteen for his body. The fellow,
who killed the officer of Newgate, very forwardly,
and like a man who was willing to deal, told him,
'Look you, Mr Surgeon, that little dry fellow, who
has been half-starved all his life, and is now half-
dead with fear, cannot answer your purpose. I have
ever lived high and freely, my veins are full, I have
not pined in imprisonment; you see my crest swells
to your knife, and after Jack Catch [1] has done, upon
my honour you'll find me as sound as e'er a bullock
in any of the markets. Come, for twenty shillings
I am your man.' Says the surgeon, 'Done, there's a
guinea.' This witty rogue took the money, and as
soon as he had it in his fist, cries, 'Bite; I am to
be hanged in chains.'     T.

No. 505.  *Thursday, Oct. 9, 1712*  [ADDISON

*Non habeo denique nauci Marsum augurem,*
*Non vicanos aruspices, non de circo astrologos.*
*Non Isiacos conjectores, non interpretes somnium :*
*Non enim sunt ii, aut scientia, aut arte divini,*
*Sed superstitiosi vates, impudentesque harioli,*
*Aut inertes, aut insani, aut quibus egestas imperat :*
*Qui sui quæstus causa fictas suscitant sententias,*
*Qui sibi semitam non sapiunt, alteri monstrant viam,*
*Quibus divitias pollicentur, ab iis drachmam petunt ;*
*De divitiis deducant drachmam, reddant cætera.* ENNIUS

THOSE who have maintained that men would be
more miserable than beasts, were their hopes con-

[1] Jack Ketch.

fined to this life only, among other considerations take notice, that the latter are only afflicted with the anguish of the present evil, whereas the former are very often pained by the reflection on what is passed, and the fear of what is to come. This fear of any future difficulties or misfortunes is so natural to the mind, that were a man's sorrows and disquietudes summed up at the end of his life, it would generally be found that he had suffered more from the apprehension of such evils as never happened to him, than from those evils which had really befallen him. To this we may add, that among those evils which befall us, there are many that have been more painful to us in the prospect, than by their actual pressure.

This natural impatience to look into futurity, and to know what accidents may happen to us hereafter, has given birth to many ridiculous arts and inventions. Some found their prescience on the lines of a man's hand, others on the features of his face; some on the signatures which nature has impressed on his body, and others on his own handwriting. Some read men's fortunes in the stars, as others have searched after them in the entrails of beasts or the flights of birds. Men of the best sense have been touched, more or less, with these groundless horrors and presages of futurity upon surveying the most indifferent works of Nature. Can anything be more surprising than to consider Cicero, who made the greatest figure at the bar and in the senate of the Roman commonwealth, and at the same time outshined all the philosophers of antiquity in his library and in his retirements, as busying himself in the college of augurs, and observing with a religious attention after what manner the chickens pecked the several grains of corn which were thrown to them?

Notwithstanding these follies are pretty well worn out of the minds of the wise and learned in the present age, multitudes of weak and ignorant persons are still slaves to them. There are numberless arts of prediction among the vulgar which are too trifling to enumerate, and infinite observations of days, numbers, voices, and figures, which are regarded by them as portents and prodigies. In short, everything prophesies to the superstitious man; there is scarce a straw or a rusty piece of iron that lies in his way by accident.

It is not to be conceived how many wizards, gipsies, and cunning men are dispersed through all the countries and market-towns of Great Britain, not to mention the fortune-tellers and astrologers who live very comfortably upon the curiosity of several well-disposed persons in the cities of London and Westminster.

Among the many pretended arts of divination, there is none which so universally amuses as that by dreams. I have indeed observed in a late speculation [1] that there have been sometimes, upon very extraordinary occasions, supernatural revelations made to certain persons by this means; but as it is the chief business of this paper to root out popular errors, I must endeavour to expose the folly and superstition of those persons who, in the common and ordinary course of life, lay any stress upon things of so uncertain, shadowy, and chimerical a nature. This I cannot do more effectually than by the following letter, which is dated from a quarter of the town that has always been the habitation of some prophetic Philomath; it having been usual, time out of mind, for all such people as have lost their wits, to resort to that place either for their cure or for their instruction [2].

MOORFIELDS, *October* 4, 1712

MR SPECTATOR,—Having long considered whether there be any trade wanting in this great city, after having surveyed very attentively all kinds of ranks and professions, I do not find in any quarter of the town an Oneirocritic, or, in plain English, an interpreter of dreams. For want of so useful a person, there

---

[1] No. 487.    [2] Bedlam was in Moorfields.

are several good people who are very much puzzled in this particular, and dream a whole year together without being ever the wiser for it. I hope I am pretty well qualified for this office, having studied by candle-light all the rules of art which have been laid down upon this subject. My great-uncle by my wife's side was a Scotch Highlander, and second-sighted. I have four fingers and two thumbs upon one hand, and was born on the longest night of the year. My Christian and surname begin and end with the same letters. I am lodged in Moorfields, in a house that for these fifty years has been always tenanted by a conjurer.

If you had been in company, so much as myself, with ordinary women of the town, you must know that there are many of them who every day in their lives, upon seeing or hearing of anything that is unexpected, cry 'My dream is out'; and cannot go to sleep in quiet the next night, until something or other has happened which has expounded the visions of the preceding one. There are others who are in very great pain for not being able to recover the circumstances of a dream, that made strong impressions upon them while it lasted. In short, sir, there are many whose waking thoughts are wholly employed on their sleeping ones. For the benefit, therefore, of this curious and inquisitive part of my fellow-subjects, I shall in the first place tell those persons what they dreamt of, who fancy they never dream at all. In the next place, I shall make out any dream, upon hearing a single circumstance of it; and in the last place, shall expound to them the good or bad fortune which such dreams portend. If they do not presage good luck, I shall desire nothing for my pains; not questioning at the same time that those who consult me will be so reasonable as to afford me a moderate share out of any considerable estate, profit, or emolument which I shall thus discover to them. I interpret to the poor for nothing, on condition that their names may be inserted in public advertisements, to attest the truth of such my interpretations. As for people of quality or others who are indisposed, and do not care to come in person, I can interpret their dreams by seeing their water. I set aside one day in the week for lovers; and interpret by the great [1] for any gentlewoman who is turned of sixty, after the rate of half-a-crown per week, with the usual allowances for good luck. I have several rooms and apartments fitted up, at reasonable rates, for such as have not conveniences for dreaming at their own house.

*N.B.*—I am not dumb.

TITUS TROPHONIUS

No. 506.     *Friday, Oct. 10, 1712*     [BUDGELL

*Candida perpetuo reside, concordia, lecto,*
*Tamque pari semper sit Venus æqua jugo.*
*Diligat illa senem quondam: sed et ipsa marito,*
*Tunc quoque cum fuerit, non videatur anus.*

MART., 4 *Epig.* xiii, 7

THE following essay is written by the gentleman to whom the world is obliged for those several excellent discourses which have been marked with the letter X [2]:

I have somewhere met with a fable that made Wealth the father of Love. It is certain a mind ought, at least, to be free from the apprehensions of want and poverty, before it can fully attend to all the softnesses and endearments of this passion. Notwithstanding we see multitudes of married people, who are utter strangers to this delightful passion, amidst all the affluence of the most plentiful fortunes.

It is not sufficient to make a marriage happy that the humours of two people should be alike; I could instance a hundred pair who have not the least sentiment of love remaining for one another, yet are so like in their humours, that if they were not already married, the whole world would design them for man and wife.

The spirit of love has something so extremely fine in it, that it is very often disturbed and lost by some

---

[1] Whole, gross.
[2] These introductory words to Budgell's paper may be by either Steele or Addison.

little accidents which the careless and unpolite never attend to until it is gone past recovery.

Nothing has more contributed to banish it from a married state than too great a familiarity and laying aside the common rules of decency. Though I could give instances of this in several particulars, I shall only mention that of dress. The beaux and belles about town, who dress purely to catch one another, think there is no further occasion for the bait when their first design has succeeded. But besides the too common fault in point of neatness, there are several others which I do not remember to have seen touched upon, but in one of our modern comedies [1], where a Frenchwoman offering to undress and dress herself before the lover of the play, and assuring his mistress that it was very usual in France, the lady tells her, that's a secret in dress she never knew before, and that she was so unpolished an Englishwoman as to resolve never to learn even to dress before her husband.

There is something so gross in the carriage of some wives, that they lose their husbands' hearts for faults which, if a man has either good-nature or good-breeding, he knows not how to tell them of. I am afraid, indeed, the ladies are generally most faulty in this particular, who, at their first giving in to love, find the way so smooth and pleasant, that they fancy 'tis scarce possible to be tired of it.

There is so much nicety and discretion required to keep love alive after marriage, and make conversation still new and agreeable after twenty or thirty years, that I know nothing which seems readily to promise it but an earnest endeavour to please on both sides, and superior good sense on the part of the man.

By a man of sense, I mean one acquainted with business and letters.

A woman very much settles her esteem for a man according to the figure he makes in the world and

[1] Steele's *Funeral*, Act iii, sc. 2.

the character he bears among his own sex. As
learning is the chief advantage we have over them,
it is, methinks, as scandalous and inexcusable for a
man of fortune to be illiterate, as for a woman not to
know how to behave herself on the most ordinary
occasions. It is this which sets the two sexes at the
greatest distance; a woman is vexed and surprised
to find nothing more in the conversation of a man
than in the common tattle of her own sex.

Some small engagement at least in business, not
only sets a man's talents in the fairest light, and
allots him a part to act in which a wife cannot well
intermeddle, but gives frequent occasions for those
little absences which, whatever seeming uneasiness
they may give, are some of the best preservatives of
love and desire.

The fair sex are so conscious to themselves that
they have nothing in them which can deserve entirely
to engross the whole man, that they heartily despise
one who, to use their own expression, is always hanging at their apron-strings.

Lætitia is pretty, modest, tender, and has sense
enough; she married Erastus, who is in a post of
some business, and has a general taste in most parts
of polite learning. Lætitia, wherever she visits, has
the pleasure to hear of something which was handsomely said or done by Erastus. Erastus, since his
marriage, is more gay in his dress than ever, and in
all companies is as complaisant to Lætitia as to any
other lady. I have seen him give her her fan when
it has dropped with all the gallantry of a lover.
When they take the air together, Erastus is continually improving her thoughts, and, with a turn
of wit and spirit which is peculiar to him, giving her
an insight into things she had no notion of before.
Lætitia is transported at having a new world thus
opened to her, and hangs upon the man that gives
her such agreeable information. Erastus has carried
this point still further, as he makes her daily not
only more fond of him, but infinitely more satisfied

with herself.  Erastus finds a justness or beauty in whatever she says or observes, that Lætitia herself was not aware of; and, by his assistance, she has discovered a hundred good qualities and accomplishments in herself which she never before once dreamed of.  Erastus, with the most artful complaisance in the world, by several remote hints, finds the means to make her say or propose almost whatever he has a mind to, which he always receives as her own discovery, and gives her all the reputation of it.

Erastus has a perfect taste in painting, and carried Lætitia with him, the other day, to see a collection of pictures.  I sometimes visit this happy couple.  As we were last week walking in the long gallery before dinner, ' I have lately laid out some money in paintings ', says Erastus.  ' I bought that Venus and Adonis purely upon Lætitia's judgment; it cost me threescore guineas, and I was this morning offered an hundred for it.'  I turned towards Lætitia, and saw her cheeks glow with pleasure, while at the same time she cast a look upon Erastus the most tender and affectionate I ever beheld.

Flavilla married Tom Tawdry; she was taken with his laced coat and rich sword-knot; she has the mortification to see Tom despised by all the worthy part of his own sex.  Tom has nothing to do after dinner but to determine whether he will pare his nails at St James's, White's, or his own house.  He has said nothing to Flavilla since they were married which she might not have heard as well from her own woman.  He, however, takes great care to keep up the saucy, ill-natured authority of a husband.  Whatever Flavilla happens to assert, Tom immediately contradicts with an oath by way of preface, and, ' My dear, I must tell you, you talk most confoundedly silly.'  Flavilla had a heart naturally as well disposed for all the tenderness of love as that of Lætitia, but as love seldom continues long after esteem, it is difficult to determine, at present,

whether the unhappy Flavilla hates or despises the
person most whom she is obliged to lead her whole
life with.                                           X.


No. 507.          *Saturday, Oct. 11, 1712*          [ADDISON

*Defendit numerus, junctæque umbone phalanges.*   JUV., Sat. ii, 46

THERE is something very sublime, though very
fanciful, in Plato's description of the Supreme Being,
that ' Truth is His body, and light His shadow '.
According to this definition, there is nothing so con-
tradictory to His nature as error and falsehood.   The
Platonists have so just a notion of the Almighty's
aversion to everything which is false and erroneous,
that they looked upon truth as no less necessary than
virtue to qualify a human soul for the enjoyment
of a separate state.   For this reason, as they recommended moral duties to qualify and season the will
for a future life, so they prescribed several contemplations and sciences to rectify the understanding.
Thus Plato has called mathematical demonstrations
the cathartics or purgatives of the soul, as being the
most proper means to cleanse it from error and to
give it a relish of truth, which is the natural food
and nourishment of the understanding, as virtue is
the perfection and happiness of the will.
   There are many authors who have shown wherein
the malignity of a lie consists, and set forth, in proper
colours, the heinousness of the offence.   I shall here
consider one particular kind of this crime, which
has not been so much spoken to.   I mean, that
abominable practice of party-lying.   This vice is so
very predominant among us at present, that a man
is thought of no principles who does not propagate
a certain system of lies.   The coffee-houses are supported by them, the press is choked with them,
eminent authors live upon them.   Our bottle-con-
versation is so infected with them, that a party-lie
is grown as fashionable an entertainment as a lively

catch or a merry story.  The truth of it is, half the great talkers in the nation would be struck dumb were this fountain of discourse dried up.  There is, however, one advantage resulting from this detestable practice : the very appearances of truth are so little regarded, that lies are at present discharged in the air, and begin to hurt nobody.  When we hear a party-story from a stranger, we consider whether he is a Whig or a Tory that relates it, and immediately conclude they are words of course, in which the honest gentleman designs to recommend his zeal without any concern for his veracity.  A man is looked upon as bereft of common sense that gives credit to the relations of party-writers; nay, his own friends shake their heads at him, and consider him in no other light than as an officious tool or a well-meaning idiot.  When it was formerly the fashion to husband a lie, and trump it up in some extraordinary emergency, it generally did execution, and was not a little serviceable to the faction that made use of it; but at present every man is upon his guard; the artifice has been too often repeated to take effect.

I have frequently wondered to see men of probity, who would scorn to utter a falsehood for their own particular advantage, give so readily into a lie when it becomes the voice of their faction, notwithstanding they are thoroughly sensible of it as such.  How is it possible for those who are men of honour in their persons thus to become notorious liars in their party?  If we look into the bottom of this matter, we may find, I think, three reasons for it, and at the same time discover the insufficiency of these reasons to justify so criminal a practice.

In the first place, men are apt to think that the guilt of a lie, and consequently the punishment, may be very much diminished, if not wholly worn out, by the multitudes of those who partake in it.  Though the weight of a falsehood would be too heavy for one to bear, it grows light in their imaginations when it is snared among many.  But in this case a man very much deceives himself; guilt, when it spreads through numbers, is not so properly divided as multiplied. Every one is criminal in proportion to the offence which he commits, not to the number of those who are his companions in it. Both the crime and the penalty lie as heavy upon every individual of an offending multitude, as they would upon any single person, had none shared with him in the offence. In a word, the division of guilt is like that of matter, though it may be separated into infinite portions, every portion shall have the whole essence of matter in it, and consist of as many parts as the whole did before it was divided.

But in the second place, though multitudes who join in a lie cannot exempt themselves from the guilt, they may from the shame of it. The scandal of a lie is in a manner lost and annihilated when diffused among several thousands, as a drop of the blackest tincture wears away and vanishes when mixed and confused in a considerable body of water. The blot is still in it, but is not able to discover itself. This is certainly a very great motive to several party-offenders, who avoid crimes, not as they are prejudicial to their virtue, but to their reputation. It is enough to show the weakness of this reason, which palliates guilt without removing it, that every man who is influenced by it declares himself in effect an infamous hypocrite, prefers the appearance of virtue to its reality, and is determined in his conduct neither by the dictates of his own conscience, the suggestions of true honour, nor the principles of religion.

The third and last great motive for men's joining in a popular falsehood, or, as I have hitherto called it, a party-lie, notwithstanding they are convinced of it as such, is the doing good to a cause which every party may be supposed to look upon as the most meritorious. The unsoundness of this principle has been so often exposed, and is so universally acknowledged, that a man must be an utter stranger to the principles either of natural religion or Christianity who suffers himself to be guided by it.  If a man might promote the supposed good of his country by the blackest calumnies and falsehoods, our nation abounds more in patriots than any other of the Christian world.  When Pompey was desired not to set sail in a tempest that would hazard his life, ' It is necessary for me ', says he, ' to sail, but it is not necessary for me to live [1] '.  Every man should say to himself, with the same spirit, ' It is my duty to speak truth, though it is not my duty to be in an office.'  One of the fathers hath carried this point so high as to declare he would not tell a lie though he were sure to gain heaven by it.  However extravagant such protestation may appear, every one will own, that a man may say very reasonably he would not tell a lie, if he were sure to gain hell by it; or, if you have a mind to soften the expression, that he would not tell a lie to gain any temporal reward by it, when he should run the hazard of losing much more than it was possible for him to gain.

No. 508.        *Monday, Oct. 13, 1712*        [STEELE

*Omnes autem et habentur et dicuntur tyranni, qui potestate sunt perpetua,
in ea civitate quæ libertate usa est.*  CORN. NEPOS, *in Milt.*, c. 8

THE following letters complain of what I have frequently observed with very much indignation; therefore I shall give them to the public in the words with which my correspondents, who suffer under the hardships mentioned in them, describe them.

MR SPECTATOR,—In former ages all pretensions to dominion have been supported and submitted to, either upon account of inheritance, conquest, or election; and all such persons who have taken upon them any sovereignty over their fellow-creatures upon any other account, have been always called tyrants, not so much because they were guilty of any particular barbarities,

[1] Plutarch's *Life*, sect. 50.

as because every attempt to such a superiority was in its nature tyrannical. But there is another sort of potentates who may with greater propriety be called tyrants than those last mentioned, both as they assume a despotic dominion over those as free as themselves, and as they support it by acts of notable oppression and injustice; and these are the rulers in all clubs and meetings. In other governments, the punishments of some have been alleviated by the rewards of others; but what makes the reign of these potentates so particularly grievous is, that they are exquisite in punishing their subjects, at the same time they have it not in their power to reward them. That the reader may the better comprehend the nature of these monarchs, as well as the miserable state of those that are their vassals, I shall give an account of the king of the company I am fallen into, whom for his particular tyranny I shall call Dionysius; as also of the seeds that sprung up to this odd sort of empire.

Upon all meetings at taverns, 'tis necessary some one of the company should take it upon him to get all things in such order and readiness as may contribute as much as possible to the felicity of the convention; such as hastening the fire, getting a sufficient number of candles, tasting the wine with a judicious smack, fixing the supper, and being brisk for the despatch of it. Know then that Dionysius went through these offices with an air that seemed to express a satisfaction rather in serving the public, than in gratifying any particular inclination of his own. We thought him a person of an exquisite palate, and therefore by consent beseeched him to be always our proveditor; which post, after he had handsomely denied, he could do no otherwise than accept. At first he made no other use of his power than in recommending such and such things to the company, ever allowing these points to be disputable; insomuch that I have often carried the debate for partridge when his Majesty has given intimation of the high relish of duck, but at the same time has cheerfully submitted, and devoured his partridge with most gracious resignation. This submission on his side naturally produced the like on ours; of which he in a little time made such barbarous advantage, as in all those matters, which before seemed indifferent to him, to issue out certain edicts as uncontrollable and unalterable as the laws of the Medes and Persians. He is by turns outrageous, peevish, froward, and jovial. He thinks it our duty, for the little offices as proveditor, that in return all conversation is to be interrupted or promoted by his inclination for or against the present humour of the company. We feel at present, in the utmost extremity, the insolence of office; however, I being naturally warm, ventured to oppose him in a dispute about a haunch of venison. I was altogether for roasting, but Dionysius declared himself for boiling with so much prowess and resolution that the cook thought it necessary to consult his own safety rather than the luxury of my proposition. With the same authority that he orders what we shall eat and drink, he also commands us where to do it, and we change our taverns according as he suspects any treasonable practices in the settling the bill by the master, or sees any bold rebellion in point of attendance by the waiters. Another reason for changing the seat of empire I conceive to be the pride he takes in the promulgation of our slavery, though we pay our club for our entertainments even in these palaces of our grand monarch. When he has a mind to take the air, a party of us are commanded out by way of life-guard, and we march under as great restrictions as they do. If we meet a neighbouring king. we give or keep the way according as we are outnumbered or not; and if the train of each is equal in number, rather than give battle, the superiority is soon adjusted by a desertion from one of 'em.

Now, the expulsion of these unjust rulers out of all societies would gain a man as everlasting a reputation as either of the Brutus's got from their endeavours to extirpate tyranny from among the Romans. I confess myself to be in a conspiracy against the usurper of our club; and to show my reading, as well as my merciful disposition, shall allow him 'till the Ides of March to dethrone himself. If he seems to affect empire 'till that time, and does not gradually recede from the incursions he has made upon our liberties, he shall find a dinner dressed which he has no hand in, and shall be treated with an order, magnificence, and luxury, as shall break his proud heart; at the same time that he shall be convinced in his stomach he was unfit for his post, and a more mild and skilful prince receive the acclamations of the people, and be set up in his room; but, as Milton says :

> These thoughts
> Full counsel must mature.  Peace is despaired,
> And who can think submission?  War then, war
> Open, or understood, must be resolved[1].

I am, Sir,
Your most obedient humble Servant

MR SPECTATOR,—I am a young woman at a gentleman's seat in the country, who is a particular friend of my father's, and came hither to pass away a month or two with his daughters.  I have been entertained with the utmost civility by the whole family, and nothing has been omitted which can make my stay easy and agreeable on the part of the family : but there is a gentleman here, a visitant as I am, whose behaviour has given me great uneasinesses.  When I first arrived here he used me with the utmost complaisance ; but, forsooth, that was not with regard to my sex, and since he has no designs upon me, he does not know why he should distinguish me from a man in things indifferent. He is, you must know, one of those familiar coxcombs who have observed some well-bred men with a good grace converse with women, and say no fine things, but yet treat them with that sort of respect which flows from the heart and the understanding, but is exerted in no professions or compliments.  This puppy, to imitate this excellence, or avoid the contrary fault of being troublesome in complaisance, takes upon him to try his talent upon me, insomuch that he contradicts me upon all occasions, and one day told me I lied.  If I had stuck him with my bodkin, and behaved myself like a man, since he won't treat me as a woman, I had, I think, served him right.  I wish, sir, you would please to give him some maxims of behaviour in these points, and resolve me if all maids are not in point of conversation to be treated by all bachelors as their mistresses.  If not so, are they not to be used as gently as their sisters ?  Is it sufferable that the fop of whom I complain should say, as he would rather have such

1 *Paradise Lost*, i, 659–662.

a one without a groat than me with the Indies? What right has any man to make suppositions of things not in his power, and then declare his will to the dislike of one that has never offended him? I assure you these are things worthy your consideration, and I hope we shall have your thoughts upon them. I am, though a woman justly offended, ready to forgive all this, because I have no remedy but leaving very agreeable company sooner than I desire. This also is an heinous aggravation of his offence, that he is inflicting banishment upon me. Your printing this letter may, perhaps, be an admonition to reform him : as soon as it appears I will write my name at the end of it, and lay it in his way; the making which just reprimand I hope you will put in the power of,

Sir,

Your constant Reader,

T.                                     and humble Servant


No. 509.        *Tuesday, Oct. 14, 1712*        [STEELE

*Hominis frugi et temperantis functus officium.*
TER., *Heaut.*, Act iii, sc. 3

THE useful knowledge in the following letter shall have a place in my paper, though there is nothing in it which immediately regards the polite or the learned world; I say immediately, for upon reflection every man will find there is a remote influence upon his own affairs in the prosperity or decay of the trading part of mankind. My present correspondent, I believe, was never in print before; but what he says well deserves a general attention, though delivered in his own homely maxims, and a kind of proverbial simplicity; which sort of learning has raised more estates than ever were, or will be, from attention to Virgil, Horace, Tully, Seneca, Plutarch, or any of the rest, whom, I dare say, this worthy citizen would hold to be indeed ingenious, but unprofitable writers. But to the letter :

BROAD STREET, *October* 10, 1712

MR WILLIAM SPECTATOR,

SIR,—I accuse you of many discourses on the subject
of money, which you have heretofore promised the
public, but have not discharged yourself thereof. But
forasmuch as you seemed to depend upon advice from
others what to do in that point, have sat down to write
you the needful upon that subject. But before I enter
thereupon, I shall take this opportunity to observe to
you, that the thriving frugal man shows it in every
part of his expense, dress, servants, and house; and
I must, in the first place, complain to you, as Spectator, that in these particulars there is at this time,
throughout the city of London, a lamentable change
from that simplicity of manners which is the true source
of wealth and prosperity. I just now said the man of
thrift shows regularity in everything; but you may,
perhaps, laugh that I take notice of such a particular
as I am going to do, for an instance, that this city is
declining, if their ancient economy is not restored.
The thing which gives me this prospect and so much
offence, is the neglect of the Royal Exchange, I mean
the edifice so called, and the walks appertaining there-
unto. The Royal Exchange is a fabric that well
deserves to be so called, as well to express that our
monarchs' highest glory and advantage consists in being
the patrons of trade, as that it is commodious for
business, and an instance of the grandeur both of prince
and people. But, alas! at present it hardly seems to
be set apart for any such use or purpose. Instead
of the assembly of honourable merchants, substantial
tradesmen, and knowing masters of ships, the
mumpers [1], the halt, the blind; and the lame, your
vendors of trash, apples, plums, your ragamuffins, rake-
shames, and wenches, have jostled the greater number
of the former out of that place. Thus it is, especially
on the evening 'Change; so that what with the din of
squallings, oaths, and cries of beggars, men of greatest
consequence in our city absent themselves from the
place. This particular, by the way, is of evil consequence; for if the 'Change be no place for men of
the highest credit to frequent, it will not be a disgrace

[1] Beggars.

to those of less abilities to absent. I remember the
time when rascally company were kept out, and the
unlucky boys with toys and balls were whipped away
by a beadle. I have seen this done indeed of late, but
then it has been only to chase the lads from chuck,
that the beadle might seize their copper.

I must repeat the abomination, that the walnut trade
is carried on by old women within the walks, which
makes the place impassable by reason of shells and
trash. The benches around are so filthy, that no one
can sit down, yet the beadles and officers have the
impudence at Christmas to ask for their box, though
they deserve the strapado. I do not think it impertinent to have mentioned this, because it speaks a neglect
in the domestic care of the city, and the domestic is
the truest picture of a man everywhere else.

But I designed to speak on the business of money
and advancement of gain. The man proper for this,
speaking in the general, is of a sedate, plain, good
understanding, not apt to go out of his way, but so
behaving himself at home that business may come to
him. Sir William Turner, that valuable citizen, has
left behind him a most excellent rule, and couched it
in very few words, suited to the meanest capacity. He
would say, ' Keep your shop, and your shop will keep
you [1].' It must be confessed, that if a man of a great
genius could add steadiness to his vivacities, or substitute slower men of fidelity to transact the methodical
part of his affairs, such a one would outstrip the rest
of the world : but business and trade is not to be
managed by the same heads which write poetry, and
make plans for the conduct of life in general. So,
though we are at this day beholden to the late witty
and inventive Duke of Buckingham for the whole trade
and manufacture of glass [2], yet I suppose there is no

[1] Alderman Thomas, a mercer, seems to have made this one of the
mottoes in his shop in Paternoster Row.

[2] ' It is a modest computation that England gains £50,000 a year by
exporting this commodity for the service of foreign nations ; the whole
owing to the inquisitive and mechanic as well as liberal genius of the
late Duke of Buckingham' (*Lover*, No. 34, by Steele). In 1670 Rossetti
and other Venetian artists came to England under the patronage of
the Duke of Buckingham, who established a manufactory at Vauxhall,
and carried it on with such success that all other nations were excelled
in blown plate-glass (*History of Lambeth*, 1786, p. 120). Advertisements
of various glass houses in London appeared from time to time in the

one will aver that, were his Grace yet living, they would not rather deal with my diligent friend and neighbour, Mr Gumley, for any goods to be prepared and delivered on such a day, than he would with that illustrious mechanic above mentioned.

No, no, Mr Spectator, you wits must not pretend to be rich; and it is possible the reason may be, in some measure, because you despise, or at least you do not value it enough to let it take up your chief attention; which the trader must do, or lose his credit, which is to him what honour, reputation, fame, or glory is to other sort of men.

I shall not speak to the point of cash itself, until I see how you approve of these my maxims in general. But I think a speculation upon 'Many a little makes a mickle', 'A penny saved is a penny got', 'Penny wise and pound foolish', 'It is need that makes the old wife trot', would be very useful to the world, and, if you treated them with knowledge, would be useful to yourself, for it would make demands for your paper among those who have no notion of it at present. But of these matters more hereafter. If you did this, as you excel many writers of the present age for politeness, so you would outgo the author of the true strops of razors [1] for use.

I shall conclude this discourse with an explanation of a proverb, which by vulgar error is taken and used when a man is reduced to an extremity, whereas the propriety of the maxim is to use it when you would say, 'There is plenty, but you must make such a choice as not to hurt another who is to come after you.'

Mr Tobias Hobson [2], from whom we have the expression, was a very honourable man, for I shall ever call the man so who gets an estate honestly. Mr Tobias Hobson was a carrier, and being a man of great abilities

---

*Tatler* and *Spectator*. George Villiers, Duke of Buckingham, as Dryden said:

> Was everything by starts, but nothing long;
> But in the course of one revolving moon
> Was chemist, fiddler, statesman, and buffoon.

[1] See No. 428.

[2] Thomas (not Tobias) Hobson, the carrier, immortalised by Milton's epitaphs. He continued his journeys to London until the year before

and invention, and one that saw where there might good profit arise, though the duller men overlooked it, this ingenious man was the first in this island who let out hackney-horses. He lived in Cambridge, and observing that the scholars rid hard, his manner was to keep a large stable of horses, with boots, bridles, and whips, to furnish the gentlemen at once, without going from college to college to borrow, as they have done since the death of this worthy man. I say, Mr Hobson kept a stable of forty good cattle always ready and fit for travelling; but when a man came for a horse, he was led into the stable, where there was great choice, but he obliged him to take the horse which stood next to the stable-door; so that every customer was alike well served according to his chance, and every horse ridden with the same justice. From whence it became a proverb, when what ought to be your election was forced upon you, to say, 'Hobson's choice'. This memorable man stands drawn in fresco at an inn (which he used) in Bishopgate Street, with an hundred pound bag under his arm, with this inscription upon the said bag :

THE FRUITFUL MOTHER OF AN HUNDRED MORE.

Whatever tradesman will try the experiment, and begin the day after you publish this my discourse to treat his customers all alike, and all reasonably and honestly, I will ensure him the same success.

I am, Sir,<br>Your loving Friend,

T.                                   HEZEKIAH THRIFT

---

No. 510.     *Wednesday, Oct. 15, 1712*     [STEELE

Si sapis<br>Neque præterquam quas ipse amor molestias<br>Habet, addas; et illas, quas habet, recte feras.<br>TER., Eun., Act i, sc. 1

I WAS the other day driving in a hack[1] through Gerard Street, when my eye was immediately catched

---

[1] 'An hack', in the original editions. The 'hack' is, of course, a hackney-coach.

with the prettiest object imaginable, the face of a
very fair girl[1], between thirteen and fourteen, fixed at
the chin to a painted sash, and made part of the landscape.   It seemed admirably done, and upon throwing
myself eagerly out of the coach to look at it, it
laughed, and flung from the window.   This amiable
figure dwelt upon me; and I was considering the
vanity of the girl, and her pleasant coquetry in acting
a picture until she was taken notice of, and raised
the admiration of her beholders.   This little circumstance made me run into reflections upon the force
of beauty, and the wonderful influence the female sex
has upon the other part of the species.   Our hearts
are seized with their enchantments, and there are few
of us, but brutal men, who by that hardness lose the
chief pleasure in them, can resist their insinuations,
though never so much against our own interest and
opinion.   It is common with women to destroy the
good effects a man's following his own way and
inclination might have upon his honour and fortune,
by interposing their power over him in matters
wherein they cannot influence him, but to his loss
and disparagement.   I do not know therefore a task
so difficult in human life as to be proof against the
importunities of a woman a man loves.   There is
certainly no armour against tears, sullen looks, or at
best constrained familiarities in her whom you
usually meet with transport and alacrity.   Sir Walter
Raleigh was quoted in a letter (of a very ingenious
correspondent of mine) on this subject.   That author,
who had lived in courts, camps, travelled through
many countries, and seen many men under several
climates, and of as various complexions, speaks of
our impotence to resist the wiles of women in very
severe terms.   His words are as follow[2] :
  'What means did the devil find out, or what instru-

[1] Cf. the *Tatler*, No. 248, where Steele says, 'It may perhaps appear
ridiculous, but I must confess, this last summer, as I was riding in
Enfield Chase. I met a young lady whom I could hardly get out of my
head, and for aught I know, my heart, ever since.'
[2] *History of the World*, Book I, chap. iv, sect. 4.

ments did his own subtlety present him, as fittest
and aptest to work his mischief by?  Even the un-
quiet vanity of the woman; so as by Adam's hearken-
ing to the voice of his wife, contrary to the express
commandment of the living God, mankind by that
her incantation [1] became the subject of labour, sorrow, and death; the woman being given to man for
a comforter and companion, but not for a counsellor.
It is also to be noted by whom the woman was
tempted.  Even by the most ugly and unworthy of
all beasts, into whom the devil entered and persuaded.  Secondly, what was the motive of her disobedience?  Even a desire to know what was most
unfitting her knowledge; an affection which has ever
since remained in all the posterity of her sex.
Thirdly, what was it that moved the man to yield to
her persuasions?  Even the same cause which hath
moved all men since to the like consent, namely, an
unwillingness to grieve her, or make her sad, lest she
should pine, and be overcome with sorrow.  But if
Adam in the state of perfection, and Solomon, the
son of David, God's chosen servant, and himself a
man endued with the greatest wisdom, did both of
them disobey their Creator by the persuasion and for
the love they bare to a woman, it is not so wonderful
as lamentable that other men in succeeding ages have
been allured to so many inconvenient and wicked
practices by the persuasion of their wives, or other
beloved darlings, who cover over and shadow many
malicious purposes with a counterfeit passion of dis-
simulate sorrow and unquietness.'

The motions of the minds of lovers are nowhere
so well described as in the works of skilful writers
for the stage.  The scene between Fulvia and Curius,
in the second act of Jonson's *Catiline*, is an excellent
picture of the power of a lady over her gallant.  The
wench plays with his affections; and as a man, of
all places in the world, wishes to make a good figure
with his mistress, upon her upbraiding him with want

[1] Enchantments.

of spirit, he alludes to enterprises which he cannot reveal but with the hazard of his life. When he is worked thus far, with a little flattery of her opinion of his gallantry, and desire to know more of it out of her overflowing fondness to him, he brags to her until his life is in her disposal.

When a man is thus liable to be vanquished by the charms of her he loves, the safest way is to determine what is proper to be done, but to avoid all expostulation with her before he executes what he has resolved. Women are ever too hard for us upon a treaty, and one must consider how senseless a thing it is to argue with one whose looks and gestures are more prevalent with you than your reason and arguments can be with her. It is a most miserable slavery to submit to what you disapprove, and give up a truth for no other reason but that you had not fortitude to support you in asserting it. A man has enough to do to conquer his own unreasonable wishes and desires; but he does that in vain if he has those of another to gratify. Let his pride be in his wife and family, let him give them all the conveniences of life in such a manner as if he were proud of them; but let it be his own innocent pride, and not their exorbitant desires, which are indulged by him. In this case all the little arts imaginable are used to soften a man's heart, and raise his passion above his understanding; but in all concessions of this kind a man should consider whether the present he makes flows from his own love or the importunity of his beloved : if from the latter, he is her slave; if from the former, her friend. We laugh it off, and do not weigh this subjection to women with that seriousness which so important a circumstance deserves. Why was courage given to man if his wife's fears are to frustrate it? When this is once indulged, you are no longer her guardian and protector, as you were designed by Nature; but, in compliance to her weaknesses, you have disabled yourself from avoiding the misfortunes into which they will lead you both, and you are to see the hour in which you are to be re-proached by herself for that very complaisance to her. It is indeed the most difficult mastery over ourselves we can possibly attain to resist the grief of her who charms us; but let the heart ache, be the anguish never so quick and painful, it is what must be suffered and passed through if you think to live like a gentleman or be conscious to yourself that you are a man of honesty. The old argument, that ' You do not love me if you deny me this ', which first was used to obtain a trifle, by habitual success will oblige the unhappy man who gives way to it to resign the cause even of his country and his honour. T.

No. 511. *Thursday, Oct. 16, 1712* [ADDISON

*Quis non invenit, turba quod amaret in illa?* OVID, *Ars Aman.* i, 175

DEAR SPEC.,—Finding that my last letter [1] took, I do intend to continue my epistolary correspondence with thee on those dear confounded creatures women. Thou knowest all the little learning I am master of is upon that subject : I never looked in a book but for their sakes. I have lately met two pure stories for a *Spectator*, which I am sure will please mightily if they pass through thy hands. The first of them I found by chance in an English book called ' Herodotus ', that lay in my friend Dapperwit's window, as I visited him one morning. It luckily opened in the place where I met with the following account. He tells us that it was the manner among the Persians to have several fairs in the kingdom, at which all the young unmarried women were annually exposed to sale. The men who wanted wives came hither to provide themselves : every woman was given to the highest bidder, and the money which she fetched laid aside for the public use, to be employed as thou shalt hear by and by. By this means the richest people had the choice of the market, and culled out all the most extraordinary beauties. As soon as the fair was thus picked, the refuse was to be

[1] See No. 499.

distributed among the poor, and among those who could not go to the price of a beauty. Several of these married the agreeables, without paying a farthing for them, unless somebody chanced to think it worth his while to bid for them, in which case the best bidder was always the purchaser. But now you must know, Spec., it happened in Persia, as it does in our own country, that there were as many ugly women as beauties or agreeables, so that by consequence, after the magistrates had put off a great many, there were still a great many that stuck upon their hands. In order therefore to clear the market, the money which the beauties had sold for was disposed of among the ugly; so that a poor man, who could not afford to have a beauty for his wife, was forced to take up with a fortune; the greatest portion being always given to the most deformed. To this the author adds, that every poor man was forced to live kindly with his wife, or, in case he repented of his bargain, to return her portion with her to the next public sale.

What I would recommend to thee on this occasion is, to establish such an imaginary fair in Great Britain; thou couldst make it very pleasant by matching women of quality with cobblers and carmen, or describing titles and garters leading off in great ceremony shopkeepers' and farmers' daughters. Though, to tell thee the truth, I am confoundedly afraid that, as the love of money prevails in our island more than it did in Persia, we should find that some of our greatest men would choose out the portions, and rival one another for the richest piece of deformity; and that, on the contrary, the toasts and belles would be bought up by extravagant heirs, gamesters, and spendthrifts. Thou couldst make very pretty reflections upon this occasion in honour of the Persian politics, who took care, by such marriages, to beautify the upper part of the species, and to make the greatest persons in the government the most graceful. But this I shall leave to thy judicious pen.

I have another story to tell thee, which I likewise met with in a book. It seems the general of the Tartars, after having laid siege to a strong town in China, and taken it by storm, would set to sale all the women that were found in it. Accordingly he put each of them into a sack, and after having thoroughly considered the value of the woman who was enclosed, marked the price that was demanded for her upon the sack. There were a great confluence of chapmen, that resorted from every part, with a design to purchase, which they were to do 'unsight, unseen'. The book mentions a merchant in particular, who observing one of the sacks to be marked pretty high, bargained for it, and carried it off with him to his house. As he was resting with it upon a half-way bridge, he was resolved to take a survey of his purchase : upon opening the sack, a little old woman popped her head out of it, at which the adventurer was in so great a rage, that he was going to shoot her out into the river. The old lady, however, begged him first of all to hear her story, by which he learned that she was sister to a great mandarin, who would infallibly make the fortune of his brother-in-law, as soon as he should know to whose lot she fell. Upon which the merchant again tied her up in his sack, and carried her to his house, where she proved an excellent wife, and procured him all the riches from her brother that she had promised him.

I fancy, if I was disposed to dream a second time, I could make a tolerable vision upon this plan. I would suppose all the unmarried women in London and Westminster brought to market in sacks, with their respective prices on each sack. The first sack that is sold is marked with five thousand pound : upon the opening of it, I find it filled with an admirable house-wife, of an agreeable countenance : the purchaser, upon hearing her good qualities, pays down her price very cheerfully. The second I would open should be a five hundred pound sack : the lady in it, to our surprise, has the face and person of a toast : as we are wondering how she came to be set at so low price, we hear that she would have been valued at ten thousand pound, but that the public had made those abatements for her being a scold. I would afterwards find some beautiful, modest, and discreet women, that should be the top of the market ; and perhaps discover half-a-dozen romps tied up together in the same sack, at one hundred pound a head. The prude and the coquette should be valued at the same price, though the first should go off the

vice, it excels all others, because it is the least shocking, and the least subject to those exceptions which
I have before mentioned.

This will appear to us, if we reflect, in the first
place, that upon the reading of a fable we are made
to believe we advise ourselves. We peruse the
author for the sake of the story, and consider the
precepts rather as our own conclusions than his instructions. The moral insinuates itself imperceptibly; we are taught by surprise, and become wiser
and better unawares. In short, by this method a
man is so far over-reached as to think he is directing
himself, whilst he is following the dictates of another,
and consequently is not sensible of that which is the
most unpleasing circumstance in advice.

In the next place, if we look into human nature,
we shall find that the mind is never so much pleased
as when she exerts herself in any action that gives
her an idea of her own perfections and abilities.
This natural pride and ambition of the soul is very
much gratified in the reading of a fable; for in
writings of this kind the reader comes in for half of
the performance; everything appears to him like a
discovery of his own; he is busied all the while in
applying characters and circumstances, and is in this
respect both a reader and a composer. It is no wonder, therefore, that on such occasions, when the mind
is thus pleased with itself, and amused with its own
discoveries, that it is highly delighted with the
writing which is the occasion of it. For this reason
the *Absalom and Achitophel* [1] was one of the most
popular poems that ever appeared in English. The
poetry is indeed very fine, but had it been much
finer it would not have so much pleased, without a
plan which gave the reader an opportunity of exerting
his own talents.

This oblique manner of giving advice is so inoffensive that if we look into ancient histories we find

[1] Dryden's satire on the intrigues of the Duke of Monmouth and
Lord Shaftesbury appeared in 1681.

better of the two. I fancy thou wouldst like such a
vision, had I time to finish it; because, to talk in thy
own way, there is a moral in it. Whatever thou may'st
think of it, prithee do not make any of thy queer
apologies for this letter, as thou didst for my last.
The women love a gay lively fellow, and are never
angry at the railleries of one who is their known
admirer. I am always bitter upon them, but well with
them.　　　　　　　　　　　　　　　　Thine,
O.　　　　　　　　　　　　　　　　　　　HONEYCOMB


No. 512.　　　*Friday, Oct. 17, 1712*　　　[ADDISON

*Lectorem delectando pariterque monendo.* HOR., *Ars Poet.* 344

THERE is nothing which we receive with so much
reluctance as advice. We look upon the man who
gives it us as offering an affront to our understanding
and treating us like children or idiots. We consider
the instruction as an implicit censure, and the zeal
which any one shows for our good on such an occasion as a piece of presumption or impertinence. The
truth of it is, the person who pretends to advise, does,
in that particular, exercise a superiority over us, and
can have no other reason for it, but that, in comparing
us with himself, he thinks us defective either in our
conduct or our understanding. For these reasons,
there is nothing so difficult as the art of making
advice agreeable; and indeed all the writers, both
ancient and modern, have distinguished themselves
among one another, according to the perfection at
which they have arrived in this art. How many
devices have been made use of to render this bitter
potion palatable? Some convey their instructions to
us in the best chosen words, others in the most harmonious numbers, some in points of wit, and others
in short proverbs.

　But among all the different ways of giving counsel,
I think the finest, and that which pleases the most
universally, is Fable, in whatsoever shape it appears.
If we consider this way of instructing or giving ad-

the wise men of old very often choose to give counsel
to their kings in fables.  To omit many which will
occur to every one's memory, there is a pretty instance of this nature in a Turkish tale, which I do
not like the worse for that little oriental extravagance
which is mixed with it.

We are told that the Sultan Mahmoud, by his
perpetual wars abroad and his tyranny at home, had
filled his dominions with ruin and desolation, and
half-unpeopled the Persian empire.  The Vizier to
this great Sultan (whether a humorist or an enthus-
iast we are not informed) pretended to have learned
of a certain dervish to understand the language of
birds, so that there was not a bird that could open
his mouth but the Vizier knew what it was he said.
As he was one evening with the Emperor in their
return from hunting, they saw a couple of owls upon
a tree that grew near an old wall out of a heap of
rubbish.  'I would fain know', says the Sultan,
'what those two owls are saying to one another;
listen to their discourse, and give me an account of
it.'  The Vizier approached the tree, pretending to
be very attentive to the two owls.  Upon his return
to the Sultan, 'Sir', says he, 'I have heard part of
their conversation, but dare not tell you what it is.'
The Sultan would not be satisfied with such an answer, but forced him to repeat word for word everything the owls had said.  'You must know then',
said the Vizier, 'that one of these owls has a son,
and the other a daughter, between whom they are
now upon a treaty of marriage.  The father of the
son said to the father of the daughter, in my hearing,
"Brother, I consent to this marriage, provided you
will settle upon your daughter fifty ruined villages
for her portion."  To which the father of the daughter
replied, "Instead of fifty I will give her five hundred,
if you please.  God grant a long life to Sultan Mahmoud! whilst he reigns over us we shall never want
ruined villages."'

The story says the Sultan was so touched with the

fable that he rebuilt the towns and villages which had been destroyed, and from that time forward consulted the good of his people [1].

To fill up my paper I shall add a most ridiculous piece of natural magic, which was taught by no less a philosopher than Democritus, namely, that if the blood of certain birds, which he mentioned, were mixed together, it would produce a serpent of such a wonderful virtue that whoever did eat it should be skilled in the language of birds, and understand everything they said to one another. Whether the dervish above mentioned might not have eaten such a serpent, I shall leave to the determination of the learned [2].                                         O.


No. 513.     *Saturday, Oct. 18, 1712*     [ADDISON

*Afflata est numine quando*
*Jam propiore dei.*                        VIRG., *Æn.* vi, 50

THE following letter comes to me from that excellent man in holy orders whom I have mentioned more than once as one of that society who assist me in my speculations. It is a ' Thought in Sickness ', and of a very serious nature, for which reason I give it a place in the paper of this day :

SIR,—The indisposition which has long hung upon me is at last grown to such an head that it must quickly make an end of me or of itself. You may imagine that whilst I am in this bad state of health there are none of your works which I read with greater pleasure than your Saturday's papers. I should be very glad if I could furnish you with any hints for

1 Pilpay's *Fables.*
2 The following advertisement appeared in No. 514 :
' A letter written October 14, dated Middle Temple, has been overlooked, by reason it was not directed to the *Spectator* at the usual places ; and the letter of the 18th, dated from the same place, is groundless, the author of the paper of Friday last not having ever seen the letter of the 14th. In all circumstances except the place of birth of the person to whom the letters were written, the writer of them is misinformed.'

that day's entertainment.   Were I able to dress up several thoughts of a serious nature, which have made great impressions on my mind during a long fit of sickness, they might not be an improper entertainment for that occasion.

Among all the reflections which usually rise in the mind of a sick man, who has time and inclination to consider his approaching end, there is none more natural than that of his going to appear naked and unbodied before Him who made him.   When a man considers that, as soon as the vital union is dissolved, he shall see that Supreme Being whom he now contemplates at a distance, and only in His works ; or, to speak more philosophically, when by some faculty in the soul he shall apprehend the Divine Being, and be more sensible of His Presence, than we are now of the presence of any object which the eye beholds, a man must be lost in carelessness and stupidity who is not alarmed at such a thought.   Dr Sherlock, in his excellent treatise upon death [1], has represented, in very strong and lively colours, the state of the soul in its first separation from the body, with regard to that invisible world which everywhere surrounds us, though we are not able to discover it through the grosser world of matter which is accommodated to our senses in his life.   His words are as follow :

'That death, which is our leaving this world, is nothing else but our putting off these bodies, teaches us that it is only our union to these bodies which intercepts the sight of the other world.   The other world is not at such a distance from us as we may imagine ; the throne of God indeed is at a great remove from this earth, above the third heavens, where He displays His glory to those blessed spirits which encompass His throne ; but as soon as we step out of these bodies, we step into the other world, which is not so properly another world (for there is the same heaven and earth still) as a new state of life.   To live in these bodies is to live in this world ; to live out of them is to remove into the next.   For while our souls are confined to these bodies, and can look only through these material casements, nothing but what is material can

[1] See No. 37.

affect us, nay, nothing but what is so gross that it can reflect light and convey the shapes and colours of things with it to the eye. So that though within this visible world, there be a more glorious scene of things than what appears to us, we perceive nothing at all of it; for this veil of flesh parts the visible and invisible world. But when we put off these bodies, there are new and surprising wonders present themselves to our views; when these material spectacles are taken off, the soul with its own naked eyes sees what was invisible before; and then we are in the other world, when we can see it and converse with it. Thus, St Paul tells us, "That when we are at home in the body, we are absent from the Lord; but when we are absent from the body, we are present with the Lord" (2 *Cor.* v, 6, 8). And methinks this is enough to cure us of our fondness for these bodies, unless we think it more desirable to be confined to a prison, and to look through a grate all our lives, which gives us but a very narrow prospect, and that none of the best neither, than to be set at liberty to view all the glories of the world. What would we give now for the least glimpse of that invisible world, which the first step we take out of these bodies will present us with? There are such things as eye hath not seen, nor ear heard, neither hath it entered into the heart of man to conceive. Death opens our eyes, enlarges our prospect, presents us with a new and more glorious world, which we can never see while we are shut up in flesh, which should make us as willing to part with this veil as to take the film off of our eyes which hinders our sight.'

As a thinking man cannot but be very much affected with the idea of his appearing in the presence of that Being whom none can see and live, he must be much more affected when he considers that this Being whom he appears before will examine all the actions of his past life, and reward or punish him accordingly. I must confess that I think there is no scheme of religion, besides that of Christianity, which can possibly support the most virtuous person under this thought. Let a man's innocence be what it will, let his virtues rise to the highest pitch of perfection attainable in this life, there will be still in him so many secret sins, so many human frailties, so many offences of ignorance, passion, and prejudice, so many unguarded words and thoughts, and, in short, so many defects in his best actions, that, without the advantages of such an expiation and atonement as Christianity has revealed to us, it is impossible that he should be cleared before his Sovereign Judge, or that he should be able to stand in His sight. Our holy religion suggests to us the only means whereby our guilt may be taken away, and our imperfect obedience accepted.

It is this series of thought that I have endeavoured to express in the following hymn, which I have composed during this my sickness [1] :

I

When rising from the bed of death
O'erwhelmed with guilt and fear,
I see My maker, face to face,
O how shall I appear!

II

If yet, while pardon may be found
And mercy may be sought,
My heart with inward horror shrinks
And trembles at the thought.

III

When Thou, O Lord, shalt stand disclosed
In majesty severe,
And sit in judgment on my soul,
O how shall I appear!

IV

But Thou hast told the troubled mind
Who does her sins lament,
The timely tribute of her tears
Shall endless woe prevent.

V

Then see the sorrow of my heart
Ere yet it be too late,
And hear my Saviour's dying groans,
To give those sorrows weight.

VI

For never shall my soul despair
Her pardon to procure,
Who knows Thine only Son has died
To make her pardon sure.

---

1 It will be observed that Addison attributes this hymn of his to the clergyman who was a member of the club.

There is a noble hymn in French, which Monsieur Bayle has celebrated for a very fine one, and which the famous author of the *Art of Speaking*[1] calls an admirable one, that turns upon a thought of the same nature. If I could have done it justice in English, I would have sent it you translated; it was written by Monsieur Des Barreaux[2], who had been one of the greatest wits and libertines in France, but in his last years was as remarkable a penitent :

> Grand Dieu, tes jugemens sont remplis d'équité ;
> Toujours tu prens plaisir à nous être propice :
> Mais j'ai tant fait de mal, que jamais ta bonté
> Ne me pardonnera sans choquer ta justice.
> Oui, mon Dieu, la grandeur de mon impiété
> Ne laisse a ton pouvoir que le choix du supplice :
> Ton interest s'oppose a ma félicité ;
> Et ta clémence même attend que je perisse.
> Contente ton desir puis qu'il t'est glorieux ;
> Offense toi des pleurs qui coulent de mes yeux ;
> Tonne, frappe, il est temps, rends moi guerre pour guerre.
> J'adore en périssant la raison qui t'aigrit :
> Mais dessus quel endroit tombera ton tonnerre,
> Qui ne soit tout couvert du sang de JESUS CHRIST.

If these thoughts may be serviceable to you, I desire you will place them in a proper light, and am ever, with great sincerity,

Sir,

O.                                            Yours, &c.

---

No. 514.        *Monday, Oct. 20, 1712*        [STEELE

> *Me Parnasi deserta per ardua dulcis*
> *Raptat amor ; juvat ire jugis, qua nulla priorum*
> *Castaliam molli divertitur orbita clivo.* VIRG., *Georg.* iii, 291

MR. SPECTATOR,—I came home a little later than usual the other night, and not finding myself inclined to sleep, I took up Virgil to divert me until I should

---

[1] A second edition of *The Art of Speaking, written in French by Messieurs Du Port Royal, rendered into English,* appeared in 1708.

[2] Jacques Vallée, Seigneur des Barreaux, born in Paris in 1602, was Counsellor of the Parliament of Paris, and gave up his charge to devote himself to pleasure. He was famous for his songs and verses, for his affability and generosity and irreligion. A few years before his death he was converted, and wrote the pious sonnet given above. In his religious days he lived secluded in Châlon sur Saône, where he died in 1673 (Morley).

be more disposed to rest. He is the author whom I always choose on such occasions, no one writing in so divine, so harmonious, nor so equal a strain, which leaves the mind composed, and softened into an agreeable melancholy; the temper in which, of all others, I choose to close the day. The passages I turned to were those beautiful raptures in his *Georgics*, where he professes himself entirely given up to the Muses, and smit with the love of poetry, passionately wishing to be transported to the cool shades and retirements of the mountain Hæmus[1]. I closed the book and went to bed. What I had just before been reading made so strong an impression on my mind, that fancy seemed almost to fulfil to me the wish of Virgil, in presenting to me the following vision.

Methought I was on a sudden placed in the plains of Bœotia, where at the end of the horizon I saw the mountain Parnassus rising before me. The prospect was of so large an extent, that I had long wandered about to find a path which should directly lead me to it, had I not seen at some distance a grove of trees, which, in a plain that had nothing else remarkable enough in it to fix my sight, immediately determined me to go thither. When I arrived at it, I found it parted out into a great number of walks and alleys, which often widened into beautiful openings, as circles or ovals, set round with yews and cypresses, with niches, grottoes, and caves, placed on the sides, encompassed with ivy. There was no sound to be heard in the whole place, but only that of a gentle breeze passing over the leaves of the forest; everything besides was buried ·in a profound silence. I was captivated with the beauty and retirement of the place, and never so much before that hour was pleased with the enjoyment of myself. I indulged the humour, and suffered myself to wander without choice or design. At length, at the end of a range of trees, I saw three figures seated on a bank of moss, with a silent brook creeping at their feet. I adored them as the tutelar divinities of the place, and stood still to take a particular view of each of them. The middlemost, whose name was Solitude, sate with her arms across each

---

1 *Georg.* ii, 488.

other, and seemed rather pensive and wholly taken
up with her own thoughts, than anyways grieved or
displeased. The only companions which she admitted
into that retirement was the goddess Silence, who sate
on her right hand with her finger on her mouth, and
on her left Contemplation, with her eyes fixed upon the
heavens. Before her lay a celestial globe, with several
schemes of mathematical theorems. She prevented my
speech with the greatest affability in the world. 'Fear
not', said she, 'I know your request before you
speak it; you would be led to the mountain of the
Muses. The only way to it lies through this place, and
no one is so often employed in conducting persons
thither as myself.' When she had thus spoken she
rose from her seat, and I immediately placed myself
under her direction; but whilst I passed through the
grove, I could not help inquiring of her who were the
persons admitted into that sweet retirement. 'Surely',
said I, 'there can nothing enter here but virtue and
virtuous thoughts. The whole wood seems designed for
the reception and reward of such persons as have spent
their lives according to the dictates of their conscience
and the commands of the gods.' 'You imagine right',
said she; 'assure yourself this place was at first
designed for no other. Such it continued to be in the
reign of Saturn, when none entered here but holy
priests, deliverers of their country from oppression and
tyranny, who reposed themselves here after their
labours; and those whom the study and love of wisdom
had fitted for divine conversation. But now it is
become no less dangerous than it was before desirable.
Vice has learned so to mimic virtue, that it often creeps
in hither under its disguise. See there! just before you,
Revenge stalking by, habited in the robe of Honour.
Observe not far from him Ambition standing alone;
if you ask him his name, he will tell you it is Emulation or Glory. But the most frequent intruder we
have is Lust, who succeeds now the deity to whom in
better days this grove was entirely devoted. Virtuous
Love, with Hymen and the Graces attending him, once
reigned over this happy place; a whole train of virtues
waited on him, and no dishonourable thought durst
presume for admittance; but now: how is the whole
prospect changed! and how seldom renewed by some

few who dare despise sordid wealth, and imagine themselves fit companions for so charming a divinity?'

The goddess had no sooner said thus, but we were arrived at the utmost boundaries of the wood, which lay contiguous to a plain that ended at the foot of the mountain. Here I kept close to my guide, being solicited by several phantoms, who assured me they would show me a nearer way to the mountain of the Muses. Among the rest, Vanity was extremely importunate, having deluded infinite numbers whom I saw wandering at the foot of the hill. I turned away from this despicable troop with disdain, and addressing myself to my guide, told her, that as I had some hopes I should be able to reach up part of the ascent, so I despaired of having strength enough to attain the plain on the top. But being informed by her that it was impossible to stand upon the sides, and that if I did not proceed onwards I should irrecoverably fall down to the lowest verge, I resolved to hazard any labour and hardship in the attempt. So great a desire had I of enjoying the satisfaction I hoped to meet with at the end of my enterprise!

There were two paths, which led up by different ways to the summit of the mountain; the one was guarded by the genius which presides over the moment of our births. He had it in charge to examine the several pretensions of those who desired a pass that way, but to admit none excepting those only on whom Melpomene had looked with a propitious eye at the hour of their nativity. The other way was guarded by Diligence, to whom many of those persons applied who had met with a denial the other way; but he was so tedious in granting their request, and indeed after admittance the way was so very intricate and laborious, that many after they had made some progress chose rather to return back than proceed, and very few persisted so long as to arrive at the end they proposed. Besides these two paths, which at length severally led to the top of the mountain, there was a third made up of these two, which a little after the entrance joined in one. This carried those happy few whose good fortune it was to find it directly to the throne of Apollo. I don't know whether I should even now have had the resolution to have demanded entrance at either of these doors,

had I not seen a peasant-like man (followed by a numerous and lovely train of youth of both sexes) insist upon
entrance for all whom he led up.   He put me in mind
of the country clown who is painted in the map for
leading Prince Eugene over the Alps [1].   He had a
bundle of papers in his hand, and producing several,
which, he said, were given to him by hands which he
knew Apollo would allow as passes, among which, methought, I saw some of my own writing, the whole
assembly was admitted, and gave, by their presence, a
new beauty and pleasure to these happy mansions.   I
found the man did not pretend to enter himself, but
served as a kind of forester in the lawns to direct passengers who, by their own merit or instructions he
procured for them, had virtue enough to travel that
way.   I looked very attentively upon this kind, homely
benefactor, and forgive me, Mr Spectator, if I own
to you I took him for yourself.   We were no sooner
entered but we were sprinkled three times with the
water of the fountain Aganippe, which had power to
deliver us from all harms, but only envy, which reached
even to the end of our journey.   We had not proceeded
far in the middle path when we arrived at the summit
of the hill, where there immediately appeared to us
two figures which extremely engaged my attention; the
one was a young nymph in the prime of her youth and
beauty; she had wings on her shoulders and feet, and
was able to transport herself to the most distant regions
in the smallest space of time.   She was continually
varying her dress, sometimes into the most natural and
becoming habits in the world, and at others into the
most wild and freakish garb that can be imagined.
There stood by her a man full-aged and of great
gravity, who corrected her inconsistencies by showing
them in this mirror, and still flung her affected and
unbecoming ornaments down the mountain, which fell
in the plain below, and were gathered up and wore
with great satisfaction by those that inhabited it.   The
name of the nymph was Fancy, the daughter of Liberty,
the most beautiful of all the mountain nymphs.   The
other was Judgment, the offspring of Time, and the only
child he acknowledged to be his.   A youth who sat upon

---

[1] *Cf.* No. 340.

a throne just between them was their genuine offspring; his name was Wit, and his seat was composed of the works of the most celebrated authors. I could not but see with a secret joy, that though the Greeks and Romans made the majority, yet our own countrymen were the next both in number and dignity. I was now at liberty to take a full prospect of that delightful region. I was inspired with new vigour and life, and saw everything in nobler and more pleasing view than before; I breathed a purer ether in a sky which was a continued azure gilded with perpetual sunshine. The two summits of the mountain rose on each side, and formed in the midst a most delicious vale, the habitation of the Muses, and of such as had composed works worthy of immortality. Apollo was seated upon a throne of gold, and for a canopy an aged laurel spread its boughs and its shade over his head. His bow and quiver lay at his feet. He held his harp in his hand, whilst the Muses round about him celebrated with hymns his victory over the serpent Python, and sometimes sung in softer notes the loves of Leucothoe and Daphnis. Homer, Virgil, and Milton were seated the next to him. Behind were a great number of others, among whom I was surprised to see some in the habit of Laplanders, who, notwithstanding the uncouthness of their dress, had lately obtained a place upon the mountain [1]. I saw Pindar walking all alone, no one daring to accost him till Cowley [2] joined himself to him; but growing weary of one who almost walked him out of breath, he left him for Horace and Anacreon, with whom he seemed infinitely delighted.

A little further I saw another group of figures; I made up to them, and found it was Socrates dictating to Xenophon and the spirit of Plato; but most of all Musæus had the greatest audience about him. I was at too great a distance to hear what he said or to discover the faces of his hearers, only I thought I now perceived Virgil, who had joined them, and stood in a posture full of admiration at the harmony of his words.

Lastly, at the very brink of the hill I saw Boccalini sending despatches to the world below of what hap-

[1] See the Lapland ode in Nos. 366 and 406.
[2] Cowley published *Pindarique Odes, written in imitation of the Style and Manner of the Odes of Pindar*.

pened upon Parnassus; but I perceived he did it without leave of the Muses and by stealth, and was unwilling to have them revised by Apollo. I could now from this height and serene sky behold the infinite cares and anxieties with which mortals below fought out their way through the maze of life. I saw the path of virtue lie straight before them, whilst Interest, or some malicious demon, still hurried them out of the way. I was at once touched with pleasure at my own happiness, and compassion at the sight of their inextricable errors. Here the two contending passions rose so high, that they were inconsistent with the sweet repose I enjoyed, and awaking with a sudden start, the only consolation I could admit of for my loss was the hopes that this relation of my dream will not displease you.          T.

---

No. 515.          *Tuesday, Oct. 21, 1712*          [STEELE

*Pudet me et miseret qui harum mores cantabat mihi Monuisse frustra.*          TER., *Heaut.*, Act i, sc. 2

MR SPECTATOR,—I am obliged to you for printing the account I lately sent you of a coquette who disturbed a sober congregation in the city of London [1]. That intelligence ended at her taking coach, and bidding the driver go where he knew. I could not leave her so, but dogged her, as hard as she drove, to Paul's Churchyard, where there was a stop of coaches attending company coming out of the cathedral. This gave me opportunity to hold up a crown to her coachman, who gave me the signal, and that he would hurry on and make no haste, as you know the way is when they favour a chase. By his many kind blunders, driving against other coaches and slipping off some of his tackle, I could keep up with him, and lodged my fine lady in the parish of St James's. As I guessed when I first saw her at church, her business is to win hearts and throw 'em away, regarding nothing but the triumph. I have had the happiness, by tracing her through all with whom I heard she was acquainted, to find one who was intimate with a friend of mine, and to be introduced to her notice. I have made so good use of

---

[1] See No. 503.

my time as to procure from that intimate of hers one of her letters which she writ to her when in the country. This epistle of her own may serve to alarm the world against her in ordinary life, as mine, I hope, did those who shall behold her at church. The letter was written last winter to the lady who gave it me; and I doubt not but you will find it the soul of a happy self-loving dame, that takes all the admiration she can meet with, and returns none of it in love to her admirers :

'DEAR JENNY,—I am glad to find you are likely to be disposed of in marriage so much to your approbation, as you tell me. You say you are afraid only of me, for I shall laugh at your spouse's airs. I beg of you not to fear it, for I am too nice a discerner to laugh at any but whom most other people think fine fellows; so that your dear may bring you hither as soon as his horses are in case enough to appear in town, and you be very safe against any raillery you may apprehend from me; for I am surrounded with coxcombs of my own making, who are all ridiculous in a manner. Your goodman, I presume, can't exert himself. As men who cannot raise their fortunes, and are uneasy under the incapacity of shining in courts, rail at ambition, so do awkward and insipid women, who cannot warm the hearts and charm the eyes of men, rail at affection. But she that has the joy of seeing a man's heart leap into his eyes at beholding her, is in no pain for want of esteem among a crew of that part of her own sex who have no spirit but that of envy, and no language but that of malice. I do not in this, I hope, express myself insensible of the merit of Leodacia, who lowers her beauty to all but her husband, and never spreads her charms but to gladden him who has a right in them. I say, I do honour to those who can be coquettes and are not such; but I despise all who would be so, and, in despair of arriving at it themselves, hate and vilify all those who can. But be that as it will, in answer to your desire of knowing my history : One of my chief present pleasures is in country-dances; and in obedience to me, as well as the pleasure of coming up to me with a good grace, showing themselves in their address to others in my presence, and the like opportunities, they are all proficients that way; and I had the happiness of being the other night where we made six couple, and every woman's partner a professed lover of mine. The wildest imagination cannot form to itself, on any occasion, higher delight than I acknowledge myself to have been in all that evening. I chose out of my admirers a set of men who most love me, and gave them partners of such of my own sex who most envied me.

'My way is, when any man who is my admirer pretends to give himself airs of merit, as at this time a certain gentleman you know did, to mortify him by favouring in his presence the most insignificant creature I can find. At this ball I was led into the company by pretty Mr Fanfly, who, you know, is the most obsequious, well-shaped, well-bred woman's man in town. I at first entrance declared him my partner if I danced at all, which put the whole assembly into a grin, as forming no terrors from such a rival. But we had not been long in the room before I overheard the meritorious gentleman above mentioned say with an oath, "There is no raillery in the thing, she certainly loves the puppy." My gentleman, when we were dancing, took an occasion to be very soft in his oglings upon a lady he danced with, and whom he knew of all women I love most to outshine. The contest began who should plague the other most. I, who do not care a farthing for him, had no hard task to outvex him. I made Fanfly, with a very little encouragement, cut capers *coupée*, and then sink with all the air and tenderness imaginable. When he performed this, I observed the gentleman you know of fall into the same way, and imitate as well as he could the despised Fanfly. I cannot well give you, who are so grave a country lady, the idea of the joy we have when we see a stubborn heart breaking, or a man of sense turning fool for our sakes; but this happened to our friend, and I expect his attendance whenever I go to church, to court, to the play, or the park. This is a sacrifice due to us women of genius, who have the eloquence of beauty, an easy mien. I mean by an easy mien, one which can be on occasion easily affected. For I must tell you, dear Jenny, I hold one maxim, which is an uncommon one, to wit, that our greatest charms are owing to affectation. 'Tis to that that our arms can lodge so quietly just over our hips, and the fan can play without any force or motion but just of the wrist. 'Tis to affectation we owe the pensive attention of Deidamia at a tragedy, the scornful approbation of Dulcimara at a comedy, and the lowly aspect of Lanquicelsa at a sermon.

'To tell you the plain truth, I know no pleasure but in being admired, and have yet never failed of attaining the approbation of the man whose regard I had a mind to. You see all the men who make a figure in the world (as wise a look as they are pleased to put upon the matter) are moved by the same vanity as I am. What is there in ambition, but to make other people's wills depend upon yours? This indeed is not to be aimed at by one who has a genius no higher than to think of being a very good housewife in a country gentleman's family. The care of poultry and pigs are great enemies to the countenance. The vacant look of a fine lady is not to be preserved if she admits anything to take up her thoughts but her own dear person. But I interrupt you too long from your cares, and myself from my conquests.

I am, Madam,

Your most humble Servant'.

Give me leave, Mr Spectator, to add her friend's answer to this epistle, who is a very discreet, ingenious woman :

'DEAR GATTY,—I take your raillery in very good part, and am obliged to you for the free air with which you speak of your own gaieties. But this is but a barren superficial pleasure; indeed[1], Gatty, we are made for man, and in serious sadness I must tell you, whether you yourself know it or no, all these gallantries tend to no other end but to be a wife and mother as fast as you can. I am, Madam,

O.　　　　　　Your most humble[2] Servant'

---

[1] 'For indeed' (folio).　　　　[2] 'Obedient' (folio).

No. 516.     *Wednesday, Oct. 22, 1712*     [STEELE

*Immortale odium et nunquam sanabile vulnus.*
*Inde furor vulgo, quod numina vicinorum*
*Odit uterque locus, quum solos credit habendos*
*Esse Deos, quos ipse colit.*          JUV., Sat. xv, 34, 36–38

OF all the monstrous passions and opinions which
have crept into the world, there is none so wonderful
as that those who profess the common name of
Christians should pursue each other with rancour and
hatred for differences in their way of following the
example of their Saviour. It seems so natural that
all who pursue the steps of any leader should form
themselves after his manners, that it is impossible to
account for effects so different from what we might
expect from those who profess themselves followers of
the highest pattern of meekness and charity, but by
ascribing such effects to the ambition and corruption
of those who are so audacious, with souls full of fury,
to serve at the altars of the God of peace.

The massacres to which the Church of Rome has
animated the ordinary people are dreadful instances
of the truth of this observation; and whoever reads
the history of the Irish rebellion, and the cruelties
which ensued thereupon, will be sufficiently convinced to what rage poor ignorants may be worked
up by those who profess holiness, and become incen-
diaries, and, under the dispensation of grace, promote
evils abhorrent to nature.

This subject and catastrophe, which deserve so well
to be remarked by the Protestant world, will, I doubt
not, be considered by the reverend and learned pre-
late [1] that preaches to-morrow before many of the
descendants of those who perished on that lamentable day, in a manner suitable to the occasion, and
worthy his own great virtue and eloquence.

[1] Dr St George Ashe, Bishop of Clogher, preached to the Irish
Protestants in London, at St Clement's Danes Church, on October
23, 1712 (No. 527, advertisement).

I shall not dwell upon it any further, but only transcribe out of a little tract, called the *Christian Hero*, published in 1701, what I find there in honour of the renowned hero, William III, who rescued that nation from the repetition of the same disasters. His late Majesty, of glorious memory, and the most Christian king, are considered at the conclusion of that treatise as heads of the Protestant and Roman Catholic world in the following manner :

' There were not ever, before the entrance of the Christian name into the world, men who have maintained a more renowned carriage than the two great rivals who possess the full fame of the present age, and will be the theme and examination of the future. They are exactly formed by nature for those ends to which Heaven seems to have sent them amongst us : both animated with a restless desire of glory, but pursue it by different means, and with different motives; to one it consists in an extensive undisputed empire over his subjects, to the other in their rational and voluntary obedience : one's happiness is founded in their want of power, the other's in their want of desire to oppose him : the one enjoys the summit of fortune with the luxury of a Persian, the other with the moderation of a Spartan : one is made to oppress, the other to relieve the oppressed : the one is satisfied with the pomp and ostentation of power to prefer and debase his inferiors, the other delighted only with the cause and foundation of it to cherish and protect 'em : to one therefore religion is but a convenient disguise, to the other a vigorous motive of action.

' For without such ties of real and solid honour, there is no way of forming a monarch, but after the Machiavelian scheme, by which a prince must ever seem to have all virtues, but really to be master of none, but is to be liberal, merciful, and just only as they serve his interests; while, with the noble art of hypocrisy, empire would be to be extended, and new conquests be made by new devices, by which prompt

address his creatures might insensibly give law in the
business of life, by leading men in the entertainment
of it [1].

' Thus when words and show are apt to pass for
the substantial things they are only to express, there
would need no more to enslave a country but to adorn
a court; for while every man's vanity makes him
believe himself capable of becoming luxury, enjoyments are a ready bait for sufferings, and the hopes
of preferment invitations to servitude, which slavery
would be coloured with all the agreements, as they
call it, imaginable.   The noblest arts and artists, the
finest pens and most elegant minds, jointly employed
to set it off, with the various embellishments of sumptuous  entertainments,  charming  assemblies  and
polished discourses : and those apostate abilities of
men, the adored monarch might profusely and skilfully encourage, while they flatter his virtue, and gild
his vice at so high a rate, that he, without scorn
of the one or love of the other, would alternately
and  occasionally  use  both,  so  that  his  bounty
should support him in his rapines, his mercy in his
cruelties.

' Nor is it to give things a more severe look than
is natural, to suppose such must be the consequences
of a prince's having no other pursuit than that of his
own glory; for, if we consider an infant born into the
world, and beholding itself the mightiest thing in it,
itself the present admiration and future prospect of
a fawning people, who profess themselves great or
mean, according to the figure he is to make amongst
them, what fancy would not be debauched to believe
they were but what they professed themselves, his
mere creatures, and use them as such by purchasing
with their lives a boundless renown, which he, for

[1] In the *Christian Hero* the paragraph proceeds thus : ' And making
their great monarch the fountain of all that's delicate and refined,
and his court the model for opinions in pleasure, as well as the
pattern in dress ; which might prevail so far upon an undiscerning
world as (to accomplish it or its approaching slavery) to make it
receive a superfluous babble for an universal language.'

want of a more just prospect, would place in the
number of his slaves and the extent of his territories;
such undoubtedly would be the tragical effects of a
prince's living with no religion, which are not to be
surpassed but by his having a false one.

'If ambition were spirited with zeal, what would
follow, but that his people should be converted into
an army, whose swords can make right in power, and
solve controversy in belief? And if men should be
stiff-necked to the doctrine of that visible Church,
let them be contented with an oar and a chain,
in the midst of stripes and anguish, to contemplate
on him, whose yoke is easy, and whose burthen is
light.

'With a tyranny begun on his own subjects, and
indignation that others draw their breath independent
of his frown or smile, why should he not proceed to
the seizure of the world? And if nothing but the
thirst of sway were the motive of his actions, why
should treaties be other than mere words, or solemn
national compacts be anything but an halt in the
march of that army, who are never to lay down their
arms until all men are reduced to the necessity of
hanging their lives on his wayward will; who might
supinely, and at leisure, expiate his own sins by
other men's sufferings, while he daily meditates new
slaughter, and new conquest?

'For mere man, when giddy with unbridled power,
is an insatiate idol, not to be appeased with myriads
offered to his pride, which may be puffed up by the
adulation of a base and prostrate world into an
opinion that he is something more than human, by
being something less. And alas! what is there that
mortal man will not believe of himself when compli-
mented with the attributes of God? He can then
conceive thoughts of a power as omnipresent as his.
But should there be such a foe of mankind now upon
earth, have our sins so far provoked Heaven, that we
are left utterly naked to his fury? Is there no power,
no leader, no genius, that can conduct and animate

us to our death or our defence? Yes, our great God never gave one to reign by His permission, but He gave to another also to reign by His grace.

' All the circumstances of the illustrious life of our prince seem to have conspired to make him the check and bridle of tyranny; for his mind has been strengthened and confirmed by one continued struggle, and Heaven has educated him by adversity to a quick sense of the distresses and miseries of mankind, which he was born to redress. In just scorn of the trivial glories and light ostentations of power, that glorious instrument of Providence moves like that, in a steady, calm, and silent course, independent either of applause or calumny, which renders him, if not in a political, yet in a moral, a philosophic, a heroic, and a Christian sense, an absolute monarch. Who satisfied with this unchangeable, just, and ample glory, must needs turn all his regards from himself to the service of others; for he begins his enterprises with his own share in the success of them; for integrity bears in itself its reward, nor can that which depends not on event ever know disappointment.

' With the undoubted character of a glorious captain, and (what he much more values than the most splendid titles) that of a sincere and honest man, he is the hope and stay of Europe, an universal good not to be engrossed by us only; for distant potentates implore his friendship, and injured empires court his assistance. He rules the world, not by an invasion of the people of the earth, but the address of its princes; and if that world should be again roused from the repose which his prevailing arms had given it, why should we not hope that there is an Almighty, by whose influence the terrible enemy, that thinks himself prepared for battle, may find he is but ripe for destruction, and that there may be in the womb of Time great incidents, which may make the catastrophe of a prosperous life as unfortunate as the particular scenes of it were successful. For there does not want a skilful eye and resolute arm to observe and grasp the occasion.  A prince, who from——[1]

Fuit Ilium, et ingens
Gloria.                        VIRG.[2]'          T.

No. 517.     *Thursday, Oct. 23, 1712*     [ADDISON

*Heu pietas! heu prisca fides!*  VIRG., *Æn.* vi, 879

WE last night received a piece of ill news at our club, which very sensibly afflicted every one of us. I question not but my readers themselves will be troubled at the hearing of it.  To keep them no longer in suspense, Sir Roger de Coverley is dead [3].  He departed this life at his house in the country, after a few weeks' sickness.  Sir Andrew Freeport has a letter from one of his correspondents in those parts, that informs him the old man caught a cold at the county sessions, as he was very warmly promoting an address of his own penning, in which he succeeded according to his wishes.  But this particular comes from a Whig Justice of Peace, who was always Sir Roger's enemy and antagonist.  I have letters both from the chaplain and Captain Sentry which mention nothing of it, but are filled with many particulars to

---

[1] In the *Christian Hero*—published before the death of King William —the sentence proceeds thus : ' A Prince who from just notion of his duty to that Being to whom he must be accountable, has in the service of his fellow-creatures a noble contempt of pleasures, and patience of labours, to whom 'tis hereditary to be the guardian and asserter of the native rights and liberties of mankind ' ; and after a few clauses summarising William's character, the book closed with a prayer that Heaven would guard his life.

[2] *Æneid*, ii, 325.

[3] In No. 1 of the *Bee* (for February 1733) Eustace Budgell, who probably was the intimate friend of Addison's to whom he there refers, said of Sir Roger de Coverley, ' Mr Addison was so fond of this character that a little before he laid down the *Spectator* (foreseeing that some nimble gentleman would catch up his pen the moment he quitted it) he said to an intimate friend, with a certain warmth in his expression which he was not often guilty of, "By God, I'll kill Sir Roger, that nobody else may murder him."'  Some have thought that this alleged exclamation referred to the story told of Sir Roger in No. 410 ; but see the note to that paper, and No. 544.

the honour of the good old man. I have likewise a
letter from the butler, who took so much care of me
last summer when I was at the knight's house. As
my friend the butler mentions, in the simplicity of
his heart, several circumstances the others have
passed over in silence, I shall give my reader a copy
of his letter, without any alteration or diminution :

HONOURED SIR,—Knowing that you was my old
master's good friend, I could not forbear sending you
the melancholy news of his death, which has afflicted
the whole country, as well as his poor servants, who
loved him, I may say, better than we did our lives.
I am afraid he caught his death the last county
sessions, where he would go to see justice done to a
poor widow woman and her fatherless children that
had been wronged by a neighbouring gentleman; for
you know, sir, my good master was always the poor
man's friend. Upon his coming home, the first complaint he made was that he had lost his roast-beef
stomach, not being able to touch a sirloin, which was
served up according to custom; and you know he used
to take great delight in it. From that time forward he
grew worse and worse, but still kept a good heart to
the last. Indeed we were once in great hope of his
recovery, upon a kind message that was sent him from
the widow lady whom he had made love to the forty
last years of his life; but this only proved a lightening
before death. He has bequeathed to this lady, as a
token of his love, a great pearl necklace and a couple
of silver bracelets set with jewels, which belonged to
my good old lady his mother : he has bequeathed the
fine white gelding, that he used to ride a-hunting upon,
to his chaplain, because he thought he would be kind
to him, and has left you all his books. He has, more-
over, bequeathed to the chaplain a very pretty tene-
ment with good lands about it. It being a very cold
day when he made his will, he left for mourning to
every man in the parish a great frieze coat, and to
every woman a black riding-hood. It was a most
moving sight to see him take leave of his poor servants,
commending us all for our fidelity, whilst we were not
able to speak a word for weeping. As we most of us

are grown grey-headed in our dear master's service, he has left us pensions and legacies, which we may live very comfortably upon the remaining part of our days. He has bequeathed a great deal more in charity, which is not yet come to my knowledge, and it is peremptorily said in the parish that he has left money to build a steeple to the church; for he was heard to say some time ago, that if he lived two years longer Coverley Church should have a steeple to it. The chaplain tells everybody that he made a very good end, and never speaks of him without tears. He was buried, according to his own directions, among the family of the Coverleys, on the left hand of his father, Sir Arthur. The coffin was carried by six of his tenants, and the pall held up by six of the quorum : the whole parish followed the corpse with heavy hearts, and in their mourning suits, the men in frieze, and the women in riding-hoods. Captain Sentry, my master's nephew, has taken possession of the hall-house and the whole estate. When my old master saw him a little before his death, he shook him by the hand, and wished him joy of the estate which was falling to him, desiring him only to make a good use of it, and to pay the several legacies and the gifts of charity which he told him he had left as quit-rents upon the estate. The captain truly seems a courteous man, though he says but little. He makes much of those whom my master loved, and shows great kindness to the old house-dog that you know my poor master was so fond of. It would have gone to your heart to have heard the moans the dumb creature made on the day of my master's death. He has ne'er joyed himself since; no more has any of us. 'Twas the melancholiest day for the poor people that ever happened in Worcestershire. This being all from, honoured Sir,

Your most sorrowful Servant,<br>
EDWARD BISCUIT

*P.S.*—My master desired, some weeks before he died, that a book which comes up to you by the carrier should be given to Sir Andrew Freeport in his name.

This letter, notwithstanding the poor butler's manner of writing it, gave us such an idea of our good

old friend, that upon the reading of it there was not
a dry eye in the club. Sir Andrew, opening the book,
found it to be a collection of Acts of Parliament.
There was in particular the Act of Uniformity, with
some passages in it marked by Sir Roger's own hand.
Sir Andrew found that they related to two or three
points, which he had disputed with Sir Roger the
last time he appeared at the club. Sir Andrew, who
would have been merry at such an incident on
another occasion, at the sight of the old man's handwriting burst into tears, and put the book into his
pocket. Captain Sentry informs me that the knight
has left rings and mourning for every one in the club.

                                                O.


No. 518.         *Friday, Oct. 24, 1712*         [STEELE

*Miserum est alienæ incumbere famæ
Ne collapsa ruant subductis tecta columnis.*
                            JUV., *Sat.* viii, 76

THIS being a day of business with me, I must make
the present entertainment like a treat at an house-
warming, out of such presents as have been sent me
by my guests. The first dish which I serve up is a
letter come fresh to my hand :

   MR. SPECTATOR,—It is with inexpressible sorrow that
I hear of the death of good Sir Roger, and do heartily
condole with you upon so melancholy an occasion. I
think you ought to have blackened the edges of a paper
which brought us so ill news, and to have had it
stamped likewise in black. It is expected of you that
you should write his epitaph, and, if possible, fill his
place in the club with as worthy and diverting a
member. I question not but you will receive many
recommendations from the public of such as will
appear candidates for that post.
   Since I am talking of death, and have mentioned an
epitaph, I must tell you, sir, that I have made discovery of a churchyard in which I believe you might
spend an afternoon, with great pleasure to yourself

and to the public : it belongs to the church of Stebon Heath, commonly called Stepney. Whether or no it be that the people of that parish have a particular genius for an epitaph, or that there be some poet among them who undertakes that work by the great [1], I can't tell, but there are more remarkable inscriptions in that place than in any other I have met with, and I may say without vanity that there is not a gentleman in England better read in tombstones than myself, my studies having laid very much in churchyards. I shall beg leave to send you a couple of epitaphs, for a sample of those I have just now mentioned. They are written in a different manner, the first being in the diffused and luxuriant, the second in the close contracted style. The first has much of the simple and pathetic; the second is something light, but nervous. The first is thus :

> Here Thomas Sapper lies interred. Ah, why !
> Born in New England, did in London die ;
> Was the third son of eight, begot upon
> His mother Martha by his father John.
> Much favoured by his prince he 'gan to be,
> But nipt by death at th' age of twenty-three.
> Fatal to him was that we small-pox name,
> By which his mother and two brethren came
> Also to breathe their last nine years before,
> And now have left their father to deplore
> The loss of all his children with his wife,
> Who was the joy and comfort of his life.

The second is as follows :

> Here lies the body of Daniel Saul,
> Spittle-fields weaver, and that's all.

I will not dismiss you, whilst I am upon this subject, without sending a short epitaph which I once met with, though I cannot possibly recollect the place. The thought of it is serious, and, in my opinion, the finest that ever I met with upon this occasion. You know, sir, it is usual, after having told us the name of the person who lies interred, to launch out into his praises. This epitaph takes a quite contrary turn, having been made by the person himself some time before his death :

[1] Wholesale, or, as might now be said, by the gross.

*Hic jacet R. C. in expectatione diei supremi. Qualis erat dies iste indicabit.*

(Here lieth R. C. in expectation of the last day. What sort of a man he was that day will discover.)[1]

I am, Sir, &c.

The following letter is dated from Cambridge [2] :

SIR,—Having lately read, among your speculations, an essay upon Physiognomy [3], I cannot but think that if you made a visit to this ancient university, you might receive very considerable lights upon that subject, there being scarce a young fellow in it who does not give certain indications of his particular humour and disposition, conformable to the rules of that art. In courts and cities everybody lays a constraint upon his countenance, and endeavours to look like the rest of the world; but the youth of this place, having not yet formed themselves by conversation, and the knowledge of the world, give their limbs and features their full play.

As you have considered human nature in all its lights, you must be extremely well apprised, that there is a very close correspondence between the outward and the inward man; that scarce the least dawning, the least parturiency towards a thought can be stirring in the mind of man, without producing a suitable revolution in his exteriors, which will easily discover itself to an adept in the theory of the phiz. Hence it is that the intrinsic worth and merit of a son of Alma Mater is ordinarily calculated from the caste of his visage, the contour of his person, the mechanism of his dress, the disposition of his limbs, the manner of his gait and air, with a number of circumstances of equal consequence and information. The practitioners in this art often make use of a gentleman's eyes, to give 'em light into the posture of his brains; take a handle from his nose, to judge of the size of his intellects; and interpret the overmuch visibility and pertness of

1 The following epitaph on Thomas Crouch, who died in 1679, is quoted in the *European Magazine* for July 1787 :

Aperiat Deus tumulos, et educat nos de sepulchris,
Qualis eram, dies isti hæc cum venerit, scies.

2 This letter was by 'Orator' Henley. See No. 396.
3 See Nos. 86, 206.

one ear, as an infallible mark of reprobation, and a sign the owner of so saucy a member fears neither God nor man. In conformity to this scheme, a contracted brow, a lumpish downcast look, a sober sedate pace, with both hands dangling quiet and steady in lines exactly parallel to each lateral pocket of the galligaskins, is logic, metaphysics, and mathematics in perfection. So likewise the *belles lettres* are typified by a saunter in the gait, a fall of one wing of the peruke backward, an insertion of one hand in the fob, and a negligent swing of the other, with a pinch of right and fine Barcelona between finger and thumb, a due quantity of the same upon the upper lip, and a noddle-case loaden with pulvil [1]. Again, a grave, solemn stalking pace is heroic poetry, and politics; an unequal one, a genius for the ode, and the modern ballad; and an open breast, with an audacious display of the Holland shirt, is construed a fatal tendency to the art military.

I might be much larger upon these hints, but I know whom I write to. If you can graft any speculation upon them, or turn them to the advantage of the persons concerned in them, you will do a work very becoming the British *Spectator*, and oblige

Your very humble Servant,

TOM TWEER

No. 519.        *Saturday, Oct. 25, 1712*        [ADDISON

*Inde hominum, pecudumque genus, vitæque volantum,
Et quæ marmoreo fert monstra sub æquore pontus.*

VIRG., Æn. vi, 728

THOUGH there is a great deal of pleasure in contemplating the material world, by which I mean that system of bodies into which Nature has so curiously wrought the mass of dead matter, with the several relations which those bodies bear to one another; there is still, methinks, something more wonderful and surprising in contemplations on the world of life, by which I mean all those animals with which every

[1] A sweet-scented powder.

part of the universe is furnished.  The material world
is only the shell of the universe; the world of life
are its inhabitants.

If we consider those parts of the material world
which lie the nearest to us, and are therefore subject
to our observations and inquiries, it is amazing to
consider the infinity of animals with which it is
stocked.  Every part of matter is peopled; every
green leaf swarms with inhabitants.  There is scarce
a single humour in the body of a man, or of any
other animal, in which our glasses do not discover
myriads of living creatures.  The surface of animals
is also covered with other animals, which are in the
same manner the basis of other animals that live
upon it; nay, we find in the most solid bodies, as
in marble itself, innumerable cells and cavities that
are crowded with such imperceptible inhabitants as
are too little for the naked eye to discover.  On the
other hand, if we look into the more bulky parts
of nature, we see the seas, lakes, and rivers teeming
with numberless kinds of living creatures.  We find
every mountain and marsh, wilderness and wood,
plentifully stocked with birds and beasts, and every
part of matter affording proper necessaries and conveniences for the livelihood of multitudes which
inhabit it.

The author of the *Plurality of Worlds* [1] draws a
very good argument from this consideration for the
peopling of every planet, as indeed it seems very probable from the analogy of reason, that if no part of
matter which we are acquainted with lies waste and
useless, those great bodies which are at such a distance from us should not be desert and unpeopled,
but rather that they should be furnished with beings
adapted to their respective situations.

Existence is a blessing to those beings only which
are endowed with perception, and is in a manner
thrown away upon dead matter, any further than as
it is subservient to beings which are conscious of

[1] Fontenelle, *Entretiens sur la Pluralité des Mondes,* Troisième Soir.

their existence. Accordingly we find, from the bodies which lie under our observation, that matter is only made as the basis and support of animals, and that there is no more of the one than what is necessary for the existence of the other.

Infinite goodness is of so communicative a nature, that it seems to delight in the conferring of existence upon every degree of perceptive [1] being. As this is a speculation which I have often pursued with great pleasure to myself, I shall enlarge farther upon it by considering that part of the scale of beings which comes within our knowledge.

There are some living creatures which are raised but just above dead matter. To mention only that species of shell-fish, which are formed in the fashion of a cone, that grow to the surface of several rocks, and immediately die upon their being severed from the place where they grow. There are many other creatures but one remove from these, which have no other sense besides that of feeling and taste. Others have still an additional one of hearing; others of smell, and others of sight. It is wonderful to observe by what a gradual progress the world of life advances through a prodigious variety of species, before a creature is formed that is complete in all its senses, and even among these there is such a different degree of perfection in the sense, which one animal enjoys beyond what appears in another, that though the sense in different animals be distinguished by the same common denomination, it seems almost of a different nature. If after this we look into the several inward perfections of cunning and sagacity, or what we generally call instinct, we find them rising after the same manner, imperceptibly one above another, and receiving additional improvements, according to the species in which they are implanted. This progress in nature is so very gradual, that the most perfect of an inferior species comes very near to the most imperfect of that which is immediately above it.

---

[1] 'Preceptive', by mistake, in the original editions.

The exuberant and overflowing goodness of the
Supreme Being, whose mercy extends to all His
works, is plainly seen, as I have before hinted, from
His having made so very little matter, at least what
falls within our knowledge, that does not swarm with
life : nor is His goodness less seen in the diversity
than in the multitude of living creatures.  Had He
only made one species of animals, none of the rest
would have enjoyed the happiness of existence; He
has, therefore, specified in His creation every degree
of life, every capacity of being.  The whole chasm
in nature, from a plant to a man, is filled up with
diverse kinds of creatures, rising one over another,
by such a gentle and easy ascent that the little tran-
sitions and deviations from one species to another
are almost insensible.  This intermediate space is so
well husbanded and managed that there is scarce a
degree of perception which does not appear in some
one part of the world of life.  Is the goodness or
wisdom of the Divine Being more manifested in this
His proceeding?

There is a consequence, besides those I have
already mentioned, which seems very naturally de-
ducible from the foregoing considerations.  If the
scale of being rises by such a regular progress so high
as man, we may by a parity of reason suppose that it
still proceeds gradually through those beings which
are of a superior nature to him, since there is an
infinitely greater space and room for different degrees
of perfection, between the Supreme Being and man,
than between man and the most despicable insect.
This consequence of so great a variety of beings which
are superior to us, from that variety which is inferior
to us, is made by Mr Locke in a passage which I
shall here set down [1], after having premised that notwithstanding there is such infinite room between man
and his Maker for the creative power to exert itself
in, it is impossible that it should ever be filled up,
since there will be still an infinite gap or distance

[1] *Essay concerning Human Understanding,* Book iii, chap. vi, sec. 12.

between the highest created being and the power which produced him :

That there should be more species of intelligent creatures above us than there are of sensible and material below us, is probable to me from hence ; that in all the visible corporeal world we see no chasms, or no gaps. All quite down from us the descent is by easy steps, and a continued series of things, that in each remove differ very little one from the other. There are fishes that have wings, and are not strangers to the airy region : and there are some birds that are inhabitants of the water, whose blood is cold as fishes, and their flesh so like in taste that the scrupulous are allowed them on fish-days.  There are animals so near of kin both to birds and beasts, that they are in the middle between both : amphibious animals link the terrestrial and aquatic together ; seals live at land and at sea, and porpoises have the warm blood and entrails of a hog, not to mention what is confidently reported of mermaids or seamen.  There are some brutes that seem to have as much knowledge and reason as some that are called men ; and the animal and vegetable kingdoms are so nearly joined that if you will take the lowest of one, and the highest of the other, there will scarce be perceived any great difference between them ; and so on till we come to the lowest and the most inorganical parts of matter, we shall find everywhere that the several species are linked together, and differ but in almost insensible degrees.  And when we consider the infinite power and wisdom of the Maker, . we have reason to think that it is suitable to the magnificent harmony of the universe, and the great design and infinite goodness of the Architect, that the species of creatures should also, by gentle degrees, ascend upward from us toward His infinite perfection, as we see they gradually descend from us downward : which, if it be probable, we have reason then to be persuaded that there are far more species of creatures above us than there are beneath ; we being in degrees of perfection much more remote from the infinite being of God than we are from the lowest state of being, and that which approaches nearest to nothing.  And yet of all those distinct species we have no clear distinct ideas.

In this system of being there is no creature so wonderful in its nature, and which so much deserves our particular attention, as man, who fills up the middle space between the animal and intellectual nature, the visible and invisible world, and is that link in the chain of beings which has been often termed the *nexus utriusque mundi.* So that he, who in one respect is associated with angels and archangels, may look upon a being of infinite perfection as his father, and the highest order of spirits as his brethren, may in another respect say to corruption, ' Thou art my father, and to the worm, Thou art my mother and my sister [1].'

---

No. 520.      *Monday, Oct. 27, 1712*      [FRANSHAM [2]

*Quis desiderio sit pudor aut modus*
*Tam cari capitis?*                    HOR., 1 *Od.* xxiv, 1

MR. SPECTATOR,—The just value you have expressed for the matrimonial state, is the reason that I now venture to write to you, without fear of being ridiculous, and confess to you, that though it is three months since I lost a very agreeable woman, who was my wife, my sorrow is still fresh; and I am often, in the midst of company, upon any circumstance that revives her memory, with a reflection what she would say or do on such an occasion; I say, upon any occurrence of that nature, which I can give you a sense of, though I cannot express it wholly, I am all over softness, and am obliged to retire, and give way to a few sighs and tears, before I can be easy. I cannot but recommend the subject of male widowhood to you, and beg of you to touch upon it by the first opportunity. To those who have not lived like husbands during the lives of their spouses, this would be a tasteless jumble of words'; but to such (of whom there are not a few) who have enjoyed that state with the sentiments proper

---

[1] *Job* xvii, 14.
[2] The touching letter which occupies this number is stated to have been written by a Mr Fransham, of Norwich, of whom some particulars will be found in *The Dictionary of National Biography*, xx, 201, and in Wright's *Life of Defoe.*

for it, you will have every line which hits the sorrow attended with a tear of pity and consolation. For I know not by what goodness of Providence it is that every gush of passion is a step towards the relief of it; and there is a certain comfort in the very act of sorrowing, which, I suppose, arises from a secret consciousness in the mind, that the affliction it is under flows from a virtuous cause. My concern is not indeed so outrageous as at the first transport; for I think it has subsided rather into a soberer state of mind, than any actual perturbation of spirit. There might be rules formed for men's behaviour on this great incident, to bring them from that misfortune into the condition I am at present, which is, I think, that my sorrow has converted all roughness of temper into meekness, good-nature, and complacency. But, indeed, when in a serious and lonely hour I present my departed consort to my imagination with that air of persuasion in her countenance when I have been in passion, that sweet affability when I have been in good humour, that tender compassion when I have had anything which gave me uneasiness, I confess to you I am inconsolable, and my eyes gush with grief as if I had seen her but just then expire. In this condition I am broken in upon by a charming young woman, my daughter, who is the picture of what her mother was on her wedding-day. The good girl strives to comfort me; but how shall I let you know that all the comfort she gives me is to make my tears flow more easily? The child knows she quickens my sorrows, and rejoices my heart at the same time. Oh, ye learned, tell me by what word to speak a motion of the soul for which there is no name. When she kneels and bids me be comforted, she is my child; when I take her in my arms, and bid her say no more, she is my very wife, and is the very comforter I lament the loss of. I banish her the room, and weep aloud, that I have lost her mother, and that I have her.

Mr Spectator, I wish it were possible for you to have a sense of these pleasing perplexities; you might communicate to the guilty part of mankind, that they are incapable of the happiness which is in the very sorrows of the virtuous.

But pray spare me a little longer; give me leave to

tell you the manner of her death. She took leave of all her family, and bore the vain application of medi-cines with the greatest patience imaginable. When the physician told her she must certainly die, she desired, as well as she could, that all who were present, except myself, might depart the room. She said she had nothing to say, for she was resigned, and I knew all she knew that concerned us in this world; but she desired to be alone, that in the presence of God only she might, without interruption, do her last duty to me, of thanking me for all my kindness to her; adding, that she hoped in my last moments I should feel the same comfort for my goodness to her, as she did in that she had acquitted herself with honour, truth, and virtue to me.

I curb myself, and will not tell you that this kind-ness cut my heart in twain, when I expected an accusa-tion for some passionate starts of mine in some parts of our time together, to say nothing, but thank me for the good, if there was any good suitable to her own excellence! All that I had ever said to her, all the circumstances of sorrow and joy between us, crowded upon my mind in the same instant; and when immediately after I saw the pangs of death come upon that dear body which I had often embraced with transport; when I saw those cherishing eyes begin to be ghastly, and their last struggle to be to fix them-selves on me, how did I lose all patience! She expired in my arms, and in my distraction I thought I saw her bosom still heave. There was certainly life yet still left; I cried she just now spoke to me: but, alas! I grew giddy, and all things moved about me from the distemper of my own head; for the best of women was breathless, and gone for ever.

Now the doctrine I would, methinks, have you raise from this account I have given you is, that there is a certain equanimity in those who are good and just, which runs into their very sorrow, and disappoints the force of it. Though they must pass through afflictions in common with all who are in human nature, yet their conscious integrity shall undermine their affliction; nay, that very affliction shall add force to their integrity, from a reflection of the use of virtue in the hour of affliction. I sate down with a design to put you upon giving us rules how to overcome such griefs as these; but I should rather advise you to teach men to be capable of them.

You men of letters have what you call the fine taste in their apprehensions of what is properly done or said. There is something like this deeply grafted in the soul of him who is honest and faithful in all his thoughts and actions. Everything which is false, vicious, or unworthy is despicable to him, though all the world should approve it. At the same time he has the most lively sensibility in all enjoyments and sufferings which it is proper for him to have, where any duty of life is concerned. To want sorrow when you in decency and truth should be afflicted, is, I should think, a greater instance of a man's being a blockhead, than not to know the beauty of any passage in Virgil. You have not yet observed, Mr Spectator, that the fine gentlemen of this age set up for hardness of heart, and humanity has very little share in their pretences. He is a brave fellow who is always ready to kill a man he hates, but he does not stand in the same degree of esteem who laments for the woman he loves. I should fancy you might work up a thousand petty thoughts, by reflecting upon the persons most susceptible of the sort of sorrow I have spoken of; and I daresay you will find upon examination, that they are the wisest and the bravest of mankind who are most capable of it.        I am, Sir,

Your most humble Servant,

NORWICH,                                      F. I.[1]
7° *Octobris*, 1712
    T.


No. 521.        *Tuesday, Oct. 28, 1712*        [STEELE

*Vera redit facies, dissimulata perit.* PET. ARB.

MR SPECTATOR,—I have been for many years loud in this assertion, that there are very few that can see or hear, I mean that can report what they have seen or heard; and this through incapacity or prejudice, one of which disables almost every man who talks to you from representing things as he ought. For which

[1] 'F. J.' (folio).

reason I am come to a resolution of believing nothing I hear; and I contemn the man given to narration under the appellation of a matter-of-fact man : and according to me, a matter-of-fact man is one whose life and conversation is spent in the report of what is not matter of fact.

I remember when Prince Eugene was here, there was no knowing his height or figure, till you, Mr Spectator, gave the public satisfaction in that matter [1]. In relations, the force of the expression lies very often more in the look, the tone of voice, or the gesture, than the words themselves; which being repeated in any other manner by the undiscerning, bear a very different interpretation from their original meaning. I must confess, I formerly have turned this humour of mine to very good account; for whenever I heard any narrations uttered with extraordinary vehemence, and grounded upon considerable authority, I was always ready to lay any wager that it was not so. Indeed I never pretended to be so rash, as to fix the matter any particular way in opposition to theirs; but as there are an hundred ways of anything happening, besides that it has happened, I only controverted its falling out in that one manner as they settled it, and left it to the ninety-nine other ways, and consequently had more probability of success. I had arrived at a particular skill in warming a man so far in his narration, as to make him throw in a little of the marvellous, and then, if he has much fire, the next degree is the impossible. Now this is always the time for fixing the wager. But this requires the nicest management, otherwise very probably the dispute may arise to the old determination by battle. In these conceits I have been very fortunate, and have won some wagers of those who have professedly valued themselves upon intelligence, and have put themselves to great charge and expense to be misinformed considerably sooner than the rest of the world.

Having got a comfortable sum by this my opposition to public report, I have brought myself now to so great a perfection in inattention, more especially to party relations, that at the same time I seem with greedy ears to devour up the discourse, I certainly don't

[1] See No. 340.

know one word of it, but pursue my own course of thought, whether upon business or amusement, with much tranquillity. I say inattention, because a late Act of Parliament has secured all party-liars from the penalty of a wager[1], and consequently made it unprofitable to attend them. However, good breeding obliges a man to maintain the figure of the keenest attention, the true posture of which in a coffee-house I take to consist in leaning over a table, with the edge of it pressing hard upon your stomach; for the more pain the narration is received with the more gracious is your bending over; besides that, the narrator thinks you forget your pain by the pleasure of hearing him.

Fort Knock[2] has occasioned several very perplexed and inelegant heats and animosities; and there was one t'other day in a coffee-house where I was, that took upon him to clear that business to me, for he said he was there. I knew him to be that sort of man that had not strength of capacity to be informed of anything that depended merely upon his being an eyewitness, and therefore was fully satisfied he could give me no information, for the very same reason he believed he could, for he was there. However, I heard him with the same greediness as Shakespeare describes in the following lines :

> I saw a smith stand on his hammer, thus, . . .
> With open mouth swallowing a tailor's news[3].

I confess of late I have not been so much amazed at the declaimers in coffee-houses as I formerly was, being satisfied that they expect to be rewarded for their

[1] By 7 Anne, cap. 17, wagers laid upon a contingency relating to the war with France were declared void.

[2] Fort Knoque or Knock, an important post at the junction of the canals of Ypres and Furnes, was taken by surprise an October 6, 1712, by Captain De La Rue, of the Confederate army, who had ascertained the weakness of the garrison during a previous visit in disguise. So well managed was the attack that Captain De La Rue lost only two men. Three French companies, and one Swiss, were taken prisoners, besides a quantity of arms. The governor of Ypres offered Captain De La Rue a large reward if he would give up the fort, but the suggestion was rejected with scorn, and the French troops retired from before the place. On the 8th, Colonel Rommingen brought men and supplies to the aid of those holding the fort, and the French gave up the idea of recapturing it. Captain De La Rue received handsome rewards from the States-General.

[3] *King John*, Act iv, sc. 2.

vociferations.  Of these liars there are two sorts.  The genius of the first consists in much impudence and a strong memory; the others have added to these qualifications a good understanding and smooth language. These therefore have only certain heads, which they are as eloquent upon as they can, and may be called embellishers; the others repeat only what they hear from others as literally as their parts of zeal will permit, and are called reciters.  Here was a fellow in town some years ago, who used to divert himself by telling a lie at Charing Cross in the morning at eight of the clock, and then following it through all parts of the town till eight at night; at which time he came to a club of his friends, and diverted them with an account what censure it had at Will's in Covent Garden, how dangerous it was believed to be at Child's, and what inference they drew from it with relation to stocks at Jonathan's.  I have had the honour to travel with this gentleman I speak of in search of one of his falsehoods; and have been present when they have described the very man they have spoken to, as him who first reported it, tall or short, black or fair, a gentleman or a ragamuffin, according as they liked the intelligence.  I have heard one of our ingenious writers of news say, that when he has had a customer come with an advertisement of an apprentice or a wife run away, he has desired the advertiser to compose himself a little before he dictated the description of the offender : for when a person is put into a public paper by a man who is angry with him, the real description of such person is hid in the deformity with which the angry man described him; therefore this fellow always made his customers describe him as he would the day before he offended, or else he was sure he would never find him out.  These and many other hints I could suggest to you for the elucidation of all factions ; but I leave it to your own sagacity to improve or neglect this speculation.  I am, Sir,

Your most obedient humble Servant

Postscript to the *Spectator*, Numb. 502

N.B.—There are in the play of *The Self-Tormentor* of Terence's, which is allowed a most excellent comedy, several incidents which would draw tears from any man of sense, and not one which would move his laughter.                                T.


No. 522.      *Wednesday, Oct. 29, 1712*      [STEELE

*Adjuro nunquam eam me deserturum,*
*Non, si capiundos mihi sciam esse inimicos omneis homines.*
*Hanc mihi expetivi, contigit: conveniunt mores: valeant*
*Qui inter nos dissidium volunt: hanc, nisi mors,*
*Mi adimet nemo.*                      TER., *Andr.* Act iv, sc. 2

I SHOULD esteem myself a very happy man, if my speculations could in the least contribute to the rectifying the conduct of my readers in one of the most important affairs of life, to wit, their choice in marriage. This state is the foundation of community and the chief band of society; and I do not think I can be too frequent on subjects which may give light to my unmarried readers in a particular which is so essential to their following happiness or misery. A virtuous disposition, a good understanding, an agreeable person, and an easy fortune, are the things which should be chiefly regarded on this occasion. Because my present view is to direct a young lady, who, I think, is now in doubt whom to take of many lovers, I shall talk at this time to my female reader. The advantages, as I was going to say, of sense, beauty, and riches, are what are certainly the chief motives to a prudent young woman of fortune for changing her condition; but as she has to have her eye upon each of these, she is to ask herself whether the man who has most of these recommendations in the lump is not the most desirable. He that has excellent talents, with a moderate estate, and an agreeable person, is preferable to him who is only rich, if it were only that good faculties may purchase riches, but riches cannot purchase worthy endowments. I do not mean that wit, and a capacity to entertain, is what should be highly valued, except it is founded upon good nature and humanity. There are many

ingenious men whose abilities do little else but make
themselves and those about them uneasy : such are
those who are far gone in the pleasures of the town,
who cannot support life without quick sensations and
gay reflections, and are strangers to tranquillity, to
right reason, and a calm motion of spirits without
transport or dejection. These ingenious men, of all
men living, are most to be avoided by her who would
be happy in an husband. They are immediately
sated with possession, and must necessarily fly to
new acquisitions of beauty to pass away the whiling
moments and intervals of life; for with them every
hour is heavy that is not joyful. But there is a sort
of man of wit and sense that can reflect upon his
own make, and that of his partner, with the eyes of
reason and honour, and who believes he offends
against both these if he does not look upon the
woman (who chose him to be under his protection in
sickness and health) with the utmost gratitude,
whether from that moment she is shining or defective in person or mind : I say there are those who
think themselves bound to supply with good nature
the failings of those who love them, and who always
think those the objects of love and pity who came
to their arms the objects of joy and admiration.

Of this latter sort is Lysander, a man of wit, learning, sobriety, and good nature, of birth and estate
below no woman to accept, and of whom it might be
said, should he succeed in his present wishes, his
mistress raised his fortune, but not that she made it.
When a woman is deliberating with herself whom she
shall choose of many near each other in other pretensions, certainly he of best understanding is to be
preferred. Life hangs heavily in the repeated conversation of one who has no imagination to be fired
at the several occasions and objects which come
before him, or who cannot strike out of his reflections
new paths of pleasing discourse. Honest Will Thrash
and his wife, though not married above four months,
have scarce had a word to say to each other this six

weeks; and one cannot form to one's self a sillier picture than these two creatures in solemn pomp and plenty unable to enjoy their fortunes, and at a full stop among a crowd of servants, to whose taste of life they are beholden for the little satisfactions by which they can be understood to be so much as barely in being. The hours of the day, the distinctions of noon and night, dinner and supper, are the greatest notices they are capable of. This is perhaps representing the life of a very modest woman, joined to a dull fellow, more insipid than it really deserves; but I am sure it is not to exalt the commerce with an ingenious companion too high, to say that every new accident or object which comes into such a gentleman's way gives his wife new pleasures and satisfactions. The approbation of his words and actions is a continual new feast to her; nor can she enough applaud her good fortune in having her life varied every hour, her mind more improved, and her heart more glad from every circumstance which they meet with. He will lay out his invention in forming new pleasures and amusements, and make the fortune she has brought him subservient to the honour and reputation of her and hers. A man of sense who is thus obliged is ever contriving the happiness of her who did him so great a distinction; while the fool is ungrateful without vice; and never returns a favour because he is not sensible of it. I would, methinks, have so much to say for myself that if I fell into the hands of him who treated me ill, he should be sensible when he did so : his conscience should be of my side, whatever became of his inclination. I do not know but it is the insipid choice which has been made by those who have the care of young women, that the marriage state itself has been liable to so much ridicule. But a well-chosen love, moved by passion on both sides, and perfected by the generosity of one party, must be adorned with so many handsome incidents on the other side, that every particular couple would be an example in many circumstances to all the rest of the species. I shall end the chat upon this subject with a couple of letters, one from a lover who is very well acquainted with the way of bargaining on these occasions; and the other from his rival, who has a less estate, but great gallantry of temper. As for my man of prudence, he [1] makes love, as he says, as if he were already a father, and laying aside the passion, comes to the reason of the thing.

MADAM,—My counsel has perused the inventory of your estate, and considered what estate you have, which it seems is only yours, and to the male heirs of your body; but, in default of such issue, to the right heirs of your uncle Edward for ever. Thus, madam, I am advised you cannot (the remainder not being in you) dock the entail; by which means my estate, which is fee-simple, will come by the settlement proposed to your children begotten by me, whether they are males or females; but my children begotten upon you will not inherit your lands, except I beget a son. Now, madam, since things are so, you are a woman of that prudence, and understand the world so well as not to expect I should give you more than you can give me.

 I am, Madam, with great respect,
  Your most obedient humble Servant,
     T. W.

The other lover's estate is less than this gentleman's, but he expressed himself as follows:

MADAM,—I have given in my estate to your counsel, and desired my own lawyer to insist upon no terms which your friends can propose for your certain ease and advantage: for indeed I have no notion of making difficulties of presenting you with what cannot make me happy without you.

 I am, Madam,
  Your most devoted humble Servant,
     B. T.

---

[1] 'Who', in original editions.

You must know the relations have met upon this, and the girl being mightily taken with the latter epistle, she is laughed out, and Uncle Edward is to be dealt with to make her a suitable match to the worthy gentleman who has told her he does not care a farthing for her. All I hope for is, that the lady fair will make use of the first light night to show B. T. she understands a marriage is not to be considered as a common bargain.     T.

No. 528.     *Thursday, Oct. 30, 1712*     [ADDISON

*Nunc augur Apollo,*
*Nunc Lyciæ sortes, nunc et Jove missus ab ipso*
*Interpres divûm fert horrida jussa per auras.*
*Scilicet is superis labor.*

VIRG., *Æn.* iv, 376

I AM always highly delighted with the discovery of any rising genius among my countrymen. For this reason I have read over, with great pleasure, the late miscellany published by Mr Pope [1], in which there are many excellent compositions of that ingenious gentleman. I have had a pleasure, of the same kind, in perusing a poem that is just published *On the Prospect of Peace* [2], and which, I hope, will meet with such a reward from its patrons, as so noble a performance deserves. I was particularly well pleased to find that the author had not amused himself with fables out of the Pagan theology, and that when he hints at anything of this nature, he alludes to it only as to a fable.

Many of our modern authors, whose learning very often extends no further than Ovid's *Metamorphoses*, do not know how to celebrate a great man,

1 Pope, then aged twenty-four, edited a volume of *Miscellanies* brought out by Bernard Lintot in 1712. This volume contained the first draft of the *Rape of the Lock*, besides translations from Statius and Ovid, and other pieces.

2 Thomas Tickell's *Poem to his Excellency the Lord Privy Seal on the Prospect of Peace*. 'That noble poem', as Addison calls it in No. 620, was published on October 28, as appears from an advertisement in No. 521. There was a second edition on November 5, 1712.

without mixing a parcel of schoolboy tales with the recital of his actions. If you read a poem on a fine woman, among the authors of this class, you shall see that it turns more upon Venus or Helen, than on the party concerned. I have known a copy of verses on a great hero highly commended, but upon asking to hear some of the beautiful passages, the admirer of it has repeated to me a speech of Apollo, or a description of Polypheme. At other times when I have searched for the actions of a great man, who gave a subject to the writer, I have been entertained with the exploits of a river-god, or have been forced to attend a Fury in her mischievous progress, from one end of the poem to the other. When we are at school it is necessary for us to be acquainted with the system of Pagan theology, and may be allowed to enliven a theme, or point an epigram with an heathen god; but when we would write a manly panegyric, that should carry in it all the colours of truth, nothing can be more ridiculous than to have recourse to our Jupiters and Junos.

No thought is beautiful which is not just, and no thought can be just which is not founded in truth, or at least in that which passes for such.

In mock-heroic poems, the use of the heathen mythology is not only excusable but graceful, because it is the design of such compositions to divert, by adapting the fabulous machines of the ancients to low subjects, and at the same time by ridiculing such kinds of machinery in modern writers. If any are of opinion, that there is a necessity of admitting these classical legends into our serious compositions, in order to give them a more poetical turn; I would recommend to their consideration the pastorals of Mr Philips [1]. One would have thought it impossible for this kind of poetry to have subsisted without fawns and satyrs, wood-nymphs and water-nymphs, with all the tribe of rural deities. But we see he has given a new life, and a more natural beauty to

[1] See No. 223.

this way of writing by substituting, in the place of these antiquated fables, the superstitious mythology which prevails among the shepherds of our own country.

Virgil and Homer might compliment their heroes, by interweaving the actions of deities with their achievements; but for a Christian author to write in the Pagan creed, to make Prince Eugene a favourite of Mars, or to carry on a correspondence between Bellona and the Marshal De Villars, would be downright puerility, and unpardonable in a poet that is past sixteen. It is want of sufficient elevation in a genius to describe realities, and place them in a shining light, that makes him have recourse to such trifling antiquated fables; as a man may write a fine description of Bacchus or Apollo, that does not know how to draw the character of any of his contemporaries.

In order therefore to put a stop to this absurd practice, I shall publish the following edict, by virtue of that spectatorial authority with which I stand invested :

Whereas the time of a general peace is, in all appearance, drawing near; being informed that there are several ingenious persons who intend to show their talents on so happy an occasion, and being willing, as much as in me lies, to prevent that effusion of nonsense, which we have good cause to apprehend, I do hereby strictly require every person, who shall write on this subject, to remember that he is a Christian, and not to sacrifice his catechism to his poetry. In order to it, I do expect of him in the first place to make his own poem, without depending upon Phœbus for any part of it, or calling out for aid upon any one of the Muses by name. I do likewise positively forbid the sending of Mercury with any particular message or despatch relating to the peace, and shall by no means suffer Minerva to take upon her the shape of any plenipotentiary concerned in this great work. I do further declare, that I shall not allow the destinies to have had an hand in the deaths of the several thousands who have been slain in the late war, being of opinion

that all such deaths may be very well accounted for
by the Christian system of powder and ball. I do
therefore strictly forbid the Fates to cut the thread of
man's life upon any pretence whatsoever, unless it be
for the sake of the rhyme. And whereas I have good
reason to fear that Neptune will have a great deal of
business on his hands, in several poems which we may
now suppose are upon the anvil, I do also prohibit his
appearance, unless it be done in metaphor, simile, or
any very short allusion, and that even here he be not
permitted to enter, but with great caution and circum-
spection. I desire that the same rule may be extended
to his whole fraternity of heathen gods, it being my
design to condemn every poem to the flames in which
Jupiter thunders, or exercises any other act of
authority which does not belong to him. In short, I
expect that no pagan agent shall be introduced, or any
fact related which a man cannot give credit to with a
good conscience. Provided always that nothing herein
contained shall extend, or be construed to extend, to
several of the female poets in this nation, who shall be
still left in full possession of their gods and goddesses,
in the same manner as if this paper had never been
written.                                        O.

No. 524.    *Friday, Oct. 31, 1712*    [—— 1

*Nos populo damus.* SEN.

WHEN I first of all took it in my head to write
dreams and visions, I determined to print nothing of
that nature, which was not of my own invention. But
several laborious dreamers have of late communicated
to me works of this nature, which, for their reputa-

1 This paper bears no signature, and the opening paragraph may
be by either Steele or Addison. The Dream is stated to have been the
joint production of Alexander Dunlop, Professor of Greek in Glasgow
University, and a Mr Montgomery, who traded to Sweden, and of
whom it is said that he disordered his wits by falling in love with
Queen Christina. Alexander Dunlop (1684–1747), born in America,
where his father, the Principal of Glasgow University, was an exile
till the Revolution, became Greek Professor at Glasgow, and
published in 1736 a Grammar, which was used for many years in
Scottish universities.

tions and my own, I have hitherto suppressed. Had I printed every one that came to my hands, my book of speculations would have been little else but a book of visions. Some of my correspondents have indeed been so very modest, as to offer at an excuse for their not being in a capacity to dream better. I have by me, for example, the dream of a young gentleman not past fifteen. I have likewise by me the dream of a person of quality, and another called the ladies' dream. In these, and other pieces of the same nature, it is supposed the usual allowances will be made to the age, condition, and sex of the dreamer. To prevent this inundation of dreams, which daily flows in upon me, I shall apply to all dreamers of dreams, the advice which Epictetus has couched after his manner in a very simple and concise precept : ' Never tell thy dreams ', says that philosopher, ' for though thou thyself mayest take a pleasure in telling thy dream, another will take no pleasure in hearing it.' After this short preface, I must do justice to two or three visions which I have lately published, and which I have owned to have been written by other hands. I shall add a dream to these, which comes to me from Scotland, by one who declares himself of that country, and for all I know may be second-sighted. There is, indeed, something in it of the spirit of John Bunyan; but at the same time a certain sublime, which that author was never master of. I shall publish it, because I question not but it will fall in with the taste of all my popular readers, and amuse the imaginations of those who are more profound ; declaring, at the same time, that this is the last dream which I intend to publish this season :

SIR,—I was last Sunday, in the evening, led into a serious reflection on the reasonableness of virtue, and great folly of vice, from an excellent sermon I had heard that afternoon in my parish church. Among other observations, the preacher showed us that the temptations which the tempter proposed were all on a supposition that we are either madmen or fools, or with an intention to render us such; that in no other affair we would suffer ourselves to be thus imposed upon, in a case so plainly and clearly against our visible interest. His illustrations and arguments carried so much persuasion and conviction with them, that they remained a considerable while fresh, and working in my memory; until at last the mind, fatigued with thought, gave way to the forcible oppressions of slumber and sleep, whilst fancy, unwilling yet to drop the subject, presented me with the following vision:

Methought I was just awoke out of a sleep, that I could never remember the beginning of; the place where I found myself to be was a wide and spacious plain, full of people that wandered up and down through several beaten paths, whereof some few were straight, and in direct lines; but most of them winding and turning like a labyrinth; but yet it appeared to me afterwards, that these last all met in one issue, so that many that seemed to steer quite contrary courses, did at length meet and face one another, to the no little amazement of many of them.

In the midst of the plain there was a great fountain: they called it the Spring of Self-Love; out of it issued two rivulets to the eastward and westward; the name of the first was Heavenly Wisdom; its water was wonderfully clear, but of a yet more wonderful effect; the other's name was Worldly Wisdom; its water was thick, and yet far from being dormant or stagnating, for it was in a continual violent agitation, which kept the travellers, whom I shall mention by and by, from being sensible of the foulness and thickness of the water, which had this effect, that it intoxicated those that drunk it, and made them mistake every object that lay before them; both rivulets were parted near their springs into so many others as there were straight and crooked paths, which they attended all along to their respective issues.

I observed from the several paths many now and then diverting, to refresh and otherwise qualify themselves for their journey, to the respective rivulets that ran near them; they contracted a very observable courage and steadiness in what they were about, by drinking these waters. At the end of the perspective of every straight path, all which did end in one issue and point, appeared a high pillar, all of diamond, casting rays as bright as those of the sun into the paths; which rays had also certain sympathising and alluring virtues in them, so that whosoever had made some considerable progress in his journey onwards towards the pillar, by the repeated impression of these rays upon him, was wrought into an habitual inclination and conversion of his sight towards it, so that it grew at last in a manner natural to him to look and gaze upon it, whereby he was kept steadily in the straight paths, which alone led to that radiant body, the beholding of which was now grown a gratification to his nature.

At the issue of the crooked paths there was a great black tower, out of the centre of which streamed a long succession of flames, which did rise even above the clouds; it gave a very great light to the whole plain, which did sometimes outshine the light, and oppressed the beams of the adamantine pillar, though, by the observation I made afterwards, it appeared that it was not for any diminution of light, but that this lay in the travellers, who would sometimes step out of the straight paths, where they lost the full prospect of the radiant pillar, and saw it but sideways; but the great light from the black tower, which was somewhat particularly scorching to them, would generally light and hasten them to their proper climate again.

Round about the black tower there was, methought, many thousands of huge misshapen ugly monsters; these had great nets, which they were perpetually plying and casting towards the crooked paths, and they would now and then catch up those that were nearest to them; these they took up straight, and whirled over the walls into the flaming tower, and they were no more seen nor heard of.

They would sometimes cast their nets towards the right paths to catch the stragglers, whose eyes, for want of frequent drinking at the brook that ran by them, grew dim, whereby they lost their way; these would sometimes very narrowly miss being catched away, but I could not hear whether any of these had ever been so unfortunate, that had been before very hearty in the straight paths.

I considered all these strange sights with great attention, until at last I was interrupted by a cluster of the travellers in the crooked paths, who came up to me, bid me go along with them, and presently fell to singing and dancing; they took me by the hand, and so carried me away along with them. After I had followed them a considerable while, I perceived I had lost the black tower of light, at which I greatly wondered; but as I looked and gazed round about me, and saw nothing, I began to fancy my first vision had been but a dream, and there was no such thing in reality; but then I considered, that if I could fancy to see what was not, I might as well have an illusion wrought on me at present, and not see what was really before me. I was very much confirmed in this thought, by the effect I then just observed the water of Worldly Wisdom had upon me; for as I had drunk a little of it again, I felt a very sensible effect in my head: methought it distracted and disordered all there; this made me stop of a sudden, suspecting some charm or enchantment. As I was casting about within myself what I should do, and whom to apply to in this case, I spied at some distance off me a man beckoning and making signs to me to come over to him. I cried to him, I did not know the way. He then called to me audibly, to step at least out of the path I was in, for if I stayed there any longer I was in danger to be catched in a great net that was just hanging over me and ready to catch me up; that he wondered I was so blind or so distracted as not to see so imminent and visible a danger; assuring me, that as soon as I was out of that way he would come to me to lead me into a more secure path. This I did, and he brought me his palm full of the water of Heavenly Wisdom, which was of very great use to me, for my eyes were straight cleared and I saw the great black tower just before me; but the great net, which I spied so near me, cast me in such a terror that I ran back as far as I could in one breath without looking behind me; then my benefactor thus bespoke me, 'You have made the wonderfullest escape in the world: the water you used to drink is of a bewitching nature, you would else have been mightily shocked at the deformities and meanness of the place; for beside the set of blind fools in whose company you was, you may now observe many others who are only bewitched after another no less dangerous manner. Look a little that way; there goes a crowd of passengers, they have indeed so good a head as not to suffer themselves to be blinded by this bewitching water; the black tower is not vanished out of their sight, they see it whenever they look up to it; but see how they go sideways, and with their eyes downwards as if they were mad, that they may thus rush into the net without being beforehand troubled at the thought of so miserable a destruction. Their wills are so perverse, and their hearts so fond of the pleasures of the place, that rather than forego them they will run all hazards, and venture upon all the miseries and woes before them.

' See there that other company; though they should drink none of the bewitching water, yet they take a course bewitching and deluding: see how they choose the crookedest paths, whereby they have often the black tower behind them, and sometimes see the radiant column sideways, which gives them some weak glimpse of it. These fools content themselves with that, not knowing whether any other have any more of its influence and light than themselves; this road is called that of Superstition or Human Invention; they grossly overlook that which the rules and laws of the place prescribe to them, and contrive some other scheme and set of directions and prescriptions for themselves which they hope will serve their turn.' He showed me many other kinds of fools, which put me quite out of humour with the place. At last he carried me to the right paths, where I found true and solid pleasure, which entertained me all the way until we came in closer sight of the pillar, where the satisfaction increased to that measure that my faculties were not able to contain it; in the straining of them I was violently waked, not a little grieved at the vanishing of so pleasing a dream.

GLASGOW, *Sept.* 29.

No. 525.     *Saturday, Nov. 1, 1712*     [HUGHES

'Ο δ' εἰς το σῶφρον ἐπ' ἀρετήν τ' ἀγὼν ἔρως,
Ζηλωτὸς ἀνθρώποισιν.     EURIP., fr. *Stheenboen.*

IT is my custom to take frequent opportunities of
inquiring from time to time, what success my speculations meet with in the town. I am glad to find, in
particular, that my discourses on marriage have been
well received. A friend of mine gives me to understand, from Doctors' Commons, that more licences
have been taken out there of late than usual. I am
likewise informed of several pretty fellows who have
resolved to commence heads of families by the first
favourable opportunity. One of them writes me word
that he is ready to enter into the bonds of matrimony,
provided I will give it him under my hand (as I now
do), that a man may show his face in good company
after he is married, and that he need not be ashamed
to treat a woman with kindness who puts herself into
his power for life.

I have other letters on this subject, which say that
I am attempting to make a revolution in the world
of gallantry, and that the consequence of it will be
that a great deal of the sprightliest wit and satire of
the last age will be lost. That a bashful fellow, upon
changing his condition, will be no longer puzzled how
to stand the raillery of his facetious companions; that
he need not own he married only to plunder an heiress
of her fortune, nor pretend that he uses her ill to
avoid the ridiculous [1] name of a fond husband.

Indeed, if I may speak my opinion of great part
of the writings which once prevailed among us under
the notion of humour, they are such as would tempt
one to think there had been an association among
the wits of those times to rally legitimacy out of our
island. A state of wedlock was the common mark for
all the adventurers in farce and comedy, as well as
the essayers in lampoon and satire to shoot at; and

[1] 'Scandalous' (folio).

nothing was a more standing jest in all clubs of fashionable mirth and gay conversation. It was determined among those airy critics, that the appellation of a sober man should signify a spiritless fellow. And I am apt to think it was about the same time that *good-nature*, a word so peculiarly elegant in our language that some have affirmed it cannot well be expressed in any other, came first to be rendered suspicious, and in danger of being transferred from its original sense to so distant an idea as that of *folly*.

I must confess it has been my ambition, in the course of my writings, to restore as well as I was able the proper ideas of things. And as I have attempted this already on the subject of marriage, in several papers [1] I shall here add some further observations which occur to me on the same head.

Nothing seems to be thought, by our fine gentlemen, so indispensable an ornament in fashionable life as love. 'A knight errant', says Don Quixote, 'without a mistress is like a tree without leaves'; and a man of mode among us, who has not some fair one to sigh for, might as well pretend to appear dressed without his periwig. We have lovers in prose innumerable. All our pretenders to rhyme are professed inamoratos; and there is scarce a poet, good or bad, to be heard of, who has not some real or supposed Sacharissa [2] to improve his vein.

If love be any refinement, conjugal love must be certainly so in a much higher degree. There is no comparison between the frivolous affectation of attracting the eyes of women with whom you are only captivated by way of amusement, and of whom perhaps you know nothing more than their features, and a regular and uniform endeavour to make yourself valuable, both as a friend and lover, to one whom you have chosen to be the companion of your life.

---

1 See Nos. 33, 479, 490, 522.
2 The name under which Waller celebrated in his verse Dorothy Sidney, afterwards Countess of Sunderland.

The first is the spring of a thousand fopperies, silly artifices, falsehoods, and perhaps barbarities; or at best arises no higher than to a kind of dancing-school breeding, to give the person a more sparkling air. The latter is the parent of substantial virtues and agreeable qualities, and cultivates the mind while it improves the behaviour. The passion of love to a mistress, even where it is most sincere, resembles too much the flame of a fever; that to a wife is like the vital heat.

I have often thought, if the letters written by men of good-nature to their wives, were to be compared with those written by men of gallantry to their mistresses, the former, notwithstanding any inequality of style, would appear to have the advantage. Friendship, tenderness, and constancy, dressed in a simplicity of expression, recommend themselves by a more native elegance than passionate raptures, extravagant encomiums, and slavish adoration. If we were admitted to search the cabinet of the beautiful Narcissa, among heaps of epistles from several admirers, which are there preserved with equal care, how few should we find but would make any one sick in the reading, except her who is flattered by them? But in how different a style must the wise Benevolus, who converses with that good sense and good humour among all his friends, write to a wife who is the worthy object of his utmost affection! Benevolus, both in public and private, on all occasions of life, appears to have every good quality and desirable ornament. Abroad he is reverenced and esteemed; at home beloved and happy. The satisfaction he enjoys there settles into an habitual complacency, which shines in his countenance, enlivens his wit, and seasons his conversation. Even those of his acquaintance who have never seen him in his retirement are sharers in the happiness of it; and it is very much owing to his being the best and best beloved of husbands, that he is the most steadfast of friends, and the most agreeable of companions.

There is a sensible pleasure in contemplating such beautiful instances of domestic life. The happiness of the conjugal state appears heightened to the highest degree it is capable of, when we see two persons of accomplished minds, not only united in the same interests and affections, but in their taste of the same improvements, pleasures, and diversions. Pliny, one of the finest gentlemen and politest writers of the age in which he lived, has left us, in his letter to Hispulla, his wife's aunt, one of the most agreeable family pieces of this kind I have ever met with [1]. I shall end this discourse with a translation of it; and I believe the reader will be of my opinion, that conjugal love is drawn in it with a delicacy which makes it appear to be, as I have represented it, an ornament as well as a virtue :

### PLINY *to* HISPULLA

As I remember that great affection which was between you and your excellent brother, and know you love his daughter as your own, so as not only to express the tenderness of the best of aunts, but even to supply that of the best of fathers, I am sure it will be a pleasure to you to hear that she proves worthy of her father, worthy of you, and of your and her ancestors. Her ingenuity is admirable ; her frugality extraordinary. She loves me, the surest pledge of her virtue ; and adds to this a wonderful disposition to learning, which she has acquired from her affection to me. She reads my writings, studies them, and even gets them by heart. You'd smile to see the concern she is in when I have a cause to plead, and the joy she shows when it is over. She finds means to have the first news brought her of the success I meet with in court, how I am heard, and what decree is made. If I recite anything in public, she cannot refrain from placing herself privately in some corner to hear, where with the utmost delight she feasts on my applauses. Sometimes she sings my verses and accompanies them with the lute, without any master, except Love, the best of in-

[1] Book iv, Epist. 19.

structors. From these instances I take the most certain
omens of our perpetual and increasing happiness; since
her affection is not founded on my youth and person,
which must gradually decay, but she is in love with
the immortal part of me, my glory and reputation.
Nor indeed could less be expected from one who had
the happiness to receive her education from you, who
in your house was accustomed to everything that was
virtuous and decent, and even began to love me by your
recommendation. For, as you had always the greatest
respect for my mother, you were pleased from my
infancy to form me, to commend me, and kindly to
presage I should be one day what my wife fancies I
am. Accept therefore our united thanks; mine, that
you have bestowed her on me, and hers, that you have
given me to her, as a mutual grant of joy and felicity.

www.ingramcontent.com/pod-product-compliance
Lightning Source LLC
Chambersburg PA
CBHW030040130726
47901CB00005BA/1179